WHERE THE HEART LEADS

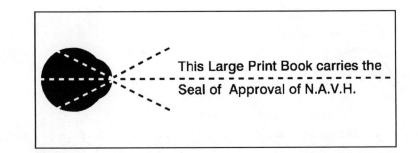

This Large Print Book carries the
Seal of Approval of N.A.V.H.

WHERE THE HEART LEADS

KIM VOGEL SAWYER

THORNDIKE PRESS

A part of Gale, Cengage Learning

Detroit • New York • San Francisco • New Haven, Conn • Waterville, Maine • London

GALE
CENGAGE Learning™

Copyright © 2008 by Kim Vogel Sawyer.
Sequel to *Waiting for Summer's Return.*
Scripture quotations are from the King James Version of the Bible.
Thorndike Press, a part of Gale, Cengage Learning.

LIBRARY OF CONGRESS CATALOGING-IN-PUBLICATION DATA

Sawyer, Kim Vogel.
　　Where the heart leads / by Kim Vogel Sawyer.
　　　　p. cm. — (Thorndike Press large print christian historical
　　fiction)
　　ISBN-13: 978-1-4104-1188-4 (alk. paper)
　　ISBN-10: 1-4104-1188-5 (alk. paper)
　　　　1. Mennonites—Fiction. 2. Large type books. I. Title.
　　PS3619.A97W45　2008b
　　813'.6—dc22　　　　　　　　　　　　　　　　　　2008036961

Published in 2008 by arrangement with Bethany House Publishers.

Printed in Mexico
2 3 4 5 6 7 12 11 10 09

For my nephews DAVID and
NATHAN.
All too soon you'll be men,
setting out on your God-designed
pathways.
Stay focused on Him
and your steps will be sure.

ONLY TAKE HEED TO THYSELF,
AND KEEP THY SOUL DILIGENTLY,
LEST THOU FORGET THE THINGS
WHICH THINE EYES HAVE SEEN,
AND LEST THEY DEPART FROM THY
HEART
ALL THE DAYS OF THY LIFE:
BUT TEACH THEM THY SONS,
AND THY SONS' SONS.

Deuteronomy 4:9

1

Boston, Massachusetts
Late May, 1904

A sharp elbow jabbed Thomas Ollenburger's ribs, his foster grandmother's all-too-familiar signal that he was doing something wrong. He stopped fiddling with the ribbon tie beneath his chin and lowered his arm to his side, but she jabbed him again, this time catching his forearm instead. He looked at her.

Although Nadine Steadman wore a smile, her eyes flashed disapproval. "Smile, Thomas. Make your guests feel welcome."

Thomas swallowed a grunt. He hadn't wanted these guests. Sure, he admitted feeling a sense of accomplishment in earning a college degree — something unique to his Mennonite upbringing — but the teachings of his sect discouraged self-pride. A party seemed too much like boasting. Nadine and he had argued when he'd stated he would rather avoid the fanfare and not attend the graduation ceremony at Boston Tech. He'd won that debate, but Nadine had insisted on throwing a celebratory party in honor of his educational achievement. So he had fanfare anyway.

Some devilishness made him whisper, *"Ach fal me no ows mein yasacht dowt no shtien."*

Nadine's smile quickly faded. "Thomas Ollenburger, you know I don't understand a word of that foreign speech." Her dark eyes dared him to leave her wondering what he'd said.

Leaning sideways to bring his head next to hers, he translated, "My face feels as if it's turned to stone." He contorted his mouth. "I've been smiling so much, my muscles are stiff."

She laughed softly and patted his arm with her gloved hand. "Thomas, you are a scamp."

Although the words could be construed as an insult, by her tone he knew he'd been forgiven. Nadine's approach was often crusty, but Thomas had learned she harbored a tender heart. Her willingness to take him in six years ago as he began high school, pay for his college education, and treat him as her own — even though he was only the stepson of her daughter-in-law rather than any blood kin — proved her generosity. He just wished she hadn't chosen a party as a way of expressing her pleasure in his accomplishment.

Dozens of guests milled through the parlor of the stately Steadman home — students, professors, church members, and neighbors. Many had entered the ornately carved oak doors as first-time visitors. But none looked as uncomfortable as Thomas had felt during his first weeks in Nadine's home.

Her three-story townhouse on prestigious Beacon Street, overlooking the Common, was so different from his simple clapboard home in Gaeddert, Kansas. His entire child-hood home had less space than the parlor of Nadine's ridiculously large residence. Even now, after six years of living beneath her tiled roof, he sometimes still experienced a sense of displacement. He wished he could set the odd feeling aside, relax, and be as at ease as his friend Harry Severt seemed to be. Right now, beside the punch bowl on the opposite side of the room, Harry conversed with two young ladies. His posture and gestures conveyed a state of complete self-assurance.

Nadine caught Thomas's elbow and gave it a little squeeze. "I believe the last of the

11

guests have arrived. You may now leave the welcoming post and mingle. Be certain to speak to each person in attendance — preferential treatment to one guest is considered impolite. Be certain to avoid any semblance of preferential treatment."

Thomas resisted growling in frustration. He'd received these instructions at least half a dozen times already — and he knew the reason. Nadine didn't want him spending all his time with Daphne Severt, Harry's younger sister who had accompanied Harry on several visits to Nadine's home. Nadine didn't seem to care for Daphne, and Thomas wasn't sure why. He admitted that when he'd first met Daphne, she'd seemed to be as pesky as his own little sisters. But lately . . . well, she'd grown into the loveliest creature he'd ever seen.

"Go ahead now," Nadine prompted. Catching her skirt between thumb and fingers, she glided across the carpeted floor with her shoulders back and chin held high, nodding and smiling as she filled the role of the perfect hostess.

Thomas cleared his throat, squared his shoulders, and edged his way around the periphery of the room. Although he did his best to appear as poised as Nadine desired him to be, his large size coupled with the crowded room made graceful movements impossible. He'd inherited his pa's height and breadth — and he never felt more monstrous than when standing beside the diminutive Daphne Severt.

Although Nadine often bemoaned the difficulty in locating suits to accommodate Thomas's frame, Daphne had once said his size made her feel protected. He scanned the room, seeking the young woman. He couldn't spend a lot of time talking to her — not with Nadine's eagle eyes observing his every move — but just a glance would satisfy him for the moment.

Daphne had arrived with Harry a half hour ago, looking beautiful in a shiny dress the same color as the ripe sand plums that grew wild on the prairie surrounding his Kansas home. Her long black hair had been pulled up into a ponytail as thick as his horse's tail, but instead of being straight, it hung in long coils that bounced when she walked. He looked for that bouncing tail of hair, and his heart jolted when he spotted it. As usual, she was the focus of attentive male gazes.

A stab of jealousy propelled him forward. "Excuse me," he muttered, weaving between clusters of guests. "Excuse me, please." He reached the group and stepped directly into

Daphne's line of vision. Her face lifted to his, and her rosy lips curved into a smile of welcome. His heart began such a raucous pounding in his chest that it threatened to dislodge the buttons of his shirt. Maybe a party hadn't been such a bad idea after all.

"Mr. Ollenburger." She stretched a hand toward him.

Placing his palm beneath hers, he bowed over the white-gloved knuckles and delivered a light kiss on the middle one. Straightening, he caught her flutter of lashes, and despite his stiff cheeks, he felt the first genuine smile of the day form on his face. "Miss Severt."

Daphne glanced at the group around her. "Please excuse me. I must speak with the guest of honor." Slipping her hand through the bend of his elbow, she turned her heart-shaped face upward. "I find myself quite parched, Mr. Ollenburger. Might you escort me to the refreshments table?"

Thomas couldn't argue with that idea. As they moved through the room together, he sensed people's gazes following them. The feeling of discomfiture grew, and he wished he could shrink at least three sizes to make himself less visible. By the time they reached the table bearing the bounty of food items, his hands were trembling, and when he tried to pour a glass of punch, he sloshed pale pink liquid over the edge of the glass's rim and spattered the linen tablecloth.

Heat burned the back of his neck, and he hunched his shoulders. "I'm so sorry."

Daphne moved closer, angling her head to meet his eyes. "Please don't apologize. And please don't let the stares of the other guests perturb you. I know what each of them is thinking."

Thomas risked a quick sideways glance, confirming a number of attentive faces aimed in their direction. "I know, too. 'What is that big clod doing with that beautiful girl?' "

She curled her fingers over his forearm. "Quite the contrary. They're thinking, 'How did that young lady manage to catch the most handsome man in the room?' "

He raised one eyebrow, silently communicating his doubt.

Her midnight eyes sparkled. "Or perhaps, 'What a perfect couple.' "

Thomas gulped. Heat crept from the back of his neck to the top of his head. He snatched up another glass, filled it with punch, and downed the cool, sweet liquid, grateful for the distraction. But unfortunately, the diversion lasted only a few seconds. When he looked once more into

15

her face, the heat returned with an intensity that made his knees weak.

"Daphne Severt," he growled, "what you do to a man . . ."

She batted her thick eyelashes. "Do tell."

He laughed, shaking his head. "Oh no. You have enough confidence already. I won't add to it."

Her flirtatious expression invited him to shower her with all the praises filling his heart and mind, but his father hadn't raised a foolish man. He wouldn't give voice to the feelings until he knew he could follow them with action. He'd be leaving soon, returning to Kansas. Now that his studies were completed, his family expected him. It felt good to be going home, but the thought of leaving Daphne filled him with regret.

Daphne lifted her cup to her lips and sipped daintily, her wide-eyed gaze never drifting from his face.

Deep regret.

When Thomas's neck blotched with color, Daphne knew she'd accomplished her goal: Thomas was smitten with her.

The first time Harry had brought Thomas to their home, she'd been intrigued. She'd been only thirteen years old then, but she'd been mature enough to recognize the differ-

16

ences between this man and the boys who generally spent time with Harry. Just standing next to him had brought a rush of pleasure. Outside, in the sunshine, his shadow completely swallowed hers. He made her feel small and feminine and safe.

A servant passed by, carrying a carved wood tray. She put her half-empty glass on the tray and caught Thomas's elbow once more. "This room is so crowded. Could we step onto the veranda for a moment?"

Thomas sucked in his lips, seeming to give her question deep consideration. He frowned, and she feared a refusal would be forthcoming. She leaned forward slightly, pressing her arm against his. "Please, Thomas? I need some fresh air."

Although his expression didn't clear, he nodded. They moved side by side through the double French doors leading to the narrow veranda that faced out over the grassy Common. Thomas tempered his wide stride to match hers, and she smiled. Such a gentleman lurked beneath his burly frame.

Thomas crossed to the iron railing and curled both of his hands over the scrolled top. Daphne retained her hold on his elbow as she took a deep breath of the spring air. "Ahh. This is much better."

Thomas chuckled. "There's no fan out

here to stir the air. It isn't any less stuffy."

"Oh, but out here we're alone." She peered up at him, offering her biggest smile. "Do you not agree that's much better?"

The blotching in his neck returned immediately.

"Thomas, must you truly return to Kansas?" She sighed dramatically.

He frowned down at her. "My family is expecting me."

"But Kansas is so far from Boston."

Thomas shifted his gaze across the Common, his expression pensive. "Yes. I know."

Determined to draw him back, she released her hold on his arm and slipped away a few feet, peering at him over her shoulder. "Will you miss me?"

"Will *you* miss *me?*"

That wasn't the response she'd anticipated. She jerked her gaze forward, folded her arms over her chest, and refused to answer. Besotted or not, she wouldn't allow him to control her. Suddenly large hands cupped her shoulders and turned her around. She had to tip her head back to look into his serious face.

"Don't play games with me, Daphne." Thomas's deep, throaty voice sounded tense. "If you'll miss me, just say so."

Daphne placed her palms against the front

of Thomas's jacket. It was a brazen gesture, but he didn't shrink away. "I shall miss you dreadfully." She whispered the words, waiting for him to respond in kind.

"I'll leave you my address. You can write to me."

Had he made a request or a demand? Daphne scowled, pursing her lips into the pout she often practiced in front of the mirror in her private sleeping chamber. "It isn't the same."

"But it will have to do," he pointed out in a calm tone that stirred her ire.

She grasped the lapels of his coat. "You are coming back, aren't you, Thomas? Harry depends on your assistance in the presidential election. He said you promised to help. You are a man of your word, aren't you?"

The blotching rose from his neck to his smooth-shaven cheeks, but this time Daphne suspected it had less to do with discomfort than with anger. How would this big man express his temper? Explode like Father, or withdraw like Harry?

Thomas drew in a deep breath, held it for several seconds, then let it out in little bursts through his nose. With each burst, the color in his face diminished. When he spoke, it was with an even, unflustered tone. "I gave my word. I'll be back."

She leaned closer.

"To assist in the campaign."

She released his lapels and pranced away, presenting her back. "Thomas Ollenburger, I —"

She didn't have the opportunity to finish, because someone threw open the French doors. Daphne spun, expecting Harry, but Mrs. Steadman stood in the opening.

"Thomas, a few of your guests are preparing to leave." The woman shot Daphne a disapproving frown before looking back at Thomas. "You should be there to tell them a proper good-bye and thank-you."

"Of course, Nadine. We were just returning. Weren't we, Miss Severt?"

Daphne nodded and forced a pleasant expression. She glided past Thomas, giving him a brief glance. "Thank you for showing me the veranda, Mr. Ollenburger. Have a safe journey to Kansas."

She returned to the parlor and sought Harry. She would fake a headache and ask him to escort her home. If Thomas were to regret the lost opportunity for a lengthy good-bye, then she couldn't tarry.

Harry was in the midst of some intense discussion with three other young men, but she captured his arm and tugged him away from the group. His fierce glower would have silenced most people, but Daphne was used to dealing with her brother. "Harry, my head is pounding. I wish to go home."

"But I haven't even had a chance to talk to Tom."

She made a great pretense of wilting, carrying one trembling hand to her forehead. "I fear I shall simply collapse if I'm not able to rest immediately."

Harry blew out a breath of frustration. "Oh, very well." He turned to the others. "I need to leave, fellows. But —"

One of the others — a student Daphne had seen before but to whom she'd never been formally introduced — stepped forward. "Harry, why don't you stay? You know Tom better than I do, anyway. I'll escort your sister home in my landau."

Harry clapped the man's shoulder. "Thank you, Wilfred. I appreciate that."

Daphne gaped at Harry. Would he truly pass her off to some skinny, pock-faced stranger?

Harry put his hand on Daphne's spine. "Daphne, you'll be in safe company with Wilfred Taylor." He pressed her forward, ignoring her angry glare. "I'll check in on you when I return."

Wilfred licked his lips and stuck out his

bony elbow in invitation. "Come along, Miss Severt."

Daphne had no choice but to place her hand in the curve of his arm. It felt like kindling compared to Thomas's broad limbs. But as she and Wilfred made their departure, she observed Thomas's clenched jaw and narrowed gaze, and satisfaction welled upward. Perhaps she possessed the victory after all.

2

Hillsboro, Kansas
Early June, 1904

The closer the rattling passenger car carried Thomas to Hillsboro, the more he shifted on the wooden seat. Sweat drenched his back, making him want to remove his suit coat and roll up the sleeves of his linen shirt. But remembering Nadine's admonition when he'd boarded in Boston — *"You're a college graduate now, Thomas. You must look the part"* — he felt certain she would ask his stepmother how he'd been dressed when he arrived in Hillsboro. He'd tangled with Nadine before; he had no desire to do it again.

The fabric of the custom-tailored black worsted suit bore wrinkles and sweat stains, and he wondered how he could look more like a college graduate in bedraggled attire than in a pair of trousers and a chambray shirt from his bag. But respect for Nadine kept him in the suit, regardless of how much he wanted to change.

The suit wasn't the only thing making him uncomfortable. Scattered emotions — eagerness to see his family, regret at not being able to say a proper farewell to Daphne, and uncertainty about what to do with the degree he'd spent three years earning — combined to make fresh perspiration moisten his forehead. *Ach, how much longer to Hillsboro?*

He snatched off his hat and dragged a wilted handkerchief over his face. The hot wind streaming through the open window peppered him with grit and coal dust. Instead of replacing his hat, he dropped it onto the seat beside him and looked out at the passing countryside.

Kansas, his boyhood home. Pasture land of gently rolling hills dotted with yucca bearing fat buds that would soon blossom. Occasional splashes of color from wildflowers. Wheat fields, the golden tips waving in the sun. Stands of wind-pruned trees, their branches full and green. It was all so familiar . . . and yet also foreign after his long time away.

Scowling, he turned from the window. He bent forward, rested his elbows on his widespread knees, and lowered his head.

Dia Gott enn de Himmel — just like his father and his father's father before him, he lapsed into German when he prayed — *I do not know where I belong now. Pa wants me home in Kansas, and a part of me wants that, too, but I have been gone for so long . . . Where am I meant to call "home"? Help me know, Lord.*

For long moments he remained in his bent-low position, his head bobbing with the motion of the train, waiting for an answer. But when the screeching of the brakes signaled the train's approach to Hillsboro, he'd received no more answers than the last time he'd prayed. Maybe when he was home, in his familiar bedroom with the sounds of the prairie soothing his troubled soul, things would become clear.

Putting one arm forward, he braced himself on the back of the seat in front of him and gritted his teeth against the vibration coming through the floorboards. He held his breath until the rapid, screeching deceleration turned into a slow *chug-chug-chug,* and then let it out in one big *whew* of relief that accompanied the train's release of steam. He glanced out the window. A small cluster of people waited on the boardwalk for the few passengers who would disembark, and his heart leaped when he recog-

25

nized his father's shaggy, wheat-colored hair — his head always inches above anyone else in a crowd.

Pa! To his surprise, tears pooled in Thomas's eyes. He plopped his hat over his own wheat-colored mop, grabbed up his bag, and raced to the door at the end of the car. He didn't bother with the metal stairs, but took a single leap that brought him flat-footed on hard-packed earth. The shock of the landing gave him momentary pause, but then he stumbled forward on tingling feet. "Pa! Pa! And Summer!"

Although Summer had been his step-mother for nine years — nearly half of his life — he still hesitated at calling her Ma. Back when she'd married Pa, he hadn't wanted to be a replacement for her deceased sons, Vincent and Tod. But now, as he called her given name, he experienced a pang of regret.

His family separated from the crowd and rushed forward, with his sisters outpacing Pa and Summer. The littlest one, three-year-old Lena, tripped and fell face first in the dirt and began to wail. Pa paused to scoop her into his arms, and stairsteps Abby and Gussie — so similar in size and appearance they could pass for twins — barreled into Thomas. He laughed at their enthusiastic welcome. They'd only been two and one years of age when he'd first left for high school and college in the East, and his visits home had been few and brief, yet each time he came home, they swarmed him like bees on a honeysuckle vine.

He lifted them off the ground simultaneously, one in each arm, and swung in a circle that made their matching yellow braids stick straight out. They clung to his shoulders and squealed, their childish voices loud in his ears. He set them down and reached for Summer. Wrapping his arms around her slender frame, he was transported back to the first time he'd dared hug her. He'd had to lift his arms to her then. This time she reached up to capture his face with her hands and give him a bold kiss on the cheek.

"Oh, Thomas, it's so good to have you home again."

The word *home* reverberated right through Thomas's heart. He swallowed hard, his arms tightening around her back. "It's good to be here."

When Thomas released Summer, Pa stepped forward with little Lena balanced on his arm. Plump tears quivered on the child's thick eyelashes, and she sucked the two middle fingers of her left hand. Thomas held out his arms to Lena, but she buried her face against Pa's neck. Her action made it impossible for him to give either her or his father a hug.

Thomas cupped the back of his sister's head of dark, tangled curls with one hand and clamped the other over his father's shoulder. A huge lump filled his throat. All of his life, he'd wanted to please this man. How would Pa feel if Thomas left Kansas for good? Forcing his voice past the lump of emotion, he managed a one-word salutation. "Pa."

Pa nodded, seeming to understand the great meaning behind the simple greeting. He responded in kind: "Son." For long moments they stood silently under the sun, with Summer, Abby, and Gussie looking on, until suddenly Lena released her father's neck and flung herself at Thomas.

"Oomph!" Thomas took a step backward when her weight hit him. The child's moist fingers dug into the back of his neck. He crossed his arms over her narrow back, holding her in place. Lena pressed her face against his collar. He heard her whisper, "You my bruvver, Thomaff."

Both Abby and Gussie beamed, clapping their hands. Obviously they'd been coaching Lena in preparation for his homecoming. Lena's valiant attempt at speaking his name brought a smile to his face and he said, "That's right." He bounced her a couple of times on his arm, making her giggle. Her fingers slid back into her rosy little mouth, and she reached for Pa. Thomas experienced a sense of loss as he relinquished her. But then Gussie and Abby danced forward, each taking one of his hands.

Pa, with Lena in one arm, picked up Thomas's bag and heaved his great shoulders in a slow shrug. "Well, now that our Thomas is here, we can go home."

Thomas fell into step between Pa and Summer, and the two little girls skipped along in front of him, getting in his way. He watched his step as he spoke. "I'm eager to get to the homestead — to say hello to Daisy and maybe take a ride before it gets dark. Are the strawflowers blooming? I'd like to take a bouquet to *Grossmutter*'s grave tomorrow — if that's all right."

A wave of sorrow accompanied his last comment. Although his dear great-grandmother had been gone more than three years now — passing away peacefully in her sleep midway through Summer's last pregnancy — Thomas still missed her with a fierce ache. He hadn't even been able to

29

attend her funeral, caught in studies halfway across the United States. But during every summer trip to Kansas, he'd spent considerable time at the tiny gravesite where *Grossmutter* rested near Summer's first husband and their four children, all of whom had died of typhoid fever as they traveled through Kansas.

Although the baby boy Summer had borne during the first year she was Thomas's new mother was also buried there, Thomas rarely sat at that grave. The infant hadn't lived more than a few minutes and hadn't even been given a name. Baby Boy Ollenburger, as his tombstone read, didn't seem real to Thomas somehow.

"*Ja,* if you want to visit *Grossmutter*'s grave, we can make that work." Pa's solemn tone reflected Thomas's thoughts.

"Thank you, Pa."

They reached the end of the boardwalk, where two wagons waited, both with horses lazing within the confines of their leather rigging. Pairs of plodding, dependable oxen had pulled his father's wagon for as long as Thomas could remember. He looked around in confusion. "Where are Arndt and Bruno?"

Summer and Pa exchanged a look that made Thomas's stomach pinch.

"Son," Pa said, his head low, "some changes we have made since last time you were home."

Why would Pa get rid of the oxen? He needed the beasts to turn the gristmill's large paddles to face the wind; horses weren't strong enough. The twinge in Thomas's middle increased. "Changes?" He looked from one parent to the other while Gussie and Abby blinked up at him.

"*Ja.*" Pa took a deep breath, as if preparing to share something of importance, but Summer touched his sleeve.

"Let's wait until we're at the house to visit with Thomas, shall we? It's warm here in the sun, and Little Lena is ready for her afternoon nap."

Pa let out his breath in a way that indicated great relief. His gaze flicked between Thomas and Summer, and he nodded his head, gently patting Lena's back as she drowsed on his shoulder. "That is sound thinking. Come."

But instead of leading Thomas to a wagon, Pa headed straight through town. Pa's brown boots thudded against the raised walkway, matching the thumping of Thomas's heart. They made two turns to reach a residential area. There, he followed Pa into a small two-story house. When he saw the

31

familiar furnishings from the homestead —
Grossmutter's and Summer's chairs, Pa's
homemade bench draped with the worn
patchwork quilt, and the handmade table
and chairs where he had eaten many meals
with his father, great-grandmother, and
Summer — he couldn't remain silent. "You
live in Hillsboro? Why didn't you tell me
you left the homestead?"

Pa shook his head, frowning when Lena
stirred on his shoulder. Instead of addressing Thomas, he turned to Gussie and Abby.
"Girls, up to your room and play for a little
bit. Stay quiet, though, while your sister
sleeps. When she wakes, your mother will
fix a snack for you."

Abby caught Gussie's hand, and the pair
scampered up an enclosed staircase that
divided the little house in two. Pa started
after them, but he paused at the base of the
stairs, peering back at Thomas with sad
eyes. "Summer will show you where you
sleep. I will put Lena in her bed, and then
we will talk."

Thomas clamped his jaw against all the
questions that burned on his tongue. He
picked up the bag Pa had left lying inside
the front door, and trailed Summer through
the kitchen to a lean-to at the back of the
house. The ceiling sloped downward at a

sharp pitch, forcing Thomas to duck to keep from hitting his head on the rafters. His old rope bed filled almost half of the room, the head and foot fitting snugly between opposite walls. Next to the head of the bed stood his chest of drawers, with a shelf above it holding many of his boyhood belongings.

For a moment, a picture of the spacious room he had occupied in Nadine's home flashed through his mind, and he grimaced. But then he noticed the neatly made bed, the colorful quilt stretched smoothly over the mattress, and the arrangement of his favorite books and childish toys on the shelf. Someone had tried to make this little room welcoming. He kept silent the disparaging thoughts. Dropping his bag, he sat heavily on the quilt. The groan of the ropes echoed the groan of his heart.

Summer linked her fingers together and stood quietly in the doorway of the lean-to. The same sadness he'd seen in Pa's eyes lingered in Summer's dark-eyed gaze.

Thomas clamped his hands over his knees. "Summer, why are you living in Hillsboro? What happened to the homestead? Who's manning the mill?"

Summer's lips trembled for a moment. "The gristmill is closed."

"Closed!" Thomas jolted to his feet, remembering too late the low height of the ceiling. His head collided with an overhead rafter, and he plunked back down. Summer rushed to him and ran searching fingers over his scalp. He gently pushed her hands aside. "I'm fine." Truthfully, his head throbbed, but that pain was minimal compared to the ache in his chest. "Why didn't Pa tell me?"

Summer sank down beside him. "He didn't want to worry you. He feared that if you knew, you would rush home before you'd finished your education."

Yes, that would be like Pa — thinking of Thomas instead of himself. But Thomas could have helped . . . somehow. "But it was operating when I was here last summer."

Summer looked to the side. "He did what he could the last two harvests, for those who brought him their wheat."

Thomas thought back, recalling how the grinding seemed to take much less time last summer than in prior years. Pa had joked that they were getting efficient, finishing early, but now he realized fewer people must have come to Pa. He drew a hand down his face. "So he sold the homestead and mill?"

Summer's expression turned sad. "No. So many people from Gaeddert have moved to nearby towns, no one was interested in purchasing the homestead. It sits empty." She paused, her throat convulsing. "It makes your father very sad."

Tears stung behind Thomas's nose as he considered how difficult it must have been for Pa to leave the house and buildings he'd constructed with his own hands. So many dreams were poured into that land, dreams carried from across the ocean and planted with high hopes. Now those dreams had been swept away like dust in a Kansas windstorm.

Summer put a hand on Thomas's knee. "Your father has a job at the steam-powered mill here in town."

Pa, who expressed pride in the three-generations-long line of self-supporting Ollenburger millers, now spent his days toiling for someone else instead of earning his way with his own mill? Thomas's chin quivered. "It's not right, Summer."

"Right or wrong," Summer said, "many of Gaeddert's residents are starting over in other communities. The town was so small, Thomas. With no more wagon trains coming through, and the difficulty in raising crops over the past few years, Gaeddert couldn't support itself any longer. Had the people allowed the railroad to come through the town, it might have survived, but . . . there was no opportunity for growth."

A shadow fell across the room, and Thomas looked up to find Pa filling the doorway. His eyes — lined at the edges, topped by thick yellow brows now streaked with gray — met Thomas's. It looked like his father had deliberately relaxed his face into an expression of complacency.

"Change is not always for bad." Pa spoke as though he'd been a part of the entire conversation, and Thomas wondered how long he'd been listening. "And here in Hillsboro, we have many familiar faces to make us feel not so lonely for our town, Gaeddert."

Summer patted Thomas's knee, sitting up straight with a smile lighting her face. "Why, yes, and one in particular will be pleased to know you're home. She asks about you often."

Thomas waited in silence.

Pa nodded. "Belinda will know soon enough you are here. The Schmidt widow and her daughters reside right there across the alley."

Thomas's mouth went dry. *Belinda* . . .

3

Sitting down to dinner reminded Thomas of how things used to be, before he left Gaeddert to attend high school and college in Boston. The smells were the same — cabbage, sausage, fried potatoes, onions, vinegar, and Summer's good homemade bread. He sat at the same worn table in a chair crafted by his father, with a familiar speckled blue plate in front of him. Holding hands around the table while Pa's rumbling voice offered grace in German brought the same feeling of belonging and contentment that had carried him through childhood. Pa's strong Mennonite faith had been a constant all his life.

With his eyes closed, Pa's voice in his ears and Summer's hand in his, Thomas momentarily forgot that he sat in a kitchen in a strange house in Hillsboro instead of his boyhood home outside of Gaeddert. But the moment Pa said amen, Lena squealed,

"I want 'tatoes!" and yanked him back to the present.

He opened his eyes to the strange kitchen, his little sisters crowded side by side on a bench across from him, and neighboring houses blocking the view from the window. Although he hadn't eaten since early that morning, hunger fled. Only the knowledge of how much it would bother his parents to have him leave the table kept him in his seat.

"So, Thomas," Pa said while scooping potatoes onto Lena's plate, "did you bring home a diploma?"

Thomas stabbed a piece of sausage. "Yes, sir. It's in my bag."

"I will build a frame for it, and you can hang it on the wall of your room."

Thomas stuck a bite of sausage in his mouth to keep from saying anything belittling about the room Pa had called his. He swallowed and forced a light tone. "I'll show you the diploma after dinner."

Pa beamed, nodding at Abby and Gussie. "You see? It is as I told you. Thomas went to school, he studied hard, and now he has paper that says he is a graduate of higher learning. You can be proud of your big brother."

The little girls hunched their shoulders and peeked at Thomas with wide blue eyes.

He waggled his eyebrows at them and enjoyed the giggles his silliness encouraged.

Summer put a serving of cabbage on each of the girls' plates before handing the bowl to Thomas. "Now that you have your degree, Thomas, what are your plans?"

Thomas stifled a groan. He knew the question would be raised, but he'd hoped they would give him a few days before asking about his future plans. He opened his mouth, ready with the pat answer he'd been giving to everyone else — *"I'm waiting to see what doors God opens"* — but Pa cut him off.

"He will do something big, for sure." Pa's eyes sparkled as brightly as his little daughters'.

"Can I go to college, too, Papa?" Abby asked.

"Me too!" Gussie added, nudging her sister with her elbow.

Pa pursed his lips and his whiskers twitched. "I hear talk of maybe a college being built right here in Hillsboro. So it might be you girls can go there when you are grown up, *ja?*" He used his fork to point at each of them in turn. "With a degree in hand, there are no limits. An educated person can do anything."

Thomas could have contradicted Pa by

saying his business administration degree qualified him for many different positions, but there were limits. Instead of arguing, however, he spread strawberry jam on a slice of bread. "It's sure good to eat Summer's cooking again. Nadine's cook is a nice lady, but she thinks everything has to be drowned in some sort of sauce." He made a great show of chewing and swallowing with relish. "This is *good.*"

Summer smiled her thanks, and the conversation shifted. Pa told Thomas how his old dog Patches now lived with the Jantz family outside of town, and Summer came close to gossiping by telling him about his old pals from Gaeddert. She mentioned Toby Kraft was planning a fall wedding, then teasingly added, "Hmm, speaking of weddings . . . is there a special girl in your life?"

Immediately Daphne Severt came to mind, but Thomas forced her from his thoughts. Daphne was young and flighty, and she wanted to stay in Boston. Then again, maybe God was calling Thomas to return to Boston. "No, but —"

"Ach," Pa cut in again, "what for would the boy be thinking of a wife already? A business he must build first, and then a wife he can take, *ja?* A man must have means of

caring for a family before he thinks of starting one." Suddenly Pa's smile faded, and silence fell. The life seemed to drain from the room as he lowered his fork to his plate.

Pa glanced around the table, his gaze crossing each face before settling on Summer. He wiped his mouth and gave his wife's hand a squeeze. "A fine meal you prepared for us, Summer. I thank you. But now I think I go check for the mail." He stood.

"I go get mail!" Lena pushed aside her plate, nearly dumping her cup of milk.

"No, no," Summer chided, sliding the half-empty plate back in front of Lena. "You need to eat your dinner."

Lena's lower lip puckered out. "I go get mail, Papa."

For a moment it appeared Pa would walk out without responding, but then he put his large hand on the child's glossy brown curls. "You want to go to mailbox with Papa?"

"I go get mail." Lena held her arms up to her father. Her dark eyes begged.

The edges of Pa's eyes crinkled. He looked at Summer. "I suppose it will not hurt her to finish her dinner later." He looked at Abby and Gussie, who sat like two prairie dogs on alert. "You would like, too, to walk for the mail?"

41

"Yes, Papa!" the pair chorused.

"Wipe the crumbs from your faces, then, and come along. The company I would enjoy."

Both Abby and Gussie swiped their napkins over their mouths and hurried to Pa's side while he lifted Lena from her seat. "We will walk to the mailbox." He took Lena's hand, stooping forward to accommodate the little girl's much shorter height. Or, Thomas suddenly wondered, was it more the weight of worry sloping his father's shoulders?

Summer watched the party leave, her lower lip tucked between her teeth. Her creased brow raised Thomas's concern. He touched her hand. She jumped and swung to face him. Immediately a smile replaced the troubled look.

"Well . . . we could have dessert, if you're ready for it. I baked an apple pie this morning, and I made sure to add extra cinnamon and a touch of nutmeg, the way you've always preferred. Or there are *gruznikje* in the cookie jar." She half stood, reaching for his dishes. "Abby and Gussie like the ammonia cookies as much as you do, but for some reason Little Lena —"

"Summer."

She stared at him, her lips parted.

"Please — sit down." To his ears, his voice

42

sounded like Pa's. He felt much older than his twenty years.

Slowly, Summer sank back into her chair.

"Is Pa expecting an important letter or package?"

"What?" Furrows appeared on her brow. "No. Why do you ask that?"

"He got up in the middle of dinner to walk to the mailbox."

Summer waved her hand. "Oh, I doubt there's any mail now that you're home, unless Nadine is missing you already. The only letters we get are the ones you or Nadine send. No, he's just . . ." She sighed, her gaze drifting somewhere beyond his shoulder, as if secret thoughts carried her away. "A walk with the girls is good medicine for him."

"Medicine to cure what?" Thomas's sharp tone made Summer's gaze jerk to meet his. A blush crept into her cheeks. "What's wrong with Pa? I know something's bothering him. What is it?"

Summer bowed her head, the slump of her shoulders reminding Thomas of his father's posture as he'd left the table. She glanced toward the door before she finally answered him. "I'm hoping your visit will bring peace to your father's heart. This move to Hillsboro has been so hard for him. He feels as though he's let us all down."

43

"Pa's never let anyone down in his whole life." The defense came naturally.

Summer's sad smile let him know she understood. "Of course not, in our eyes. But in his? When he had to close his mill . . ." Tears appeared in Summer's eyes. "I've never seen him so despondent, Thomas. He left a portion of his heart at the homestead with the mill, and I'm at a loss as to how to help him recover it."

Several different fears dashed through Thomas at once, and he voiced one. "Are you doing all right financially?"

"Oh, yes." Summer nodded emphatically. "Your father would never leave us wanting for anything. Even though we have additional expenses here in town — rent for the house and at the livery where the oxen and your Daisy are boarded — our needs are met. That isn't the issue."

"It's because he has to work for someone else — isn't it." Thomas forced the words past a knot in his throat. Even though Pa wasn't a boastful man, he took pride in being a business owner in his beloved country of America. Surely it pierced his heart to serve under someone else's leadership.

"That isn't it, either." Summer's expression turned thoughtful. "No, it's deeper, Thomas. I believe he feels as though he's lost a part of himself. He wanted so much to leave the mill to his children — he considered it his legacy. And now, here we are in Hillsboro, and the mill stands idle. It hurts him."

Thomas nodded slowly. He considered the difficulties faced by farmers, and he remembered the promises made by Thomas Watson, the Populist candidate for the presidency, to ensure the future success of farmers in the Midwest. Although many from the college believed Theodore Roosevelt would win, Thomas supported Watson. Surely by helping put Watson into office, he'd be making a stride toward improving the lot of area farmers and, in so doing, improve things for his own father.

Knowing how the Mennonites felt about political involvement, he couldn't voice his intention to assist in the campaign to Pa, but Summer would understand. He opened his mouth to share his plans with her, but Pa's booming voice carried into the kitchen.

"No mail in the box."

Gussie and Abby scampered in, their faces sweaty but smiling. Pa followed more slowly, Lena still clinging to his hand. "But a *goot* walk we had, for sure, and Gussie found a four-leaf clover. Show your mama."

Gussie thrust out her dirty fist and opened

45

it to reveal a wilted scrap of green. "Papa says they bring good luck. I'm gonna put it in my storybook and keep it forever."

"What a wonderful idea." Summer smoothed wisps of Gussie's bedraggled blond hair away from her face. "Go put it away now, and then you girls can have some pie, hmm?"

Gussie dashed from the room, and the others returned to their seats at the table. Thomas watched Pa for a few moments, his body relaxing a little when he saw his father's tranquil countenance. Pa picked up his fork and resumed eating as if no interruption had transpired.

As soon as Gussie clattered back into the room, Summer rose and carried the pie to the table. She looked at Thomas, her lips tipping into a teasing grin. "How large should I cut your slice?"

But Thomas put his palms against the table edge and pushed himself back. "I think I'd rather wait and have pie later, if you don't mind. The long train ride, and all the sitting, has me eager to stretch my legs. I'd like to take a walk around the area, get acquainted with . . . the town."

Pa paused midbite. "Do you want some company for your walk?"

"No, Pa." Eagerness to be alone made his

words come out too clipped. He softened the statement with a smile. "You had your walk already. Now it's my turn." He took a moment to tweak his little sisters' curls, place a kiss on Summer's cheek, and squeeze Pa's shoulder before stepping out the back door.

In the yard, he let his head drop back, and he sighed. The early evening sky was light, but the shadows were long, letting Thomas know he had about an hour of daylight left. He looked right and left, taking in the clusters of houses. Everything close together. Like Boston, he thought, even though most Bostonians would scoff at the comparison.

He had anticipated the open space around the homestead — the prairie stretching in all directions. The feeling of confinement that often plagued him in the big city now struck again, tempting him to find the livery, saddle Daisy, and head straight out of town. But a ride could wait until tomorrow. For now a walk would do.

Belinda Schmidt hummed as she stacked the clean, dry plates one on top of the other. The melody skipped a note when she ran her thumb over the tiny nick at the edge of one china plate — the result of careless

47

stacking on a previous day. Mama took such pride in the dishes her own mother had brought from Russia, and it saddened Belinda to see the nick. To avoid scratching the delicate rose design hand-painted in the center of each plate, she placed a square of soft flannel between each layer before transferring the stack to the glass-front cabinet in the dining room.

She passed Malinda, who hunched over the table polishing the silverware. Belinda cringed at the wheezing breaths her sister expelled with every scrub of the soft cloth over the silver finish. Malinda's contorted face spoke clearly of the difficulty of the task, and Belinda considered volunteering to take over. But unwillingness to receive a tongue-lashing for treating Malinda like a helpless child kept her silent. Even when the spoon fell from Malinda's hand to clack against the tabletop and Malinda exploded in a shout of displeasure, Belinda hummed and pretended not to notice.

Belinda had learned early to step carefully around Malinda. Her sister had always been mercurial, her emotions bouncing up and down like a rubber ball. But the fever that had struck in her early twenties, leaving her with a damaged heart, nearly constant pain, and the bitter sting of abandonment from a fiancé who couldn't accept her weakened physical state had brought out a resentful spirit that robbed her of the upward bounce. Belinda couldn't remember the last time she'd seen her sister smile, and trying to cheer her only angered her.

With nine years separating the girls in age, they had never been close, but Belinda had harbored hope they might develop a loving relationship after Papa passed away last winter. Instead, Malinda had pulled further into bitterness. She rarely spoke kindly even to Mama these days.

Belinda turned the little brass key, securing the cabinet door, and returned to the kitchen to finish cleaning up. A creak overhead let her know Mama was in the small attic. Again. Belinda grasped the lip of the sink, lowered her head, and closed her eyes. *Lord, bring healing to Mama's heart. She misses Papa so, but it's not healthy for her to sit beside the trunk of his clothes and relive past days. She needs to move forward.*

A dog barked outside, and Belinda looked out the window. A dark figure moved through the alley — a man, tall and wide-shouldered, his head down and hands thrust deep in his pockets. She recognized him by his size. *Herr* Ollenburger. No other man in town carried such proportions.

His posture exuded sadness, and Belinda's heart caught in sympathy. So many of Gaeddert's former residents seemed to have lost their sparkle. She leaned closer to the open window, watching as he turned into the backyard of the house across the alley. If he glanced her way, she would reward him with a cheery expression.

To her delight, his chin angled in her direction. She called a greeting. "Good evening! Did you enjoy —" She drew back in embarrassment when she realized the man wasn't *Herr* Ollenburger after all. He was as big-boned and square-jawed as her neighbor, but this man was younger and had no beard. And now she noticed he wore a suit — matching pants and jacket — instead of the clothes of a working man.

Recognition dawned, and Belinda gasped. She hadn't seen him more than half a dozen times in the past six years, but her heart set up a patter she feared Malinda would hear in the next room. Pressing her hand to her throat, she whispered, "Thomas."

Although he couldn't have heard her raspy voice, he remained still, seeming to look right at her. She stared, her pulse pounding beneath her trembling fingers. Then the rumors were true — he was back. Back for good? His previous visits had been short, only a few weeks during summers to help his father grind the farmers' bounty, a bounty that had diminished with the scarcity of rain and the abundance of insects. Belinda vacillated between remorse for the farmers' loss and joy for the opportunity to feast her eyes once more on Thomas Ollenburger.

"Hmmph."

At the scornful snort, Belinda jumped. Her sister stood behind her, Malinda's rounded shoulders giving her the appearance of an elderly woman even though she'd only turned thirty a few months ago. "If it isn't Mr. College Man himself." Her tone was caustic.

Belinda gave her sister a frown. "Malinda, you shouldn't be unkind."

"Look at him." Malinda continued as if Belinda hadn't spoken. "Wearing a suit to take a walk, as if he were someone of great importance. Has he no idea how ridiculous a big ox like him looks in city clothes?"

Belinda bit back a sharp retort. Defending Thomas would only lead to further criticism. She took a calming breath and offered a benign rejoinder. "I'm sure his parents are very happy to have him home."

Malinda turned from the window to look at Belinda. A knowing smirk climbed her

51

face. "His parents aren't the only ones, are they, Belinda?"

Fire filled Belinda's cheeks, but she couldn't turn away.

Malinda's lips curled in contempt. "Oh yes, Mama and I are fully aware of your infatuation with Thomas Ollenburger. Papa knew, too, and disapproved, I can tell you that. A miller's son . . . and you know the grief that particular miller caused Papa with his self-righteous attitude. Never would Papa bless a union between you and Ollenburger's son."

Belinda bit the inside of her lip, though she wanted to rise to *Herr* Ollenburger's defense. Although Papa had often railed about Ollenburger's supposed self-righteousness, Belinda had never witnessed anything but a godly attitude from the gentle man. She'd never understood why Papa had held such animosity toward *Herr* Ollenburger.

Malinda grasped Belinda's upper arm with a trembling grip. "But even with Papa's blessing, it would be pointless. Even if Thomas were to return your feelings of affection, he's a city man now. He'll never stay here. And you wouldn't leave Mama and me, would you, Belinda?"

The desperation on Malinda's face made

Belinda want to recoil, but a sudden move could send her sister toppling. Malinda glanced out the window, and her hold relaxed, allowing Belinda to slip away.

"He's gone," Malinda said matter-of-factly.

Belinda spun toward the window. The yard was empty. To her chagrin, tears pricked her eyes.

"It's better this way." Her sister spoke in the kindest tone Belinda had heard in months. "Let him go." She hobbled out of the kitchen, her steps plodding.

Belinda closed her eyes, envisioning Thomas as she'd viewed him through the window: his familiar farm-boy frame attired in a big-city suit. He'd always been more handsome than any other boy in their small school, and the suit only emphasized his masculinity.

Her sister's voice echoed in her mind: *"Let him go."* She sighed. *How can I let him go when he has never been mine to hold?*

4

Thomas resisted the urge to knock before stepping through the back door of the house where his family now lived. All was quiet, the kitchen as tidy as Summer had always kept their little house outside of Gaeddert. In the center of the table, a blue-checked cloth covered a lump of something. Curious, he crossed to it and lifted an edge to find a wedge of pie, obviously left for him.

Built-in cabinets stood along one wall. He found a fork in the second drawer he opened. Just as he pushed the drawer shut, Pa stepped into the kitchen doorway.

"You are home."

The word *home* echoed through Thomas's mind, creating a rush of rebellion. This house was not his home! But he wouldn't hurt Pa by voicing the thought. He put the fork on the table, then removed his jacket and hung it on the back of the chair before sitting down. Tossing the checkered cloth aside, he looked at his father. "I walked farther than I'd planned, but I found my way back again."

Pa chuckled. "You probably followed your nose, *ja?* You smelled the cinnamon in the pie?"

Thomas took a bite. Flavor exploded on his tongue, and he eagerly forked up another mouthful. Pa sat across from him, watching him eat. Not until Thomas had finished the pie and pressed the back of the fork's tines against the plate to get every crumb did Pa speak.

"*Prautsijch* I am of you, son."

Yes, Pa, I know you are proud of me.

"An educated man you are, just as your mother wanted. She would be so happy."

It pleased Thomas that Pa would speak of his mother. Even though she had died before Thomas could truly know her, and even though he had a stepmother he loved, Pa still spoke of Thomas's mother, keeping her alive for him.

"And Summer, too. All of us — you have made us proud."

Thomas swallowed. How proud would Pa be if he returned to Boston?

"I wait up because I need to tell you I will not be here all day tomorrow. Today I meet the train, but tomorrow I must work."

55

Summer had indicated Pa had more expenses in town than he'd had at the homestead. Although he would have liked a couple of uninterrupted days with his father, Thomas understood. "That's all right. I'll probably spend the day getting reacquainted with my sisters and visiting *Grossmutter's* grave. Then, after the weekend, I'll think about a job."

Pa's face lit. He leaned his elbows on the table. "What business will you start?"

Looking into his father's hopeful face, Thomas didn't have the heart to admit he had no desire to start a business in Hillsboro. Hillsboro already had everything it needed to meet the needs of the residents. If Gaeddert wasn't dying, then maybe . . . He chose words he knew his father would accept. "I'm not sure yet, Pa."

Pa nodded, his face serious. "Well, you pray about it. For sure, that is best thing to do. Summer and me, we pray for you, too. You must follow the path God wants for you — that is always best."

Thomas came close to asking whose idea college had been — God's or Pa's? Thomas didn't resent his education — he knew he'd been given a tremendous advantage — but the years away had been far from idyllic. Homesickness had given him stomachaches;

his difficulty in adjusting to city life had aged him beyond his years. And now he was an educated man, expected to do wonderful things — and he didn't know what things he wanted to do.

Pa rose and stretched his arms straight out, balling his hands into fists. He yawned, his gray-streaked beard bristling. "*Ach,* to my room I better go before I fall asleep here. Why am I so tired when no work I do today?"

Thomas stood and rounded the table. "Good night, Pa." Nostalgia tugged at his heart. *"Schlop die gesunt."*

Pa snorted with laughter. "You sound like my *kjleen Jung* again with those words. *Ja,* I will sleep well, for sure, with you under my roof." His deep chuckle rumbled. "I say *Schlop die gesunt* to your sisters when tucking them in each night. Abby and Gussie say it back to me, just as you always did, but Little Lena, she has some trouble with the words. She says 'slop in the zoont.' "

Thomas laughed. "She'll learn, in time." For a moment he wished his father had left the nighttime wish to sleep well a tradition between only the two of them, but then he realized that would be selfish. His sisters would enjoy the tradition of *Schlop die gesunt* as much as he did.

"*Schlop die gesunt,* boy." Pa opened his arms, and Thomas stepped into the embrace, giving his father as many thumps on the back as Pa gave him. As a little boy, Thomas had wanted to grow up to be just like his pa. Now, watching his father's broad back go around the corner toward his bedroom, he wondered how he could be like Pa — thinking of his family first — and still honor his word to Harry Severt and the Populist Party members.

Thomas spent the following morning with his sisters, giving them piggyback rides, letting them beat him at checkers, and reading them a dozen Bible stories from a big picture book. But after lunch, when Summer put Lena down for a nap and instructed Abby and Gussie to sit at the table and practice writing their letters on well-used slates, he headed downtown.

He deliberately skirted the mill, unwilling to witness his father working under someone else's leadership. Guilt stabbed at his avoidance, yet he knew Pa would want to introduce him to everyone, and he wasn't in the mood to smile and be polite. He needed some time alone.

Summer had indicated that Daisy was boarded at the livery. He had no trouble locating the stable. He entered the huge building and scanned the stalls. Daisy spotted him first, nodding her head and whickering. Hurrying to her stall, he laughed out loud when she pawed the ground and continued bobbing her head in excitement.

"Hey, girl! It's good to see you, too."

The livery owner wandered over, and Thomas introduced himself. "I'm going to take Daisy for the afternoon."

"That's fine. Need a saddle?"

"Yes, sir, if you have one I could borrow. Otherwise, I can ride bareback."

The man dragged a worn saddle and blanket from the back of a stall and, after looking Thomas up and down, said, "I figure you can saddle her yourself."

In a few minutes, Thomas swung himself onto Daisy's back and aimed her north out of town. The afternoon sun beat down on his uncovered head, and sweat soaked through his cotton shirt, but he didn't mind. The farther he got from town, the more he relaxed, reveling in the open space and endless blue sky. But he felt his stomach clench when the homestead came into view. Daisy picked up her pace, eager to be back in her familiar territory.

"Whoa, girl." Thomas gave a gentle tug that brought Daisy to a halt. The horse nickered, expressing her displeasure at the delay. But Thomas discovered he didn't want to go to his childhood home. Not when he couldn't stay. Not when nothing waited for him except memories. He turned Daisy's head and clicked his tongue. "C'mon. Let's go visit *Grossmutter* instead."

The gravesite, surrounded by a time-washed picket fence, waited just off the road that led to Gaeddert. Thomas ground-tied Daisy and left her munching prairie grass while he stepped inside the fence and crossed straight to Lena's headstone. Crouching down, he touched the wooden cross Pa had carved with *Grossmutter*'s name and the dates of her birth and death.

The information seemed incomplete, but how would a person encapsulate all of the living and loving that took place between the two dates? No headstone was large enough to hold all that would need recording. He traced his finger over the tiny dash between *January 3, 1817,* and *March 17, 1901,* as he thought about how much the old woman had meant to him. Before Summer came into their lives, she had been the only mother he'd known. All of his little-boy memories included his gentle, steadfast great-grandmother.

His gaze drifted to the house sitting

silently several hundred yards away. His family had teasingly called the house "Nadine's vacation cottage." Although it had been built for Summer, she had lived in it only a few months before marrying Pa. After that, Nadine had used it during her twice-a-year visits until the time Thomas moved in with her in Boston. Even though the house sat empty most of the time, today it seemed dismal without occupants.

Thomas turned back to *Grossmutter*'s cross, wondering again why she had chosen to be buried in this little plot with Summer's first husband instead of the cemetery near the *Kleine Gemeinde* — the little church in Gaeddert where she had attended worship services with Pa, Summer, and himself. Maybe, he surmised, it was her way of letting Summer know she had fully accepted her as part of the family, even though Summer was not Mennonite.

Still on his knees, he spent time tidying the little graveyard — plucking weeds, smoothing the ground where a rabbit or some other small animal had tried to dig a burrow in the hard earth. When the graves were clean, he searched for flowers. Beside the slow-moving Cottonwood River, he located several clusters of wild violets, their velvety petals as deeply hued as a cloudless sky at dusk. He picked a handful to place at the base of *Grossmutter*'s cross.

His task complete, he gathered Daisy's reins and pulled himself into the saddle. "Well, c'mon, Daisy. Let's head back."

When he reached Hillsboro, he slowed Daisy to a measured *clip-clop* and surveyed the town in the late afternoon sunlight. As a boy, he had come with Pa to Hillsboro when they needed to make use of the train station, whether picking up goods or retrieving visitors. Of course, he had also been delivered to Hillsboro on a railcar when he'd come home for summer visits between school years. But those times were few, so his memories of the town were fuzzy. Yet it seemed to him that the town had grown even since his last time here.

For sure it's grown — half of Gaeddert is here now.

He scanned the front windows of each place of business, looking for HELP WANTED placards. As he passed a general merchandise store, a woman with a broom in hand stepped out onto the boardwalk. She swished the straw bristles against the walkway, stirring up a cloud of dust, and she released a mighty sneeze.

Automatically, Thomas called, *"Gesundheit."*

The woman's face angled upward in search of the voice, and Thomas realized the woman was his childhood classmate, Belinda Schmidt. Why had he bothered to bless her? Recollections of her snooty faces and snide comments rushed through his mind, and he clicked his tongue to hurry Daisy along.

But she rushed to the edge of the boardwalk. "Thomas Ollenburger!"

His father hadn't raised him to be impolite. With a sigh, he gave Daisy's reins a tug that wheeled the horse to face Belinda. "Hello. How are you, Belinda?"

She ran her hand over her hair, smoothing back a few stray wisps that had slipped loose of the simple bun. "I'm fine, thank you. I had heard you were back."

He wondered why she didn't mention seeing him through a window of her house last night. Then again, maybe that hadn't been her face in the window, after all. He remembered Summer mentioning Belinda often asked about him, and an odd discomfort held him tongue-tied.

She didn't seem to notice. "I hear you finished college and have a degree now."

In Gaeddert, everyone had known everyone else's business. Hillsboro was bigger, but apparently, as Pa would say, hens still clucked. Belinda's mother, *Frau* Schmidt, had been the noisiest clucker of all. He managed a nod.

"Ekj graute'learen jie."

He hadn't expected congratulations from Belinda. He forced his lips into a tight smile of thanks.

Her smile beamed bright enough for both of them. "You must feel proud of yourself. It is quite an accomplishment to hold a college degree."

He waited for a spiteful comment to follow about him being too big for his britches or being too smart for his own good — her favorite barbs as a child. But to his surprise, she simply stood, squinting into the sun as she waited for his reply. He cleared his throat. *"Dank."* Glancing at the white apron that covered her simple dark blue calico dress, he motioned toward the store. "Do you work here?"

For a moment she ducked her head, bringing into view the straight part in her honey-colored hair. Working as a clerk would be a comedown for a Schmidt, he would think, and her pose seemed to reflect his thoughts.

Then she met his gaze again, giving a slight nod. "*Ja.* After Papa died, we moved into Hillsboro. I've been working here ever since to help care for Mama and Malinda."

Thomas remembered Malinda Schmidt, too, even though she was several years older than he and Belinda. She was as mean-faced as her parents. Pa had always excused Belinda's bad behavior by saying she didn't know how to be kind because no one in her house showed her how. Thomas always thought she could look to others in the community for good examples, if she'd wanted to. Maybe she'd finally done so. Today she seemed pleasant enough.

"Well, I need to get Daisy to the livery. It's good to see you, Belinda." He stretched the truth on that statement.

"You, too." She sounded sincere. She raised her hand in a wave, then returned to sweeping, but he sensed her gaze on his back as he rode on.

In the livery, he returned the saddle and blanket to the stall where they belonged. Then he gave Daisy fresh water and hay and spent some time grooming her with a brush he found on a shelf. It didn't appear that the livery owner had taken the time to use a curry brush on the horse lately. Perhaps he'd take that up with Pa later.

He entered the house through the back door, expecting to see Summer in the kitchen or the girls at the table enjoying an afternoon snack. But the house was quiet.

65

He looked around, scowling, and spotted a piece of paper tacked to the doorframe of his room. He pulled it loose and read the short note. Summer had taken the girls to meet Pa and walk home with him.

So he was alone. He took advantage of the solitude to retrieve paper and a pen from the little desk in his parents' bedroom, feeling like an interloper as he entered the room. But he knew if they were here, they'd allow him access.

Items in hand, he sat at the kitchen table — he didn't feel comfortable using the desk in their room — and quickly penned a letter to Harry. He considered writing to Daphne, letting her know how to reach him since he hadn't realized he would be living in Hillsboro rather than in Gaeddert. But he knew Harry would tell her. Besides, it was probably best if Thomas didn't encourage her by writing too much. Daphne was a girl who saw what she wanted and went after it.

He knew she wanted him.

The thought made his hand still. An image of Daphne filled his mind. She was so beautiful. When she looked at him with her big, brown eyes, something inside of him melted. She fascinated him more than any girl he'd ever met. Did that mean he wanted her, too?

With a grumble of irritation, he returned his attention to the letter, writing:

There are very few job opportunities here, which will pave the way for me to return to Boston. I need to spend at least a couple of weeks with my family, but then I will look into coming back.

A lump filled his throat when he thought about leaving so soon. Yet he knew the longer he stayed, the harder it would be for his father to let him go again. A short visit was best for all of them, and not finding a job would provide a good excuse for returning to Boston, one his parents would understand.

After reading the letter again, he considered adding *Greet Daphne for me* but decided against it. Instead, he signed his name and blotted the ink. Just as he put the pen and inkpot back in the desk, he heard the front door open.

"Thomas?" Pa's voice boomed.

"I'm here, Pa." He stepped from the bedroom into the front room.

Pa caught his arm and gave it a squeeze. "*Goot* news, son. I talk to *Herr* Barkman — owner of this house and the one rented by the Schmidts — and he tell me he can make use of you as a roofer. You go see him first thing Monday. You can earn a wage that will give you money to start your own business. This is very *goot* news, *ja?*"

Thomas slipped the folded letter into his pocket and forced a tight smile. "Sure, Pa. Good news."

5

Daphne stood at the top of the winding staircase, her hand draped over the carved rail, and listened for a reply. When she didn't receive one, she called again, "Harry!"

"Daphne." Mother's scolding voice carried from her dressing room. "Must you insist on that unladylike bellowing?"

Daphne released a huff of displeasure. "Mother, how else am I to locate Harry in this cavern of a house?" The three-story brick country home with its attached conservatory provided any number of corners in which Harry could conceal himself. Yesterday she had searched for nearly an hour before locating him in the window seat of the library, snoozing with a book in his lap. Bellowing would have saved a tremendous amount of time.

The prestige of the country estate outside of Boston wasn't lost on Daphne. She adored the fact that Father was wealthy enough to afford this gabled home with multiple verandas. Her sleeping chamber, decorated in shades of ecru, mossy green, and wild plum, with its own private balcony, was so scrumptious it saddened her to think of marrying and leaving it. Yet the house had its drawbacks, the main one being the difficulty in locating someone who didn't want to be located. Like her ridiculous brother.

On slippered feet, she padded to the highest of the three stairway landings. Leaning well over the railing, she peered to the marble tiled foyer below and bawled, "Ha*aaaa*ry!"

The sound of pounding feet let her know he'd heard her. She hastened down the stairs and met him at the bottom, matching his scowl with one of her own. "Where have you been?"

He ran a hand through his dark hair — his familiar gesture of irritation. "What do you need, Daph? I'm about to drive down to the campaign headquarters."

Daphne experienced a rush of excitement at her brother's words. Although she had no interest in politics, unlike many of her friends who marched in parades and waved signs to demand the right to vote, going to

70

campaign headquarters sounded important and exhilarating. "For what purpose?"

He shifted his weight to one leg, pushing back his jacket to prop his hand on his hip. "Whatever the captain needs." His clipped tone spoke clearly of his impatience to get going.

Daphne wanted to ask to go along. If the campaign headquarters proved boring, she could spend some time in one of the many dress shops or perhaps visit a friend. But she knew her brother well enough to know he would refuse her in his present state of ill humor. So she returned to the reason for summoning him. "I wondered if you'd heard from Thomas."

"He's only been gone a week and a half. I don't expect to hear from Tom so soon."

Daphne wrinkled her nose. "Why do you insist on using the shortened version of his name?" A man of Thomas's proportions needed a name to match. "*Tom* is simply not apropos."

Harry shrugged. "He's Tom to me and nearly all of the fellows from school. It doesn't bother him, so I don't know why it should bother you." Straightening the lapels of his jacket, he said, "If that's all you needed, then —"

"Are *you* planning to write to *him?*"

71

Harry blew out a mighty breath of aggravation. "Daphne, I have no reason to correspond with Tom right now. He's spending a few weeks with his family, and then he'll be back to help with the campaign. Now, please. I need to get going."

Daphne stomped her foot as Harry turned and headed for the back of the house. Brothers could be so annoying! She charged after him. "Can you not wait one more minute?"

He came to a stop, but he let his head drop back and kept his gaze aimed upward. Hands on his hips, he barked, "What?"

She had intended to ask him to delay his drive into town for the length of time it would take her to write a quick message and address an envelope. But his impatient reaction fired her own temper. With another stomp of her foot against the polished floor, she tossed her head and clenched her fists. "Never mind. Go ahead and take care of your oh-so-important business!"

If she'd thought her behavior would soften him, she was wrong. Without a word, he hurried out the back door.

"Oh!" Daphne glared at his disappearing back. Then she spun and stomped back up the stairs to her room. Once there, she gave the door a slam that she hoped echoed all the way to the carriage house. Flouncing onto the bed, she folded her arms across her chest and stewed.

The strong need to communicate with Thomas took her by surprise. She'd never been so smitten with a man before. But her fascination with Thomas, which had only grown as she matured from child to woman, was firmly imbedded. She wouldn't call what she felt for Thomas Ollenburger love. Not yet. But she could see it developing into that overwhelmingly beautiful emotion, given time and togetherness.

How many times had she and her friends swooned in silliness over some boy who wandered by? In hushed tones, they had discussed the intimacies of courtship, giggling like the schoolgirls they were as they contemplated the wonderment of *being in love.* Daphne even imagined herself besotted a time or two, just for the sake of experimentation. But her infatuation with Thomas Ollenburger was . . . different. Deeper. Real.

She threw herself backward onto the mattress. Catching a pillow, she hugged it to her chest and stared at the lace canopy of her four-poster bed. Why was it so difficult this time to be apart from Thomas? Even when he had lived in Boston, many days would slip by without her seeing him; he'd spent weeks of every summer back in Kansas with his family, and she'd never before fretted about the time apart. So why the intense desire for his presence now?

Tossing the pillow aside, she rose from the bed and crossed to her balcony. She curled her fingers around the warm iron railing and closed her eyes. The day of Thomas's party, when she'd stood on the balcony of Nadine Steadman's home with him, came back to her. A sense of urgency had filled her then, and now she realized a fear girded the urgency.

Thomas now had his degree. His schooling was complete. He truly had no reason to return to Boston, save the presidential campaign with which he had promised to help — and that would all be over in November. Her heart lurched. Then she might never see him again.

He needed something — someone — to hold him in Boston permanently. Or at least until which time she was certain of her feelings for him. She popped her eyes open, nibbling her lower lip as her thoughts churned. Long-term commitments involved . . . what? Relationships, naturally. And jobs.

Jobs! Of course, a job — a job better than

anything he could possibly locate in that little town in Kansas — would be motivation enough to keep him here. She raced through her room, down the hallway, and pounded on her mother's dressing-room door. "Mother, I must take the barouche to the city to see Father."

"See here, *Herr* Barkman. Here is my son, Thomas, just as I promised."

Pa pressed Thomas forward to shake the man's hand, making Thomas feel like a ten-year-old again.

"A strong, dependable worker he will be for you."

Herr Barkman and Thomas exchanged a firm handshake while Pa went on, making Thomas's ears burn. "A job he needs, but not for forever. My Thomas has . . ." Pa took in a deep breath. His next words came out humbly. "A college degree, so his own business he will start one day soon. But it takes money to do this. So that is why he needs the job."

"*Ja*, Peter, you have told me this already." *Herr* Barkman winked and poked Thomas on the shoulder. "I think your father is big-headed over your accomplishment, but we cannot blame him, can we?" He stroked his beard, squinting against the bright morning sun. "Your father says you will not need a job long, but I could use you for a little while. I have a roof that needs replacement. Leaks real bad. The last man I hired quit after only one day. He was afraid of high places. Do high places frighten you?"

"No, sir."

"You are familiar with repairing roofs?"

Thomas was no expert, but he knew he could fix a roof. From the time he was big enough to wield a hammer, he'd worked side by side with Pa on everything from putting up walls to hammering down shingles. He nodded. "I'm familiar with most carpentry jobs."

Herr Barkman looked satisfied. "So I can count on you to see it through?"

Thomas held his breath. He'd sent his letter to Harry already, and he hated to disappoint his friend. But looking at Pa's face, he knew he couldn't disappoint his father, either. How long could it take to repair a roof? Maybe a week? Surely, he could wait that long. "You can count on me."

"Goot. Goot." The man gave Thomas a hearty clap on the back. "Well, then, let us get you working. There is a wagon waiting behind my house with cut shingles in the bed, as well as a ladder, tools, and nail keg — everything you need. You know where is

76

the Schmidt house?"

Aware of Pa's watchful gaze, Thomas carefully guarded his expression. "Yes, sir."

"You will see the pocks from last spring's hailstorm. Replace all the damaged shingles." The man twisted his lips. "It will be most all of them."

Most all of them equated to a good-sized job — more than a week, for sure. Thomas set his jaw and smacked his hat onto his head. "Then I better get started. Bye, Pa. See you at lunch."

Working right across the alley from his folks' house had its advantages, Thomas discovered. While he tore loose damaged shingles and tossed them into a pile on the ground, his little sisters provided entertainment with their enthusiastic chasing game. As a youngster, he had often played *Eene, meene, Maun* on the playground. He wiped the sweat from his forehead and grinned as Gussie snatched Abby around the middle and crowed, *"Eene, meene, Maun! Botta enna Paun! Kjees enne Kiep! Du best jriep!"*

Standing, Thomas waved his hat and called, "Good job, Gussie!"

The girls giggled, waved at him, and then took off again for another round. Thomas turned back to his task, whistling a merry tune. He had no idea what tagging someone had to do with butter in a skillet or cheese in a basket, but it was obvious his sisters enjoyed the game as much as he had as a child. The sound of their laughter carried him through the first hour of removing shingles.

Midmorning, Summer crossed the alley with a jug of ginger water and a plate of oatmeal cookies. He eagerly climbed down the ladder to enjoy a few minutes in the shade. Summer handed him the jug and asked, "How is the job going?"

Thomas swallowed, backhanded his moist lips, and grimaced. "I'm afraid it's going slow. Most of the shingles need to be replaced, but at least the hailstones didn't damage much of the sheeting." At her puzzled look, he added, "The boards underneath the shingles."

"Ah." She nodded, holding out the plate of cookies. "Well, I know you'll do a good job. The Schmidts should appreciate it."

At that moment the back door of the Schmidt house opened. Malinda Schmidt stood in the doorway. "Have you finished for the day?"

Thomas nearly laughed. "Finished? Oh, no. There's still much to do."

Her frown caused deep furrows around her mouth. "The sounds of whistling, scraping, and thudding are giving Mama a horrible headache."

Thomas had no idea how he would repair their roof without making noise. He looked helplessly at Summer.

Summer offered Malinda a kind smile. "The roof must be repaired, Malinda."

"Can you not come down off the roof to place the shingles on the pile? The steady crack of shingles hitting the ground is *en Fe'druss.*"

Thomas stared at the woman in disbelief. They found the sounds of his working annoying? Surely it was less annoying than a leaking roof. He opened his mouth to inform Miss Schmidt of the ridiculousness of her request, but Summer interrupted.

"Perhaps *Frau* Schmidt could put some cotton in her ears to block the sounds. Or you are welcome to come sit in my parlor while Thomas works."

Malinda huffed and slammed herself inside the house.

Summer sighed and put her hand on Thomas's arm. "Don't take offense."

Thomas forced a light laugh and brushed his hands together, ridding himself of the remaining cookie crumbs. "I learned a long time ago not to pay attention to anything a Schmidt says. Her words are water off a duck's back."

Summer returned to her house, and Thomas climbed back onto the roof. He made no effort to tiptoe, and he continued to toss the shingles rather than climb down the ladder and place them quietly in a pile, as Malinda Schmidt had suggested, but he did stop whistling. Every now and then Malinda appeared in the yard, her face turned upward with a hand shielding her eyes, a sour expression on her face. Each time, he gave a wave and returned to work.

By the time the sun was straight overhead, Thomas had cleared a third of the old shingles on the back half of the house. He stood, hands on hips, surveying the stripped area. If a rain came, the Schmidts would have a mess with the sheeting unprotected. Should he spend the afternoon shingling the area he'd just cleared? He shifted his gaze to the sky. The cloudless expanse of endless blue gave no threat of rain, but he knew wind could stir up a storm quickly on the plains of Kansas.

"Boy!"

Thomas jerked then flailed to keep his balance on the steeply pitched roof. His balance restored, he turned slowly to find his father and Belinda Schmidt in the middle of the Schmidts' backyard, looking upward.

At the horrified look on Belinda's face, he released a little laugh. He inched his way to the roof's edge and crouched, elbows on knees. "You thought I was going to fall, didn't you?"

"A mountain goat you are not," Pa said, shaking his head. "It is time to see what Summer has fixed for our lunch."

Thomas wouldn't argue about eating. Accustomed to sitting in a classroom during the day, a morning's hard labor had built his appetite. He climbed down the ladder to the security of even ground. Walking toward Pa, he slapped at his dust-coated trousers.

He heard a small sneeze from somewhere beside him. Belinda held her fingers beneath her nose, obviously fighting off another sneeze.

"Gesundheit," Pa said.

Belinda sniffled. "Thank you, *Herr* Ollenburger. I must have caught a cold. I've been sneezing a lot lately."

Thomas flicked a surprised glance in her direction. Her sneezing seemed to be related to dust, and he'd just created a cloud of it by slapping at his filthy pants. Yet she hadn't pointed a finger of blame.

"Sneezing clears the head," Pa said, chuckling. "So you will be fine now."

Belinda peeked past Pa to Thomas. "I

didn't realize *Herr* Barkman had hired you to repair our roof, Thomas."

Pa beamed. "*Ja,* a job Barkman gave him. So now he earns a wage."

Long-legged for a woman, Belinda was tall enough that her head reached Thomas's chin. Perspiration glowed on her forehead and nose, yet she showed no signs of moving into the comfort of shade. "So you'll be staying in Hillsboro, then, Thomas?"

Thomas knew whatever he said would be repeated. He chose his words carefully. "I've promised to see that your roof is repaired."

Belinda's fine brows came down, the scowl a familiar sight from their childhood. But a moment later, her expression cleared and she gave a nod. "Of course. There aren't many job opportunities in Hillsboro, and you'll want to find something more suited to your degree, I'm sure."

When Thomas didn't answer, Belinda shifted her attention to Pa.

"*Herr* Ollenburger, I will be going to the mangle house this afternoon. If *Frau* Ollenburger has sheets or clothes to be mangled, I would be happy to take them for her."

Pa threw back his head and hooted. "*Ach!* One does not often hear the word 'happy' when speaking of mangling."

Thomas, thinking of the effort it took to

push and pull the box of rocks over cloth-wound rollers, agreed with Pa.

Belinda smiled, tipping her blond head. "It isn't the task of mangling that gives me pleasure, but I do appreciate the comfort of pressed, softened sheets on my bed. Besides, *arbeit macht das Leben süz.*"

"For sure, work sweetens life," Pa agreed, his grin wide. He scratched his beard, winking in Belinda's direction. "I tell Summer what you say about the mangle house. But maybe she decides to sweeten her own life with the mangling, hmm?"

Belinda and Pa laughed softly together, as if sharing a joke. A weight pressed in Thomas's chest. He felt oddly alone standing under the sun while his pa and Belinda Schmidt enjoyed a shared moment of amusement. He opened his mouth to suggest they head in for lunch, but suddenly Pa's expression turned serious.

His arms crossed over his chest, Pa said, "How is your mother doing now, Belinda? I have not seen her in Sunday service for many weeks."

Immediately, Belinda lost her sparkle. Her shoulders slumped, and she ducked her head. "Mama is . . . having a hard time, *Herr* Ollenburger. I'm worried about her."

"Well, losing her husband is a hard thing."

Pa's kind, serious tone brought Belinda's head up. "We will keep praying for her heart to heal. And I will send Summer over with some *honigkuchen*. That will be *goot, ja?*"

Belinda's eyes flew wide. "Oh, no! Honey cookies take so much effort, and your wife has three little girls to care for each day." She swallowed hard. "Besides, Mama wouldn't eat them. I can hardly get her to eat anything."

Pa's frown expressed concern. "Not eating is normal when one has suffered loss." He stroked his beard again, his expression solemn. "Well, if no cookies we send, at least we send Summer. She understands your mother's pain of loss. Maybe she can give words of comfort."

Belinda blinked rapidly. "Thank you, *Herr* Ollenburger. Perhaps a visit from Summer would do Mama good."

Pa gave Belinda's shoulder an awkward pat. "We will be praying. God restores joy."

A sad smile appeared on Belinda's face. "Thank you." She backed up, waving her hand toward her house. "I'd better go in. I need to put a meal on the table. Good-bye, *Herr* Ollenburger."

Thomas followed Pa across the alley toward the back door of the little house. "Since when are you friends with Belinda

84

Schmidt?"

Pa gave Thomas a puzzled look. "Have I been her enemy?"

"No. But friends? With the Schmidts?" Thomas raised one brow. He could never remember *Herr* or *Frau* Schmidt making any effort to befriend Pa. Especially after he took Summer as his wife — a woman not raised in the Mennonite faith — the Schmidt family had looked down their noses at the Ollenburgers.

Pa frowned. "We must not judge, Thomas. Belinda is a fine girl. She cares for her mother and sister, and all without complaint." He pointed a finger, making Thomas wish he could shrink into the sparse blades of grass. "You do not hold grudges based on her behavior as a little girl. She is no longer that little girl, and the Bible tells us to forgive seventy times seven."

Thomas cleared his throat, offering a meek shrug. "Sure, Pa. I don't hold a grudge."

Pa's expression cleared. He threw his arm around Thomas's shoulders and herded him through the door. "Then let us eat and return to work. It is *goot* for man to labor hard, *ja?*"

Thomas followed Pa to the kitchen, where his little sisters dashed forward to grab Pa's legs and beg to be held. Thomas stood to the side, feeling left out again. As he watched his father stoop down to catch all three girls in a hug, he suddenly wondered why Belinda hadn't wished him good-bye before scampering off into her own house.

And then he wondered why it bothered him.

6

The aroma of dinner greeted his nose as Thomas stepped through the back door. As he had come to expect over the past several days, his sisters raced across the floor to climb all over him, bantering and giggling in their excitement to have him home again. He responded by swinging Abby and Gussie in a circle, then tossing Lena in the air and catching her again.

His littlest sister wrapped her arms around his neck and squealed. Thomas carried her to the table while Abby and Gussie tugged at his sleeves, begging, "Again, Thomas! Swing me again!"

He sent Summer a helpless look, and she shook her head, laughing. "Come, girls, let your brother be." She plucked Lena from his arms and slid her into her chair at the table. "He's worked long and hard today. He deserves a rest and some quiet."

On tiptoes, their hands covering their giggling lips, Abby and Gussie crept to their chairs and sat, peering at Thomas with sparkling eyes.

Summer winked at Thomas. "They enjoy having you here."

Thomas smiled, but he wanted to groan. Was it kind to let his sisters get accustomed to his presence when he'd be leaving soon? The Schmidts' roof was almost complete. One more day of hard labor, and he should be free to return to Boston.

Rolling up his sleeves as he went, he joined Pa at the washstand near the sink and soaped his arms to the elbow. With he and Pa crowded side by side, it was a tight fit, but they managed to get their hands clean.

After Pa's prayer, Summer dished food onto the girls' plates before handing the bowls to Pa and Thomas. Thomas, observing how his little sisters obediently kept their hands in their laps until everyone had been served, appreciated the training Summer had given them. They were as well-mannered as any high-class Boston child.

A thought hit him: If Pa and Summer were to move to Boston, the whole family could be together. Pa no longer had his mill, so nothing held him in Kansas. If they all moved to Boston, Thomas wouldn't need to feel guilty about leaving. The little girls, with their proper behavior, would fit neatly in Nadine's world. Perhaps he should suggest it.

Then Pa said, "No pickles? Or *kraut?*"

Summer arched a brow. "Isn't there enough food on the table to fill you?" The center of the table overflowed with platters of fried pork, noodles, potatoes, carrots, and sliced home-baked bread. Jars of jam and a molded pat of butter crowded between platters.

"*Ach,* a meal is not a meal without something sour," Pa said.

Thomas could imagine Nadine's sour look at his father's request for pickles.

Summer laughed softly. "Very well. I'll get some pickles from the pantry." She ran her hand over Pa's shoulders as she moved past him, her slender fingers tweaking a thick hank of hair behind his ear. When she put the pickle jar in front of Pa's plate, she leaned forward and delivered a kiss on his whiskered cheek.

He smiled, forking two fat pickles onto his plate. "*Dank,* Summer."

Another sweet laugh provided her reply.

Thomas, looking on, experienced a rush of envy. Someday he wanted what Pa had with Summer — a loving, tender, God-ordained relationship with a woman. He had witnessed friendship turning to love between his father and Summer. Over the years of their marriage, despite facing rejection from some community members who couldn't accept Summer's non-Mennonite upbringing, the heartache of losing their firstborn child, and now the loss of their home, the love had never flickered.

From *Grossmutter*'s stories, he knew his mother and Pa had been childhood friends before declaring their love for one another. It seemed to Thomas that friendship was key in providing a sound base for a marriage. The thought made Daphne flit into his mind. She wasn't a friend, exactly — more an acquaintance. He thought backward in time and scowled, realizing he'd never really considered a girl a friend. Maybe it was time he looked a little harder at the females in his circle of acquaintanceship.

Summer picked up a jar from the middle of the table. "Belinda made the gooseberry jam. The Schmidts have a bush growing in their side yard." She made a face as she spooned thick, seedy preserves onto a slice of bread. "I don't have the patience to pick berries surrounded by thorns, but I do appreciate Belinda's diligence. It's quite tasty."

She offered the jar to Thomas. "Try some. The jam is a thank-you for visiting her mother."

Thomas looked at the jar's contents, seeing instead an image of Belinda — tall, honey-haired, in a simple dress and apron, swishing a broom's bristles over a wooden porch floor. Then a second picture intruded: Daphne — diminutive, dark-haired, fashionably attired, sipping punch from a cut-glass cup. Two such different images.

Pa spoke around a bite of pork. "How is *Frau* Schmidt?"

Summer put down her fork and sighed. "Not well at all. I understand why Belinda is so concerned. The woman is lost in melancholy. And Malinda is so caught up in her own grief, she doesn't help at all. Poor Belinda carries a full load between working at the general merchandise store, caring for the house, and trying to maintain a positive spirit. And she's suffered loss, too. Her mother doesn't seem to recognize anyone's pain but her own, however, and we all know how self-centered Malinda has always been."

Thomas glanced out the kitchen window. Across the expanse of their backyard and separating alley, the glow of a lantern lit the window of the Schmidts' kitchen. Was Belinda sitting down to dinner with two uncommunicative women? His heart lurched in sympathy.

"You keep going over to visit," Pa said, giving Summer's hand a squeeze. "Time it takes for hearts to heal, but we know healing comes. *Frau* Schmidt needs the reminder, and she needs to see *Be'weiss* of a healed heart." He smiled warmly at Summer. "What better testament is there than a woman who has been restored to joy?"

More pictures of Belinda tried to crowd through Thomas's mind — pictures he didn't want to explore. Pa had told him not to carry a grudge, and he'd committed to letting go of his past dislike of Belinda Schmidt. But this wave of sympathy was sending his heart in directions he didn't want it to go.

Thomas set down the jar without helping himself to preserves. "Dinner was very good, Summer. Thank you. But may I be excused? I believe I'd like to take a walk and stretch my legs."

Abby stood up eagerly. "May I go, too, Thomas?"

Gussie leaned forward, her bright eyes begging. "And me?"

Lena echoed, "And me!"

Thomas shot his parents a look he hoped

communicated his desire to be alone.

Pa caught Lena's waving fist. "You girls go for a walk with me."

"But we want to go with Thomas!" Abby and Gussie chorused the complaint.

Pa shook his head, his expression firm. "Not this time, *kjinja*." His tone softened as he added, "If there are letters, I will need your help to get them home safely."

The girls sighed but voiced no more arguments.

Thomas pushed away from the table. "I'll see you later." He strode out the back door. Heading to the narrow alleyway between yards, he planned to steer clear of the main streets and walk along the outskirts of town. But as he passed a small shed on the corner of the lot directly behind his parents', he heard something that brought him to a halt.

He tipped his head, listening intently. The wind rustled leaves in the trees that lined the alley. Night sounds — a turtledove's coo, a dog's distant bark, the gentle lullaby of the wind — tried to mask the noise, but he heard it again. A sound of distress. Weeping.

He crept to the shed and put his ear against the planked door. The sound came from inside. He considered moving on, letting whomever it was have privacy, but in the end he couldn't. Someone needed help or comfort.

He tapped lightly and gave the door a push. The hinges squeaked, and a path of light fell across the dirt floor of the tiny building. In the corner, nearly hidden by shadows, Thomas glimpsed a woman crouching forward over her lap, crying into her apron.

Belinda Schmidt.

"Poor Belinda carries a full load." Apparently Belinda's load had finally overwhelmed her.

He cleared his throat, then whispered, "Belinda?"

She burrowed forward into her lap. Sobs convulsed her, but the sounds that had captured his attention ceased.

He took a step into the shed. "Is there anything I can do?"

With a jerky motion, she sat upright and turned her face toward him. Her eyes were red and puffy, her blotchy cheeks moist. She'd obviously been crying for quite a while. The sight of her misery touched Thomas more deeply than he could understand.

Summer's comments returned to him. *"She's suffered loss, too."* Although Thomas hadn't cared a great deal for *Herr* Schmidt, the man had been Belinda's father. Now he was gone. Having lost his own mother and *Grossmutter,* he understood her heartache.

He moved forward a few more steps but maintained a respectful distance. His hands deep in his pockets, he asked again, "Can I do anything . . . to help?"

To his surprise, a short, humorless laugh rang out. "Oh, Thomas . . . that's funny."

He crunched his brow.

Lifting her apron, she mopped her face. The cloth hid her face from view, but he heard her murmur, "How very, very funny." She dropped the apron and laughed again.

Thomas took a shuffling step backward. Could she be addlepated? Her comment made no sense.

Her shoulders rose and fell in a mighty sigh. Although the crying had ceased, her chin still quivered, as if she had a tenuous grip on control. She faced him again. "You — of all people — asking if you can help, after the way I . . ."

Thomas removed his hands from his pockets and crouched, propping his elbows on his knees for balance. The minimal light filtering through the open door and cracks in the siding created a gloomy, oppressive setting. He was eager to escape, yet something held him captive. Maybe Belinda was right — something was funny.

"I'm really all right," she said. Her voice sounded hollow and stuffy, but the tone was matter-of-fact. "It's just that sometimes I need . . . release. I can't cry in front of Mama or Malinda — it upsets them. So I come out here."

Thomas thought about the selflessness of her act. He nodded slowly. "My pa says God gave us tears to express the feelings underneath."

Belinda blinked twice, looking at him. "My father didn't have patience for tears." She dropped her gaze and toyed with her apron. "Maybe that's why I have so many tears now. I've been storing up."

Thomas had no idea what to say in response.

Suddenly her chin bounced up, and she fixed him with a panicked look. "Please don't say anything to your parents about finding me here. If your stepmother mentions it to my mother, she —"

"Don't worry." Thomas held out one hand. "Your secret is safe with me."

Belinda sucked in her lips, examining his face. Her shoulders relaxed. "Yes. You were always truthful as a child. I can trust you."

He met her gaze. "But I do think you need to find some help. Sitting out here crying doesn't make anything better, does it?"

Belinda sighed. "Apparently not. Mama has been crying for weeks, and she's no better than the day we put Papa in the ground. And Malinda . . ." She sighed again, a sound heavy with unspoken burdens.

From his position near the door, Thomas couldn't touch Belinda, but he had the urge to stretch out his hand and take hers. To offer comfort. Instead, he linked his fingers together and cleared his throat.

"I remember when Summer first came to live on our property." He kept his voice low. Many memories pressed for release, but he pushed them aside. "She was sad. I even wondered if she had lost the ability to smile. But over time, with prayer, with Pa's patient teaching, and . . ." He hesitated. He didn't want to take too much credit, yet he knew he had played a role in Summer's recovery from deep sorrow. Finally he said, "And with me growing to love her and need her, she found a reason to live again. To love again. God planted the willingness to love again in her heart. That doesn't mean she's forgotten her other children or her husband, but she's been able to put the past behind her and move forward. It will happen for your mother . . . and you, too."

Belinda stared at him, her expression

unreadable. For long moments they remained in silence. The light had dimmed a bit, indicating the setting of the sun. A turtledove cooed his soft evening song, harmonizing with the sweet whisper of wind.

Finally Belinda said, "Thank you, Thomas."

Her voice, soft and tremulous, had a strange effect on him. His stomach turned a somersault. He pressed his palms to his thighs. "Y-you're welcome. You'll be all right now?"

She stood, straightening her skirt with impatient, embarrassed motions. "Yes. I'll be fine. But I need to . . ." She glanced toward the doorway, which he blocked.

His neck flooded with heat. "Oh." He stepped aside.

She moved past him, but when she reached the opening she paused and peered up at him. Her blue eyes, dark in her pale face, held him captive for three interminable seconds, and then without a word she hurried across the yard and closed herself in her house.

Thomas remained in the shed's doorway for several more seconds, trying to understand the odd feelings coursing through him. For the first time, he had looked at Belinda Schmidt and seen something besides his childhood nemesis. He had seen . . . a woman. And an attractive woman, at that.

Shaking his head, he stalked out of the shed and closed its door with a firm *click*. A glance at the rising moon told him he'd used up the time he meant to spend walking. He jammed his hands into his pockets and turned back to his parents' house, but his mind remained on the house across the alley. On Belinda.

The moment he stepped into the kitchen and closed the door, Abby came running with Gussie on her heels.

"I want to give it to him!" Gussie squealed.

"No, me! Papa let me carry it!" Abby responded, holding a square of white — an envelope, he realized — away from Gussie's reaching hands.

Thomas strode forward and plucked the envelope from Abby's grasp before the two managed to destroy it with their tussle.

Abby stuck out her lower lip. "I wanted to *give* it to you, and you *took* it." She folded her arms across her skinny chest and glowered up at him.

Thomas tapped the top of her head with the envelope and waggled his eyebrows. "Well, now I've got it, so all is well."

With a giggle, Abby dropped her sullen pose and scurried away. Gussie chased after her. Chuckling, Thomas watched them disappear around the corner before turning his attention to the envelope.

In the upper left-hand corner, he read the name — *Miss Daphne Severt* — and his stomach turned another somersault.

7

Seated on his bed and leaning forward, Thomas angled the pages to catch the lamp's glow so he could read Daphne's letter. Once, twice, and then again. By the third time, he nearly had it memorized.

The letter was surprisingly brief. A mere three paragraphs in length. Short paragraphs. Daphne always had so much to say, and it was a surprise that she didn't write long, chatty letters. It also seemed wasteful to use an embossed sheet of stationery — which added weight and expense to the mailing — on what could have fit neatly on a penny postcard. But, he had to admit, her three brief paragraphs gave him much food for thought.

Harry spends every day at campaign headquarters. He looks forward to you joining him in the battle to put Thomas E. Watson in the White House.

Eagerness made Thomas's heart thud. Watson's backing of the Farmers' Alliance, which worked to prevent deflation of agricultural prices, had won Thomas's support. Raised by a man who made his living from the bounty of farmers, Thomas had a personal stake in protecting the livelihood of those who raised crops. He puzzled over Harry's zealousness for this particular candidate, but he supposed Harry's reasons weren't as important as his actions.

My father has several positions at the Boston Beacon for which you would be qualified. I am certain the wage would be sufficient to secure your interest.

Thoughts of working for the Severt family newspaper brought a rush of excitement. As Daphne said, the wage would no doubt far exceed what he currently made from *Herr* Barkman. But more than that, it would be a challenge and a chance to use the skills he'd acquired in college.

Boston is terribly lonely without your presence, my dear Thomas. I await your hasty return.

The shortest paragraph gave him the biggest jolt. The thought of Daphne Severt longing for his return made him feel flattered. There certainly could not be a lovelier woman than Daphne. And she wanted to spend time with Thomas, the big, clumsy son of a Mennonite miller.

He looked again at the words *my dear Thomas,* and his chest constricted until he could hardly draw a breath. *Her* dear Thomas . . . Her *dear* Thomas . . . The words made him feel so special. So . . . *desired.*

He carried the letter to his nose and sniffed, hoping for an essence of Daphne — she always held the subtle fragrance of oranges. But no citrusy scent lingered on the page. Disappointed, he lowered it to his lap. The absence of the distinctive aroma made his heart pine for the presence of the delicate woman. Leaving the page unfolded, he propped it against a stack of books on his bureau top so he could see the neat lines of script.

Lying back on his bed, he linked his hands behind his head and stared at the simple letter. Plans raced through his head.

Talk to Pa about the job opportunity in Boston.

Finish up the last section of the Schmidts' roof.

Contact Nadine about moving in with her

again — or contact Harry about locating a small apartment.

Make travel arrangements.

A light tap on his door interrupted his thoughts. He sat up and called, "Come in."

The door cracked open, and Summer's face appeared. "Were you sleeping?"

"No, not yet."

She pushed open the door a little more and stood in the doorway. "I wanted to say thank you."

He crunched his brow. He couldn't think of anything he'd done to warrant thanks.

"These past days, having you home again, has brought a measure of peace to your father's heart. He was so afraid you would be disappointed in him."

Thomas opened his mouth, but she held up her hand.

"As you know, he wanted you to have the gristmill, and now it's gone. But seeing you willingly accept the job of roofing and getting to spend his evenings with you has eased his heartache. It's given him a fresh outlook on his situation here." She moved into the room and leaned forward to kiss Thomas's cheek. "I know it isn't the kind of job you want to have, and he knows it, too, but for now . . . you're making him very happy. So thank you, Thomas."

A lump filled Thomas's throat. "I'd do most anything for Pa." *But can I forgo my commitment to Watson's campaign and a job opportunity in Boston?*

A soft smile rewarded his words. She cupped his jaw with her hand, the touch tender. Then she slipped from the room, closing the door behind her.

Thomas spent a restless night, dreaming repeatedly that his arms were tied to horses being driven in opposite directions. The desire to please Pa battled against the tug of a future in Boston. By the time the morning sun sent light through the slit in his curtains, he still had no firm answers. He only knew he couldn't leave Pa. Not yet.

"Good-bye, Mama. Have a good morning." Belinda placed a kiss on her mother's cheek. "I'll be home at noon to fix you some lunch."

Mama lay in her bed with her graying hair in tangles across the pillow. Her skin appeared sallow, her cheeks sunken from weeks of refusing food. Although her eyes were open, she didn't so much as glance at her daughter.

Belinda swallowed tears. "I love you, Mama."

Her mother rolled to her side, facing away

from Belinda, and pulled the covers to her chin.

Belinda sighed and left the room. Across the hall from Mama, scuffling sounds came from Malinda's room. Her sister was awake. Belinda tapped lightly on the door.

"What do you want?" Malinda called from inside the room.

"May I come in?" Belinda maintained a pleasant tone.

"No. I'm not dressed."

Belinda closed her eyes, resisting the urge to sigh. "Would you please try to convince Mama to get up and eat some breakfast? I left toasted *zwieback* on the table." Mama had always relished dipping the crusty halves of the leftover two-level rolls in coffee.

A long silence followed, during which Belinda wondered if Malinda had drifted back to sleep. Finally a brusque reply came.

"Fine. *Au'dee.*"

"Good-bye," Belinda offered in return, then headed down the narrow hallway and out the front door to walk to work. When she reached the road, she heard a sound that immediately brought a smile to her lips — laughter. Loud. Boisterous. Full of joy.

Like a magnet, the sound pulled her, leading her between two houses, across the alley, and alongside the house rented by the Ollenburgers. When she reached the corner of the house, she stopped, suddenly unwilling to intrude into the merriment. But another burst of laughter urged her forward a few inches, just enough to peek around the edge of the house.

The scene that greeted her made her feet itch to rush around the corner and join the fun. Peter Ollenburger and all three of his little girls frolicked on the dew-kissed grass. Belinda clamped her hand over her mouth to hold back her own laughter. Their shadows, stretched long by the morning sun, wove in and out as the children dashed back and forth in a dance of uninhibited glee.

The girls' high-pitched giggles carried over *Herr* Ollenburger's deep belly laugh. He tickled and teased, his fingers poking ribs and tugging curls, while the girls darted away and then back again, their bright faces begging him without words. But Belinda heard the words in her imagination: *Me, Papa! Now me!*

Had she ever played this way with her own father? No, of course not. Papa had been too stern, too formal to allow himself to play. Not even in the house, with no watching eyes, would he have behaved in anything less than a dignified manner. And look what they had lost out on because of it. What wonderful memories the Ollenburger girls were building. Belinda wished she had similar memories on which to reflect now that her father was gone.

Instead, she remembered Papa's coldness, Mama's criticism, Malinda's constant ups and downs. Their lives reflected an inward misery that had matched her own until the day three years ago when she had asked Jesus into her heart. Why hadn't her parents, who claimed to love God, shown evidence of the joy of the Lord rather than being trapped in the dictates of *do*'s and *do not*'s? With a sigh, she opened her eyes for one last glimpse at the Ollenburgers' fun.

Herr Ollenburger dropped on his back in the grass, his arms straight out from his sides. All three girls dove on top of him, the littlest one burying her hands in his beard. His arms wrapped around the squealing group, and he rocked back and forth, his deep chuckle rumbling.

Belinda, with tears stinging her eyes, crept away. While she performed her duties at the mercantile, she replayed images from the morning scene. Why did the playful romp have such a hold on her? A longing rose up and held with a pressure in her chest that became a physical ache. She wanted what the Ollenburgers had. Love. Laughter. *Fun.*

At noon, she hurried to the end of Main Street, her heart pattering with hope that her path would cross that of *Herr* Ollenburger and Thomas when they met for lunch. To her delight, she reached her backyard just as Thomas climbed down from the roof to join his father. She lifted her skirts slightly and ran to them.

"Hello!" She sounded breathless, but she knew it wasn't because of the brief run. Suddenly she questioned the wisdom of speaking with *Herr* Ollenburger and Thomas. Now that she stood side by side with the men, her evening crying bout — and Thomas's kindness — came back to haunt her. Would he feel uncomfortable around her?

Herr Ollenburger waved in greeting. "Hello, Belinda. I must thank you for the *goot* gift of jam you give to my wife." He patted his belly, chuckling. "It was *dääj goot* on Summer's fresh-baked bread."

His compliment sent a shaft of warmth through her middle. "I'm so glad you enjoyed it."

Thomas said, "How are you today?"

She read the meaning behind the simple question. Had she recovered from her sadness? Although nothing in her family had

109

changed, she'd been allowed a glimpse of happy times. Watching it wasn't the same as living it, but it was better than not knowing happiness existed at all.

She offered a trembling smile and slight nod. "I am fine, *dank.* And you?"

"I'm fine."

"*Ja,* fine, and Thomas is nearly finished with your roof, Belinda," *Herr* Ollenburger said with pride in his voice. "Just the tarring of cracks, and a rainproof roof you will have."

Thomas's head jerked toward his father, his jaw dropping slightly in an expression of confusion. "Tar?"

Herr Ollenburger delivered a light slap to Thomas's shoulder. "Why, of course, tar. How else do you seal all the little places where water can leak through?"

"Oh." Thomas looked at the roof and heaved a sigh. "Of course."

Eager to see his smile return, Belinda said, "Thank you, Thomas, for your hard work." He merely nodded in response, his eyes troubled.

Herr Ollenburger added in a jovial tone, "And I thank you, Belinda, for the newspaper your family shares with us. One of last week's papers has an article about Plymouth Rock chickens which I find very *intra'ssaunt."*

Apparently he had found the article interesting enough to memorize nearly all of it, and the man's lively retelling of the merits of the new breed of chickens brought a smile to Thomas's face, which Belinda mirrored, her heart trembling at the change in his countenance.

When *Herr* Ollenburger said, "And now we must go to lunch," she experienced a sense of loss for two reasons — she didn't want to go into her somber house after the light-hearted conversation, and she didn't want to leave the Ollenburgers.

This time, it wasn't just Thomas who held her captive. She wanted time with *Herr* Ollenburger. She saw in the big, burly man the kind of father she wished she'd known as a child. One who would play and laugh and simply spend time with his children. Although Belinda had loved her father, she'd never really known him. The thought left her feeling sad and empty inside.

"Belinda!" *Herr* Ollenburger's booming voice carried a cheerful note as he put his arm around his son's shoulders and turned toward his own house. "Have a *goot* day!"

She nodded and scurried to her back door. To her surprise, Malinda shuffled past her into the yard, carrying a basket. Without

111

a word, her sister crossed to the sagging line that extended from the corner of the house to the little shed on the corner of the neighbor's property. Snatching out a handful of tea towels from the basket, she began flinging them one by one over the line.

A smile grew on Belinda's face at the sight of her sister under the noonday sun. Malinda hadn't ventured outside the house for weeks. Surely this was a good sign.

"Malinda!"

Malinda peeked between two towels. "What?"

The harsh tone chased the smile from Belinda's face. "It . . . it's good to see you outside."

Malinda thrust aside the wet items with a swipe of her wrist and leaned forward, panting with the small exertion, to scowl at Belinda. "With you gone all the time, laundry isn't getting done. I had to do it."

Stung, Belinda considered reminding her sister they wouldn't have money coming in if she didn't go to work every day. Once more she wondered what had happened to the money Papa earned over the years. Mama insisted they were destitute and worried constantly about being sent to the home for orphaned or penniless people outside of Hillsboro.

Instead of saying something that would start an argument, Belinda stepped forward and touched her sister's arm. "Thank you for doing the laundry, Malinda."

"I haven't started lunch. You put the skillet on the shelf instead of leaving it on the stove." Malinda barked the words then swung her arm, plucking a shirt from the basket. The grunt of effort it took to throw the wet article of clothing substantiated Malinda's lack of strength.

Guilt sat heavily in Belinda's chest. She tried so hard to accommodate her sister, yet more often than not she failed. She backed up two steps, waving her hand toward the house. "I'll get lunch started. It will only take a few minutes."

In the kitchen, her hands busy cutting up potatoes and onions to fry with links of sausage, Belinda looked across the alley to the Ollenburgers' kitchen window. When their family sat down to sup together, did they discuss the day? Express appreciation for the contributions each made to the household? Enjoy a pleasant time of fellowship? Somehow, based on her observation of *Herr* Ollenburger with his little girls, she doubted a meal at their table mimicked one in her family's dining room.

Even though Mama hardly ate a bite, Belinda still set the table the way her mother always preferred — with their finest dishes arranged just so on a linen cloth of creamy white spread across the table. They never ate in the kitchen, even though the room had adequate space for a small table; instead, they always used the dining room between the parlor and kitchen. She knew many families only used their dining rooms when guests came for a meal, but Mama had always insisted on formality.

But then Belinda remembered that Summer, *Herr* Ollenburger's second wife, had been raised in the city of Boston. So maybe the Ollenburgers sat down to a formal setting, too. Maybe she, Malinda, and Mama weren't the only ones who ate without speaking and carefully blotted their mouths between bites.

For some reason, Belinda needed to know. Somehow, if the Ollenburgers did *something* just like her own family, then she could bear it. Maybe she was building the Ollenburgers up in her head too much and, in so doing, putting her own family down. But for what reason could she barge in on her neighbors in the middle of a meal?

Mama plodded into the kitchen, her hair uncombed, wearing Papa's old bathrobe over her nightclothes. She looked into the skillet and released a sigh. "Potatoes. Can we have tomatoes instead? Stewed tomatoes would taste so good."

Shocked, Belinda dropped the knife into the tin basin and spun, taking hold of her mother's shoulders. "If I find you stewed tomatoes, Mama, you will eat?"

Her mother shrugged. Belinda interpreted the response as a yes.

Surely, Summer Ollenburger had canned tomatoes stored in her pantry. And the woman would cheerfully share a jar if Belinda told her Mama wanted to eat. Giving her mother's shoulders a quick squeeze, she said, "Stay here, Mama. I'll be right back." Then she dashed out the back door and across the yards to the Ollenburgers' house.

8

Thomas closed his sisters' storybook. Pa usually read them a bedtime story and listened to their prayers, but he'd left the house right after dinner and still hadn't returned. So the girls had begged Thomas to read to them instead. Lena fell asleep midway through the story about a cat who brought gifts to the king's castle to win favors for his master, but both Abby and Gussie remained alert to the end.

He placed the storybook back on its shelf while they slipped to their knees beside the bed and recited a list of God-blesses. Then, the prayers done, they bounced onto the mattress and pulled up the covers. Thomas leaned forward and gave them each a kiss on the top of the head. "Good night," he said, straightening. *"Schlop die gesunt."*

Abby's eyes grew round in her pixie face. "You said Papa's words."

Gussie's forehead scrunched in confusion.

"How come you know *schlop die gesunt?*"

Thomas grinned. "Well, your papa is my papa, too, you know. When I was your age, he said *schlop die gesunt* to me."

Abby nodded, her expression serious. "And Papa says we'll say it to our children someday."

With a giggle, Gussie added, "You'll be a papa, Thomas, but we'll be mamas."

Thomas tucked the covers up to his sisters' chins, his heart pounding in his chest at the thought of tucking his own children into bed someday. The task done, he extinguished the lamp and crept from the room.

In the hallway, he paused and leaned against the wall. He tried to imagine his own children. Bright-eyed and golden-haired like Abby and Gussie, or dark-haired and dimpled like Little Lena? Odd how golden-haired children made him think of Belinda and dark-haired ones led his thoughts to Daphne.

He pinched his brow when he remembered Belinda knocking so timidly on the door at noon today to request a jar of Summer's tomatoes. She had such a strange look in her eyes as she stood in the doorway, examining his family at the kitchen table. When she'd left, she'd looked disappointed, but he couldn't imagine why. She'd gotten what she'd come for.

With a shake of his head, he removed the thoughts of Belinda and focused once more on the future, on becoming a father. The idea of being a papa appealed to him, especially teaching a child about the Bible and growing things and nature, the way Pa had taught him. But where would he raise his children — in a city like Boston, or a small community like Gaeddert? So much depended on —

"Thomas?" Pa's voice, carrying from downstairs, kept him from completing the thought.

Forced to set aside his musings, he hurried down the enclosed staircase to the parlor where his father waited. "Yes, Pa?"

Pa's face beamed, his beard bristling with the stretch of his grin. "I have gift for you." He brought his hand from behind his back and thrust a square package wrapped in brown paper at Thomas.

Thomas took the package, and he knew instantly what the paper contained. "You finished the frame."

Pa nodded. Summer stepped beside him and looped her hand through his elbow. Pa patted her hand, still looking at Thomas. "*Ja,* I finished. A fine frame it is — oak

118

stained the color of an acorn's hull. There is even glass to protect your diploma from dust."

Thomas peeled back the paper and admired Pa's handiwork. The frame's corners fit perfectly, the wood sanded smooth. "Whose woodshop did you use?"

Pa raised one shoulder in a shrug. "The lumberyard let me use their machines and tools."

Thomas imagined his father, alone in the lumberyard, working to complete a gift for his son. He swallowed. "It's perfect, Pa. Thank you."

"Come. Let us put the diploma in the frame and see how it looks."

Thomas allowed his father the privilege of putting the hand-lettered sheepskin in the frame. When the back was secured, Pa held the framed certificate at arm's length and admired it. Thomas's tongue itched with the desire to tell Pa about the job opportunity in Boston, but not wanting to disrupt his father's pleasure in this moment, he remained silent.

Pa sighed and handed the frame back to Thomas. "*Ach,* son, how nice it is to see your name on that certificate. All the years apart, when so muchly we missed you, I would think of the day when you would be a graduate of higher learning. It kept the deep ache away and made the separation bearable." He clamped his big hand over Thomas's shoulder, tears winking in his lined eyes. "And now you are graduated, and you are home, and you will have your own business."

Before Thomas could reply, Pa clapped his hands together and said, "So where do you want to hang it? On this wall, or over here, where people standing outside the door will see it?"

Thomas considered saying, "I'll hang it in my apartment in Boston," but he couldn't. Not when his father looked like a little boy on Christmas morning. He pointed. "How about here?"

Pa nodded. "I will fetch hammer and tack."

But Summer stopped him. "Banging will wake the girls, Peter. Let's wait until morning."

Pa heaved a sigh of defeat, but he said, "As always, my wife is the sensible one. We wait until morning." With his arm around Summer's waist, he guided her from the room.

Thomas watched his parents move to the stove, where Summer poured a cup of coffee and offered it to Pa. They stayed there, quietly sipping and talking together, but Pa's last comment echoed through Thomas's mind. *"As always, my wife is the sensible one."* Of course! Thomas should talk to Summer about his plans. Summer could make Pa understand why Thomas needed to return to Boston. Why hadn't he thought of this sooner?

9

The miserable job of tarring took nearly three weeks, waylaid by two summer showers and three days of winds so gusty only a fool would venture onto a roof. But at the end of the first day of July, Thomas's boss handed him his pay and made a sad face. "Thomas, you have been a good worker, but I am afraid I have some bad news."

Thomas slipped the pay envelope into his pocket and waited.

Herr Barkman crossed his arms and rocked on the worn heels of his boots. His head low, he said, "I have no more jobs waiting for completion since the Harms boys decided to do their own repairs. This means . . ."

He didn't need to finish. Thomas understood. "It's all right, *Herr* Barkman. As Pa told you when I took the job at the Schmidts' place, I wasn't seeking a permanent job. So don't feel badly about letting me go." He hoped his tone reflected the proper amount of respect and regret, but underneath he felt like celebrating. He hadn't found a moment alone with Summer to present the idea of his returning to Boston. But now he could just talk to Pa — Pa wouldn't expect him to remain in Hillsboro if he didn't have a job.

The boss gave Thomas's hand a firm shake. "As I said, Thomas, you are a good worker. You find another place needing workers, I will make a recommendation for you."

"Thank you." Thomas left Barkman's house and walked to the mill to meet his father, eager to head home so they could discuss Thomas's return to Boston. But when he saw his father's concerned face after telling him his job had ended, Thomas didn't have the heart to bring up the idea of leaving. Instead, they walked in silence to the house, Pa's occasional heavy sigh and sidelong glances communicating his desire to make things better for his son.

When they reached the yard, Pa stopped Thomas with a hand on his arm. "Son, sorry I am about the job. But do not be disheartened. Another job we will find for you. You will get the money to start your business."

Thomas took a deep breath. "Pa, about another job —"

"So sorry I am for not being able to keep my mill." Tears glistened briefly in the corners of Pa's eyes. "Then at least we would have something to keep you going."

Thomas thought his heart might break at his father's distress. How could he tell this man he loved and admired that, even if the mill was still in operation, he might not stay? The mill was everything to Pa — sharing it with Thomas had been his dream. Thomas couldn't shatter his father by telling him his heart was calling him far from the prairie.

"Pa . . ." Thomas licked his lips, considering his words carefully. "You don't need to worry about me. I'm a grown man now. I . . . I can see to my own needs."

Unexpectedly Pa threw his arms around Thomas and tugged him close, banging his big hand on Thomas's back. "*Ach,* you are a man grown, for sure, but you are still my boy — *mein eensje Sän.* I cannot help but feel concern for you."

Thomas returned Pa's embrace with something akin to desperation. Pa's words, *"my only son,"* pierced Thomas like a sword. For the first time since the day they laid the tiny body of his baby brother in the ground, Thomas wished he wasn't the only son.

Then he wouldn't have to carry so much . . . responsibility.

Pa released Thomas and drew his hand down his beard, removing all evidence of sadness and smiling broadly. "Well, now we go in and see what Summer has cooked for our dinner." He slapped his belly and chuckled. "Always ready to eat, I am."

Thomas forced a light laugh and clapped his hand on his father's shoulder, and they headed into the house together.

After dinner, Thomas retreated to his little room and picked up the letter from Daphne. He traced his finger over the words, *My father has several positions at the* Boston Beacon *for which you would be qualified.*

The murmur of his parents' voices carried from the kitchen, where Pa dried the dishes Summer washed. He could walk out there, show them the letter, and bring an end to his inner turmoil. He groaned. That action would mean the beginning of his father's turmoil.

He folded the page into a square, jammed it into his shirt pocket, and jolted from the bed, remembering to keep his head low until he cleared the sloping beams. "Pa. Summer," he said as he entered the kitchen, "I'm going for a walk."

Summer reached for the last of the dirty

plates. "Would you go to the post office and check our box? It's been almost three weeks since I've heard from Nadine. I expect news from her soon."

"Of course." He turned toward the back door. Just as his hand closed on the doorknob, he heard a clatter of footsteps behind him. Abby and Gussie careened into the kitchen, followed by Lena, who was slowed by the blanket she dragged.

Gussie caught his hand and suspended herself from it. "Where are you goin', Thomas?"

"To the post office."

"Oh! May I go, too? Please? Please?" Gussie begged, and both Abby and Lena took up the cry.

Thomas had originally wanted to go alone, but looking into his sisters' hopeful faces — and realizing he might not have much more time with them — he relented. "All right. But Lena will have to leave her blanket behind." He hid his smile when she promptly dropped the rumpled square of faded blue wool. "And all of you will have to stay with me." He coupled the warning with a stern look at Gussie. Her adventurous nature made her the most inclined to run ahead.

Gussie put on an innocent look. "I'll stay

with you."

He swallowed his smirk. "Then let's go."

They set out together, Lena's moist hand tucked securely in Thomas's grasp and the older two girls skipping in front of him. Abby and Gussie swung their clasped hands between them and sang a children's rhyme called *Rea, rea Jrettje.* Listening to their high-pitched voices transported Thomas to his own childhood. In his memory he heard his dear great-grandmother's voice reciting the rhyme, followed by her sweet laughter as he threw his hands in the air and repeated the final line, *"Diesem riet de Kopp auf, onn schmeit'm wie!"*

Suddenly Gussie whirled and raced to his side, grabbing his free hand. "Thomas, how come in the song they give some children porridge but tear one's head off and throw it away?"

Thomas snorted a laugh. To him, the rhyme had just been nonsense. But Gussie's serious face told him she weighed the meaning of each word. He supposed the thought of stirring porridge and sharing it with some, but throwing away one child's head rather than feeding him could be frightening to a little girl — especially since her mother put porridge on the breakfast table at least twice a week.

He asked, "Are you worried it might be your head that gets thrown away?"

Gussie stared at him with wide blue eyes. "It won't happen . . . will it?"

Thomas tapped the end of her nose with his finger. "It only happens to little girls who don't clean up their porridge bowls, so as long as you eat all your porridge, you'll be safe."

A bright smile burst across Gussie's face. "Thank you, Thomas!" She dashed ahead to join Abby once more.

Thomas chuckled and peered down at Lena. "Your sister is silly."

Lena blinked in response, her baby face so sweet and innocent, Thomas couldn't resist picking her up and carrying her the remainder of the distance. They retrieved a single letter from their box at the post office — from Nadine, as Summer had anticipated — and Thomas experienced a brief stab of regret that Daphne hadn't written again. But, he reminded himself, why should she? He hadn't yet replied to her first letter.

He frowned as he left the post office and aimed the girls toward home, putting Lena back down to walk. Her short legs slowed the process, and by the time they reached their yard, the house's shadow stretched clear to the street. "Go on in and give this letter to your mama," Thomas instructed, placing the letter in Abby's waiting hand. "And, Gussie, you tell Papa I'll be back a little later." When Lena dawdled, he gave her a little pat on the bottom to hurry her along.

As soon as the three girls were safely inside, he set off again, this time alone so he could collect his thoughts and finally find a way to break the news to Pa about a job waiting in Boston. With his hand pressed to the pocket where Daphne's letter was stashed, he kept his eyes on his feet. Dust scuffed up with each step.

His head down, he didn't see the person step into his pathway until it was too late. A quick glimpse of a blue skirt and the pointed toe of a black lace-up shoe brought him to an abrupt halt. He reared back, catching the back of his heel on the edge of the slightly raised sidewalk. Before he could catch himself, he sat down in someone's yard. The force of his backside hitting the ground sent the air from his lungs in an audible *whoosh!*

His gaze bounced from the shoes to the woman's face. Belinda Schmidt held both hands over her mouth. Her blue eyes — round and horrified — probably mirrored his own expression, and despite himself, he laughed.

At his laughter, she lowered her hands, and a sheepish look crept over her face. "I'm so very sorry. I wasn't looking where I was going."

He shrugged, pushing to his feet and dusting off the seat of his pants. "No harm done. I did little more than dent my pride."

She giggled, and the light-hearted sound sent a spiral of satisfaction through his chest. He added, "Besides, it was as much my fault as yours. I wasn't watching where I was going, either."

Belinda tipped her head, one gold strand of hair slipping free of its bun and curving along her cheek. "Lost in thought?"

Thomas hadn't had enough time alone to thoroughly lose himself in thought. "I —" He noticed the wooden wagon in the street beside her. The bed of the wagon was heaped with thick bundles wrapped in brown paper and tied with white string. He pointed. "You've got quite a load there."

Belinda glanced at the wagon and chuckled. "Yes, but I'll empty it soon." He sent her a puzzled look, and she said, "I do ironing for the laundress in town. I'm delivering today's load."

"So you need to hurry on." Thomas couldn't decide if he was disappointed or relieved at the prospect.

"No, not particularly. To be honest," she said, the sheepish look returning, "it's nice just to stand and *brisle* with someone for a little while."

Thomas would never understand females and their need to talk. "You work all day in the merchandise store, you come home to a mother and sister . . . Don't you get enough chatting?"

Belinda's face clouded, and Thomas regretted the question. He started to apologize, but she answered in a solemn tone. "I very rarely chat just for the sake of chatting, except with your stepmother. Or your father. They're very kind and always have time for me."

So that was why she showed up at his house so regularly. Still, it seemed odd that someone Belinda's age would spend more time with his folks than with anyone else. Curiosity made him ask, "Don't you spend time with the young people in town? Quite a few of our Gaeddert classmates now live in Hillsboro."

The corners of Belinda's lips tipped downward. "Thomas, you well know I didn't endear myself to others when we were children. Now that we're grown, the friendships are already formed, and they

131

don't have room for someone else — especially when their memories of that 'someone else' aren't pleasant."

Thomas grunted in irritation, refusing to acknowledge he'd felt the same way about Belinda when he'd first returned to town. "That seems *je'rinj* to me."

Belinda offered a sad shrug. "It may be petty, but I don't blame them. Besides, I don't have much time for *brisling.* Not with Mama and Malinda needing my attention."

Thomas thought about Belinda's day — filled with work at the merchandise store, caring for her mother's home, and then ironing in the evenings. Little wonder she seemed to carry an aura of sadness. When did she find time for something fun? Without stopping to think about the possible ramifications, he said, "Independence Day is this coming Monday. Does your family have plans?"

Belinda's eyes flew wide. "N-no. The store will be closed in celebration of the holiday, but . . . I'll probably catch up on our family laundry or bake bread."

Thomas made a face. "That doesn't sound like much of a celebration. Pa and Summer are planning a picnic. Why don't you come?"

For long moments Belinda stood in silence, the lashes of her unblinking eyes throwing a shadow across her cheeks. Finally she said, "Are you sure? Mama . . . and Malinda . . ."

At that moment Thomas wasn't altogether sure he wanted the company of the sour-faced Schmidt women, but he couldn't turn back now. "All of you. It should be fun. Lots of food, games for the kids, and Pa even squandered some of his hard-earned money and ordered Roman candles to shoot off after the sun goes down."

Belinda's mouth dropped open. "Fireworks? I . . . I've never seen fireworks."

"Well, then you have to come."

She sucked in her lips, clearly uncertain.

Thomas stepped forward and touched her hand. "Belinda, you and your family would be very welcome. Will you come?"

Why it meant so much to him to bring a little joy into Belinda's life he wasn't sure. He only knew she needed it and he wanted to provide it. Finally she gave a little nod. "Yes. Thank you. I'll . . . I'll talk to Mama."

"Good." He leaned over and picked up the knotted end of the rope attached to the wagon. "Now, where does that laundress who's waiting for the ironing live?"

She reached for the rope, her cheeks stained with pink. "I can take it."

He shook his head. "It's getting dark, and

133

you shouldn't wander the streets alone. I'll go with you and then walk you home."

The pink in her cheeks brightened to red. Heat in his own face told him he was blushing, too, but he wouldn't leave a woman alone on the streets at dusk. Not even Belinda Schmidt.

10

Most of the house was dark by the time Thomas returned from delivering Belinda's ironing and then walking her home, but a yellow glow in the kitchen window indicated someone was still up. When he stepped through the back door, he found Summer surrounded by three iron tubs of water and a towering mound of dirty clothes.

She greeted him with a mock scowl. "*There* you are. This night-wandering must be a habit you acquired in Boston. You were always early to bed when you were a boy." She lifted one of Pa's shirts from a pile on the floor. "Your father waited for you. He had some news concerning a job. But it can wait until morning, I suppose."

Thomas crossed to the crock that served as a cookie jar and removed the lid. "I would have been back sooner, but I ran into Belinda Schmidt" — he grinned, realizing his words were literal rather than figurative

— "and helped her deliver a wagonful of ironing." He fished two fat ammonia cookies from the crock and replaced the lid with a soft *clank.*

Summer shook her head and dropped a shirt into the tub closest to her knees. "Ironing yet . . . That girl is going to work herself to death." A puzzled look crossed her face. "I've not been able to determine why Belinda is working at all. Her family seemed well-to-do when her father was alive, but since his death, it's as though they're impoverished." Then she raised her shoulders and added, "But I suppose that isn't my business. I do admire Belinda for being willing to support her mother and sister. I only wish her sister would help by at least taking over the housework. And I worry about her. I'm afraid she'll spend her whole life tending to *Frau* Schmidt and Malinda."

Thomas finished the first cookie and brushed crumbs from his shirtfront. "I invited her family to our picnic on the Fourth. Is that all right?"

Summer separated Pa's pants from the girls' dresses. "I discussed the picnic with her mother over a week ago and encouraged her to come with Belinda and Malinda."

Thomas scowled. "Belinda knew nothing

136

about it."

With a soft huff of displeasure, Summer shook her head. "I should have known to mention it to Belinda. I'm glad you said something."

"I feel sorry for her." Thomas examined the remaining cookie in his hand but saw only Belinda's sad eyes. He glanced up to find Summer fixing him with a speculative look. "What's the matter?"

She just smiled. "Nothing." She returned to sorting, placing each item into its appropriate tub to soak. "I hope they'll come. They could all benefit from taking a break from mourning." Then she put her hands on her hips and assumed a stern air. "But right now, young man, I need your dirty clothes. I didn't want to invade your privacy by going into your room and seeking them out myself. So would you please retrieve whatever items need to be washed?" With an arched brow, she let her gaze rove from his head to his toes and back. "Which includes the pants and shirt you're wearing."

Thomas popped the last bite of cookie into his mouth and grinned. "Yes, ma'am." And while they were alone, perhaps they could discuss Boston.

He quickly changed into his nightshirt and

robe, then gathered up all of his dirty clothes. Heat filled his face as he stepped back into the kitchen with his hairy legs and bare feet sticking out from beneath the hem of the nightshirt. His stepmother had seen him in his nightclothes many times when he was a boy, yet he felt somehow exposed standing before her now in such informal attire.

But she simply took the items from his hands and said, "Thank you. Now *schlop die gesunt,* son."

That was his cue to go to bed. *Maybe that was best.* Summer looked tired.

Thomas awakened to the sound of his father whistling. He cocked his head, straining to determine whether anyone else was up with Pa. He detected no other voices.

Throwing back the light cover, he shimmied into a pair of pants, tugged on a shirt, and headed to the kitchen. He spotted Pa leaning over one of the tubs of water, preparing to lift it. Thomas dashed forward. "Here, Pa. Let me help."

"Dank." Pa stepped to one side of the tub and took hold of the handle. "The load is easier with two backs instead of one."

He and Thomas carried all three tubs to the backyard, where Summer would do her scrubbing later in the morning. Thomas brushed his hands together, looking at the contents of the tubs. He shook his head. "What a task to wash all this!"

Pa chuckled. "*Ja,* and it is more with you here. We both are so big — our clothes are bigger, so a third tub she uses now."

Thomas glanced into the tub holding his father's shirts and pants. He glimpsed his own clothes tangled up with Pa's, and his heart gave a leap. He slapped his shirt where the breast pocket would be and sucked in a sharp breath.

Pa stared at him in concern. "Son?"

Thomas plunged his hands into the tub, digging out the shirt he'd worn yesterday. He grimaced when he located the letter from Daphne, still folded in the pocket, but now soggy from its overnight soak in the tub. Would it dry out and still be readable? He tried to unfold it but only managed to tear the paper.

Pa stepped forward, his fingers pinching his beard. "This is something important?"

Thomas nodded, but he didn't elaborate. He pressed the square against his leg, absorbing some of the moisture with the fabric of his pants.

Pa held out his hand, and Thomas plopped the paper onto his father's palm. They both stood, staring at the crumpled wad. "Maybe . . ." Pa worked his jaw back and forth, squinting. "Maybe when it is dry, you can unfold it."

Thomas gritted his teeth. "Unfolding it won't fix it. Look at it — it's all stained and blotchy. The ink ran." He looked into the tub again. "I hope the ink didn't transfer to your clothes. If it did, I'll replace everything."

"That is not needed," Pa said, rotating his palm slightly to turn the paper to receive the sun's rays. "Work clothes have stains — a few more will not matter."

"I suppose."

"So what is this important paper I hold?" Pa searched Thomas's face.

At last — his chance. Taking a deep breath of fortification, Thomas readied his thoughts.

"Oh, good!" Summer's cheerful voice cut in before Thomas could form a word. She stepped through the back door into the yard, her gaze drifting across the waiting tubs. "Thank you for getting those out of the way so I can fix breakfast." She slipped beneath Pa's arm and smiled up at him. "*Panküake* this morning?"

"Ach, what is better than pancakes for Saturday breakfast?" Pa asked.

Summer looked between Pa and Thomas. "Have you told him about the mill?"

Pa slapped his forehead. "*Nä!* I almost forget. I go see my boss last night, and he says he can use you until all harvest grains are ground. It is only a short job, but still a job." Pa bounced the ruined letter on his open palm, his grin broad.

A wave of frustration filled Thomas's chest. He took the letter from Pa and opened his mouth, ready to share about the job opportunity offered on the page.

"Mama, Papa!" Gussie burst through the back door, her nightgown flapping. Her wide blue eyes matched her excited voice. "Little Lena tried to climb out of her crib and she fell! *Komm flucks!*"

Both Summer and Pa dashed after Gussie, and Thomas followed. Even though Lena's injury was minor — a bruise on her forehead and scuffed skin on one palm — the fright from her tumble required a great deal of comfort. By the time the little girl had been calmed, Thomas's sodden letter was forgotten, and he didn't have the heart to bring it up again.

By the morning of the Fourth of July, Thomas nearly fumed with frustration, and he didn't feel much like celebrating freedom. He felt trapped by circumstances, and he wasn't sure how to fix the situation. Was this God's way of telling him to remain in Hillsboro? Would he be stuck in this small town forever?

The morning passed quickly as Thomas helped Pa prepare the backyard to receive guests. With Abby, Gussie, and Lena darting between them and slowing their progress, he and Pa laid boards across borrowed sawbucks to use as tables. Summer covered them with lengths of red-and-white-checked cloth, giving the yard a festive appearance. Pa pounded iron stakes into the ground so the men could play horseshoes, and Thomas set a washtub in the shade and filled it with water so the kids could bob for last fall's wrinkled apples. Quilts dotted the ground, providing more places to sit, and the smells that carried from Summer's kitchen made Thomas's mouth water and his stomach churn with desire for the evening to arrive so they could indulge in all the special dishes.

Midafternoon, to Summer's obvious joy and Thomas's surprise, all three of the Schmidt women paraded across the alley to join the Ollenburgers. Belinda carried a fresh-baked apple-raisin pie, and Malinda presented a basket of cherry *plauts* that

142

brought a cheer from Abby and Gussie. Although not allowed to drink coffee, the little girls both loved the fruit-laden miniature cakes baked to accompany a cup of the strong brew.

Summer placed both sweets on the table designated to hold the food and gave hugs to all three women, although neither Malinda nor *Frau* Schmidt reciprocated. Summer made a show of admiring the pie and *plauts.* "You didn't need to bring anything, but these look delicious."

"Thank you." Malinda spoke with stiff lips, as though forming the words was painful. She looped her hand through her mother's elbow and led her to the side of the house, where makeshift benches of boards laid over barrels provided shaded seating. The pair remained there, perched like two birds on a wire, until all of the guests had arrived.

Frau Schmidt and Malinda kept to themselves, but Belinda appeared to enjoy mingling. Thomas observed her sitting down on a quilt with two or three other ladies. It gave his heart a lift to see her smile and hear her soft laugh. The invitation might have been offered on a whim, but he was glad he'd followed the impulse.

He didn't do a great deal of visiting,

however. For the most part, he hovered on the fringes of the groups, playing with his little sisters when they begged and answering questions if someone addressed him directly, but he kept himself detached as much as possible. He couldn't explain why he needed his distance; he only sensed that if he involved himself too much, it would create a new complication when it was time to return to Boston.

As the sun neared the horizon and the activities slowed down, Malinda and *Frau* Schmidt finally left their spots on the bench and approached Belinda. "Mama is tired," Malinda said in a strident tone. "We need to take her home now."

Belinda's face fell. "But we haven't seen *Herr* Ollenburger fire off the Roman candles yet." She gestured to the tables scattered with dirty plates, empty serving dishes, and crumpled napkins. "And I thought I would help *Frau* Ollenburger clean up."

From his spot where he leaned against a tree, Thomas read Malinda's aggravation in the pursing of her lips. "She wants to go home *now*." *Frau* Schmidt didn't add a word but clutched her bony hands at her waist.

Belinda sighed. "Well, let me get our things, then, and —"

"Belinda." Thomas pushed off from the

tree and approached the women. Slipping his hands into his trouser pockets, he assumed a relaxed air he hoped would put *Frau* Schmidt at ease. Once plump and outspoken, the older woman's skin now hung from a thin frame and she appeared ready to shatter at the slightest provocation. "We won't be able to fire the Roman candles until it's full dark. Go ahead and walk your mother home and get her settled for the evening, and then you can come back." He shifted his gaze to Malinda, who stared at him with mistrustful eyes. "You, too, Malinda. I'm sure you'd enjoy the fireworks."

Belinda looked at her mother. The hopefulness in her face tugged at Thomas's heart. "Would that be all right, Mama? I'll help you ready yourself for bed, and then I'll come back?"

Frau Schmidt didn't reply, but she did give a quick nod.

Belinda lifted her beaming face to Thomas. "I'll return shortly. Thank you, Thomas."

Thomas, Abby, and Gussie helped Summer carry the dishes to the kitchen; then he and Pa took down the tables. They left the quilts on the ground, and people settled in little groups, waiting for the sun's glow to disappear over the rooftops so the fireworks could begin. Thomas looked frequently toward the Schmidts' house. Would Belinda return, or would her sister insist she remain with her mother? She would probably be able to see the fireworks from a window, but it wouldn't be the same as enjoying the show with her neighbors.

Pa was ready to begin when the Schmidts' back door burst open and Belinda emerged. She trotted to Thomas's side. "Did I miss it?"

"Not yet. Pa's just getting started."

"Oh, good!" Her voice held pure joy.

They stood side by side beneath the swaying branches of the oak tree and watched Pa press a thick paper tube into a mound of sand. Thomas held his breath. Pa lit a match, held it to the wick until a sizzle indicated it caught, then backed up quickly. At the first explosive *pop!* followed by a burst of color about twenty feet in the air, Thomas let out his air in an exultant cry. "Woo-hoo!"

Similar exclamations sounded across the yard. Pa had purchased six candles, and each candle contained six blasts of shimmering light. All too soon, the last burst faded against the night sky, and it was time for everyone to go home.

Pa rounded up the little girls, who were

tired and cranky, and took them inside. Summer began folding quilts, and Belinda helped her. Thomas took the quilts in turn and made a neat stack beside the back door. Each time he took a quilt from Belinda's hands, she flashed him a smile as bright as the stars that shot from the Roman-candle tubes.

When the last quilt was folded, Summer sighed. "That was fun, but I'm exhausted." A screech sounded from the house, and Summer frowned. "It sounds as if Little Lena is having trouble settling down. Excuse me." She hurried into the house, leaving Belinda and Thomas alone under the moonlight.

Thomas stuck his hands in his pockets. "Well —"

"Thank you for the invitation, Thomas. I had a wonderful time."

"I know."

She tilted her head in silent query. In the shadows, he could barely make out her features.

Leaning against the house, he said, "I watched you visiting with the other ladies. I could tell you enjoyed yourself. I . . ." He paused, wondering if he'd said something he shouldn't have. He cleared his throat. "I'm glad you had fun." She needed it.

For a moment she sucked in her lips. Then she said, "I watched you, too. It didn't appear you enjoyed yourself as much as I did."

He straightened, his hands coming from his pockets. "Why do you say that?"

A shrug lifted her shoulders. "You were very helpful, but not very . . . involved." When he didn't respond, she added, "You seemed many miles away in your thoughts."

Visions of Boston — a newspaper office, campaign headquarters, his friends, and Daphne Severt — danced through Thomas's brain. "I was thinking about . . ."

"Boston?"

Her softly voiced query struck like a lightning bolt. "Am I so obvious?"

She smiled. "I would imagine after living in a large city, coming back here must be very dull."

"No, that's not it." Could he trust her with information about the job offer? Maybe saying the words to Belinda would give him the courage to repeat them to his parents. "I'm just thinking about something that's waiting for me in Boston, and I'm eager to explore it."

"Oh?" She managed to convey a great deal of interest in the simple query.

"Yes. A job. At a newspaper office — the *Boston Beacon*."

"Impressive." Not a hint of sarcasm colored her tone. "When do you start?"

Thomas blew out an angry breath and stalked across the yard to the oak tree. Pressing his palm to the rough bark, he cleared his throat. "That's the problem. I can't start until I go back to Boston, and I . . . *can't* . . . go back to Boston."

She followed him. The tips of her fingers landed lightly on his forearm, and he looked at her. Tree branches blocked the glow of the moon, casting speckled blue shadows across her upturned face. Her forehead crinkled in curiosity. "Why not?"

Thomas set his jaw, battling resentment. "Pa wants me here."

"He said that?"

"Not in so many words, but —"

"Then what has he said?"

Thomas snorted in annoyance. "How proud he is of my college degree. How wonderful it will be when I start my business. How happy it makes him to have me under his roof again."

"Well, of course." Belinda's calm, matter-of-fact tone did little to placate Thomas. "But none of that means he expects you to stay here forever. He knows you have a college degree. He wants you to use it. If that means using it in Boston, then surely —"

"You don't understand." Thomas barked the words. "How can you? You aren't an only son, carrying your father's dreams around your neck like a millstone."

Belinda cringed, and immediately Thomas regretted his outburst. He reached out to touch her shoulder, then changed his mind, pulling his hand back with a sharp jerk. He swallowed hard. "Belinda, I'm sorry. That was unkind. I didn't mean it."

She blinked rapidly, as if clearing tears. When she replied, her voice was low and measured. "My father had no sons, so he wanted grandsons. He gave up on Malinda — he realized she was *onnpaussant* . . . unsuitable . . . for motherhood between her health problems and her unpredictable moods. So it was left to me to marry and give him grandsons.

"Instead I'm taking care of Mama and Malinda. So I understand about not fulfilling a father's expectation. But I'm doing what is best for Mama, Malinda, and me . . . for now." She seemed to gain strength as she spoke.

Taking a step closer to him, she said, "Your father's greatest dream is for you to follow God's will in your life, Thomas. I know, because he's told me. He believes your college education will open the door

God has planned for you. So if you believe that door waits for you in Boston, he'll understand. It will be hard for him to watch you go, but he won't stand in your way."

At that moment a second voice — deep and thick with emotion — sounded across the yard.

"*Ja,* boy, she is right. And you should have come to me long ago."

11

Belinda sidled sideways a few steps, her gaze darting back and forth between father and son. "I-I need to turn in now. Thank you again for inviting me to your picnic and letting me watch the fireworks. Good night, Thomas. *Herr* Ollenburger." She turned and scurried off.

Pa watched Belinda go, waiting until she was inside her house before facing Thomas. "Son, I am shamed."

Guilt smacked Thomas. He stepped forward. "Pa, I —"

"You think I hold you back?"

The pain in his father's voice made tears sting behind Thomas's nose. "Not hold me back, Pa, but . . ."

"Tell me, boy."

Thomas swallowed. "You're so happy to have me here. I don't want to hurt you by leaving."

Pa's sigh was laden with remorse. "*Ach,*

son, for sure it makes me happy to have you here. You are my son. I love you. Having you near brings me joy. But keeping you here out of selfishness? That I do not want to do." He shook his head. "I make a big mistake if this is what I make you feel I am doing."

Pa moved forward, stopping a mere three feet from Thomas. Heavy shadows fell over Pa's face, but Thomas read clearly a mix of pride and anguish in his father's eyes. "I send you to school — to a college — so you can make best use of the *goot* head the Lord gave you. A *goot* head is a gift. Gaining knowledge is a privilege. The Lord does not want us to squander either our gifts or our privileges. If you have chance to use these things at a newspaper office in Boston, then that is what you must do."

Thomas whispered hoarsely, "Y-you *want* me to go to Boston?"

Pa shook his head slowly. "What I want and what is best may be two different things, boy. You know sometimes God takes us places we do not see as best, yet His purpose must be fulfilled." He paused, his jaw working back and forth as he peered sharply into Thomas's eyes. "Do you believe God has opened this door to you in Boston?"

Thomas sought an honest answer. He felt obligated to return to Boston to honor his commitment to help in the campaign — that much he knew. But was this job God's plan for his life or was it just . . . happenstance? He couldn't be sure. He flung his arms wide. "Pa, I don't know if it's what God intends for me to do. But I want to go — I want to see where it takes me."

For long moments Pa stood silently, seeming to examine Thomas. His lowered brows and wrinkled forehead told of his inner conflict, and Thomas waited for a lecture on seeking and following God's will. But when Pa spoke in a soft, tender voice, it was far from what Thomas expected.

"You are a grown man — no longer my little boy. When you were little, I tell you what to do and I expect you to do it. But now? Look at you, standing tall as me and in possession of a certificate from a college that proves you have sense in your head." Pa licked his lips. "I will not tell you what to do, Thomas. This you must decide on your own. If you think this job in Boston is where you should be, then you must go."

Thomas sucked in a sharp breath, but Pa had more to say.

"See, in the Bible it advises to train up a child in the way he should go. I have done that as best as I know how. My job . . . is done. Now your job begins — to seek God's will and stay in it. I trust you to do that."

As Pa finished speaking, the back door opened, sending a misshapen rectangle of yellow light across the lawn. Summer's shadow created a black form in the center of the pale rectangle. "Peter? Thomas?"

Pa turned toward the house. "*Ja,* Summer, still out here we are. We will come in soon."

The door closed, sealing them once more in a cloak of gray. Pa put his big hand on Thomas's shoulder and squeezed. "Tomorrow, when businesses open downtown, you go send a telegram to this newspaper office to say you're coming, and you buy your train ticket. You go to Boston. You seek your path."

"And . . . and you won't be hurt?" Thomas held his breath.

"*Ach,* son, of course it hurts to see you go. I love you, and I miss you when you are not here. But that is the way of life — people coming and going. A poor excuse for a father I would be if I held you back and kept you from blooming." The hand on Thomas's shoulder squeezed then fell away. "To bed now. I am tired, and I must speak to Summer about your leave-taking." He turned and headed to the house, his plodding steps and sloped shoulders mute evidence of his heartache.

"Daphne?"

At her father's voice, Daphne tipped her head in acknowledgement but continued to press her fingers to the piano's ivory keys.

"I received an intriguing telegram message at work this afternoon."

Daphne's hands stilled on the piano keys. She peeked over her shoulder. Harrison Severt, Sr., sank into his favorite parlor chair and fixed Daphne with a piercing look. She turned the stool to face her father, crossed her ankles, and rested her clasped hands in her lap. "Oh?"

Father snorted, his eyes narrowing. "Don't play cat and mouse with me, Daphne. You know very well who sent the message."

Daphne's heart pounded, but not in trepidation of her father's wrath. No, the pounding heart was an indication of excited delight. Placing a finger against her lips, she gave a few thoughtful taps. "Could the sender possibly be Harry's good friend Thomas Ollenburger?"

Her father scoffed loudly, just as Daphne expected. "You are cunning, my dear. I have the sneaking suspicion not only I but this

156

Ollenburger are dancing at the ends of your puppet strings. A shame you weren't a boy — I could use someone with your expertise for manipulation at the office."

Not for the first time, Daphne experienced a pang of resentment. Her father's cavalier attitude concerning her gender hurt, yet she wouldn't trade her female status. A woman gifted with manipulation could move mountains no man's brute strength could touch.

"So will you put him on staff?" Daphne now asked, using a deliberately light tone.

"I don't see where I have much choice, considering the boy already believes a position is waiting." He shrugged. "As it turns out, one of the men in advertising decided to move back to his home state of North Carolina, leaving me with a proofreading position to fill."

Daphne flipped her wrists outward. "Perfect!"

Father pointed a finger at her, his thick brows forming a sharp V. "But if this Ollenburger proves inept, Daphne, his pay will be taken from your monthly allowance until it is repaid in full."

Daphne had expected this. Father always presented a consequence to exercise his control. She blinked in innocence. "Why, certainly I'll be responsible should Thomas fail to meet your expectations. But" — she angled her chin high — "I have no fear of losing one penny of my allowance. Thomas will so impress you, he'll soon be one of the most trusted members of your staff."

Father slapped his knee. "Well, I suppose we shall see." He rose and left her to her piano playing. However, once he departed from the parlor, instead of resuming the song he'd interrupted, she pushed her feet against the carpet to give the stool a spin as she released a squeal of delight.

Thomas is coming!

Slamming the soles of her slippers against the floor, she brought the whirling ride to an end and dashed up to her room. Behind her closed door, she hugged herself and spun another happy circle. Dizzy from her wild dance and uncontrolled excitement, she flung herself across the bed and laughed out loud for joy.

When Thomas hadn't replied to her letter, she'd suffered so many moments of worry. He was so different from Harry's other friends. Maybe her letter wouldn't have the intended effect. A simpering look and flutter of eyelashes sent most males bowing at her feet, ready to do her bidding. But not Thomas.

She shivered as she considered his physical attributes — the breadth of his shoulders, his great height, and his hands that could easily span her waist if ever he found the nerve to try.

Closing her eyes, she pressed her face into her pillow and allowed her imagination to carry her to sweet dreams.

Two days after sending the telegram to the owner and chief editor of the *Boston Beacon* — little more than a month after his return to Hillsboro — Thomas packed his bags and prepared for another train ride.

While he packed, his little sisters sat in a sorrowful row on his bed, watching him. Their silence, so unlike the unending jabber to which he'd become accustomed, pierced his heart. But they cheered somewhat when he took three prized books from the shelf above his bureau and gave them each a good-bye gift. He knew it would be a few years before they would be old enough to read and enjoy such stories as *The Prince and the Pauper, Arabian Nights,* and *Tattered Tom,* yet seeing their faces brighten made him feel better.

His carpetbags stuffed and ready, he said, "You girls go get your breakfast now. When it's time to go, you can help me carry my things to the station."

They trailed out in a row, and Thomas followed. Before he could sit at the table, several light taps sounded on the back door. Summer started toward it, but he held up his hand. "Feed the girls. I'll get it."

Belinda Schmidt stood on the grassless spot of ground right outside the door, holding a small wicker basket that she offered to him with a trembling smile. "I heard you were leaving. So I — I baked you some *honigkuchen* to take along."

He remembered her response when Pa suggested Summer could bake honey cookies for Belinda's mother — she had said they were too much trouble. The thought of her taking the time to make him these cookies brought a lump to his throat. Accepting the basket, he managed a nod. "Thank you."

She peeked past him to the breakfast table, where his family sat. Her face flooded with pink. "I'm sorry — I interrupted." She turned to dash away, but Thomas stepped outside and let the door slam behind him.

"Belinda, wait!"

Hesitantly, she turned back, her eyes wide and glimmering. Was she going to cry?

"I . . . I'm glad I had the chance to tell you good-bye. I've enjoyed our times of visiting."

She sucked in her lower lip, blinking

rapidly. "I have, too. I . . . I'll miss . . ." One tear rolled down her cheek. "I'll pray for you, Thomas, that things will go well for you . . . wherever your heart leads."

Thomas drew in a deep breath. He hated the thought of her solemn life filled with days meeting everyone else's needs except her own. Suddenly it became very important that she continue reaching out to people, the way she had done with him.

"Belinda, remember there are many neighbors close by. You can talk to any of them, if you'll just do it. Don't shut yourself away, all right?"

"I'll try." But her tone didn't indicate much enthusiasm.

He stepped closer to her, glancing over his shoulder to make sure they were alone. "And would you do a favor for me?"

She tilted her head to the side, her expression curious.

"Would you write to me now and then? Summer will give you the address for Mrs. Steadman — that's where I'll be staying. Tell me how my sisters and Summer and Pa are doing. I know my leaving is hard on Pa. I want to make sure . . ."

She nodded enthusiastically. "I can do that."

Suddenly embarrassed, but not sure why,

he rushed on. "Summer writes to me, of course, but I suspect she tells me what she thinks I want to hear, not what's really happening, so —"

"Thomas." Belinda's tone held a hint of humor. "I'll write, and I'll be honest."

He puffed his cheeks and blew out a breath.

"But don't worry. Your parents are strong people with a lot of faith. They'll be all right."

Thomas nodded. He thought about her family, and how much they leaned on her. "And you? Will you be all right?" Embarrassment seared his face as he heard his own question. Would she assume he thought she wouldn't survive without his presence?

She bowed her head for a moment, chewing again on her lip, but when she lifted her face and looked at him he saw only calm acceptance in her eyes. "I'm strong and have a lot of faith, too. It isn't easy right now with Mama so deeply mournful, but mourning passes. One day, she'll throw off her melancholy. Things will be fine."

Thomas didn't know what to say then. Good-bye was appropriate, yet he held the word inside.

She said it for him. "Good-bye, Thomas. Have a safe journey, and God be with you."

Then she turned and hurried away, leaving him standing alone on the dew-kissed grass with a little basket of *honigkuchen* in his hands.

12

Nadine and her trusted, longtime servant, Clarence, were waiting at the train station when Thomas arrived in Boston. Even though Thomas had anticipated his foster grandmother retrieving him from the station, he still experienced a brief stab of disappointment. Harry and Daphne knew he was coming. Couldn't they have met him, too?

Nadine gave him a quick, impersonal hug while Clarence smiled from behind her shoulder, his chocolate-colored face reflecting his pleasure at having Thomas with them again. As soon as Nadine released Thomas, Clarence took the bags. Nadine slipped her hand through Thomas's elbow, and they weaved between disembarking passengers and their welcoming throngs to Nadine's familiar carriage.

"Your room is exactly as you left it," Nadine said once they were settled in the leather seats and the horses carried them over Boston's cobblestone streets. "I suspected you would return." She gave a quick shake of her head. "As much as I enjoy my visits to your parents and their little prairie home, I couldn't imagine residing there permanently. And now, after tasting all the city has to offer, you've discovered that truth for yourself, hmm?"

Thomas shrugged. "For now." Remembering how withholding his plans from Pa had created heartache, he added, "I don't know if I'll stay permanently, but I'll be here at least through the presidential election."

Nadine caught the window ledge of the carriage as the vehicle rounded a corner. "Oh, you'll choose to remain. Opportunities are abundant here, nonexistent there," she said with assurance. "You may as well begin calling yourself a Bostonian, Thomas."

After the carriage rolled to a stop, Thomas allowed Clarence to carry his bags to the house, but he took over when they reached the stairs. Being much younger and stronger, he couldn't allow the elderly servant to carry two heavy bags up the curving staircase.

When he put his foot on the first riser, Nadine said, "Unpack, and then I'll have Mildred draw you a bath. Dinner will be ready promptly at seven, as always."

Thomas swallowed a chuckle. Nadine wouldn't come right out and tell him she didn't want his smelly, travel-rumpled presence at the table, but her suggestion managed to communicate the message anyway. He nodded his agreement and headed up the stairs.

In his room, he plunked both bags on the brocade bedcover and unbuttoned the flap of the largest bag. He began transferring shirts and pants to the drawers of the tall bachelor's chest. When he picked up a stack of shirts neatly folded by Summer, something pricked his hand. Puzzled, he put the stack on the bed and withdrew the source of the prick — a piece of tablet paper, folded into a lumpy square.

He unfolded it, and something flitted to the floor. Dropping to one knee, he scanned the patterned carpet and located a dried four-leaf clover. His heart seized. A gift from Gussie. On the paper was a childish scrawl:

Dear Thomas, here is my 4 leef clover so you will hav good luck in boston. I love you Thomas. Your sister Agatha (Gussie)

Still on one knee, he closed his eyes and

relived the moments on the boardwalk outside the station in Hillsboro before he'd boarded the train four days ago. He and his family had created a little circle with each departure for another year of schooling, but this time it had felt different. This time Thomas wasn't sure when — or if — he'd be back.

He pictured each face, from little Lena's to Pa's. They'd all done their best to smile when bidding him farewell, but they'd failed dismally. As had he.

He fingered the dried clover, Gussie's gift, and homesickness slammed into him as hard as it had his first year in Boston. With a sigh, he folded Gussie's note back around the clover, pushed to his feet, and put the paper and gift in the top drawer of the chest.

"Well, Gussie, let's see if it brings me luck in Boston," he said aloud. Then he set his jaw against the quiver in his chin and finished unpacking.

The next morning Thomas put on his best double-breasted pinstripe suit with its matching vest and trousers. He grunted as he leaned forward to fasten his shoes — the fashionable skinny fit of the trouser legs didn't match well with his muscular thighs and calves. The crisp, new celluloid collar poked the underside of his clean-shaven chin, providing another element of discomfort. But he determined to show the owner of the *Boston Beacon* that he could be as much a gentleman as any other Bostonian.

Nadine beamed her approval when he entered the dining room for breakfast. "You look like a true newspaperman, Thomas." She lifted her tea cup, smoothing down the thick ruffles of her morning gown before taking a sip. She gestured to the chair across the table. "Sit down. Everything is still hot."

He slid into his seat, tossed a napkin across his lap, and filled his waiting plate with fluffy scrambled eggs, bacon, sausage, and muffins loaded with raisins and nut-meats, all of which had been kept warm in silver footed trays with heavy lids — so different from the mismatched crockery bowls at home. He pushed away the thoughts of Hillsboro, offered a quick prayer, and began to eat.

He ate as quickly as possible, aware of the ticking pendulum clock and the *clink* of his fork against the china plate — their intrusions loud in the otherwise silent room. Unlike Pa and Summer, Nadine wasn't given to conversation over a meal.

When he was finished, he wiped his mouth and rose. "I probably won't be here for the noon meal. And I may make arrangements for dinner with some friends, too, so don't hold anything for me."

Nadine clinked her tea cup into its saucer. "But, Thomas, you've only just returned! Mildred has planned a coming-home dinner with all of her specialties."

Thomas withheld a groan. He'd grown to love the rotund housekeeper who spent half of her day in the kitchen, but Mildred's "specialties" always left him feeling as bloated as a calf that had eaten wet alfalfa. "I'm sorry, but —"

"Let's make a compromise." Nadine stood, fixing Thomas with a firm look. "Invite your friends to come here for dinner. Mildred and I will set a table for — how many? Six? Eight?"

Thomas drew in a deep breath, prepared to argue, but one of Pa's admonitions played through his head: *Boy, respect your elders.* He released the breath and said through clenched teeth, "No more than six."

Nadine clapped her palms together twice. "Very well. A party of six. I'll look forward to it. We so rarely hosted events for your circle of acquaintanceship when you were in school. It seemed you always had studying to do. But now it's time for your friends to see my home as your home, and a party is just the event to make that clear."

Unwilling to squelch her excitement, Thomas held back a second argument that rose in his throat.

Nadine bustled around the table, catching his elbow and propelling him toward the front door. "Hurry on, now. You mustn't keep your new supervisor waiting." She straightened his silk tie, gave him a quick pat on his cheek, and pushed him through the door. Even with the solid door closed behind him, he heard her shrill cry: "Mildred! We must prepare for a party!"

Thomas hailed a cab, wondering where he would find four people to join him for Nadine's dinner party.

After a long discussion of his duties at the newspaper office, Harrison Severt, Sr., walked Thomas to a noisy, dismal office next to the large typesetting room on the lowest level of the four-story building. It wasn't what Thomas had envisioned when he received Daphne's letter, but he hoped he managed to hide his disillusionment as his new boss escorted him to an empty desk jammed against the ends of two face-to-face occupied desks in the center of the cracked concrete floor.

"Here is where you will work," Mr. Severt said, raising his voice above a rhythmic *whiz-*

bump. "You will share duties with Wallace Todd and Clark Phillips." He slapped the scarred desktop with his open palm, and the desk vibrated with the blow.

Thomas cringed, wondering if the desk would topple. When it didn't, he nodded a silent hello to the young men who sat in silence at the nearby desks. Scattered pages nearly hid the butted wooden surface of their desktops.

"Have a seat," Severt ordered, pointing to the empty wooden chair.

The chair's legs screeched against the floor as Thomas eased it away from the desk. The wooden back bumped against the wall, leaving a sixteen-inch gap into which Thomas squeezed himself. Without conscious thought, he hunched his shoulders forward in an attempt to fit better in the small space.

"Break at noon." Severt gave a brusque nod and stalked out of the room.

Without a word, Clark lifted a pile of pages from the corner of his desk and handed them to Thomas. Thomas picked up a pencil and leaned over the papers. His job was to read each advertisement carefully in a search for print errors. With Severt gone, Clark and Wallace joked with each other as they worked. They tried to pull

Thomas into their conversations a few times, but he resisted, focusing on the task at hand. *Oabeide fer späle* — work before play — he'd always been taught, and avoid play completely when drawing a wage.

A few minutes before the noontime break, Harry and Daphne arrived to welcome Thomas back to Boston and invite him to a little street-side café for lunch. Since Wallace and Clark overheard the invitation, Harry asked if they'd like to come, too. On the way to the café, Thomas realized he now had enough people to fill the chairs for Nadine's dinner party, so he asked if they would like to attend. To his relief, all four accepted.

Even though the luncheon was meant to be a celebration for Thomas, the other three men did most of the talking, which suited Thomas fine. He ate little, for there was something else on which to feast his eyes. Daphne looked wonderful in a shiny dress of softest pink, with a matching bonnet bearing rows of ruffled lace. He admired the contrast of the pale pink against her black hair. The wide satin ribbon tied into a bow beneath her chin called attention to her heart-shaped face and bright eyes.

Daphne seemed to be content to simply sit and stare into his eyes. She hardly touched the salmon patties and iced asparagus spears arranged artfully on her plate. Occasionally her gaze flitted to one of the other three men as she offered a quick smile or soft giggle in response to something one of them said, but each time her attention returned quickly to Thomas.

All too soon, he needed to return to the office. Harry paid for everyone's meals, and then he captured Thomas's arm, earning a scowl from Daphne. "So, Tom, on the way back, let's talk politics, shall we?"

Thomas glanced over his shoulder to see Wallace and Clark fall into step on either side of Daphne. He gave her what he hoped was an apologetic grimace. Her pursed lips communicated her own displeasure at this formation. But Thomas knew he and Harry had a lot of catching up to do concerning the campaign, and they certainly wouldn't be able to do it over dinner that evening. Nadine frowned at discussing politics or religion during social events.

Thomas nodded at Harry. "Catch me up on what's been happening at campaign headquarters."

By the time they reached the newspaper office again, Thomas had agreed to accompany Harry to the headquarters following their evening meal to help prepare flyers for distribution. At the front doors, Wallace and Clark offered thanks to Harry for the lunch, wished Daphne a pleasant afternoon, and sauntered inside.

Harry looked at Daphne. "Have a cab driver take you home, Daph. I need to talk to Father, and then I'll spend the afternoon at headquarters." He disappeared inside without waiting for her to reply.

Thomas, knowing he was due back at his desk, started to follow, but a gentle grasp on his arm delayed him.

"When might I have a moment of time alone with you, Thomas?"

Did she know how beguiling she was? Actually, he suspected she knew full well . . . "One day soon." Although he had given a noncommittal response, a part of him wanted to promise her the moon.

She folded her arms across her chest, her white-gloved fingers tapping against her elbows. "And you haven't even thanked me for letting you know about the job opportunity here."

Heat rose from his neck to his hairline. "Uh, I apologize. I should have responded to your letter, but —"

She waved one small hand, dismissing his words. "I trust you'll enjoy being a part of Father's newspaper?"

174

Thomas's ears still rang from the incessant *whiz-bump* of the machines in the typesetting area. His shoulders ached from slumping over the desk. But at least he had a job worthy of a college graduate. "Very much," he said, adding honestly, "although I hope to eventually be able to do something besides check advertisements for accuracy."

Daphne's eyes twinkled. "Father starts all inexperienced new workers in either delivery or advertising. Delivery is the lowest position, and you were spared that. Be thankful." Her smile seemed to tease him. "But if you work hard and show initiative, you'll have the opportunity to work your way up." She touched his arm again, her fingers sending warmth through his sleeve. "I have confidence you will be on the highest level with the managing editors before the year is out."

Thomas couldn't even promise he would be in Boston by the time the year was out. He stepped toward the door, and her hand slipped from his arm. "I thank you for your confidence, but if I'm to earn my way to the highest level, I need to get back to work." He touched his forehead with his fingers in lieu of tipping a hat. "I will see you at Mrs. Steadman's at seven o'clock sharp."

"That you will, Mr. Ollenburger." She waggled her fingers at him and whirled, her skirts flaring behind her.

The image of Daphne's sashaying skirts interfered with Thomas's focus the remainder of the day, earning a few ribald remarks from his co-workers. He set his jaw and refused to respond to their goading, but he could hardly wait for seven o'clock when he would have time at the dinner table with Daphne.

To his delight, Nadine didn't assign seats when his guests arrived, giving him the opportunity to place people where he wanted them. He graciously gave Nadine the seat at the head of the table, then instructed Harry, Wallace, and Clark to sit on Nadine's right. He took the seat immediately to Nadine's left, with Daphne beside him. Just having Daphne so close, where his elbow lightly bumped hers as he cut his beef roast, made his heart thud against his ribs like Daisy's hooves against the hard-packed prairie when he gave her free rein.

Although he'd worried Nadine might disapprove of having Daphne in her home, she acted the perfect hostess, engaging each person in conversation that included nothing of a personal nature. Thomas appreciated her taking charge because his tongue felt too thick for his mouth, and he was sure he wouldn't be able to form a coherent sentence given Daphne's close proximity.

They ate and conversed their way through Mildred's main courses, and then the smiling cook carried in a towering three-level torte that brought a round of politely restrained cheers from Thomas's guests.

Nadine beamed at their delight. "This is Mildred's special recipe and contains a secret ingredient in the cream filling that she has never deigned to share even with me. I trust you will enjoy it."

Based on the reactions of the guests, Nadine's trust was well placed. Wallace even boldly asked for a second helping, but Thomas noticed Daphne picked at her dessert, consuming less than half of the portion on the crystal dessert plate. Then he looked at his own serving and realized he'd left as much uneaten as she. He wondered if the reason for her diminished appetite was similar to his. How could he even think about putting food in his belly when he felt so full of Daphne?

When all had reached their limit, they pushed away from the table, offering appreciation to Nadine for her hospitality.

"You are all very welcome, and of course you are invited to visit Thomas anytime. It is so good to have young people in the house." Nadine's gaze touched each member of the visiting party, although Thomas noted it skipped past Daphne more quickly than the men. "Now, if you'll excuse me, I will retire to the parlor. Feel free to remain here and visit if you desire."

"Thank you, Mrs. Steadman," Harry said, rounding the table to commandeer Thomas away from Daphne. "But we have work to do, and I need to steal Tom."

Nadine looked pointedly at the pendulum clock on the wall behind her. "At this hour?"

Pressure constricted Thomas's breathing. Her words made him feel like a child.

"I'm afraid so." Harry managed to express regret with his tone. "You see, we have a presidential election to win, and time is of the essence. We can't waste a single minute if we plan to see our candidate become the United States' twenty-seventh president!"

Nadine asked Thomas, "And whose cause have you championed, my dear?"

Harry clapped Thomas's back and answered for him, "The finest candidate, of course — Mr. Thomas Watson!"

Nadine's face pinched into an expression of distaste. "Watson?!"

13

Thomas stared at his foster grandmother. Given her penchant for avoiding conversations involving politics, he had no idea she was even aware of the parties, let alone the candidates. Yet her tone let him know she was not only knowledgeable but held a strong opinion.

"You are campaigning for *Thomas Watson?*" Somehow she made the name sound like a curse.

Thomas sent Harry a startled glance before looking again at Nadine. "Yes, ma'am."

She shook her head, her brows low. "Not while you reside under my roof, young man."

"But why?" Thomas started to explain the man's views concerning the protection of farmers, but Nadine thrust her hand outward in a bid for silence.

"I will not discuss my personal views

concerning Mr. Watson" — once again she spat his name — "but I demand you withdraw your support immediately."

Thomas took a step back. Aware of their audience, embarrassment made his knees weak, but he maintained an even tone. "I'm sorry if my preference for our next leader is upsetting to you, Nadine, but as you've often pointed out, political views are personal. Just as you are entitled to your choice for president, I am entitled to mine."

Nadine glowered, her lips pressed together so tightly they nearly disappeared. "Very well. I concede that, as an adult, you are entitled to your preference. However, I will not have that man's name mentioned again in my presence. Do you understand, Thomas?"

Harry edged to Thomas's side and took his elbow. "Come on, Tom," he whispered, his wary gaze pinned to Nadine's face. "Give her some time to simmer down. You two can talk later."

Thomas nodded. With the same respect he'd always used when addressing his foster grandmother, he said, "I will return by eleven o'clock, Nadine, and I will lock the door behind me when I come in."

Nadine whirled away, but not before Thomas heard her mutter, "You'll be fortunate if the door is *unlocked* for your entry. Thomas Watson, indeed."

The moment Nadine left the dining room, Daphne erupted in giggles. Harry glared at her, and she covered her mouth with her hands, bringing an end to the chortling. "I'm so very sorry. It was a nervous reaction. I truly see nothing humorous here."

"I would hope not." Harry gave his sister one more scowl, then turned to Thomas. "Listen, Tom, you might need to consider finding yourself an apartment rather than living here if she's going to dictate how you spend your time."

Thomas shook his head. "I'm sure we'll manage to work things out. Nadine can be —" he sought a word both truthful and kind but found only — "*baulstiarijch,* but —"

A blast of laughter came from Daphne again. Despite himself, he laughed, too. Why had the *Plautdietsch* word crept into his sentence? Apparently, a part of him remained in Hillsboro, speaking Low German with the Mennonite members of the community.

Daphne's bright eyes danced. "What on earth did you just say?"

Thomas pinched his chin, stifling his smile. "I said she was headstrong."

Daphne gave an emphatic nod. "Oh my,

181

yes!" She peered toward the doorway where Nadine had disappeared. "I wholeheartedly agree!"

Harry flicked Daphne's shoulder with the backs of his fingers. "And you should know headstrong when you see it."

Daphne whirled on her brother. "Harrison Edward Severt, I —"

Thomas stepped forward. "We're wasting time. As I said, Nadine and I will work out our differences concerning the campaign. If we're going to accomplish anything this evening, we need to get going."

Belinda tapped lightly on the Ollenburgers' back door. Although the hour was late, a light still glowed, and a shadowy figure moved back and forth past the window. Someone was awake.

The door flew wide, and Summer Ollenburger gestured Belinda into the kitchen. The woman offered Belinda a quick hug and her usual welcoming smile. "Good evening! What brings you out? Is everyone all right at your house?"

The concern in *Frau* Ollenburger's tone gave a lift to Belinda's heart. Sometimes it seemed to her that the Ollenburgers cared more for her mother than even Malinda did. "Everything is fine, *Frau* Ollenburger.

Thank you." Her statement wasn't quite true — neither Mama nor Malinda could be considered "fine," yet she knew *Frau* Ollenburger would understand. "I hope I'm not intruding, but —"

"Belinda, you are never an intrusion." *Frau* Ollenburger squeezed Belinda's arm. "Come in, sit at the table and talk to me while I finish my ironing."

Belinda sank onto the simple wooden bench beside the rough-hewn table. The Ollenburgers' belongings all seemed so homey — friendly rather than formal. She supposed it matched their open, welcoming hearts. "I could iron for you, if you like. I do it for other people."

Frau Ollenburger's elbow jutted upward as she pressed the iron against the shirt splayed across the ironing board. "You have more than enough to do without adding my ironing to the list. Besides" — she sent a twinkling smile in Belinda's direction — "the task is pleasant. I like the clean smell that rises when I press the iron to the fabric, and I like seeing the wrinkles replaced with a smooth appearance. It reminds me of how lives contain a sweet essence and are straightened out when we submit to following God's will."

Belinda stared at *Frau* Ollenburger, her

thoughts whirling. How long had it been since she'd sought God's will for her own life? Her prayers seemed to be begging ones: make Mama better, help Malinda smile, grant strength to get through the days . . . Shamed, she made a silent promise to more actively seek God's will.

"I'll think about that the next time I iron." Belinda released a rueful chuckle. "Since I iron every evening, I will have lots of chances to think!"

Frau Ollenburger laughed along with her as she deftly folded the crisply ironed shirt and set it aside, then reached for another one. She gave it a snap that sent it neatly across the waiting board. Iron in hand, she peeked at Belinda. "What can I do for you this evening?"

"Oh!" Belinda jumped to her feet. "I came to see if you would give me Thomas's address in Boston." At her neighbor's speculative look, Belinda's stomach fluttered with a rush of self-consciousness. "He said I should write to him — keep him up-to-date on what's happening here in Hillsboro. I . . . I hope that's all right."

Frau Ollenburger set the iron on the back of the stove. "It's perfectly all right, Belinda. I'm glad you and Thomas will be corresponding. I think it will do his heart good to hear from one of his schoolmates from Gaeddert." She slipped around the corner, and her whispered voice was followed by a low-toned mumble. Belinda's discomfort grew as she realized *Herr* Ollenburger's sleep had been disturbed. She tangled her hands in her apron while battling the urge to flee out the back door.

Frau Ollenburger returned with a folded piece of paper in her hand, which she offered to Belinda. "Here you are. Thomas is staying with my mother-in-law, so just address the envelope to Thomas in care of Mrs. Nadine Steadman."

Belinda slipped the paper into her apron pocket. "I'll do that. Thank you, *Frau* Ollenburger."

"You're welcome."

Belinda turned to leave.

"And Belinda?"

She looked over her shoulder. "Yes, ma'am?"

Frau Ollenburger moved forward and touched Belinda's arm, bringing her all the way around. "When you write, please tell him all is well here." She glanced toward the doorway that led to the front of the house then lowered her voice. "We miss him dreadfully — his father most of all — but if Thomas knew how much he's missed it

185

would only worry him. We mustn't say anything that might pull him away from God's plan for his life. Guilt has a way of tugging one off course."

Did *Frau* Ollenburger think she would mislead Thomas? Then a second thought came to her — how often had Malinda employed guilt to keep Belinda from leaving her and their mother? Had she allowed her sister to tug her away from God's plan? The thought froze her in place for a moment.

"Belinda?" *Frau* Ollenburger's brow furrowed. "Are you all right, dear?"

Belinda gave a start. "Oh! Of course, I'm fine. I just . . . got lost in thought for a moment." She shook her head a little, bringing herself back to *Frau* Ollenburger's comment. "I wouldn't tell Thomas anything untruthful, but I'll not persuade him to do something he shouldn't."

She bid *Frau* Ollenburger good-bye and slipped out the door. Under the stars, she tipped her head back and released a long sigh toward heaven. Her brief visit with her kindly neighbor had given her much to consider. She pressed her hand to her pocket, feeling the crunch of paper. Although she had planned to finish the letter to Thomas before going to bed, she decided to talk to her heavenly Father instead.

"Oh, Thomas, it has been such a lovely afternoon." Daphne wrapped both hands around Thomas's forearm and clung, pressing her cheek briefly to his bicep. "A pity one can't demand the sun hold its position to delay the night from falling."

She loved the way his eyes crinkled when he smiled. He guided her along the park's rock-paved pathway, and she knew he was curtailing his long-legged stride to match her much shorter one.

"It wouldn't surprise me to learn you made demands of the sun, Daphne. You make demands of other things."

The teasing undertone held no offense, but Daphne fluttered her eyelashes at him and offered a slight pout anyway. "Pray tell, what demands have I made of you?"

Thomas paused, tipping his head to the side. His eyes twinkled merrily. " 'I should *so* enjoy a walk through the botanical garden.' " His attempt at a lilting voice failed, but Daphne recognized the words as her own. He tipped his head the opposite way. " 'Oh, Thomas, mightn't we ride in a swan boat?' "

She gave his arm a light slap with her folded Japanese fan and urged him onward.

"Now, you know very well those were not demands but mere suggestions. Suggestions, I might add, you heartily endorsed."

"You're right. But —" his voice caught, the timbre deepening — "it doesn't matter much to me what we do. I just enjoy having time together."

Her heart tripped happily at his confession. She snugged her cheek to his arm once more. "Oh, Thomas — me too."

They walked in silence along pathways lined with explosions of dahlias, cannas, and pansies. Set against a neatly-clipped carpet of emerald green, the flowers lent an air of festivity, and Daphne could barely contain the desire to twirl in a circle. What could be better than strolling through a flower-laden park on the arm of the man she loved?

Yes, over the past hours, Daphne had determined she most definitely loved Thomas Ollenburger.

Since his return to Boston, they hadn't had much time alone together. Between his daytime hours at the newspaper office and his evenings helping with the campaign, he had little free time available. She had been forced to snatch moments at his noonday break on the days she managed to make her way into the city, or to sneak a few sentences of conversation at campaign headquarters when Harry allowed her to accompany him. Those unsatisfactory, rushed, far-too-infrequent minutes had fed her desire for a long, uninterrupted expanse of time with this man who made her heart feel too big to fit comfortably within her chest.

And after two weeks, she'd finally gotten it — an entire Saturday afternoon with Thomas. His gentlemanly attentiveness combined with his altogether pleasing physical attributes made him the perfect choice for a suitor. Now, as the sun slipped toward the horizon, their time together neared its end, and Daphne wasn't ready to bid him good-night.

They reached the ornate iron gate that opened out onto the street, and Daphne pulled back on Thomas's arm. "Let's not go just yet. Look . . ." She pointed to a carved wooden bench tucked beneath the trees and surrounded by bright pink heliotrope. "Can we sit for a little while before you take me to meet Harry's carriage at the headquarters?"

At the word *headquarters,* Thomas grimaced, but he led her to the bench and seated himself beside her. Leaning forward, he propped his elbows on his knees and peered across the grounds where the trees' shadows created splotches of deeper green on the grassy carpet.

"I hope Harry won't be upset about me not working on the campaign today."

The worry in his tone rankled her. Did he regret his day with her? Yet she wouldn't spoil their time by fussing at him. She opened her fan with a flick of her thumb and waved the painted silk panels beneath her chin, giving herself time to calm her temper. She deliberately shifted so her skirts brushed against his trouser leg. "Harry shouldn't fault you for a day of relaxation. With the exception of the dinner party hosted by Mrs. Steadman the day after your return, you've worked *all* the time."

After a quick, lopsided grin, he said, "A man who refuses to labor is considered slothful."

She raised one eyebrow. "Is that one of your small-town folklores?"

His lips twitched. "No. Actually, it's from the Bible, the book of Proverbs."

"Oh." She raised her shoulders in a blithe shrug, increasing the tempo of the fan. "I've never read that book."

Thomas's brows crunched downward. "Never? Don't you attend church?"

"Why, certainly! At Christmas, of course, and Easter. But Sunday is Father's only day away from the office. We rarely leave the house on Sunday."

Thomas's look of dismay made her believe she'd insulted him, although she had no idea how. But she acted quickly to make amends. Dropping the fan into her lap, she took one of his hands and held it between her palms. She pretended to examine it with all seriousness. "As for these hands . . . slothful?" Another flutter of her lashes encouraged pink to blotch his neck. "I think not, Thomas."

He withdrew from her grasp, sliding the palm down the length of his thigh before linking his fingers together. His neck faded to its normal color as he stared across the lawn.

Daphne sighed, lifting the fan once more. "Perhaps tomorrow you could ride out to the estate and join my family for a late breakfast? Cook makes a positively scrumptious cinnamon cake laden with pecans and brown sugar, and Father always insists on ham, bacon, eggs, and waffles, so there will be sufficient food to satisfy your grand appetite."

Thomas's deep blue eyes held conflicting emotions — longing, most certainly, but something else, too. Remorse? Confusion? For long moments he held her captive with the intensity of feeling dancing through his sky-colored eyes. Then his expression suddenly changed to mirth. A light chuckle rumbled from his chest. "Here I thought I'd minded my manners when dining with you, but you still spotted my big appetite."

Daphne giggled, matching his light-hearted tone. "As if someone of your size could hide something like that." She lowered her chin, peeking at him over the top of the fan in a deliberately flirtatious look. "I trust you would also enjoy the . . . company . . . at my father's estate."

"Oh." He swallowed then cleared his throat. "Of course, I'd enjoy the time with . . . your family."

Daphne whisked nonexistent dust from her skirt. "And perhaps you'd have the opportunity to visit with Harry about the campaign. He could inform you what transpired today in your absence."

Thomas heaved a sigh. "Truthfully, I probably need to worry less about Harry than about Nadine." He twisted his lips into a wry grin. "She and I have been getting along as well as two tomcats in a gunnysack ever since Harry told her I was helping with Watson's campaign."

Daphne sat up, curiosity straightening her spine. "I find her reaction puzzling. Has she strong political opinions?"

"No, she's always steered away from political discussions, insisting politics is a topic polite people should avoid. So when I ask her why she's so opposed to Watson, she refuses to answer, telling me I need to figure it out for myself. There's got to be something upsetting her, though. I wish I knew what it was."

Daphne offered a supportive squeeze of her hand on his arm. "She'll tell you when she's ready. In the meantime, be patient with her. She's old and set in her ways, but she loves you — that will bring acceptance in the end."

Thomas sucked in his lips for a moment, seeming to consider her words. Then, with a shake of his head, he said, "I'll talk to her one more time, and if she doesn't agree to stop badgering me, I'm going to accept Harry's offer to locate an apartment for me." He sounded rueful when he added, "She might love me, but she's making things very uncomfortable."

14

As Thomas stepped through the front door of Nadine's home, his heart felt tangled in knots of confusion from his time with Daphne. Her confession at the park about never attending church had taken him by surprise. *"Be ye not unequally yoked together with unbelievers,"* the Bible admonished, and Thomas had learned to honor it. But at the end of the evening, as he'd graced her glove-covered knuckles with a kiss, his heart had catapulted into his throat. The lump of longing was still there.

He latched the door behind him and then pressed his forehead against it, eyes closed. God wouldn't allow him to feel drawn to a woman of whom He disapproved, would He? People in Gaeddert had certainly disapproved of Pa spending time with Summer when she first arrived in town, yet things had worked out between them. Wouldn't things work out, then, for him and

Daphne?

Someone spoke his name from behind him. He jumped and spun around, slamming his elbow against the doorjamb. Sucking in a sharp breath, he rubbed his elbow. "Yes, Nadine?"

Dressed in a navy blue evening gown with a high collar, the pale skin of Nadine's face almost gave the appearance of an apparition in the muted light filtering through the wide parlor doorway. She arched one brow and glanced at his elbow. "Are you all right?"

He lowered his hand even though the spot still throbbed. "Just fine, thank you. I . . . I tried to be quiet."

"I've been waiting for you."

Despite her genial tone, a sense of foreboding gripped Thomas. "Oh?"

"Yes. Please . . ." She held her hand toward the parlor. "Shall we sit?"

Thomas followed her into the parlor, waited until she seated herself in her favorite embroidered chair, then settled into the center of the settee. Hoping to appear more relaxed than he felt, he propped his right ankle on his left knee and leaned fully against the stiff backrest of the uncomfortable seat.

"I trust you had a pleasant afternoon?"

"Yes, ma'am. The botanical gardens are

beautiful." Thomas wondered if the remainder of the evening would put a damper on the day's remembered pleasures.

Nadine's eyebrows shot up. "Botanical gardens? I thought you spent the day at the . . . campaign headquarters."

Had she hesitated or did he only imagine it? He rubbed his dry lips together before responding. "No. I spent the day with Daphne Severt."

"Ah." A quick moue of displeasure crossed Nadine's face. "I'm not sure that's any better than campaigning for Watson. . . ."

Despite himself, Thomas smiled. "Why not? She's a lovely girl." He almost sighed with pleasure as he recalled Daphne's sweet face turned up to his as they drifted across the lake in a swan-shaped boat while several of the real birds floated along beside them. Then he remembered her comment about never attending church, and his heart contracted.

"Lovely, yes. But spoiled." Nadine spoke matter-of-factly without a hint of malice, but also without warmth. She shook her head. "I can see nothing of lasting value coming from your relationship with Daphne Severt, Thomas. All of her appeal is superficial — skin deep." Now her tone took on an edge. "When choosing a life's mate, there must be more than physical attraction."

Thomas frowned. "I know."

"Do you?"

He sat silently as resentment built within him. While he loved Nadine, her interference in his life was becoming tiresome. Besides, her words too closely mirrored the concern that had already struck him. He shoved aside his own worries about Daphne and focused on Nadine. By reminding himself she had no one to fuss over but him, he found the patience needed to hold his tongue. He swallowed and managed a terse response. "Yes, I know."

She leaned her head back and closed her eyes for a moment. Her body seemed to relax, her tightly held fingers opening so her hands lay limply in her lap. "Ah, Thomas, you think me foolish and overbearing, don't you?"

He certainly wasn't going to answer that!

Opening her eyes, she fixed him with a tender look. "But in truth, I'm concerned for you. I was young once, too, as was my son, Rodney, and your stepmother, Summer. Rodney and Summer married for the sake of attraction, you know, and although they were committed to each other, I'm aware of their lack of true happiness together. Summer loves you dearly — she would want more than a superficial relationship for you."

Thomas leaned forward, dropping his foot to the floor. "I appreciate your concern, Nadine. But there's no reason to worry. I haven't made any commitment to Daphne. I just enjoy my time with her." Heat crept up his neck once again as he recalled the evening he walked Belinda Schmidt home after delivering her load of ironing. If he were truthful, his time with Daphne was different than his time with Belinda, although both had been enjoyable.

"One more word of advice from an old woman, hmm?" She nodded, as if he'd spoken an agreement. "Make a determined effort to acquaint yourself with Daphne Severt's character. I'm certain it will not be easy — she has been doubly blessed with external beauty, which would distract the most mature gentleman — but for the sake of avoiding heartbreak, you must try."

"I'll try," Thomas promised, eager to move to another topic.

She took a deep breath. "About your involvement in the Watson campaign —"

Thomas wished they could return to discussing Daphne. He released a derisive grunt. The disrespectful behavior would have appalled his father, but he couldn't stop himself. "Nadine, please, I don't understand why —"

"No, you do not." Her eyes blazed, but he wondered if her reaction had as much to do with his impolite grunt as it did with Watson. "You do not understand at all."

He deliberately gentled his voice. "Then please explain it to me."

"I will not waste one second of my lifetime trying to explain myself to you."

Plopping back into the seat, he threw his arms wide, forgetting his determination to be gentle. "Then how will we ever reach a compromise on this issue?"

"There is no compromise." For a moment, he thought he saw a tear glisten in Nadine's eye, but she blinked and it disappeared. She continued in an unemotional yet firm tone. "Although my behavior of late no doubt gives you reason to question it, I am not a suffragist. Certainly, if given the opportunity to vote, I would exercise that right and cast my ballot, but I will never join parades or rabble-rouse to be granted the privilege. In truth, although my Horace was a staunch Republican, I have no strong political affiliations."

Her statements only served to increase Thomas's confusion. "Then why —"

"It is not for *political* reasons that I question your support of this particular candidate." She continued in the same unflappable, even voice, as if Thomas hadn't spoken. She paused, unblinking, fixing Thomas with a look he felt certain bored a hole through him. "What was my advice to you concerning Daphne Severt?"

Thomas frowned, trying to recall her exact words. He paraphrased, "To look below her surface for the truth of who she is."

Nadine nodded, looking satisfied. "Yes, that's exactly right." She rose, crossing to stand directly in front of him. She reached out and plucked up his hand, squeezing it between her soft palms just as Daphne had done not long ago. "And, Thomas, that is what you must do with Mr. Watson — look below his surface for the truth of who he is. Then you decide whether he is worthy of your support and admiration." Releasing his hand, she left the room without a backward glance.

Thomas sat staring at the doorway where Nadine had exited, processing her puzzling statement. Look below Watson's surface to the truth? He'd already done so, or he wouldn't be involved in the campaign to elect him to office. The man's stand that farmers should be protected went straight to the core of who Thomas was — the son of a man who made his living from what farmers sowed. Supporting him made sense. Didn't it?

He rubbed his hand down his face, suddenly very weary. His day in the sun, combined with the emotional upheaval of the final hours, had sapped his energy. He was too tired to pick through Nadine's comments for nuggets of wisdom. Pushing to his feet, he started for the stairs, and once more someone calling his name brought him to a halt.

Mildred bustled forward, her brown face wreathed in a warm smile. "Here you go, Mr. Thomas — a letter came in the mail for you." She pointed to the upper left-hand corner and winked, her double chin tripling with her broad grin. "From a lady, I see. Someone special?"

Thomas glanced at the name — Belinda! Yes, Belinda was special, but not the way Mildred implied. "A friend from home." He took the envelope and slipped it into his breast pocket.

Mildred seemed to wilt for a moment, then shrugged her rounded shoulders. "Well, friends is a good place to start," she said as if reassuring herself.

Thomas allowed a chuckle and headed up to his room, taking the stairs two at a time.

Mildred's parting comment rang through his mind. Pa and Summer had started with a good, solid friendship, and he'd never seen a more contented couple. However, when he thought of solidifying a friendship, it wasn't Belinda he thought of — it was Daphne.

"Ollenburger!"

Thomas jerked upright and spun around in his seat. The advertisement he had been checking for errors skidded off the desk and floated to the floor. He picked it up before replying. "Yes?"

The wide-eyed errand boy waved his hand, beckoning Thomas to the hallway. "Mr. Severt wants a word with you. He says for me to bring you to his office."

Thomas placed a glass paperweight over the advertisement and followed the boy up the concrete steps to the main lobby and then to the elevator. His heart pounded. In the month of his employment at the *Boston Beacon,* he had never been summoned to the owner's office. As the elevator operator tugged the cable, carrying the enclosed box and its occupants to the fourth floor, Thomas's hands began to sweat. He shoved them into his pockets, hoping to remove the moisture.

The elevator groaned to a stop, and the errand boy slid the iron door open. "Come on," he said to Thomas in an impatient tone, as if urgency propelled him. The boy's shaggy hair bounced with his jogging pace as he led Thomas to a pair of double doors at the end of a short, marble-floored hallway. "He's in there." The boy spun and trotted to a bench where he seated himself, his hands in his lap and his gaze aimed straight ahead.

Thomas knocked on the right-hand door. A brusque "Enter!" gave him permission to open the door.

The hinges made no sound when Thomas pushed the heavy door open. In the center of a spacious room lined with hip-high bookcases and narrow windows that stretched above the cases to the high ceiling, Mr. Severt sat behind a massive maple desk. He bent forward, his thick eyebrows low, his hand busily scribbling on a sheet of yellow paper. Thomas hovered in the doorway until the man set the pen aside and looked up.

"Ollenburger. Come in. Sit."

Thomas lowered himself onto one of the guest chairs, grimacing when the joints creaked with his weight. He resisted the urge to tug at his tight collar. Mr. Severt's collar had been unfastened, its pointed ends springing out on either side of his face. His jacket hung on the back of his tall chair, and his shirt sleeves were rolled to his elbows, exposing thick, hairy forearms. Even though Thomas had visited the Severt estate the past two Sundays — Mr. Severt's lone day off — he'd not seen the man in such an informal state. The sight made him want to avert his gaze.

Mr. Severt linked his hands together and rested his elbows on the edge of his messy desk. "How long have you been with the *Beacon,* Ollenburger?"

"Four weeks now, sir."

"Happy here?"

The man's clipped manner of speaking, as if he considered Thomas an intrusive stranger, created an unsettled feeling in Thomas's gut. Given the time they'd spent chatting over his cook's elaborate breakfasts in his ostentatious dining room, it seemed odd he would be so stiff and cold now. Maybe, when in his office, he saved his words for his articles.

Thomas cleared his throat and replied, "Yes, sir, I'm quite satisfied with my employment."

Mr. Severt grunted, and fresh sweat broke out across Thomas's back. Had he said something displeasing? Suddenly his boss thumped his hands onto the desktop, scattering papers. "Satisfied? In proofreading? Have you no other aspirations?"

Thomas swallowed. "Well, of course, sir, I hope to eventually move into a higher position, but —"

"Good to hear that." The man relaxed into his high-backed chair, his piercing gaze pinned to Thomas's face. "I must say, I haven't regretted Daphne coercing me into putting you on staff." He released an indulgent chortle, shaking his head. "She's been able to keep every penny of her allowance."

Thomas blinked. Daphne had *coerced* her father into hiring him? And what did her allowance have to do with anything?

"Not a one of the advertisements you've proofed has printed with an error. And the occasional rephrasing has met my approval every time. You seem to have a keen eye and a way with words — a worthy combination in the newspaper business."

Still reeling from the comments about Daphne, Thomas didn't reply.

"Harry has spoken well of you, and what I've observed during your visits to our home has substantiated all of Harry's claims."

His mouth dry, Thomas remained silent. Unease prickled the hairs on the back of his neck as he thought about the man observing him, forming opinions, while Thomas was unaware of the scrutiny.

"I believe I'm wasting your talents as an advertising proofreader. I'd like to offer you a position as editorial copy editor. The position means a considerable pay raise and a private office on the third floor. Better than the basement, hmm?"

Despite his earlier confusion, Thomas couldn't stop a grin from growing. Even without the pay raise, the change appealed to him — if for no other reason than the view. All he could see from the tiny window in the office he now occupied was people's feet passing by and an occasional pigeon tapping at the glass. He glanced toward the windows in Severt's office. A touch of blue sky over rooftops and — he stifled a chuckle — roosting pigeons. Some things would be the same.

"So . . . are you interested?"

Thomas swallowed. "I'd be foolish to say no, sir."

"Indeed." He rose abruptly, pushing his sleeves to his wrists and deftly clipping gold cufflinks into place. Thomas looked out the window as the man hooked his collar, huffing with the effort. Then Severt snatched up his coat, jammed his arms into it, and buttoned it across his broad middle. Rounding the desk with a brisk pace, he ordered, "Follow me."

Thomas trailed Mr. Severt out of the office. When they entered the hallway, the errand boy sat straight up, his hands poised to push himself from the bench. Severt ignored the boy, stomped directly to the elevator, and pressed the brass buzzer. In moments the elevator doors squeaked open, and Severt gestured Thomas to enter.

"Floor three," Severt barked to the elevator operator, his eyes on the doors rather than his employee.

A few tugs lowered the elevator, and Thomas followed his boss down a hallway lined on both sides by windowless doors spaced approximately twelve feet apart. Severt walked directly to the fourth door on the right and opened it without knocking.

"Perkins!"

Thomas remained outside the door, peering into the room. He experienced a lurch of sympathy when the man behind the desk nearly toppled out of his chair in surprise. Obviously he'd been napping.

Severt jerked his thumb over his shoulder to indicate Thomas's presence. "This is Ollenburger. He'll be taking your position. Pack your personal effects, collect your final pay from the clerk, and be out by four o'clock." Without waiting for a response, he whirled on Thomas. "Ollenburger, if you have any personal items at your desk in the basement, see to them now. Plan on assuming this office Monday morning at nine o'clock." His face retained its stern countenance as he asked, "I assume you will be out to see Daphne this evening?"

Thomas's face flushed as he sensed Perkins' fierce attention. It was Friday — payday — which meant Daphne would expect to see him. He offered a nod.

"Very well. Make sure you thank her for her persuasive recommendation." Severt thrust out his hand.

Too startled to do otherwise, Thomas shook it.

The man clapped him on the back and broke into a smile. "Congratulations, son." He strode away, leaving Thomas standing uncertainly in the office doorway with Perkins' hard glare piercing him and the title "son" echoing in his memory.

15

Daphne held the curling tongs to her hair, counting to ten to be certain the heat would penetrate enough to create a curl without singeing her hair. She slid the tongs free, smiling in satisfaction at the perfect coil that fell along her neck to join the abundance of glossy spirals.

With a scowl of concentration, she separated another strand and twisted it around the metal barrel of the tongs. Her maid, Nancy, had offered to do the curling, but Daphne had refused. She and she alone would be responsible for every detail of preparation for Thomas's arrival. Her arms ached from the effort involved in curling her hair — for over an hour she'd been alternately heating and using the tongs — but it was worth it. Thomas was worth it.

Her heart skipped a beat at the thought of his name. As had become their custom since their walk through the botanical gardens two weeks ago, he would soon drive out, pick her up, and take her to dinner. Her Friday evenings with Thomas were unquestionably the best part of her week because he was all hers — no sharing with Harry or worrying about a servant eavesdropping on private conversation.

Sometimes she wished he would splurge on days other than payday, but he had the notion that he needed to send a portion of his pay to the church his family attended in a little town in Kansas, a portion to Mrs. Steadman — even though she vehemently argued against taking it — and then set back a portion into a savings account. He didn't spoil her with gifts or take her to extravagant locations, and sometimes she puzzled why she allowed him to get by with it.

"Because just being with him is enough," she admitted aloud. The scent of scorched hair reached her nostrils; with a cry of alarm, she jerked the tongs free. She'd completely forgotten to count! Clenching her teeth, she gingerly fingered the strand, then slumped with relief. Although it felt a bit stiff, she didn't think she had done permanent damage. Determined to stay focused, she set thoughts of Thomas aside long enough to finish curling her hair.

But the moment she released the final

spiraling coil and dropped the tongs onto her messy dressing table, she allowed herself to consider the evening ahead. A smile grew on her face as she recalled Father's nonchalant comments at breakfast that morning.

"Yes, Daphne, you were right about the Ollenburger lad. He's proven competent. In fact, he'll be offered a promotion. I've been looking for the right man to replace that inept excuse for a copy editor, Perkins." Father shook his head in frustration. "*You* would do a better job than Perkins has done!"

She had ignored the insult in light of his final comment.

"Yes, indeed, Ollenburger has potential. I see a bright future in store for him."

A delicious shiver slid down her spine — how good it felt to have Father's approval! But how she wished she could have been in the office when Father told Thomas the news of his promotion. Tonight she would insist he replay every minute, every emotion.

Stepping in front of the mirror, she practiced her response to the appreciation she was certain he would shower on her when he learned of how she had helped him secure a prestigious position at the *Beacon*. Convinced she had found the perfect expression of humble acceptance, she turned this way and that, admiring her reflection. The summer frock of buttery yellow silk, embroidered with delicate daisies and a lavender-winged butterfly, provided a perfect backdrop for her black hair and dark eyes. Certainly Thomas would be so taken by her feminine appearance in this beautifully crafted gown, he would melt at her feet.

Daphne sank onto the little embroidered bench at the foot of her bed, carefully spreading her skirts over her knees to avoid creasing the fabric. Pressing her cheek to the downy comforter covering the thick feather mattress, she closed her eyes and released a sigh of pure contentment. Such a wonderful future awaited her and Thomas. With Father's admiration of Thomas's work ethic, other promotions would surely follow this first one. In no time at all, Thomas would have the means to propose to her!

Popping her eyes open, she looked at the clock on the wall. Another forty minutes yet before he would arrive. She willed the time to pass quickly.

The moment Clarence drew the carriage to a stop in front of the Severt estate, Thomas hopped out. "I might be a few minutes, Clarence."

The man nodded, the silver streaks in his black hair glistening under the early evening sun. "I'll be here when you need me, Mr. Thomas."

Thomas gave a quick wave, then made his way slowly up the long brick walk that led to the ornately carved double doors. In past visits, he had trotted to those doors, eager to see Daphne, unwilling to waste a precious minute of time with her despite the discomfort that worried at the back of his mind concerning their relationship. The more time he spent with her, the easier it became to ignore the twinge of doubt.

But this evening his feet moved as if his shoes were crafted of lead. An odd dread filled his stomach. Although he'd debated with himself all afternoon, he still wasn't sure how to approach Daphne concerning her father's unusual comment about being coerced into hiring him. If it was true — if he had the position at the newspaper only because Daphne had forced her father to hire him and not due to Thomas's own abilities — he didn't think he could continue working there.

As he lifted his hand to pound the brass lion's-head knocker against its circular plate, a longing to pray for peace and assurance rose up within him, but he ignored the feeling. Prayer wouldn't change what had already taken place. He'd just have to make the best of what would come next.

The door swung open, and the Severts' butler invited Thomas to enter the foyer.

"Good evening. I'm here for —"

"Miss Daphne," the man interrupted, not so much as a hint of a smile softening his austere expression. The Severts' household staff members carried a far more formal air than Clarence and Mildred, who served Nadine faithfully and cheerfully. "I shall retrieve her directly."

The man walked with wooden movements up the stairs and disappeared around the top bend. Thomas remained just inside the door on the marble-tiled floor. He held his hat in his hands, staring at the polished toes of his boots while he wondered what he would say when she came down. The *pat-pat* of feet on carpet captured his attention. Daphne . . .

As always, her beauty made his breathing quicken, and he allowed his gaze to travel from her beaming face to her slender hands. One of her hands draped gracefully over the staircase railing; the other held her sunshiny skirt just high enough to expose shapely ankles graced by ribbon ties on white slippers. With a gulp, he returned his focus to her smile and the shiny curls that bounced on her narrow shoulders. She came directly to him and held out one hand, fully expecting a kiss. Without hesitation, he bent forward and pressed his lips to the center knuckle. Her fingers curled over his, giving an almost indiscernible squeeze.

He jerked upright, slapping his hat onto his head.

"You are punctual, as always," she said brightly. "I thought perhaps today you might be tardy given the excitement at the *Beacon.* Have you already settled into your new office?"

"Not until Monday."

She affected an adorable little pout — one of her most familiar expressions. "Ah." Then she giggled softly. "Of course, whether your belongings have been transferred to the third floor or not, we know the promotion is for sure. So we have cause to celebrate! Have you chosen a special place of dining this evening?"

"Actually, no."

"No? Whyever not?"

Thomas swallowed hard. Her fingers still held to his hand. He gave a gentle tug, guiding her out the front door to a wicker settee tucked in shadow beneath an overhead balcony. "Before we go, I need to know

215

something."

She seated herself, placed her linked hands in her lap, and lifted her expectant, open gaze to him. He paced the width of the settee twice before sitting beside her. Yanking his hat from his head, he ran his hand over his hair and plunked the hat on the seat next to his hip. He cleared his throat, met her gaze, and finally blurted, "Did your father really want to hire me?"

She reared back, her hand rising to rest against the lacy bodice of her gown. "What an odd question." She shook her head, giving him an indulgent look. "Thomas, my darling, does Harrison Severt strike you as the kind of man who performs actions against his own will?"

Over the past weeks, Thomas had learned Daphne was a master at answering questions indirectly, which turned the topic away from the one he intended. He wouldn't allow her to dissuade him this time — this was too important. "Daphne, please answer me. Did your father hire me at your request?"

Daphne tilted her lips upward, her eyes sparkling. "You needn't be equivocal, Thomas. Simply offer your thank-you and let us be off for dinner." She started to rise.

Thomas caught her hand. "You admit it,

then? Your father didn't hire me because he thought I was an able candidate, but because you . . . coerced him?"

The flash in her eyes set off a warning in the back of Thomas's brain. But just as quickly as it flared, the fire died and she offered her familiar sulky expression. "What an ugly word. Why, as if Father could be coerced by a mere woman! I'm not entirely sure who has just been insulted more — Father or myself."

A sense of remorse rose within Thomas's chest, but he refused to allow it to overshadow his desire for the truth. "I didn't intend to insult you, but I can't keep a position I didn't earn on my own merits."

"I fail to see why not."

Thomas's brows jerked downward. How could she be so oblivious?

She shrugged, her eyes wide and innocent. "Perhaps I did influence Father when it came to hiring you. He sees numerous applicants every week, young men eager to join the staff and make names for themselves in the newspaper world. Mentioning your name gave you an advantage over those others and brought you to the forefront of Father's attention."

A band seemed to surround Thomas's chest, squeezing as Daphne admitted his fear — she *had* coerced her father.

"But," she continued blithely, unaware of his inner turmoil, "once on staff, only your own efforts would *keep* Father's attention. Father hires and fires at will — and he is not hesitant to send someone packing."

Thomas remembered Mr. Severt's treatment of the hapless Perkins. He nodded slowly.

She placed her hand on his wrist, and he wondered if she felt his pounding pulse. "Thomas, let me assure you that this promotion from advertising proofreader to editorial copy editor is something you earned yourself. Father would never offer such a prominent position based on the say-so of his daughter."

For a moment, a look of hurt flickered in her eyes, but it disappeared so quickly he wondered if he had imagined it. Her fingers tightened on his wrist. "You *earned* this promotion, Thomas, so celebrate it, as I so heartily celebrate it."

Looking into her sincere face, Thomas melted. "Of course I celebrate it. I'm grateful for the opportunity."

Her dark eyes shone, and she leaped to her feet. She snatched up his hat and pressed it into his hands. "We have so many reasons to rejoice, Thomas! Such wonderful things are happening!"

Suddenly the closing line from Belinda Schmidt's last letter ran through Thomas's mind: *Every day, I pray God's will for you.* He sucked in his breath as he wondered, *What is God's will for my life?*

Daphne caught his hands, tugging him from the bench. "Let's go."

On the carriage ride to town, Daphne continued to bubble. "And think of what the promotion means for you, Thomas. Of course there is the prestige of editing Father's writings — Father trusts only a handful of employees with his own work. With the increase in pay, you can afford to move from Mrs. Steadman's home. Independence now awaits you, Thomas, and independence opens the door to . . ."

Although she didn't complete the sentence, Thomas understood. If he had his own place of residence, he could establish a family of his own. He released her name on a low growl. "Daphne . . ."

"What?" It seemed she feigned innocence.

Thomas shook his head, trying to rein in his thoughts. Was a commitment to Daphne God's will? He hadn't prayed before accepting the position of editorial copy editor, and he couldn't remember praying about pursuing a relationship with Daphne. Confusion filled him. His breath rushed out so rapidly, he felt as if his chest might collapse. Thoughts rolled through his mind like tumbleweeds across the prairie, without direction or control: This new position meant independence . . . his own apartment . . . an opportunity to rise in prestige . . . a sufficient salary to support a family.

The final thought reverberated, growing in volume with each echo. Support a family . . . a family . . . *a family!*

Daphne pinned her gaze to his but remained silent. The secret promises shining in her dark eyes made Thomas's mouth go dry. *A family* . . . The longing to have all his father had — a home with a wife and children — once more filled him.

He grabbed hold of her hands and opened his mouth to share his desire, but the carriage rolled to a halt and Clarence called, "Mister Thomas? We at the restaurant."

With reluctance, Thomas released his hold on Daphne. The opportunity for a private conversation had passed, but there would be time later. He gestured to the door. "Let's eat." When she tucked her little hand between his elbow and rib, her upper arm brushing against his as he escorted her into the restaurant's dining room, he experienced a jolt of reaction so strong it might have been electricity coursing through his veins. There was so much he wanted to discuss with her.

16

The contents of the letter took the air from Belinda's lungs. Had she not been already seated, her legs might have given out beneath her.

Across the parlor, Malinda lifted her attention from the embroidery hoop. "What is it now?"

Her sister's impatient tone suggested she was often forced to listen to a series of complaints. Belinda admitted with a humorless chuckle that complaints were offered regularly in the house, but they were always offered *by* Malinda rather than *to* her. Knowing her sister awaited an answer, Belinda waved the single page. "Thomas. He received a promotion at the newspaper. He is now copy editing editorials for the paper's owner."

Malinda's scowl didn't relax. "So?" She leaned back over her work, jabbing the needle in and out as if through a sheet of iron rather than muslin.

Belinda sighed, lowering her gaze to Thomas's neat script. She resisted the urge to share her thoughts. Malinda wouldn't understand and would no doubt belittle her. Rather than subject herself to verbal abuse, Belinda stayed silent. But how her heart ached. She had hoped Thomas's stay in Boston would be brief and he would return to Hillsboro to be near his parents. Near her. But with this new job, it became more likely he would make Boston his permanent home.

As she read the remainder of the letter, a pressure built behind her eyes until she could no longer contain her emotions. She jolted to her feet, crumpling the letter into her pocket.

Malinda's head shot up. "Where are you going?"

"Outside." Belinda headed toward the back of the house.

"You're being foolish." Malinda's strident tone followed. "Moping won't bring him back here. And even if he were here, he doesn't care for you. Those letters are due to obligation, not devotion. Do you hear me, Belinda?"

Belinda ignored her sister and charged out the back door into the sultry late August evening. She sucked great gulps of air, an attempt to calm herself. But tears still clouded her vision. Choking back a sob, she stumbled across the browning grass to her familiar place of refuge and closed herself inside. The stifling heat of the windowless shed matched the oppressive weight in her chest. Dropping to her knees, she moaned, "Heavenly Father, why . . . ?"

She curled her hand over the crushed letter in her pocket, recalling the paragraph that had twisted her heart with despair. *With this increased income, I can now move into my own place. I found a cottage that suits my needs. I'll be living in it by the end of the month. I trust Daphne will also find it acceptable even though it's much smaller than her family's estate. But if she's to be the wife of a lowly copy editor, she'll have to become accustomed to a more humble dwelling.*

Thomas had mentioned Daphne before — the younger sister of his college friend. Belinda was familiar with the name, but not until this letter had she realized the extent of Thomas's interest in the young woman. Or maybe, she acknowledged with a pang of self-recrimination, she had overlooked the truth in order to hold on to hope that Thomas would one day see her as more than a casual friend.

Foolish, Malinda had said. Yes, Belinda had been foolish indeed thinking her letter-writing would bind Thomas to her. How could she have let herself believe for even one minute he would feel as connected to her through her letters as she did with him? Despite his moments of kindness during his brief time in Hillsboro, she was still Belinda Schmidt, the girl who had tormented him throughout his growing-up years. Their past — and her behavior — would always be a stumbling block between them.

Belinda raised her face to the planked ceiling overhead. She glared at the weathered gray boards. "Is it too much to ask for a little happiness? Neither Mama nor Malinda appreciates all I do for them. I thought — I thought Thomas appreciated my letters, but now . . ." She swallowed, her chest heaving with the effort of holding back sobs. "Now I see he's just used me, too, to meet his own need for information. He never c-cared for m-me . . ."

Pain stabbed so fiercely, Belinda couldn't contain it. Doubling over, she wrapped her arms across her stomach, rocked herself, and allowed the tears to flow. Between bouts of wracking sobs, she poured out her hurt in a mingled torrent of complaints, regrets, and requests. Then, finally spent, she drooped against the rough shed wall and peered upward once more. A small crack between two overhead boards allowed in a slender beam of early evening sunlight. Shimmering dust motes danced through the shaft of white.

She squinted, focusing on the glittering bits of grit, fascinated by the play of light on each miniscule particle. How could dirt — just plain old ugly dirt — take on the appearance of diamonds when drifting through a beam of light? For reasons beyond her understanding, a small candle of hope lit within her breast. Could all of the heartache of these days — Malinda's surliness, Papa's death, Mama's despondence, the thankless hours of toil — be somehow transformed into something pleasant? Something of beauty?

A portion of a verse from the book of Isaiah suddenly filtered through Belinda's mind. She whispered the words aloud. " 'Give unto them beauty for ashes.' "

Eager to confirm the thought, she pushed to her feet and raced to the house. She closed herself in her bedroom, opened her Bible, and searched until she located the text in Isaiah's sixty-first chapter, the third verse. She read the entire scripture aloud, pronouncing each word carefully.

" 'To appoint unto them that mourn in Zion, to give unto them beauty for ashes, the oil of joy for mourning, the garment of praise for the spirit of heaviness; that they might be called trees of righteousness, the planting of the Lord, that he might be glorified.' "

She closed her eyes for a moment, soaking up the meaning of the passage. God could replace unhappiness with joy — the verse clearly confirmed it. Opening her eyes, she focused on the words that had called to her in the shed. *"Beauty for ashes . . ."* Certainly all she had now was ashes — gray, useless wisps of burnt dreams and desires. But what was faith if not a belief that God would do what He promised? She scanned the words again: *"Beauty for ashes . . . Joy for mourning . . . Praise for the spirit of heaviness . . ."* She underlined the final words with a trembling finger: *"That he might be glorified."*

Closing the Bible, she pressed her hands to the worn leather cover. Could all of the difficulties of the past year be a way of testing, of growing her, so that she might bring glory to her Lord? Gulping, she remembered her outpouring in the shed — the bitter complaints she had hurled at her heavenly Father. Had she failed Him by giving in to despair?

Slipping to her knees, she begged forgiveness, then admitted in a ragged tone, "It just hurts so much, God, to feel . . . cast aside . . . by everyone. I need to be loved and appreciated. Please, can't you send someone who will meet my needs even as you give me strength to meet the needs of my mother and sister?" Clenching her fingers so tightly they ached, she begged, "Give me beauty for ashes, Father. A little beauty, please . . ."

A frantic pounding at her door brought her to her feet. She rushed to the door and flung it open. Malinda stood in the hallway, her chest heaving with rapid breaths and her eyes wild. Belinda grasped her sister's arms. "What is it?"

"Belinda." Malinda's harsh whisper sent a shaft of fear through Belinda's breast. "It's Mama. Something's wrong."

The telephone jangled, interrupting dinner. Nadine looked toward the door leading to the kitchen and scowled. Thomas covered his rueful smile with his napkin. At least she was scowling at something besides him. The past two weeks had been difficult, facing his foster grandmother's constant disapproval of his choice to move into the cottage. She didn't seem to realize her scolding only made him more determined to leave.

Mildred appeared in the doorway, her round face showing concern. "Mr. Thomas? The call is for you." She wrung her hands in her apron. "From Hillsboro."

Thomas sent a startled look at Nadine. He'd never received a telephone call from Kansas. His parents communicated through letters or an occasional telegram. They didn't use the telephone. His heart set up a thud of trepidation. Wiping his mouth, he followed Mildred to the kitchen and picked up the earpiece. Leaning close to the mouth horn, he hollered, "Hello, this is Thomas."

"Son." A crackle of static underscored Pa's grave voice.

Thomas pressed his palm to the wall next to the telephone. His legs quivered. "What's wrong?"

Pa's voice was low. "Of course you would think right away something is wrong. And you would be right. There has been a death."

Summer? One of the girls? Thomas's knees buckled, and he nearly went down.

"*Frau* Schmidt died in her bed this afternoon."

The relief was so great, Thomas sank against the wall, his shoulders slumping low as he dropped his chin. Then guilt brought

229

him upright. He should feel grief for Belinda, not deliverance for himself. "What happened?"

A long pause made Thomas wonder if the connection had broken. Then Pa's voice came again, subdued. "She refused to eat for many weeks. The doctor says . . . she willed herself to die."

A chill went down Thomas's spine. How awful for her daughters, to know their mother had chosen to leave them. "How —" He swallowed the knot in his throat. "How is Belinda?"

"She is holding up for Malinda's sake, but I see much pain in her eyes. Pray for her, son."

Thomas swallowed again. "I will, Pa. You tell her she's in my prayers."

Pa informed Thomas when the burial would be, and then they disconnected the call. Thomas walked on wooden legs back to the dining room and sat. Nadine raised her brows in silent query, and Thomas shared the news.

"Ah. So sad." Nadine shook her head, clicking her tongue against her teeth. "Death is a difficult thing to bear, especially for one at such a young age. Your friend Belinda will be much in need of support." She raised one brow. "This *is* the Belinda who writes to you regularly, is it not?"

Thomas nodded. He pushed his plate aside, his hunger gone. "If you'll excuse me, Nadine, I believe I'd like to take the carriage and go for a ride."

For once Nadine didn't question him but merely waved her hand in dismissal. He headed to the small carriage house at the rear of Nadine's property and secured the horse in its rigging. In a few minutes, he sat in the driver's seat, guiding the horse through the streets of Boston. The typical evening traffic greeted him, and he decided he'd rather avoid others. He aimed the carriage for the edge of town.

After a few minutes, he realized he'd chosen the road that led to the Severt estate. By accident or design? He supposed it didn't matter whether the selection was intentional or not. Suddenly he needed to share the hurt he carried for Belinda's loss, and who better to unburden him than his sweetheart, Daphne?

He turned the carriage into the lane and drew the horse to a stop in front of the house. Even before he could hop down, the front doors opened and Daphne stepped outside. Her face glowed with open delight.

"Thomas!" She rushed forward, catching his hands. "What an unexpected pleasure!

What brings —" Her eyes widened. "Oh, my. I can tell by your expression. Something is wrong." She gave his hands a tug, leading him to the wicker settee surrounded by potted flowers. "Come. Sit down."

Thomas sank gratefully onto the padded cushion. Daphne seated herself gracefully beside him, her full skirts falling across his knee. "Please tell me what has you troubled. Has Mrs. Steadman been chiding you again about the cottage?"

Truthfully, Nadine didn't let a day go by without voicing her opinion about the foolishness of him spending his money on rent when he could live free of charge beneath her roof. But he'd learned to nod and ignore her. Besides, that complaint seemed petty in light of Belinda's loss. He shook his head.

"Then is it the campaign?"

Thomas snorted. Although he'd spent every evening at campaign headquarters and continued to give Watson his full support despite Nadine's disapproval, the election seemed of no greater consequence than Nadine's fussing about the cottage. "I received some unpleasant news from home."

"Tell me."

His stomach churned when he thought about Belinda facing her mother's service and burial without the support of family or friends. Malinda would be useless, and few people in the community had reached out to her. Although he had encouraged her to make friends, he knew from her letters she was too busy with her responsibilities to take time to socialize. How alone she must feel.

"A friend of mine . . ." His head hung low as sympathy weighed him down. "Her mother died."

"Her?"

The sharp note brought Thomas's head up. "Yes. Her name is Belinda Schmidt. We went to school together, and —"

Daphne's expression became a scowl of displeasure. "I wasn't aware you had a *friend* named Belinda."

At the bite in her tone, Thomas withdrew by sliding sideways several inches. Her skirt slipped from his trouser leg, and she smoothed it even closer to her own knees. He explained, "We grew up in the same community, but we didn't become friends until this past summer."

Daphne's eyes snapped, but she pressed her lips together and sat in silence.

"She's written to me since I came back to Boston, kept me up-to-date on what was happening in Hillsboro. She lives right across the alley from my parents."

A chill seemed to creep across the balmy air. Thomas recognized the signs of jealousy, but surely Daphne understood there was no reason to be envious of Belinda? He clasped her hand and held it even though she tugged slightly to free herself. "Daphne, listen to me. Belinda lost her mother. Her father is already gone. All she has is an older sister who has never been stable and now struggles with her health, so she is no help at all. I'm concerned for Belinda."

Daphne managed to wriggle her hand loose. She clutched her fingers together and pressed them to her lap, fixing Thomas with a haughty glare. "Well, I'm sure *Belinda* appreciates your great concern. Perhaps you should go back to Mrs. Steadman's and pen her a lengthy letter, telling her how much you *care*."

Thomas's chest felt tight, his face hot. "I don't *care* for Belinda. Not the way you're intimating. As I said, she's a friend. I realize you don't know her, but can't you feel any compassion for her at all?" And couldn't she feel any compassion for the way *Frau* Schmidt's death had impacted him?

Daphne rose, lifting her chin. "I fail to see why you should expect me to feel compassion for a woman with whom I have no relationship. And I fail to see why you are so affected by her loss unless" — her cool tone carried recrimination — "you harbor a deeper caring than you are willing to admit."

Thomas stood and warned, "Daphne, I don't appreciate your insinuation."

Daphne stamped her foot, glowering upward. "And I do not appreciate your overt concern for another woman! You are courting *me*. No other woman should hold any part of your attention."

Thomas's anger welled, building a band of constriction around his chest. Rather than blast her with his frustration, he turned toward the buggy.

Two small hands caught his elbow and clung, the fingers digging into his flesh. He paused, taking in a deep breath before turning his head to look into her face. She held to his elbow as she peered at him with wide, sad eyes glistening with tears.

"Thomas, you think me cold and uncaring, don't you? Truth be known, I've suffered that accusation before. But it isn't the case. Not really. I care so dearly for you. I only ask that you care as much for me. That you put me before all others." The velvety color of her eyes deepened as tears swam. "I couldn't bear it if something — or someone else — came between us. You do understand, don't you, Thomas?"

Yes, he understood. This was possessiveness — wanting Thomas all to herself. Hadn't he experienced the same feeling when other men had admired Daphne? Selfish jealousy had struck him when he feared Daphne's attention belonged to someone other than him.

Then, without warning, his father's voice rang through Thomas's head, advice from long ago: *"Son, if you put God first, your family second, and yourself third, you will be blessed."* Should selfish jealousy exist in Thomas's heart? Should he accept it from Daphne?

"I understand, Daphne. But . . ." He swallowed hard.

She pressed her hands to her bodice and met his gaze with an imploring look that cut to his heart. "But . . . what?"

He didn't know how to explain what he was thinking. "Nothing. I . . . I need to go." He turned toward the carriage.

Daphne's hand caught his sleeve. "Thomas, this Belinda —"

He sighed. "You have no reason to be jealous of Belinda," he said quietly. "She and I are just friends."

Daphne's expression relaxed. Her fingers curled around his forearm. "I'm sorry I misjudged your intentions. I just love you so . . ."

The fervency of her gaze moved Thomas. He captured her in an embrace. Holding her to his beating heart, with her arms wrapped around his middle, he found the comfort he'd sought. He would forgive her hasty reaction. She was young and impetuous, and her emotions carried her away. Her love for him drove the passion of jealousy. He could forgive her foolishness.

Pressing his lips to the top of her head, he whispered, "You are very important to me, Daphne. You know that, don't you?"

Still nestled in his arms, she sighed. "I know. I'll never be so silly again." She lifted her face to him, her eyes shining with something akin to victory. "No one will ever come before me. Right, Thomas?"

Pa's advice once more winged through his memory. But Thomas closed his eyes and held tighter to the woman in his arms.

17

A gust of wind peppered Belinda with particles of dust. The tiny bits stung the bare skin on the back of her neck. Beside her, Malinda sagged with grief and exhaustion. Belinda slipped her arm around her sister's waist.

"Malinda, let's go home now," she whispered, the whistle of the wind adding harmony to her soothing tone. "It's time for us to say good-bye to Mama."

Malinda jerked free of Belinda's touch and dropped to her knees beside the fresh grave. Her hands pressed into the mound of moist, dark dirt covering the pine box that held their mother's body, and her face contorted in agony. "No*ooooo!*" Her moan carried above the ceaseless wind.

Belinda knelt, too, catching her sister's hand. "Malinda, please . . ." She could hardly bear to see Malinda's heartbreak, yet even as she tried to offer comfort, she longed for someone to comfort her.

Malinda slapped Belinda's hand, her face twisting into a fierce scowl. "Leave me be! I'll not leave Mama!" She threw herself across the grave, her face buried in the bend of her elbow.

Belinda rose, her wind-tossed skirts and burden of pain making her clumsy. How would she convince Malinda to come home? The burial service had ended over an hour ago. All of the mourners had already gone. One by one, they had climbed into their wagons and headed back to their own homes. Even the minister had gone at Belinda's insistence. She had been certain, once all had departed, Malinda would see the sense of saying her final good-bye and returning to Hillsboro.

She glanced over her shoulder and spotted *Herr* Ollenburger and his wife waiting in the slice of shade cast by their wagon. Belinda knew they were ready to leave. They had graciously transported Belinda, Malinda, and the coffin carrying Mama's body to the gravesite near the Gaeddert *Kleine Gemeinde.* Though she had not told her so, Belinda was certain Mama would want to be buried next to Papa in the church's tiny cemetery. Kind *Herr* Ollenburger had said they could stay as long as they needed to find peace, but Belinda feared peace would never come. Not for Malinda. And without Malinda's acceptance, Belinda had no peace, either.

Closing her eyes against the sting of tears, she whispered, "Please, heavenly Father, help me."

A warm hand closed around her elbow. She opened her eyes and found *Herr* Ollenburger at her side. His tender gaze brought a new rush of tears. She clung to his arm, drawing strength from his presence. "Oh, *Herr* Ollenburger, I don't know what to do. Malinda refuses to leave."

Without a word, the big man nodded. Stepping forward, he wrapped his hands over Malinda's shoulders. "Come now, Malinda." He spoke in Low German, his rumbling voice calm and soothing. "Time it is for us to go."

Malinda didn't move, but she didn't argue. Gently, *Herr* Ollenburger lifted Malinda from the grave. Then, with a smooth movement, he scooped her unresisting form into his arms. He carried Malinda as easily as he would carry one of his little girls. To Belinda's amazement, Malinda threw her arms around the man's neck and buried her face in the curve of his shoulder. For a brief moment, Belinda considered collapsing just

240

for the opportunity to be scooped up in that same manner.

At the wagon, he set Malinda in the back, and she immediately drew her arm up and curled against the hard side of the wagon, making no protest about being taken away from the grave. *Herr* Ollenburger assisted his wife into the wagon, then he held his hand to Belinda.

She clasped his wide hand with both of hers. "Thank you," she whispered.

He nodded, a sad smile on the corners of his lips. "Come now. Let us take you home."

At Belinda's home, *Herr* Ollenburger once more lifted Malinda and carried her, placing her on her bed when Belinda guided him to the bedroom. Belinda smoothed her sister's sweaty, tangled hair and murmured, "Rest now. I'll bring you some dinner in an hour or so."

Malinda rolled to her side, reminding Belinda of the way her mother had shut out her attempts at comfort and assistance. With a sigh, she trailed behind *Herr* Ollenburger down the hallway to the parlor. *Frau* Ollenburger had also entered the house, and she came forward to put an arm around Belinda.

"Now, Belinda, you get some rest. Remember, church ladies will bring meals over for the remainder of the week, and Mr. Ol-lenburger and I are right across the alley. If you need anything, whether day or night, you come to us. Will you, dear?"

Belinda blinked rapidly to control the rush of tears. "I . . . I will. Thank you for . . . everything. I don't know how I would have survived the last few days without you."

"It will take some time," *Frau* Ollenburger said quietly, stroking Belinda's back, "but you will heal, Belinda. You will move forward. You and Malinda will be fine."

Although Belinda wanted to believe the woman's kind words, she wasn't so sure. A thought winged through Belinda's mind — a selfish one: If she were always responsible for Malinda, how would she ever form a family of her own? The desire to be a wife and a mother was strong inside her. Would she forever set aside her own longings to meet the needs of someone else?

Frau Ollenburger took Belinda's hands. "Life is often hard, and it can seem very unfair. You've suffered many losses, yet haven't you also learned that God is faith-ful? He sustains us, yes, Belinda?"

Even in the midst of her heartache, Be-linda recognized her kind neighbor's pres-ence as a kiss from heaven.

Frau Ollenburger continued, "Before I

leave today I will pray with you that He will give you peaceful rest. Rest is good medicine. Shall we pray now?"

Belinda, eager to experience peaceful rest, bowed her head without a word.

When she had finished praying, *Frau* Ollenburger gave Belinda a long hug and a kiss on the cheek. "Now, remember. You run across the alley if you need anything. Any time, day or night."

Belinda forced a smile. "I'll remember. Thank you." She walked the older woman to the door, then watched her cross the alley to her own home. When she disappeared into her house, Belinda finally closed her own back door. She turned and faced the silent, empty kitchen, and tears pressed for release.

Determinedly, she blinked the tears away. "I don't have time for tears. I have work to do," she told herself. Moving to the hallway, she paused for a moment outside of Malinda's door. Silence greeted her. She offered a silent prayer of gratitude. If Malinda slept, it would make the next tasks easier.

Entering her mother's room, she crossed quickly to the bed and worked automatically, humming, forcing her mind to other things. She stripped the quilt and sheets, bundling them into a big wad in her arms.

She moved briskly down the hallway and dumped the pile of bed coverings on the floor of the pantry, out of sight.

Back in the bedroom, she faced the bureau. Papa had used the bottom two drawers, Mama the top ones. Sucking in a deep breath of fortification, she tugged open the top drawer. Neatly folded items, long unworn, came into view. Mama had worn the same black dress or her nightgown since Papa's death.

Belinda fingered the simple collar of one dress, remembering how the deep green hue had brightened Mama's pale hazel eyes. Her chin quivered. Swallowing, she pushed aside the memories and set to work. A musty smell rose from the clothes in the drawers, and Belinda wrinkled her nose as she removed items to make stacks on the uncovered feather mattress. Dresses in one stack, aprons in another, undergarments in a pile by the door.

When the drawers were empty, she dumped the undergarments in the burn barrel in the alley, then returned for Mama's clothes. Although she had intended to take them to *Frau* Ollenburger and ask her to give them away, she now discovered a reluctance to part with them. She stacked the aprons on top of the dresses, then hugged the whole pile close, her breath coming in little spurts as she battled tears. Unable to face letting them go, she marched to the hallway and tugged the rope that released a narrow ladder.

Arms full, she precariously made her way to the tiny attic where Mama had spent so much time mourning over Papa's clothes. The familiar handmade Russian chest sat in the middle of the floor with its top up, just as Mama had left it. How many times had she found Mama up here, her tears dampening Papa's shirts and jackets?

For a moment Belinda faltered — would she be creating a shrine by saving her mother's clothing? Then she shook her head. She wouldn't be climbing that little ladder to visit her parents' items. She only needed time to heal before giving everything away.

Leaning forward, she arranged Mama's clothes on top of Papa's in the big chest and then slowly lowered the lid, sealing everything inside together. Turning, she sat on the lid and peered around the steeply roofed space. The air was dead, heavy with dust. No window illuminated the area, the only light coming from the hole in the floor where the ladder descended, so shadows fell heavily. Despite the stuffy surroundings, Belinda shivered. How had Mama endured it up here, day after day? Certainly the closed, lifeless room had added to her sense of despair.

Unwilling to explore that thought any further, Belinda rose and started for the ladder. But a second box — a much smaller chest with a silver flap on the front — captured her attention. Tucked well back in the shadows where the underside of the roof met the attic floor, it was nearly hidden. Ducking low, Belinda approached it, squinting in the meager light. Where had she seen this chest before? Dust coated its top, yet several scuffs indicated fingers had recently opened the box and examined the contents.

Belinda tried lifting the silver latch, but it held tight. She poked her finger in the black keyhole, wondering where a key might be. She hadn't seen one in any of Mama's bureau drawers. A quick search through the clothing chest proved fruitless. Curiosity drove her from the attic to her mother's room. Feeling like a burglar, she looked in the carved wooden box on the bureau top that held Mama's watch and hairpins and then in the little drawer of the table beside the bed. Only Mama's Bible and some loose pages of stationery sat in the drawer.

Belinda scratched her head, wondering

where else to look, when she remembered a ring of keys on a hook inside the pantry door. She retrieved the ring, then went back into the attic. On her knees in front of the little chest, she tried each key in turn, but none opened the box. Puzzled, she sat back on her heels and stared at the mysterious little chest.

"What is in there?" she wondered aloud.

"What . . . do you think . . . you're doing?"

Malinda's rasping, broken voice came from behind Belinda's shoulder. Belinda spun around on her knees. Malinda clutched her hands to her chest, her shoulders heaving from the exertion of climbing the attic ladder.

Belinda scrambled to her feet and guided her sister to the Russian trunk. Pressing Malinda onto its lid, she asked, "Are you all right, Malinda? Why are you up here?"

Malinda continued to gasp for breath, but she glared fiercely at Belinda. "I came . . . to see . . . what you were doing." She pointed her finger, her eyes narrowing. "Snooping! I caught you . . . snooping!"

Belinda frowned. "I wasn't snooping. I was trying to figure out what that little chest is. I know I've seen it before."

"It's mine." Malinda leaned over her own

lap, coughed hard, and then sat straight up again. Her eyes flashed fire. "It's my box. You leave it alone."

Belinda put her hand on Malinda's shoulder. "All right, Malinda. I won't bother it. Now, please, calm down before you make yourself sick."

For several minutes Belinda rubbed Malinda's back, praying for the heaving breaths to slow. Finally, with a shudder, Malinda pushed herself to her feet. She grabbed Belinda's upper arms and leaned close.

"That's my box, Belinda. *Mine.* Don't bother it again." With a little shove, she released Belinda and descended the ladder without another glance at her sister.

Belinda, her heart pounding, shot one more look toward the chest before leaving the attic. What did Malinda own that required such secrecy?

18

Thomas turned the key in the lock of the heavy wooden door, securing his new home. He had moved into the cottage in Back Bay the first week of September. Tucked between a six-story apartment building called a "French flat" and twin townhomes, the simple mortar-and-brick cottage looked like a mushroom amidst oak trees, but Thomas didn't mind. He'd been raised in a small, cozy home, so the four-room residence suited him.

He headed down the sidewalk with a long-legged stride, breathing in the moist air. The essence of salt water on the breeze left a tang on the back of his tongue that had become familiar during his years of living in Boston, yet it also left him lonely for the smell of the Kansas prairie.

He thrust his jaw at a determined angle and refused to allow the brief thought of Kansas to take root. There were numerous reasons to remain in Boston: the presidential election was still two months away; he'd committed to renting the cottage until the first of the new year; and he had a job that provided for him better than anything waiting in Gaeddert or Hillsboro.

"And Daphne Severt resides in Boston," he added aloud.

Temptation to count the days until the election — his self-imposed waiting period before officially requesting Daphne's hand in marriage from her father — hit him hard, but he resisted. He didn't want anything to cloud this otherwise sunny day.

Rounding the corner, he lifted his hand to hail an approaching cab. The driver brought his horse to a halt at the curb, and Thomas climbed aboard. During the ride to the newspaper office, Thomas's mind ran over all of the blessings of the past weeks — the new job with its enviable upper-office position and increased salary, the camaraderie of his co-campaigners, a beautiful woman who loved him, and a cozy home to bring that woman to when the time was right.

Yes, everything was coming together very nicely for him in Boston. Apparently little Gussie's four-leaf clover had done its duty. He'd have to send her a letter and express his appreciation. Imagining how Gussie would gloat at receiving the first letter mailed from his new address, a grin tugged at his cheeks. Then he chuckled as he envisioned his humble cottage with its hodgepodge of furnishings.

Nadine had graciously allowed him to take the bedroom suite from the room he'd occupied during his school years as well as anything he wanted from the cluttered basement. He had been shocked at the things stashed in the basement — apparently Nadine had never thrown away a stick of furniture in all her years of living in the big townhouse — but he'd expressed only appreciation.

Thanks to her generosity, his parlor held a settee and two chairs with mismatched, marble-topped end tables. A table and four chairs filled the corner that served as a dining room. The second bedroom contained a sleeping couch, rocking chair, and desk. Eventually that room would serve as a bedroom for his children — at that thought he tugged his collar, suddenly overly warm — but for now he used it as a makeshift office for after-hours work.

The cab rolled to a stop outside the newspaper office. Thomas paid his fare plus a tip and hopped out. He strode into the building, considering the wisdom of purchasing his own means of transport. No carriage house existed behind the cottage, but the sizable lawn provided a space to park a vehicle. Daphne had coyly suggested he look at motorized automobiles, and the idea was tempting. Wouldn't it be fun to drive a horseless carriage? Pa, Summer, and the little girls would enjoy a ride, he was sure, and he could imagine Belinda Schmidt's eyes bugging out if he pulled into town behind the wheel of an automobile.

Briefly, he wondered how Belinda was doing. He hadn't heard from her since her mother's death, and he realized with a stab of guilt, he hadn't written to her, either. He stood still, his eyes aimed straight ahead, unseeing, as he chastised himself for being so neglectful of his friend's needs.

"You comin' in?"

The voice pulled Thomas from his reverie. He looked to find the elevator operator holding the door open for his entry. With a nod, Thomas stepped into the elevator and automatically requested, "Floor three, please."

But the young man shook his head. "No, sir. Mr. Severt requests a meeting with you. I'm to take you to the top floor."

Uh oh. Was his everything-is-going-well-in-Boston idea about to be destroyed? Even though he'd served as Mr. Severt's personal editor for several weeks, he rarely had face-to-face visits with the man. Severt handed Thomas his written drafts, barked his expectations, then left him to work. If Thomas performed to his boss's satisfaction, he heard nothing; if he failed, he heard plenty. Given his boss's penchant for withholding positive comments, Thomas had no expectation for a pleasant encounter.

The elevator doors slid open, revealing the fourth floor, and Thomas made his way down the hallway to Mr. Severt's office. The door stood slightly ajar. He raised his fist to knock, but before his knuckles connected with the wood, a voice ordered, "Come in, Ollenburger. Prompt, as always."

The gruffly worded approval eased a bit of the tension in Thomas's shoulders. He entered the room, crossed directly to the desk, and offered his hand. Severt, a pen clenched in his stained fingers, remained hunched over a sheet of paper and didn't even look up. Papers scattered across the desktop told of feverish writing. Without a word, Thomas sank into the chair opposite the desk.

After a few moments, Severt set the pen aside, stretched his arms over his head, and acknowledged Thomas's presence with a tired smile. "Had to get my thoughts down before they escaped."

Thomas understood. If someone interrupted him while he was editing, it took several minutes to bring his focus fully back to the task.

Severt yawned and leaned back in his chair, linking his hands behind his head. "Ollenburger, I am about to open a can of worms the likes of which Boston has never before seen."

Thomas raised his eyebrows.

Severt released a deep chuckle. "That's what newspaper editorial writers do — stir things up. Make people look at a situation differently than they have before. Change things. And I intend to stir until I've changed the minds of every resident of Boston, of Massachusetts, of the entire United States of America!"

How did one respond to such boldness? Uncertain, Thomas replied with a hesitant, "Th-that's a worthy aspiration, sir."

Another blast of laughter chased away Thomas's words. The man grinned then slapped his palms to his desktop. "But the U.S. of A. doesn't need to be apprised of my intentions just yet. Sometimes ideas need to come in like a fox approaching a henhouse — without the chickens' knowledge."

More confused than ever, Thomas simply nodded.

"But once the fox is in . . . feathers fly! The balance of the coop is upset. And, best of all, the fox always wins. Well, Ollenburger, I am the fox, and I — shall — win!"

Thomas cleared his throat, swallowed, and braved a question. "What, exactly, are you winning?"

The man stared as if Thomas had lost his sense. "Why, the election, of course! The presidency will be given to my candidate." A cunning look crossed Severt's face. "And then the changes will come. Things will revert to the way they should have remained. . . ." His voice trailed off, his gaze drifting to the window.

Thomas waited for him to complete the thought, but after several seconds he said, "What is my role in this . . . invasion of the henhouse?"

Severt jerked around, looking startled, and then he burst out laughing. "Your role in the invasion . . ." The man rocked in his chair, still chuckling, while seconds ticked by, and Thomas wondered if his boss had imbibed spirits before coming to work that morning. "Your role is crucial, Thomas. You will be editing my work for errors, of course, but more importantly, for understanding of the message. You're a farm boy, Ollenburger, raised in a simplistic, rural setting. You have a different way of examining things than those raised in the city. The message I have penned must be understood and absorbed by both educated and common men."

Despite his efforts to remain poised, Thomas's brow pinched into a frown. Was Severt trying to insult him?

"Yes, subtlety this first week." Severt's tone turned pensive as he stroked his mustache. "A hint of what's to come without being blatant. Allow the truth to be revealed in small bites, easily digested. . . ."

"Sir?"

Suddenly Severt scowled and pointed at Thomas. "This country was turned upside-down by Lincoln, but upside-down can be turned right side up again. And I intend to do whatever I can to turn it to right. Do you understand?"

In all honesty, Thomas didn't understand. But rather than appear foolish, Thomas nodded. "I'll do my part, too."

"Good!" The man's expression cleared. He tamped several handwritten pages together and thrust them across the desk at

Thomas. "There are three editorials there, intended for the next three Saturday editions, marked clearly by sequence. Read them in order, mark your reactions, and then return them to me at the end of the day. Take the entire day." His thick brows came down, an almost ominous tone creeping into his voice. "It is of the utmost importance that the meaning be grasped by the readers. Three editorials . . . any more would be excessive. These three must suit the intended purpose."

Thomas nodded. "Yes, sir."

"The articles will be wired to every major newspaper from coast to coast, Ollenburger. Do you understand the importance of careful editing?"

Thomas rose, holding the stack of pages in front of him like a shield. "Yes, sir. Thank you, sir." Instead of using the elevator, he took the enclosed stairway to the third floor. Curious, he glanced at the scribbled text. A quote opened the first editorial: *"Men and women are what they are largely because of the stock from which they sprang."* The statement instantly grabbed Thomas's attention, and he plodded slowly through the pages, reading each word with care. By the time he reached his office, he'd finished the first of the three drafts.

In his office, he removed his jacket and hung it on the back of his chair before sitting. He leaned his elbows on either side of the second draft and carefully read each word for clarity.

So-called "equality" leads to societal chaos. Our standing as a world leader is threatened by the acceptance of inferior races as "equal" to those who founded this country. . . .

A sick feeling flooded his stomach. Even a *farm boy* like himself caught the meaning. His hands shook. He dropped the sheets, rose, and paced the office. Severt's face — stern and intense — appeared in Thomas's memory. The man trusted him. He must complete the task.

Swiping sweat from his forehead, Thomas sank into his chair and reread each draft in turn. At the final sentence in the third draft — *Only one candidate will return this nation to its proper balance: Thomas Watson!* — Thomas slumped against the back of his chair.

No, there had to be some mistake! Whispering a silent, hopeful plea that he would discover he'd misinterpreted Severt's intention, he leaned over the drafts once more.

His reading complete, he put his head in his hands. Never in all of his conversations with his boss had he guessed such ugly ideas lurked in the man's heart. Never at the campaign headquarters had he picked up any inkling of Watson's intention to lord one race over another.

He pushed away from the desk and snatched up his jacket. A celluloid button with an attached red, white, and blue ribbon was pinned to the left lapel. He read aloud the simple message arched above the black-and-white drawing of Watson's profile on the button. "Watson — Candidate of Choice." He'd believed that by campaigning for Watson he was benefiting his father and all other common men in the agricultural business. But now?

He unpinned the button, dropped it in a desk drawer, and then slipped his arms into his jacket. Severt expected a response by the end of the day concerning the comprehension of his drafts. Before Thomas could address his boss, he needed to speak to someone at headquarters about Watson. And about Severt.

19

Daphne pressed the six-inch length of ribbon to the bottom edge of a *Watson for President* celluloid button and held it while she counted silently to ten. The glue soaked through the porous ribbon, dampening her fingertips, and she released a small whimper of irritation. After setting aside the finished button, she wiped her fingers on a rag lying next to the pile of cut ribbon on the table, then reached for another button from the small box at her elbow.

When Harry had asked her to come in and construct buttons for the final round of distribution, Daphne had eagerly agreed. Being in town meant being in closer proximity to Thomas. Sometimes Thomas dropped by the campaign headquarters on his noon break, and although he exercised great restraint when in public places, she always recognized the pleasure that lit his eyes when he spotted her. It wouldn't be long, she was certain, and Thomas would ask Father for her hand in marriage.

Her fingers trembled at her bold thought, and she attached the ribbon at an angle rather than straight down. Harry, the perfectionist, would surely scold. Well, she decided with a shrug, maybe his dissatisfaction would lead to assigning her a less monotonous task. Yawning, she plopped the imperfect button in the completed stack while glancing toward the double doors leading to the sidewalk.

Her mouth still wide in the yawn, she nearly swallowed her tongue when the left door swung open and Thomas stepped through. Snapping her jaw shut, she leaped from her chair and placed her back to him, frantically fluffing her wrinkled skirt. She scowled at the glue splotches dotting the pale green, but there was no cure for it now. Perhaps if she smiled brightly enough, he wouldn't notice.

With a deep breath, she fixed her face into a welcoming smile and spun around. But her shoulders deflated. Rather than approaching her table, Thomas had joined two men at a desk in the far corner of the room. With a small stomp of one slippered foot against the polished wood floor, she plunked her hands on her hips. For several seconds she stewed, waiting for Thomas to turn and notice her. When he didn't, she huffed in frustration and charged across the room to his side.

She arrived in time to hear him say, ". . . makes no sense to me. Before I continue with this campaign, I need to understand Watson's position."

"Position on what?" Daphne tugged at Thomas's arm.

Thomas removed her hands with a slight frown. "Daphne, go sit down, please. I'll talk to you when I'm finished here."

Had he ever spoken to her so abruptly? Rebuffed, she took two backward steps, her face filling with heat. "A-all right. Fine." She hurried back to the table. With each step, her indignation grew. Why, he had just treated her as Father always did — as if she didn't have enough sense to engage in meaningful conversation!

She sat, staring across the room at Thomas. He ran his hand over his hair, leaning close to the other two men, his arms flying out in gestures of agitation. Something certainly had him in a dither. Observing his uncharacteristic display, her heartbeat slowed to a normal rhythm. She would overlook his rude treatment given his obvious state of anxiety, but she intended to make sure this dismissal of her presence was a one-time occurrence.

It seemed hours passed as she watched, waiting, before the other two campaigners returned to their posts, leaving Thomas alone. He stood for long moments, his head down, hands thrust deep into his pockets — the perfect pose of dejection. Daphne considered going to him, but his previous command held her squirming in her seat.

At last he lifted his head, his shoulders heaving in a mighty sigh, and then he turned and crossed the room to her table. He sat heavily across from her and lifted one of the beribboned buttons from the stack. "Watson, indeed . . ."

Despite herself, Daphne giggled. At his scowl, she mimicked, "Watson, indeed . . . For a moment, I felt as though I were in Mrs. Steadman's parlor, listening to her harangue you about the campaign."

A knowing grin twitched at Thomas's cheeks. "Yes. Well. It seems Nadine was right all along."

Daphne tipped her head. "Oh? About what?"

"About Watson." Thomas propped his elbows on the table edge, his head slung low. He looked so sad, Daphne reached across the table to take his hand. He glanced at her with surprise in his eyes, but he didn't pull away. "She told me to look beneath the surface to the truth of who Watson was, and I thought I had. But I see now I was wrong. Very wrong."

"About what were you wrong?" To her delight, Thomas curled his fingers around her hand. The warmth of his palm pressed to hers made her heart flutter.

"Watson's character. And —" Suddenly his neck blotched with color and he jerked his hand free.

Daphne's heart sank. "Thomas?"

For long moments he stared at her. An intense fire burned in his eyes, deepening the color to a stormy blue. Alarm created an unpleasant taste on the back of Daphne's tongue. What thoughts lurked behind his dark gaze?

When he spoke, the words were uttered in a hoarse whisper that told clearly of inner torment. "Daphne, Watson believes in separation of the races."

Daphne stared at him, unblinking, for a few startled seconds, waiting for him to add to the simple comment. When no other concerns were voiced, she nearly laughed with relief. "Why, Thomas, is that what has you upset? To think I feared something dreadful had occurred!"

He shook his head, frowning. "Something dreadful *has* occurred. I've been campaigning for a man whose values I —" His face twisted into an expression of loathing. "To consider one man of more value than another just because of his skin color . . ."

Daphne placed her hand over Thomas's wrist and squeezed gently. His pulse pounded beneath her fingers. He had worked himself into a fine state. She slipped her hand beneath his, gratified when he responded by clasping her fingers. In a soothing tone, she said, "Well, *someone* has to be in control, Thomas. Surely you see the sensibility of retaining a hierarchy of social levels."

Thomas seemed to freeze, his hand within hers stiffening. The color in his neck rose higher, and his nostrils flared with a great intake of breath. "Are you suggesting a return to slavery?"

She squeezed hard on his hand. "Of course not *slavery*. Men should be paid a fair wage for their service, but allowing them to be in positions of authority over us —"

"Them?" Thomas yanked his hand from her grasp, his tone cold. "Meaning colored people?"

"In this case." Daphne held out her hands.

"Thomas, pray tell, what is the problem here?"

Thomas turned away, staring across the room at the bustle of activity, yet seeming to look past it. The muscles in his jaw twitched. As the color drained from his face, it seemed to take his energy with it. He slumped in his chair. When he faced her again, the cool recrimination in his eyes made her feel as though she were looking into the face of a stranger.

"Your father holds the same beliefs as Watson — that colored people are inferior to white people."

Slowly, Daphne nodded, her breath held so tightly her chest ached.

"And you — do you agree with that view?"

Daphne's lips parted, her breath escaping. She rubbed her dry lips together before answering. "Is the view I hold of importance to you?" A part of her hoped her view held great importance — that Thomas truly cared about what she thought. Father certainly didn't put much stock in anything she said.

"Your view is very important. I need to know."

"Then . . ." She lifted her chin in an attempt to appear confident when underneath she quivered with apprehension. "I believe

Father is right. There is a need for social hierarchy, and the highest positions of hierarchy rightfully belong to white men of means."

"White men of means have superiority." Thomas stated it bluntly, as if seeking her confirmation. His emotionless tone gave her the courage to press on.

"Yes."

"Over colored people."

"Of course."

Thomas's eyes narrowed. "You said 'of means.' Does that mean white men of lesser financial wealth hold lesser value?"

Daphne exploded with a huff of displeasure. Why was he creating such an issue over something so inconsequential? "Yes. Father is highly educated, wealthy, a man of influence. That entitles him to leadership. Superiority, as you put it."

In the same even, detached voice, he said, "So your father, with his money and education, is *better* than my father, who has no more than a basic education and little wealth."

Daphne winced. "Well, when stated in that manner, it sounds uncivilized, but in truth . . . yes. My father is better than your father."

Although Thomas spoke calmly and im-

267

passively, fiery splotches decorated his neck, indicating strong emotion. "There is no finer man than my father."

Daphne hid her smile. He sounded like a recalcitrant child issuing a challenge in the schoolyard. Teasingly, she said, "And if you were to ask Harry, he would say the same thing about *our* father." She waited, but no answering grin came in reply. With a sigh, she said, "I understand your strong feelings. Yet you must see that, in many ways, my father *is* superior to yours. Perhaps not in a moral or personal sense, but most certainly in a social sense."

"And me?"

The clipped question took Daphne by surprise. "What about you?"

"Are you better than me?"

Heat built in Daphne's cheeks. "W-why, of course not! You . . . you're every bit as educated as Harry, and —"

"But I grew up in a little town, raised by an uneducated miller who still struggles with the English language. I don't have endless wealth and likely never will. You were raised in Boston by a man of great financial means. Socially, are you superior to me?"

Daphne didn't care at all for the route the conversation had taken. "Now you're being insulting."

He waved his hand, dismissing her feeble attempt at redirection. "I want an answer, Daphne." Thomas leaned forward, his eyes flashing. "Just this morning your father reminded me of my humble upbringing. So tell me . . . Am I less than you because I grew up on the prairie of Kansas rather than in a big city? Am I less than you because my father doesn't have much money? Am I less than you because —"

"Thomas, please! You are scaring me." Daphne blinked rapidly as tears flooded her eyes. "Why are you treating me in this manner?"

Though no thought of manipulation had prefaced her reaction, she realized by Thomas's response to her tears that she'd chosen the right tactic. He sat back in his chair, his stern face relaxing into an expression of remorse. He opened his fists and reached for her. After a moment's hesitation, she offered her hands, and he clasped them gently, sweetly, the way she had come to expect.

"I'm not angry with you, Daphne." The tender timbre of his deep voice let her know her Thomas had returned. "But I'm angry at myself for being so blind."

Confusion struck again. Before she could question him, he continued in a sad, resigned tone that chilled her even more than his fury of moments ago.

"You see, Nadine tried to warn me. But I wouldn't listen to her. I ignored my own conscience, too. But I can't ignore —" He lowered his head, drawing in a breath that raised his shoulders. His fingers tightened around hers, and he raised their joined hands, pressing his lips to her knuckles. Then, abruptly, he let go, almost as if he'd found her taste unpleasant. A chill of abandonment briefly shook her frame.

"I've made a terrible mistake, Daphne. And somehow I must right it. The first step is to" — he rose, taking a physical step backward — "distance myself from you. You . . . are . . . far too distracting. You keep me from seeing what's right. As for the next steps . . ." He swallowed, causing his Adam's apple to bob. "I must return to the office. Good-bye, Daphne."

He strode away, leaving her bewildered and sorrowful. *"Good-bye, Daphne."* The words resonated in her head. He'd said them dozens of times before, at each leave-taking — yet today they held something new. Something final. This good-bye, she realized, was meant to be a permanent one.

20

Thomas bypassed the elevator and used the staircase to return to his office. The stale air in the enclosed concrete stairway felt heavy and dead, and by the time he'd completed the first flight, his chest ached. But, he conceded, the ache might have more than one source.

Conflicting emotions coursed through him, almost making him collapse. Had he really considered marrying someone whose ideals and values so opposed his own? Why hadn't he seen, as Nadine had instructed, beneath Daphne's surface? Today, listening to her spout the nonsense about one man being of greater value than another, she had appeared . . . ugly.

Didn't the Bible he'd read from childhood indicate God was no respecter of persons? That slave was equal to master, servant no less than his employer? Even the Jews and Gentiles were declared the same in God's eyes. And if God viewed all men equally, what right did men have to place one race as inferior to another?

Mr. Lincoln — one of the greatest men to ever live, Pa claimed — had declared all men equal. *All* men. A battle had been fought to unite the country in this belief. Equality. Freedom. His own people, the Mennonites, had come to America for those very ideals! Pa called the United States of America the land of opportunity — freedom to live, work, and worship as each man saw fit. Here, in the land of opportunity, there was no place for the social hierarchy that existed in other countries.

With a great intake of breath, Thomas forced himself to complete the second flight of stairs, and with each upward step, his conviction grew. He might not be as rich, powerful, or educated as some, but thanks to the upbringing of a simple miller, he knew right from wrong. Social hierarchy — holding one man in lordship over another — was *wrong*.

Rounding the corner for the final flight, his fingers curled tightly over the metal handrail, he paused. A part of him longed to cry out for comfort, for peace, for help — but the words remained at bay. Why ask God for help now when he hadn't consulted

Him in any of the decisions that led to his discovery of Watson's and Daphne's character?

No, this problem he would need to solve for himself. Pa always said, *"If a mess you make, son, clean it up."* So Thomas would clean it up. He stepped out of the stairway and gulped the fresher air, eager to clear his lungs. Standing in the hallway, allowing his heartbeat to return to normal after his long climb, he considered the task ahead.

Mr. Severt wanted Thomas's feedback on the editorials. Well, Severt would get feedback . . . and something more.

Belinda watched as Summer Ollenburger paused in scrubbing her daughter's dress on the washboard and lifted her shoulder to push the hair from her eyes. "Have you heard from Thomas recently?" Summer asked.

Belinda wrung the excess water from a towel, gave it a brisk snap, then clipped it to the clothesline. The task completed, she faced her neighbor and forced the painful answer. "No, ma'am. It has been several weeks."

Frowning, *Frau* Ollenburger turned her attention back to the dress. She scrubbed with more force than Belinda believed necessary, considering she held one of Lena's small frocks rather than one of *Herr* Ollenburger's work shirts. "I hoped you had. He hasn't written to us, either. Gussie got a brief note, which she shared with all of us, but since then . . . I'm concerned about him. I haven't even heard from Nadine."

Belinda reached into the rinse tub for another towel. A tiny prickle of gladness teased, knowing Thomas hadn't written to his family — at least she wasn't the only one who had been left wondering how he fared. Then guilt struck — she shouldn't be glad of the Ollenburgers' worry. She said, "I'm sure he's just very busy with his new job and his new home." She didn't add, *and Daphne Severt.* It pained her to even think of Thomas with Daphne — and she couldn't bear to speak the words aloud.

"Busy I understand," *Frau* Ollenburger countered, giving the dress a final push down the length of the washboard and then lifting it from the sudsy water. She dipped the gingham dress into the rinse tub as she continued. "But neglectful is unlike Thomas. In all the years he lived in Boston, he never allowed more than a week to pass between letters. His father has lain awake nights, worrying. Not even all of Peter's reading about Plymouth Rock chickens — a topic with which he has become completely enamored — has removed his concern."

"Is he still talking about chickens?" Belinda couldn't help smiling. Imagining the big man's fascination with the domesticated fowl painted an amusing picture.

"Oh, yes." *Frau* Ollenburger glanced up from the washtub, a wry grin on her face. "There have been times in the past weeks that I've regretted teaching him to read English. He even wrote to North Carolina for a pamphlet on the care of Plymouth Rocks." She gestured to their small yard. "Where would I keep chickens?" With a soft laugh, she turned her attention back to the wash. "But at least it has provided somewhat of a distraction for him. As for me, I'm tempted to make a telephone call to Thomas from the bank."

"Does Thomas have a telephone?" Belinda clipped the last towel to the line, peeking over her shoulder at her neighbor.

Frau Ollenburger gave a dress a twist to dispel extra water, flopped the frock over the line with a quick flick of her wrists, then flung her hands outward. "I don't know! He might have one. I'm sure it isn't as uncommon in Boston as it is here." She pointed her finger at Belinda, as if scolding.

275

"But I know Nadine has one, and if I were to call her, she'd let Thomas know in no uncertain terms how his lack of attention is affecting everyone at home."

Holding back a giggle, Belinda faced the clothesline. She had never witnessed *Frau* Ollenburger's anger before, if one could call the outburst angry. Though stronger than anything she'd previously seen from the woman, the eruption was mild compared to Malinda's frequent stormy blasts. Belinda didn't find the woman's emotional display amusing, but her reference to Nadine Steadman brought a hint of merriment. Based on past letters from Thomas, she knew *Frau* Ollenburger's former mother-in-law was a formidable force.

"I'm sure Mrs. Steadman could convince Thomas to write."

No answer came. Belinda shifted to face her neighbor. The sadness in *Frau* Ollenburger's face stirred Belinda's sympathy. She crossed the rough ground to take her friend's hand. "Don't fret. He'll write. He's busy now, carving his own pathway, but it doesn't mean he never thinks of you."

Frau Ollenburger captured Belinda in a tight hug. "Thank you, dear one. You always know just the right thing to say." For a moment she cupped Belinda's cheeks with her soft hands, smiling. "I won't fret. But I will continue to pray that our wayward boy finds the time to let his pa know he's doing well. We'll all fare better when we know."

A blush built in Belinda's face. Did *Frau* Ollenburger mean to include her when she said *our wayward boy,* or was the gentle pat on her cheek mere coincidence? The woman dropped her hands and turned to the washtubs.

"Well, let's empty these tubs in the garden." With a teasing smirk, she added, "There's nothing growing that is in need of a drink, but habits are hard to break. I can't make myself dump water in the alley where it's wasted on weeds."

Belinda laughed and caught hold of the handle on the opposite side of the tub. It felt good to work under the early fall sun with *Frau* Ollenburger. Although she had enough of her own duties to fill her days, she spent as much time as she could with the Ollenburgers. Their friendship became increasingly important as Malinda slipped further and further into melancholy, reminding Belinda of her mother's sad journey toward death.

The water sloshed across the empty garden plot, soaking into the rich dirt. Belinda stared at the disappearing pool of sudsy water, wishing it were as easy to toss away troubles and sorrows.

Frau Ollenburger's concerned voice brought Belinda back to the present. "You look overtired, Belinda. Are you catching a cold?"

"No, ma'am. I'm fine."

"I probably should have insisted you rest instead of helping me this afternoon. You go on home now. Lie down. Then you and Malinda join us for the dinner meal."

"Oh, no, I —"

Frau Ollenburger's firm nod stilled Belinda's words. "It's the least I can do for the help you gave me with my washing. Go on now." She gave Belinda a gentle nudge toward her home. "I'll see you at dinnertime."

Belinda obeyed, a part of her rebelling but most of her rejoicing at the opportunity to sit at the Ollenburgers' table, another opportunity for her to pretend she was a part of their family. Those moments of pretending were the happiest of her days.

"Drivel. Pure drivel!" Father slammed his fist against the table next to his plate. His water glass bounced with the force of the blow.

From the other end of the table, Mother

chided, "Harrison, please. We will all suffer indigestion if you don't calm yourself."

Daphne exchanged a look with Harry. Father had come home in the worst temper they'd seen in ages. And she knew Harry was as distraught as she over the cause.

"The effrontery of that lad to write his own editorial, in complete opposition to mine." Father ignored Mother's mild reprimand and continued in a blustering tone. "Rebutting my words as if we were involved in a written debate! He dared to compare my viewpoint to that of capitalist Russia, as if I were persecuting a particular group of people. Persecution? Bah!"

Daphne cringed when he raised his fist in preparation for another mighty thud.

"Harrison!" At Mother's high-pitched cry, Father's fist froze midair. Mother glanced toward the door leading to the servant's hallway then sent a stern look at her husband. In a whispered tone, she said, "I must insist you lower your voice. Our reputation shall be damaged with talk amongst the servants if you cannot control your emotions."

Daphne relaxed in her chair. This time Father would listen. He valued his reputation, and they were all aware how servants loved to spread salacious tidbits about their employers. If caught, they could be sent packing, yet they still indulged in story-sharing whenever possible. The more influential the person involved in the gossip, the faster the story spread. Anything involving Father would be choice tittle-tattle.

Father lowered his hand to the table slowly, as if fighting his own muscles. His frown deepened until he resembled an angry bull. Hissing through his teeth, he held himself to a fierce growl that carried only to the ears of those around the table. "The boy's action borders on insubordination. I will not tolerate defiance among my employees!"

Harry leaned forward. "Father, did Thomas refuse to edit your writings?"

Father stared at Harry, his thick brows so low his eyes squinted. "No. He did an exemplary job in editing, as always, but —"

"How can you call it insubordination when he did what you asked him to do?"

Daphne silently cheered. How she wished she could ask such a question and set Father back in his chair! But if she had made the query, Father wouldn't be sitting in thoughtful introspection; he'd either wave his hand in dismissal or glower in disapproval.

She replayed Thomas's good-bye, and relief washed over her. Surely his solemn farewell had been based on a belief he would be discharged the moment he placed his own editorial on Father's desk. The good-bye had nothing to do with her and everything to do with Father. If only Father would see that Thomas had done nothing wrong, everything would return to normal. She sat with her lips pressed tightly together and waited for Father to reply.

But only a grunt sounded, followed by Father snatching up his fork and knife and digging into his now-cold dinner. Harry winked at Daphne, and they also turned their attention to their food. When they had been excused, Harry caught her elbow and guided her to the backyard pergola situated well away from the house. He pressed her onto a bench and leaned against the railing, fixing her with a serious look.

"What do you know about the editorial Tom wrote?"

Daphne threw her hands outward in a silent gesture of innocence. "Not a thing! Father mentioning it at dinner is the first I heard of it. But Thomas visited me at headquarters earlier today, quite upset not only with Watson, but with Father, as well." She didn't add that his concerns had trickled over onto her. "The fact that he wrote out his opinion of injustice doesn't surprise me."

"It surprises me." Harry released the top button of his shirt and slipped his hands into his trouser pockets, affecting a relaxed pose that didn't match his scowl. "Tom's never been one to stir up trouble. He was the peacemaker amongst our chums — in fact, we all jeered at him for it. Big enough to beat anyone into submission, but he preferred talking out differences and finding a compromise. He said he was taught to be at peace with all men, inasmuch as was possible."

Yes, Thomas's penchant for gentleness was one of his most endearing qualities, in Daphne's opinion. She had never feared him, despite his large size. Except . . . Her smile faded when she remembered his fierce attack this morning. What immense emotion must have boiled beneath the surface for him to react so strongly.

Harry went on quietly, as if speaking to himself. "Always, there was something different about Tom — a maturity, even when we were young. We'd goad him about being a country boy, call him a hayseed, and even then he'd just smile and say something that disarmed the malicious intent. Yet he always jumped to the defense of anyone else being tormented."

Suddenly Harry straightened, one hand popping out of his pocket to sock the air. "Why, that's it! Tom could never abide anyone being left out or mistreated. He told me one time that 'his people,' whatever that meant, had suffered oppression because of their religion. Why, this editorial he wrote must be out of his belief that —" Harry stormed out of the pergola, heading in the direction of the carriage house.

Daphne jumped up so fast she felt dizzy. She grabbed a vine-woven post with both hands and leaned forward. "Harry!"

He whirled, his feet still moving as if eager to continue. "What?"

"Where are you going?"

"To talk to Tom — talk some sense into him."

She released the post and scrambled down the two wooden steps. "I want to accompany you."

"No."

"But surely I could —"

"No!" His stern look silenced her protest. "This might turn unpleasant. I plan to be very straightforward with Tom, and likely he'll be straightforward back. With you in the middle of it, we won't be able to speak plain, man-to-man. This isn't a time for sugar-coating. His entire future is at stake."

"But my future is at stake, too! Please, Harry!" She clasped her hands beneath her chin.

Her brother's expression softened. He walked toward her and brushed her cheek with his fingertips. "Don't worry, Daph. I'll make sure Tom sticks around for us. He — he's like a brother to me. My best pal, ever since he walked into biology class and said he couldn't believe we'd cut up a pig just to look at its innards when the only thing inside a pig that interested him was ham, chops, and sausage."

They laughed softly together, and Daphne felt closer to her brother than ever before in those moments.

Harry finished in a hoarse whisper. "I don't want to lose his friendship."

Tears filled Daphne's eyes. "And I don't want to lose *him*." She waved her brother away. "All right. Go alone so you can speak man-to-man. And tell him . . . tell him I love him still."

21

Thomas jumped at a sudden series of thuds on his front door. He glanced at the partially completed letter on his desk and decided getting his thoughts down was more important than whatever the person outside needed.

He leaned back over the desk, pen tip against the page. But the pounding came again, more insistent. A voice called, "Tom! Open up or I'll break the door down!"

Harry. Thomas smacked his pen onto the paper and pushed away from the desk. He stomped to the door, swung it wide, and issued a gruff warning. "If you break the door down, you'll pay for it."

Harry charged over the threshold without waiting for an invitation, spun to face Thomas, and started speaking before Thomas could even secure the door. "What are you trying to do? Get yourself sacked?"

"I take it your father told you about the

editorial I wrote this afternoon."

Harry ran his hand through his hair. He shook his head, pacing the floor. "Oh yes, you were the topic at our dinner table. Father was ready to call out a firing squad." He whirled on Thomas. "What compelled you to do such a foolish thing? You had to know Father would be angry. I've never known you to deliberately incite ire. Why now?"

Recalling his conversation with Daphne and the emotional pain that followed, Thomas hesitated before answering. He valued his friendship with Harry, which had been years in the making. It pained him to think he would lose this friend, yet he knew he couldn't stay silent on the concept of social hierarchy. Not if it meant the deliberate intimidation of an entire race of people.

He answered carefully. "I suppose I never had a reason to incite ire before."

Harry laughed — a harsh, brittle sound. "You don't have a reason now."

"Yes, I do. Wrongs need to be fixed, and it's a sorry man who refuses to fight for right."

Harry snorted. "Fight for right . . . Right is subjective, Tom. Besides, what Watson wants benefits us."

"Us? Including me?"

"Of course, including you!"

"How am I a part of this 'us'?"

Harry flung his arms wide, his expression incredulous. "Are you colored? Are you Jewish? No! So this isn't your battle, Tom. Father's editorial had nothing to do with you."

"Because I'm not colored or Jewish."

"That's right."

Thomas grimaced. He crossed to his secondhand sofa and sat, his elbows on his knees and his hands clasped. He kept his gaze aimed downward and said, "No. But I'm poor. And that's just the next step up, isn't it?"

A soft expletive exploded from Harry as he moved to the chair at the end of the sofa and slumped into the seat. "I don't think of you as poor."

Thomas lifted his head to look directly into Harry's eyes. "You don't think of me as poor only because I lived with Nadine. But if you'd visited Gaeddert and seen my pa's house, you would never have chosen me for a friend. Admit it, Harry. Your father's belief that white men of wealth are superior is your belief, too."

Red streaked Harry's cheeks, his gaze darting sideways briefly before returning to Thomas. "That doesn't matter because you don't live in Gaeddert anymore. You live in Boston, and you have the opportunity for at least the illusion of wealth if you keep working your way up at the paper. No one would have to know you were brought up on a farm in Kansas."

Thomas laughed, but the sound held no amusement. "Harry, I'm not ashamed of my upbringing." The words caused a part of a verse from the book of Romans to flit through Thomas's mind: *"I am not ashamed of the gospel . . ."*

"I'm not saying you should be ashamed." Harry straightened in his seat, his tone convincing. "But there's no reason to boast about it, either. Why give people a reason to look down on you?"

Thomas bolted from his seat. "That's just it, Harry. Why should people look down on me because I'm not wealthy? Why does a fancy house and a large bank account make one man better than another? What difference is there in the color of skin? Skin is only this deep!" He pinched his thumb and finger together, indicating a scant difference.

Harry rose, too, his eyes snapping with fury. "I don't know why it matters, but it does! It always has! And you can't change it, so why sacrifice your job and your opportunity for high standing in this community over a bunch of —"

Thomas lunged, catching Harry's shirtfront. "Hold your tongue!"

Harry set his lips in a grim line and glared. For several seconds Thomas held tight, his face only inches from Harry's, the unspoken disparaging term hanging in the air like a vile stench.

Abruptly, Thomas released his hold and stepped back. He drew a deep breath and released it bit by bit, willing his anger to calm, inwardly reminding himself Harry was his friend. His *friend.* Not his enemy.

A cloak of tension fell over the room. Harry stood with his hands balled into fists, his jaw clenched so tightly the muscles twitched. The heaviness in Thomas's chest made breathing difficult. *Why, Lord? Why did you not let me see? Why did you not keep me from becoming involved in a campaign to elect a man with reprehensible morals?*

Pa's voice, from a day long past, whispered a response to Thomas's inner torment. *"Son, choices a man makes, and not always does he choose the right. This is why we seek daily the Lord's guidance."*

Belinda's familiar ending to each of her written communications followed Pa's admonition: *"Every day, I pray God's will for you."*

Thomas swallowed hard, shame and regret churning his belly. How disappointed his parents would be to know how far off course he'd gone. Despite his pa's wise counsel and steadfast example, he had chosen this pathway without consulting his heavenly Father. And now he must suffer the consequences.

At last Harry cleared his throat and broke the silence. "Tom, for as long as I've known you, you've championed the downtrodden. I never completely understood it, yet at the same time, it seemed an admirable quality." His chin jutted forward. "But you'd be a fool to let your personal feelings cost you the opportunity my father gave you. Apologize to him. He can be arrogant, but underneath he's a reasonable man. You have worked hard and proven to be an excellent copy editor — I've heard him say so. Given your past efforts, he'll forgive your lapse in judgment and allow your employment to continue."

Thomas squared his shoulders. "I'm more concerned about seeking forgiveness from *my* Father, and His opinion is the one that matters most."

Harry frowned, clearly confused.

"I will speak to your father," Thomas promised, ushering Harry toward the door, "on Monday, first thing."

Harry paused in the doorway. "You could speak to him Sunday, when you come to the estate for brunch. Daphne will expect you."

Thomas held his breath for a moment, wavering. But he shook his head. "I can't come out Sunday. I . . . I'll be accompanying Nadine to service." Saying the words out loud brought a rush of peace that had been too long absent from his heart.

Harry's eyebrows shot high. "But Daphne —"

"Daphne will have to understand."

"You'll disappoint her. She loves you, you know."

Thomas met Harry's steady gaze. "I know. And —" he swallowed — "I love her, too. But there's someone else I answer to first." A lump filled his throat as he thought about the number of times an elusive emotion had tried to tug his heart elsewhere. He recognized that tug now, and he would not continue to ignore it. "There's a relationship I've neglected for far too long, and I can't allow myself to let anyone, including Daphne, interfere with it again."

Harry shook his head as if clearing cotton

from his ears. "You make no sense."

"I'll explain later, after I've spoken to your father. Now, please, Harry, I need some time alone."

Harry shot Thomas one more frustrated look before releasing a grunt of displeasure. "Fine. I'll go. But think long and hard about what you're giving up."

Thomas nodded. He'd thought of little else since that morning. "I will. Good-bye, Harry." He closed the door behind his friend and then leaned against it with his eyes closed and his heart pounding. He stood to lose several important relationships if he continued as his conscience dictated, yet there was also something comforting about his decision. *Thank you, Lord, for awakening me in time. Help me make the right choices from now on.*

When he opened his eyes, his gaze settled on the doorway of the small second bedroom — the bedroom where he had imagined his children residing. With determination, he pushed aside the thought and reminded himself that his letter awaited completion. He crossed to the desk, sat down, and picked up where he'd left off. *So, considering everything that has happened, Pa and Summer, I've decided . . .*

■ ■ ■ ■

"Daphne, stop moping or leave the breakfast table."

Father's stern reprimand forced Daphne's head up. She stopped dragging her fork through the small serving of eggs on her plate and forced a startled look. "Moping?"

Father muttered a mild oath and shook his head. "Yes, moping! Having to look at your pouting face makes me dyspeptic." He popped a sausage in his mouth and chewed violently.

Daphne considered telling him his disposition had been unbearably bad-tempered since Friday evening, but she managed to squelch the comment before it left her lips. Still, she hinted at the true cause of her father's ill-humor with a whispered admission. "I miss him."

Harry met her gaze from across the table with a sympathetic smile that eased a bit of the ache in her heart. But Father's derisive harrumph quickly chased the comfort away. Unable to abide the worry that had kept her up much of the night, she blurted, "Father, do you intend to release Thomas from his duties at the *Beacon*?"

Father paused with a piece of sausage

suspended on the fork's tines beneath his chin. His brows formed a sharp V. "Daphne, that is hardly your concern." He jammed the sausage into his open mouth.

"On the contrary, it is very much my concern." Her quivering fingers lost their hold on the fork. It clattered against her plate. She clutched her hands in her lap and continued in an impassioned tone. "If he has no employment, he will be unable to remain in Boston. If he returns to Kansas, I will surely —"

Father smacked his fork onto the table. "Wither up and die?"

Despite his contemptuous expression, Daphne drew herself up in the chair and pressed one hand to her beating heart. "It feels as though I could!"

"Bah!" Father planted his elbows on the table and leaned closer to Daphne. The grease along the bottom edge of his mustache glistened in the morning sun that streamed through the breakfast room's bay window. "Boston teems with eligible men — most of whom possess much stronger pedigrees than this Thomas Ollenburger." With a wave of his hand, Father turned his attention back to his plate.

As he picked up his fork, Daphne grabbed his wrist. "So you *do* intend to dismiss him."

Father jerked his arm free, sending the fork flying to the floor. "Stanton!" He bellowed the servant's name. When the man appeared in the doorway, Father barked, "Fork." The servant scuttled away and Father turned his glowering gaze on his daughter. "My intentions are not your affair, Daphne. Leave business to those who know how to conduct it. No more of this topic."

Daphne leaped from her chair, nearly colliding with Stanton, who returned with a fork held on a linen napkin. The servant took a backward step as she slung her napkin onto her plate. "I have no appetite, so I shall leave the table. But know this, Father — if you send Thomas away, I shall never forgive you. I love him, I know he loves me, and his *pedigree* matters not one whit! If I cannot marry Thomas, I shall die an old maid!"

She fled, but not quickly enough to avoid hearing Father's snide comment. "Females . . . overly dramatic."

Harry said something in reply, but Daphne didn't pause to discover whether he defended or disparaged her. She raced up the stairs and past her parents' room, ignoring her mother's query as to the reason for her unladylike dash down the hallway. After slamming the door, she turned the key in the lock. She had no expectation of anyone coming after her, but it gave her measure of control to turn that key and block out the world.

Throwing herself across the bed, she gave vent to the tears she had kept dammed all through the long night when she lay awake, hoping Thomas would change his mind and come to brunch as he'd done for so many weeks. She'd held the tears at bay to avoid greeting him with red eyes and a blotchy face should he come. But with his absence, her reason to avoid the emotional torrent no longer existed, so she reveled in the release of a long, heaving, soggy cry.

When her tears dried up, she mopped her face clean with the hem of her dressing gown then dropped the garment in a crumpled heap at the foot of her bed. Stepping out onto her balcony in her nightclothes, she stood and looked across the lawn. The open expanse made her feel small and alone — which was just as she had felt in the breakfast room with only Father, Harry, and the servants for company. The loss of Thomas's company had cast a pall on the room, and if she found one breakfast without him so melancholy, how would she survive years without him?

22

At the preacher's closing amen, worshipers left their seats to file down the aisles and spill out into the churchyard to visit. The weather remained dry and warm, even though September neared its end, providing a pleasant atmosphere for conversation.

Belinda rose slowly, wishing she didn't have to leave the chapel. It had been so satisfying to be in the house of the Lord, lifting her voice in song and listening to the Bible taught with heartfelt conviction. She had no desire to return to Malinda's taciturn company. *God, I've been praying for Malinda to change for so long. When are You going to answer?*

Small arms captured her from the side, and she looked down into the smiling face of Abby Ollenburger. She turned in the aisle to see *Frau* Ollenburger, with Lena in her arms. "The girls love the aprons you sewed for them," *Frau* Ollenburger said.

Abby scampered to Gussie's side. Resembling mirror images, the little girls held out the embroidered skirts of their new aprons and offered giggling curtsies.

Belinda laughed and leaned forward to give them each a hug. "You look like little angels. It was a joy to use that snowy white organdy at long last. Mama's had it for years — she purchased it to embroider fancy dresser scarves for Malinda's hope chest, but . . ." Her voice drifted away, her enjoyment at seeing the little girls in their Sunday aprons tarnished by unpleasant memories.

Frau Ollenburger touched her arm. "It was thoughtful of you to use it for the girls. Please thank Malinda for allowing it."

Belinda nodded, but she knew she wouldn't say anything to Malinda. Her sister would be furious to know Belinda had touched anything from the trunk in the attic. Malinda would rather moths ate the items in that trunk than see them put to good use.

Though they remained obediently silent, Abby and Gussie danced in place, eager to race outside with the other youngsters. *Frau* Ollenburger gave them a stern look. "You may go, but mind your manners. Keep your aprons nice."

"Yes, Mama!" they chorused, and the pair

scampered off, their blond curls bouncing.

Lena cupped her mother's face with both pudgy hands. "I go pway?"

Frau Ollenburger chuckled and lowered the little girl to the floor. "Go ahead, but stay close to your sisters." She waited until Lena exited the wide doorway before turning back to Belinda. She winked. "You said they look like angels, but they are typical children. Always wanting to play."

"Let them play." Belinda stared wistfully after them. "They'll be grown up soon enough, with no time for play." A touch of bitterness colored her tone, and heat built in her cheeks when *Frau* Ollenburger gave her a puzzled look. Before her friend could ask questions, Belinda added, "And speaking of no time for play . . . I must go home and put a meal on the table. Malinda will expect me."

Frau Ollenburger opened her mouth to speak, but another voice cut her off.

"Summer?" *Herr* Ollenburger stood in the doorway. He held Lena, and Abby and Gussie stood at his side. "Come now. We must hurry home." He tipped his head to include Belinda. "You come, too, Belinda."

Curious, Belinda hurried after *Frau* Ollenburger. Excited chatter from the yard greeted them as they stepped outside. *Frau*

Ollenburger looked up at her husband. "Peter? What is it?"

"A fire." *Herr* Ollenburger's tight voice matched his concerned face.

Belinda sniffed the air. The acrid odor tickling her nose proved her neighbor's words true.

"Men have run already for the fire wagon."

Belinda's heart began to pound. The last rains had been in late June. As dry as it was, a fire could spread rapidly. She clutched her hands together against her rib cage. "Do you know where it is?"

"No. But from the smell, in town, for sure," *Herr* Ollenburger replied. Still holding Lena in one arm, he put his free arm around his wife's waist and guided her toward the sidewalk. Glancing back at Belinda, he added, "Come. We must go home and ready tubs with water, just in case."

Belinda caught hold of Abby's and Gussie's hands and trotted down the sidewalk behind her neighbors. Silently, she prayed protection for anyone in the path of the fire. The smell of smoke seemed to grow stronger as they walked, and when the little girls started coughing, she knew it wasn't her imagination that the smoke was getting thicker.

They rounded the final corner to the Ollenburgers' block. A cloud of smoke hung heavy in the still air. The fire was very near! Clanging bells from the fire wagon sounded from behind them, and they scurried into a yard to watch the horse-drawn wagon roll by. It wheeled around the far corner, heading toward the street on which Belinda lived.

"Oh, Peter!" *Frau* Ollenburger came to a stop and pointed.

Belinda followed the woman's pointing finger and gasped. Flames licked along the roofline of her home! Her heart vaulted into her throat. "Malinda!" Shaking off the little girls' icy hands, she started running. But strong arms caught her and pulled her back. She fought against the restraining arms, but they held tight.

"Belinda! You must not try to go in there!" *Herr* Ollenburger commanded sternly.

Belinda pushed hard on his chest, groaning with the effort to break free. "But I have to get Malinda!" She threw back her head and screamed her sister's name.

Herr Ollenburger shook her and spoke in rapid *Plautdietsch.* "The men will know she is in there! Never does she leave — all of the town knows this! You stay with Summer." He pushed her into *Frau* Ollenburger's arms. Touching his wife's cheek briefly, he said, "I will go see to Malinda. You throw

301

water on the back side of our house. If flames come through the alley, you run for safety." He ran between houses, disappearing from sight.

The three little girls stared at their mother in mute horror. *Frau* Ollenburger crouched before them, gathering them near. "Girls, I want you to stay right here. Don't leave this yard. You are safe from the fire here. Abby, keep hold of Lena. Gussie, you help. Keep Lena right here until either your papa or I come for you. Do you understand?"

Wide-eyed, the girls nodded and chorused, "We understand." Little Lena began to cry, and Abby pulled her into an embrace. The three sat together in the dusty yard, unmindful of soiling their new white aprons.

"Come, Belinda." *Frau* Ollenburger looped arms with Belinda, and they ran to the back of the Ollenburgers' home. They filled bucket after bucket with water, splashing it as high as they could throw on the back side of the house. That task complete, they watered the dry yard.

Aware of the activity across the alley yet strangely separated from it, Belinda kept her focus on the task at hand: fill a bucket, carry it several feet, throw the water; repeat the process. Over and over, with eyes burning and lungs aching, she worked to protect the Ollenburgers' house from the fire. Finally, *Frau* Ollenburger caught her arm.

"The wagon is leaving," she said in a quiet, hoarse voice.

Belinda looked at her house. No more yellow and orange tongues danced at windows or roofline. Puffs of smoke rose from the charred wood, but although the smell was still strong, the danger seemed to be over. She stood with *Frau* Ollenburger, waiting until *Herr* Ollenburger plodded slowly around the damaged house.

Soot coated his church suit and streaked his cheeks above his beard. His hair, wet with sweat, lay plastered to his head. He might have been a chimney sweep returning home after a hard day's work. His red-rimmed eyes settled on Belinda, and he slowed for a moment, his spine stiff. Then he came directly to her and cupped her shoulders.

She stared into his dirty, concerned face. "*Herr* Ollenburger? M-my sister?"

His large fingers curled more tightly over her shoulders. She gripped his wrists for support while she awaited a reply. He drew a deep breath, giving his head a slight shake. "I do not know."

Belinda sent a startled glance at *Frau* Ollenburger, who furrowed her brow in confusion. "I don't understand. Where is Malinda?"

Again, he shook his head. "She must have run away when the fire started. She was not in the house."

Two simultaneous, conflicting emotions — relief and worry — struck Belinda with vehemence. Clinging to his wrists, she begged, "What do you mean? Where could she be?"

Herr Ollenburger coughed. "I do not know. Several church members agreed to go looking."

Frau Ollenburger interjected, "I'll bring the girls home now." She hurried off, leaving Belinda and *Herr* Ollenburger alone.

He cleared his throat several times before speaking again. "Let us go to the house and wait for a report from the men." He steered her toward his own house.

Belinda dug in her heels. "I'll go to my house. If she returns, she'll —"

"You cannot." Although kind, the man was firm. "Your house is not safe. The fire started in the attic, probably from a candle. All that new tar Thomas put on the roof was like fuel. There was much damage from flames. The ceiling has partly fallen, and more could fall down on you. To our house you will come. Thomas's room is empty —

304

you will use it. Come, Belinda."

Belinda wanted to argue more, but she discovered she didn't have the strength. With a nod, she allowed *Herr* Ollenburger to guide her to his home.

She slept fitfully all afternoon, curled on Thomas's rope bed. Often the voices of neighbors who had stopped by the Ollenburgers' home awakened her, but when no one indicated Malinda had been found, Belinda chose to shut out the world for a little longer.

By evening, however, her body refused more sleep, so she plodded into the kitchen. *Herr* Ollenburger sat at the table, and *Frau* Ollenburger stood at the stove, stirring something that smelled wonderful.

Herr Ollenburger glanced up when Belinda entered the room. He patted the spot at the table next to him. "*Goot,* you are awake. Sit down here and we will talk."

Belinda sat down, accepting a cup of coffee from *Frau* Ollenburger. "No word on Malinda yet?"

Herr Ollenburger's sad eyes answered without words.

Belinda pushed the coffee aside. "Where can she be? You're sure she wasn't in the house? Maybe she . . ."

"She was not in the house. Everything was

305

carefully searched. She must have run away." He patted Belinda's clenched fists. "But she will come back when she realizes all is safe again. Do not worry, Belinda. Trust the Lord to watch over her."

"That's right." *Frau* Ollenburger ladled thick soup into bowls and then carried them to the table. "We don't know where she is right now, but God knows. We've been praying all afternoon for Him to guide her safely home."

Belinda waited until *Herr* Ollenburger blessed the simple meal before speaking again. "But home to what? If I'm not there, she won't stay."

"We have neighbors watching," *Frau* Ollenburger said.

"But unless I am there —"

"Belinda, I must insist you do not go into your house alone." *Herr* Ollenburger's stern voice reminded Belinda of her own father. "The house is unsafe, and another tragedy we do not need. Summer and I have discussed it while you sleep, and we want you to stay here, with us."

Swallowing a protest, Belinda offered a compromise. "Then I will pay you rent for the privilege of staying here until I can find someplace for Malinda and me."

"No. No rent." Herr Ollenburger shook

his head. "You stay as a friend in need. And when Malinda comes back, she stays here, too."

Belinda's heart leaped at their kindness. Tears stung her eyes as she whispered, "It's too kind."

"Nonsense," *Frau* Ollenburger inserted. Her familiar, playful grin lifted Belinda's spirit. "Besides, you can be of help to me."

Belinda gave an eager nod. "Of course! I can —"

"You can talk about Plymouth Rock chickens with Peter."

Herr Ollenburger burst out laughing, and Belinda couldn't help but join in. The release felt wonderful. The girls, apparently beckoned by the happy sound, pounded down the stairs and into the kitchen. Dressed in flannel nightgowns with their hair tied in little pin curls, they looked adorable. All three ran directly to Belinda.

"Are you staying? Huh, Belinda? Will you sleep in Thomas's bed and be here every day?" The questions tumbled on top of one other.

Still laughing, Belinda held out her arms and tugged all three into an awkward embrace. Looking over the tops of their heads to their smiling parents, Belinda gave a nod. "Yes, I'll stay."

"Goody! Goody!" Breaking loose of Belinda's hold, the three hopped around in a happy dance.

Frau Ollenburger stood and rounded up the girls as efficiently as a mother hen gathers her chicks. "All right, now, you need to go back to your beds. Come."

When the kitchen was quiet again, Belinda voiced a practical question. "What about my things? I can stay here, but I'll need my clothing, at least. Was everything ruined?"

Herr Ollenburger took a bite of stew, his expression thoughtful. "Some things we could probably . . ." He looked at his wife. "How you say it? Savage?"

She smiled. "Salvage."

He nodded, facing Belinda again. "Some things we salvage. The smell of smoke all will hold, but we can scrub and let things sit in the sun. That will help." He frowned, his eyes narrow. "Since it began in the attic, the ceiling came down over the hallway. A big trunk came with it. The trunk is probably ruined. But other furniture? Maybe some we can —" he grinned — "salvage."

The big trunk held Mama's and Papa's clothes. Remembering something else that was in the attic, she asked, "Did you see a small trunk, about this size" — she held out her hands to indicate a foot and a half distance — "come down, too?"

"*Nä,* only the big one."

"Maybe it's still up there," Belinda mused aloud.

"In the attic?" *Herr* Ollenburger shook his head. "*Nä.* Two men go into the attic to spray water around. They only find emptiness."

Belinda's heart skipped a beat. Malinda must have taken it with her when she escaped. The trunk was obviously important to her sister. *What,* she wondered again, *could be in that little trunk?*

23

When Thomas arrived at the newspaper building Monday morning, he stopped briefly by the mailroom to drop off his letter for posting and then headed to his office. A gunnysack, crumpled into a wad, created a bulge in his jacket pocket. If Mr. Severt burst in and sent him packing, as he'd done to the office's previous occupant, Thomas would have something in which to transport his personal belongings.

He'd felt sorry for Perkins the day Severt tossed him out the door, but he doubted anyone would sympathize with him. From the silent stares of his co-workers when he'd walked through the lobby, he guessed they all knew what he'd done and counted him foolish for blatantly going against their boss.

Well, he reasoned as he dropped his jacket over the high back of his chair, there was a Bible verse about the world's wisdom being foolish in the sight of God. He hadn't broken any biblical mandates by writing out his opinion of social hierarchy, so he'd just have to trust that, somehow, things would work out for the best for him — whether in Boston or Kansas.

The mail would go out midmorning, and his letter should arrive in Hillsboro by the end of the week. He'd shared his various options with his parents, and by the time the letter reached them, final decisions would be made. He wished he could communicate with Pa more quickly, to ask him to pray. But then he reminded himself Pa would be praying for him every day anyway, as would Summer. And Belinda.

He slid into his seat at his desk, only to spot a note tacked directly to the desktop: *SEE ME.*

No signature was required. Thomas knew by whom he'd been summoned.

For a moment, apprehension fluttered through his middle. But then he closed his eyes, said a silent prayer for strength to face the consequence of his actions, and pushed away from the desk. He slipped his arms into the sleeves of his jacket, removed the gunnysack from his pocket and dropped it on the desk, and then he headed for his boss's office.

He found Mr. Severt waiting in the open-

311

ing of the double doors of his top-floor office. Arms folded, scowling, collar firmly buttoned beneath his chin, the man presented a formidable appearance that sent the elevator operator scuttling right back into his cubby.

Severt waved one hand and barked, "I've been waiting. Let's go." He turned and stomped into his office.

Thomas glanced at the errand boy, who stared with wide eyes. He paused long enough to wink at the lad before he trotted through the yawning doors. Once Thomas was inside the office, Severt commanded, "Close 'em."

Thomas followed his directions. He crossed to the opposite side of the man's massive desk and waited until Severt pointed to a chair. The moment Thomas's backside touched the seat, Severt launched into a lengthy and scathing tirade about company loyalty, following directions, and personal integrity. Thomas sat in silence, nodding occasionally, his gaze never wavering from Severt's red face.

Finally the man ran out of words. He leaned back, linked his hands over his stomach, and said, "So, do you understand what I expect of my employees?"

"Yes, sir." Thomas stood. His boss tipped

his head to maintain eye contact. "I appreciate the opportunity to work here. I've learned a great deal, and my pa always says experience is never wasted. So thank you." He stretched out his hand, waiting for Severt's return shake.

But Severt pushed Thomas's hand away. "What are you doing? Quitting?"

Thomas drew back in confusion. "Aren't you releasing me?"

A snort blasted from the man, and he pointed to Thomas's chair. "Sit."

Thomas lowered himself slowly onto the chair's edge.

"I probably should take you by the back of the jacket and toss you onto the street after the hullabaloo you've caused."

Thomas squirmed.

"But I'm not going to."

He sat bolt upright. "Sir?"

"No." Severt leaned forward to rest his elbows on the desk edge. "I'm not at all pleased you chose to add an unsolicited addendum to my editorial. I found the text slanderous, narrow-minded, and highly prejudicial — the very thing you accused me of being. And yet . . ." He stroked his mustache, his piercing gaze pinning Thomas in place. "It was also very well-written."

Thomas held his breath.

Severt slashed his hand through the air. "Now, I don't swallow an ounce of the equality nonsense you spouted, but I do admire the way you put words together. Filled with emotion. Stirring. Thought-provoking."

Thomas stared at his boss, hardly able to believe his ears.

"Your abilities are being wasted simply editing my words, young man. I didn't realize you had taken writing courses at the university."

"I . . . I didn't. I took business classes."

"Then where did you learn to write?"

Thomas lifted one shoulder in a slow shrug. "I guess all the reading I did as a boy helped. . . ."

Severt gave a brusque nod. "I suppose. Given your knack, you should be doing your own writing. Reporting. Does that interest you?"

"A . . . a journalist?" Thomas's mind whirled at this unexpected turn.

"Facts only," Severt said. "None of this self-serving drivel you poured onto the page for my benefit. You wouldn't be writing editorials but fact-based articles." He rocked in his chair, the rhythmic squeak keeping time with Thomas's racing heart. "No pay increase . . . yet. Not until I see what you can do."

Thomas wanted to joyfully accept, but he'd learned his lesson. A decision of such magnitude required a great deal of thought and prayer. "I . . . I can't agree right away, sir. I need time to think about this."

Severt frowned. "How much time do you need?"

Thomas licked his dry lips. "I-I'm not sure. Maybe . . . a week?"

For long moments, Severt glared at him. Thomas waited, expecting the man to act on his earlier threat to catch the back of his jacket and send him out the door. But finally his boss shook his head, leaned back, and threw his arms outward. "Fine. A week. But no more! And while you're thinking, edit these." He thrust a handful of pages into Thomas's hands.

"Yes, sir." Thomas started to leave.

"Ollenburger!"

Thomas turned back.

"Remember what I said about loyalty." The man's dark eyes sparked. "I'm giving you a second chance — something I rarely offer. I *never* offer third chances."

Thomas understood. "Sir, if I decide to remain in your employ, a third chance won't be necessary." Severt's writings in hand, Thomas left the office.

■ ■ ■ ■

After only three days of living under the Ollenburgers' roof, Belinda felt as though she'd been a lifelong member of the family. Peter and Summer, as they insisted she call them, treated her like one of their own, allowing her to perform household duties and including her in family discussions.

The little girls clamored for her attention, and she delighted in cutting dresses and bonnets from scraps of wrapping paper for Abby and Gussie's paper dolls or reading Lena stories before tucking her in for her afternoon nap. Watching the girls interact created a bittersweet ache in her chest. She wished she and Malinda had enjoyed similar times together while growing up, yet being a part of the Ollenburger sisters' circle of acceptance brought her great joy.

Although community members rode out on horses each day to search for Malinda, she still hadn't been found. Belinda's worry magnified with each passing day, yet she tried to do what Peter suggested and leave Malinda in God's hands.

"He knows where she is. When the time is right, He will lead her back again." Peter's faith, which matched his size, gave Belinda the courage to trust, too.

As the days slipped by, Belinda found herself looking ahead. While her constant prayer was for the safe return of her sister, she caught herself wondering what she would do if Malinda was never found. She had given up her job at the mercantile after Mama's death so she could stay close to Malinda, earning money by taking in more ironing and sewing for neighbors.

Even though the Ollenburgers didn't ask her to contribute to the family income, she felt an obligation to help out. Returning to work seemed best. Even when Malinda returned, if they stayed with the Ollenburgers, her sister would have company all day and she could be away to work. Belinda decided she needed to discuss the situation with Summer.

Friday morning, Belinda stood by the door while Summer gave Abby and Gussie each a good-bye kiss and sent them off to school. She held Lena's hand, keeping the three-year-old from dashing after her sisters, as she was prone to do.

"Tell your sisters good-bye," Belinda encouraged the little girl.

Lena, swinging Belinda's hand, called, "Bye-bye, sissies!"

Abby and Gussie waved and scurried

down the sidewalk.

When Summer closed the door, Belinda scooped Lena into her arms and followed Summer to the kitchen, where she began clearing the table of dirty breakfast dishes. Belinda set Lena on the kitchen floor with a pile of well-worn wooden blocks before joining Summer.

While Summer washed and Belinda dried, Belinda broached the subject of finding a job. Summer sent her a sidelong glance, her lips tweaked into a teasing grin. "Am I not keeping you busy enough?"

Belinda laughed. "My days here have been pleasantly full, even though you expect much less of me than if I were keeping my own house." She shook her head and admitted, "I'm downright lazy compared to how much I worked taking care of Mama and Malinda."

"You've earned a break." Summer handed Belinda the last plate and began scrubbing silverware.

"But eventually Malinda will come back, and I'll need to take care of our needs." Belinda carefully stacked the clean plates on their shelf. The beautiful plates from Mama's cabinet were packed away in a box under Thomas's bed. Belinda was grateful she had been able to save the plates, although the glass in Mama's bow-front cupboard had been shattered.

"We can worry about that when the time comes," Summer said. She dropped the silverware into the rinse pan with a clatter. Drying her hands on a towel, she faced Belinda. "May I ask a nosy question?"

Belinda turned from the shelf and nodded.

Summer pursed her lips for a moment, as if gathering her thoughts. Then she spoke in a hesitant voice. "Your father was a . . . well-to-do businessman. Yet your mother and sister depended on you to provide for them. Did your father not leave any means of provision for your mother?"

Belinda crossed to the dry sink. "I have wondered about that myself." She lifted silverware from the pan one piece at a time, rubbing each piece dry before handing it to Summer. "I once asked Mama about Papa's money, but she snapped at me that finances were private and shouldn't be discussed. Yet, she insisted I work in order to bring in money to pay our rent and for our food, constantly reminding me that without my support, we would starve or be homeless."

"Well," Summer replied, placing the silverware in one of the kitchen's built-in drawers, "perhaps the money was lost when your father's business closed in Gaeddert. Some-times that happens. When Peter closed the mill and we faced the expenses of moving into Hillsboro, we had very little money left on which to live."

"I suppose that's possible." Belinda chewed her lower lip, her brow puckered thoughtfully. "But I still found it strange that he hadn't put something aside. Papa's business did well, and he didn't squander money — even though Mama begged for new things every year." She chuckled softly. "Of course, she did wear him down more often than he probably would have liked. Mama could be very persuasive." Her laugh ended in a sigh, chasing away the brief mo-ment of light-heartedness. "I appreciate you and *Herr* Ollenburger letting me stay here and being willing to welcome Malinda when we find her. But she and I will need to find our own place eventually. I'll need money to pay for our house and the furnishings to fill it, since so many of our things were ruined in the fire. So . . . I do need to look for a job."

Summer leaned against the cupboard and watched Lena build a block tower for a few moments before turning back to Belinda. "Eventually, yes, you'll want to look for a job. But let's not rush into it, shall we? Why don't we wait until we find Malinda and get her settled into her new routine here. She'll want you close by for a few days at least, I'm sure. You don't have any expenses right now, so there's no need to hurry into job-hunting, is there?"

Belinda considered Summer's suggestion. She knew a change in routine would be difficult for her sister, and having Belinda nearby would help ease the transition. A part of her balked at continuing to live on the generosity of her neighbors, yet she knew Summer had spoken wisely. Finally she nodded. "All right. I'll wait until we find Malinda."

Summer beamed her approval. "Good."

"But standing around waiting for her to show up is driving me mad." Belinda forced a light laugh to cover her underlying worry. "Do you suppose Thomas would mind if I took Daisy for a ride to Gaeddert? It's the only place I can think of that Malinda would go."

"The men have searched your old house and your father's business in Gaeddert several times," Summer reminded her.

Belinda raised one eyebrow. "But I know Malinda better than anyone else. Maybe she'll come out of hiding for me. It would also give me a chance to visit Mama's and

Papa's graves."

Summer touched Belinda's cheek. "Very well. The livery owner knows you, so he won't question you borrowing the horse. Will you be back by lunchtime?"

"I don't know," Belinda answered honestly. "Don't plan anything for me, just in case."

For a moment, she thought Summer would argue, but then the woman simply nodded. "Very well. I'll say a prayer for you to find her. And would you mind stopping at the gravesite where Thomas's great-grandmother is buried while you're out? It has been quite a while since we could go. I just want to assure myself things are all right there."

"I'd be glad to." Belinda stepped forward and gave Summer an impulsive hug. After kissing the top of Lena's glossy head of curls, she walked quickly to the stable, asked the liveryman to saddle Daisy, and set out. Riding with her knee hooked over the saddle horn, she held Daisy to a canter to avoid being bounced out of her seat.

"Lord," she prayed aloud to the accompaniment of Daisy's rhythmic, clopping hooves, "let me find Malinda. Let her be well, and let her be willing to come back with me."

As difficult as it was to care for her sister, the desire to find her nearly overwhelmed Belinda. Malinda was her only family. She loved her and truly wanted her back, safe and sound. Choking back a sob, she finished her prayer on one trembling word: "Please?"

24

Belinda looked in the window of every empty building in Gaeddert, hoping for a glimpse of her sister. The few residents remaining in town chatted willingly with Belinda, but no one had seen Malinda. They all indicated they were watching for her, and each promised to send word immediately if she was spotted.

Abandoning her search, Belinda led Daisy to the *Kleine Gemeinde.* For a few moments she stood, staring at the white clapboard church building, her heart aching. Even though it had only been a few months since services were cancelled due to the lack of a minister, the church already showed signs of neglect. Two cracked windows, a sagging porch rail, and paint peeling along the foundation gave mute evidence of the lack of care.

Belinda turned away from the church and looked down the street at the sad row of abandoned businesses, the windows of several boarded over. The empty boardwalks and wagonless street painted a dismal, heartbreaking picture of abandonment. Had this really been a thriving town only a few short years ago? How quickly things could change.

Belinda's vision blurred. With a sigh, she wiped the tears from her eyes. Crying wouldn't bring back the town or its people. She might as well complete her errands and move on.

She left Daisy at the edge of the boardwalk and walked behind the church to its adjoining cemetery. Stepping carefully between headstones, she made her way toward her parents' side-by-side graves in the back corner of the cemetery. Dry leaves in browns, yellows, and russets crunched beneath her feet, and the wind tapped emptying tree branches together. The sounds created a mournful melody, and Belinda folded her arms across her chest to ward off a sudden chill.

When she reached the twelve-inch-high iron fence surrounding the Schmidt plot, she lifted her skirts to avoid catching the hem and stepped over the fence. She rounded Papa's tall stone and came to an abrupt halt, drawing in a startled breath.

Clusters of dried wildflowers, their stems meticulously braided together, lay at the base of each stone. Belinda dashed forward and snatched up one bouquet. She looked around wildly. Malinda had been here!

With reverence, she placed the bouquet back where she'd found it, then lifted her skirts and raced to Daisy's side. Using a split rail fence as a ladder, she climbed onto Daisy's back and gave the horse a little nudge in the ribs. "Come, girl, we'll go check the grave plot for Summer and then hurry back. Peter needs to know what I found!"

Daisy eagerly trotted down the road out of town. The house Summer had built before marrying Peter stood midway between Gaeddert and Hillsboro, flanked by the slow-moving Cottonwood River and the road. If she hadn't made that promise to Summer, she would have bypassed the house completely, but Summer had done so much for her — the least she could do was check the graves and tidy things, if need be.

When Daisy reached the lane that led to the house, Belinda didn't even have to coax the horse to turn. The horse trotted directly to the shade beside the house and nodded her great head, giving a snort as if to express pleasure at the opportunity to visit the bungalow.

Belinda grabbed the porch railing and swung herself down. She rubbed Daisy's nose and instructed, "Just stay right here. I won't be long." Then she scurried to the small grave plot. The little wooden gate was off its hinges, resting against the homemade picket fence. Belinda frowned. If the gate had come loose on its own, it would have fallen into the grass. Someone had to have placed it there against the fence.

She stared at the gate, wondering if Peter or Thomas would have done that. Surely either of them would have fixed it rather than set it aside. A funny tingle went down her spine, and her heart picked up tempo. Slowly she turned from the grave plot to look toward the house. A slight movement at the far corner of the house — more a shadow than anything of substance — caught her attention.

Squinting against the early afternoon sun, Belinda strained to make sense of the brief glimpse. Then, while she watched, someone peeked around the house. Even though her face was filthy and her hair flew in wild disarray, Belinda recognized her at once. With a cry of joy, she dashed forward. "Malinda!"

■ ■ ■ ■

Thomas rose from the floor and sat on the edge of his bed. Hunching forward, he rubbed his knees. While he'd been in prayer, he hadn't noticed any discomfort, but now that his weight was off of his knees, they ached like a bad tooth. Still, he smiled. Pa had once told him the apostle Paul was called Camel Knees because he spent so much time in prayer. Thomas had a long way to go to earn that title, but it felt good to be back in daily communion with his heavenly Father.

He had prayed especially hard the past few days, seeking God's will about the job opportunity Mr. Severt had offered. He needed to let his boss know on Monday whether he would take the reporting position, and he still didn't know what to do. If he were to follow his impulses, he would pack his bags and return to Kansas immediately. In Kansas, it would be easy to push aside memories of Boston, the presidential campaign . . . and Daphne Severt.

A streak of pain stabbed him at the thought of her name. He'd also prayed for God to remove his affection for Daphne from his heart, but that prayer, too, had gone unanswered. Even though he hadn't seen her once in the past week, she still filled his thoughts and intruded in his dreams. He tortured himself repeatedly by replaying their last conversation in an attempt to make her distasteful, but the effort failed. The images that tormented his mind were far from unpleasant. He missed her.

Pushing off from the bed, he entered the parlor and picked up a book from the table beside the sofa. It was a children's book, but Nadine had recommended it because it featured a little girl named Dorothy from Kansas. If he liked it, he would probably send a copy to his sisters. He sank into the center of the sofa and tried for the third time to read, but the fanciful elements failed to hold his attention.

With a huff of disgust, he slapped the book onto the table and crossed to the window. Dusk had fallen, shrouding his yard in deep shadows. Hands in his pockets, he peered across the dark landscape and allowed his thoughts to drift past the residential area to the campaign headquarters, where no doubt frenetic activity took place as Election Day loomed near. In a little more than two weeks the United States would name a new president. He prayed it wasn't Thomas Watson.

Guilt weaseled its way through his middle. He'd broken his promise to aid in the campaign. But knowing what the man advocated, he could no longer support Watson. Going against his conscience was worse than breaking a promise, and he knew he'd done the right thing by withdrawing. Still, an element of unease remained. A man was only as *goot* as his word, Pa always said.

Thoughts of Pa led him to Hillsboro. If he returned, what job awaited him there? According to Pa's latest letter, Pa was set on trying to get a chicken farm started on the old homestead. Thomas supposed he could help, but for how long? Did he really want to be a chicken farmer? He wrinkled his nose. He knew he didn't. Not forever.

But Hillsboro held one big draw: his parents and little sisters. And in the Mennonite community of Hillsboro, he'd no doubt be able to find a Christian woman — maybe even Belinda Schmidt. He could settle down, start his own family.

He puffed his cheeks and blew out a breath of relief that he'd never verbalized his intentions to marry Daphne. Had he asked her father for her hand, he'd have a bigger burden of regret than the one he already carried. A betrothal was taken seriously.

"Thank you, Lord, for giving me a second chance to seek your will in a life's mate." The words slipped out in a heartfelt whisper. No matter how he pined for Daphne, he would not concede to his desire to see her. He would not disappoint his Maker by becoming unequally yoked with an unbeliever. Lowering his head, he closed his eyes and offered another prayer.

"Father, open Daphne's heart to accept your Son." He paused, searching his heart for hidden motives. Did he want Daphne to discover God's Son for his good, so he could pursue her once more, or did he want it for her good? Convinced his intentions were pure, he finished, "Bring her into a relationship with you, and then guide her on the pathway you have planned for her. Amen."

With the release of Daphne into his Father's hands, Thomas turned from the window, sat on the sofa, and once more picked up the book, opened it, and read aloud, " 'Chapter One, The Cyclone . . .' "

Daphne bent her knees, hiding the book in her lap. Should Father open the door and peek in, as he'd begun doing in the past days for some reason she couldn't fathom, he would see her reclining in her bed but wouldn't know she had sneaked in contraband.

Father heartily disapproved of women authors, claiming their emotionally-based disposition made them unsuitable for something as serious as writing. But Daphne's friend Rosemary Robbins, who marched in women's rights parades and who openly poohpoohed the dictates of society, had lent her a novel called *To Have and to Hold*.

Written by an American author named Mary Johnston, the book told the story of a Colonial soldier who unwittingly purchased a wife already claimed by another man. The book was full of adventure and heartbreakingly romantic moments. She could barely set it aside when the young wife, Jocelyn, eloquently persuaded the governor to free her husband, Ralph, who was mistaken to be a pirate. Yet despite getting lost in the pages, the moment she lifted her attention from the book, she thought of Thomas.

The familiar sting of tears made the words on the page waver. She closed her eyes, willing herself to gain control. She hadn't realized a body could manufacture so many tears. Ever since last Sunday, when Thomas had failed to arrive for his usual brunch with her family, tears had been her companion. Her appetite had fled. Her chest ached continually. If he didn't return, surely she would, as her father had scornfully predicted, wither up and die.

Thinking of Thomas benefited her not at all. Determinedly, she fixed her focus on Ralph's capture by Indians. But just as she once more engrossed herself in the story, the squeak of a turning doorknob brought her chin up. Father poked his head into the room. Daphne quickly flopped the coverlet over the book and pushed herself higher on her pillows. "Yes, Father?"

"You're still awake."

A statement, not a question, but Daphne nodded. "Yes, sir."

He came into the room, stopping at the carved footboard of the four-poster bed. With his hand curled around one turned corner post, he gave her a stern look. "Your mother says you refused dinner."

Daphne shrugged. "I wasn't hungry."

"This is becoming a bad habit, Daphne." Father didn't bother to soften his tone. "Avoiding eating will not affect Thomas Ollenburger."

Daphne flinched at the brusque mention of her dear heart's name. "I can't help it. When I try to swallow . . . it refuses to go down."

"Nonsense. You could eat if you wanted

to. Your behavior won't garner the attention you seek."

Daphne hid a bitter grin. His actions belied his words, because here he stood, in her bedchamber, showing her more attention than she could ever remember receiving in times past. She threw aside the covers and pulled herself from the bed. When she stood before him in her nightclothes, his face suddenly filled with red.

She gave herself a cursory glance, taking in the layers of white cotton backlit by the soft glow of her bedside lamp. Although the voluminous gown showcased nothing of what was underneath, it could be considered indecent. But Daphne didn't care. He had come to her, admonished her. Now he would listen.

"Father, when you came home so angry with Thomas —"

"Daphne, must we discuss —"

"Yes!" She clasped her hands together beneath her bodice. "Yes, we must. Until I am assured that Thomas will remain in Boston — remain in my life — I cannot eat or sleep. I'm weary of crying and feeling glum."

Her father lifted his face to the ceiling, his lips twisting into a grimace of displeasure.

She dashed forward and shook his arm.

"Please, Father. I know you think me melodramatic, but truly, my heart is breaking. Can't you tell me what transpired between the two of you? Why, if as you said, you kept him in your employ, has he continued to distance himself from me?"

Father pointed to the bay window of the room, where two chairs and a round table formed a seating area. Daphne interpreted the gesture as a command to sit, and although she preferred to remain standing, she decided her obedience might elicit greater cooperation from her father. On the way to the chairs, she lifted her dressing gown from the foot of the bed and slipped it over her nightgown.

Although Daphne sat, Father paced with his hands clasped behind his back. "Daphne, I know you are smitten with this boy, and I understand the reasoning."

Daphne smiled, envisioning Thomas's handsome face and tall, strong form.

"Yet this separation is no doubt for the best, for both of you."

Her smile quickly fled. "But why? You've spoken highly of Thomas. You have always praised his work ethic and appreciated his efforts at the newspaper. When he has visited the house as a guest, you've treated him warmly."

"Yes, I have," her father concurred, "but welcoming him as a guest and approving of him as an employee does not equate with accepting him as a son-in-law."

"But, Father!"

"Daphne, hush and listen." Father sat in the opposite chair, crossed his legs, and rested his laced fingers on his knee. He might have been in a business meeting instead of in the midst of a heart-to-heart talk with his child. "I have offered Thomas a position on the paper, which he would be wise to accept. It would be to my benefit, as well, to keep him in my employ because, as I've indicated previously, he performs his duties skillfully and is above reproach.

"However, he is not of our circle. Yes, he and Harry have become chums, as youth are prone to do, but they are men now. Men go their separate ways. Ollenburger cannot change his station in life any more than Harry can change his. Especially after Harry assumes leadership at the *Beacon,* it will be necessary to curtail any kind of friendship, or it will be detrimental to the overall workings of the newspaper."

Daphne stared at her father, his image swimming with the rush of tears. "Father, are you saying Thomas isn't good enough to continue a friendship with Harry?"

Father's mustache twitched briefly. "That is exactly what I am saying. The boyish alliance must end." He pointed at her. "And your infatuation with him must come to an end, as well. It can go no further than what I've allowed thus far. I presumed you would tire on your own of that overgrown bumpkin. I should have intervened long ago."

The tears spilled down Daphne's cheeks in a torrent of agony. "But I love him, Father!"

"Love isn't enough to bridge the differences between you." Father's matter-of-fact, emotionless tone crushed her. "After reading his rebuttals to my editorials concerning Watson's election, I am more convinced than ever that he will never fit into our world."

"Then why did you offer him a better position at the paper?"

Father's eyes widened in disbelief. "Daphne, I never allow personal feelings to interfere with what is of benefit to my business."

Miserably, Daphne bowed her head. *Of course.* She had hoped Father's decision to retain Thomas had been in response to her plea. She should have known it would have nothing to do with her. She longed to rail at him, to accuse him of cold-heartedness and insist he leave her room, but the ache in her throat made speech impossible.

Father reached across the small table and grazed Daphne's hand with the tips of his cold fingers. The touch, no doubt intended to offer comfort, instead sent tremors through Daphne's frame. "I must insist, Daphne, that you allow Thomas Ollenburger to go his separate way."

Daphne pressed her hands to the scrolled armrests of the chair and pushed herself upright. Her fickle legs quivered beneath her, but she clenched her fists and willed herself to remain upright. Looking steadily into her father's face, she dared voice a defiant question. "And what if . . . what if I choose to pursue him instead?"

Father's forehead pinched into a scowl of fury. He cupped her cheek with one hand, his fingers biting into the flesh beneath her jaw. "That, my daughter, would be a mistake."

Daphne waited until he left the room before she rubbed away the remembrance of his touch.

25

On Sunday morning, Daphne knelt on the floor of her bedroom with one eye shut, peering through her keyhole. A cramp throbbed in her neck, and her open eye felt dry and itchy, but she remained in the spot until Father and Mother passed her room and headed downstairs. Once she was sure they were in the breakfast room, she pushed to her feet, slipped her door open, and stepped into the hallway.

On tiptoe, she crept to Harry's room and tried the doorknob. She sucked in her breath. Locked! Crossing to the railing that overlooked the lower floor, she listened intently. The gentle clink of silverware against china plates let her know her parents were occupied. Treading as softly as possible, she returned to Harry's door, raised her knuckles, and rapped gently. She cringed at the sound, holding her breath until she heard Harry's cough.

Bending forward, she put her face next to his keyhole. "Harry?" She pressed her ear to the door and listened. No reply. Clenching her fists, she called again in a hoarse whisper: "Harry!"

Snuffles told her he'd awakened. The padding of feet sounded, and she jumped back as the door swung open. Her brother growled, "What do you want?"

She placed her hand over his mouth and shoved him back into the room. He pushed her hand aside, and she whacked her finger against her own lips to stifle the anticipated outburst.

"Harry, I need your help." Yesterday, while sequestered in her room, she'd plotted a way to see Thomas. On Sundays Father rarely left the house, so he wouldn't miss the barouche, but given his recently adopted habit of visiting her room, he might miss *her.* She needed someone to cover for her absence, and the only available person was Harry.

Harry ambled back to his bed and sat at the foot, his widespread knees creating a hammock of his nightshirt. He ran his hand down his face. "With what?"

Daphne sent one more furtive look down the hallway before closing his door and rushing to stand before him. "Getting into town. I need to see Thomas."

He groaned. "Oh, Daph . . ."

"Please, Harry." She made a steeple of her hands and pressed her fingertips to the underside of her chin.

"How will you —"

"Fred can take me in the barouche to Thomas's cottage. I know Father won't miss the horse or carriage, but I need you to keep him busy so he won't come looking for me."

Harry shook his head, yawning. "Won't work, Daphne."

She huffed. "Why not?"

"Because Tom won't be at his cottage."

"How do you know?"

Harry scratched his head, leaving his hair standing in disheveled ridges. "I talked to him Friday — stopped by the *Beacon* to see if he'd decided whether or not to start reporting for the paper. Also invited him to brunch —"

Daphne's heart skipped a beat.

"— but he refused because he had plans."

She swallowed the sorrow that threatened to transform into a surge of tears. "If you know his plans, then tell me. Where will he be? I will go to him, wherever he is!"

Harry eyed her with one dark brow arched higher than the other. "Even Mrs. Steadman's?"

341

Daphne took a step backward.

Glancing at the clock ticking atop his cherry highboy, he shrugged. "He's probably at church right now with Mrs. Steadman, and then he'll spend the afternoon with her."

Daphne deflated. She hadn't figured Thomas's foster grandmother into the situation. How could she speak privately with him at Mrs. Steadman's place? All her careful plotting shattered, she sank onto the bed next to Harry.

He put his arm around her. "Listen, Daphne, I know it's hard for you to accept, but Tom . . . he's not coming around anymore. He might not even stay in Boston. He told me he's praying about the job Father offered, but he isn't sure where God means for him to be."

Daphne stared, openmouthed.

Harry nodded. "That's right — he's waiting for *God* to tell him what to do. And if he doesn't take the job, he'll probably return to Kansas right away. So maybe you'd better —"

Daphne leaped from the bed and spun to face her brother. "I won't forget him! I can't! I-I love him too much to let him go!"

For several long seconds Harry sat silently with his forehead furrowed. At last he stood.

Throwing his arms outward, he said, "All right, Daph. I'll keep watch so Father and Mother don't discover your absence, but I think you're making a mistake." His mouth contorted, giving Daphne a glimpse of her brother's heartache. "You're setting yourself up to be hurt. For whatever reason, Tom doesn't want to associate with us anymore."

She raised her chin. "I'll not believe it until I hear it myself from his lips."

Thomas helped Nadine from the carriage, secured the door, and called, "Thank you, Clarence."

Clarence chirruped to the horse, and the carriage rolled away from the curb and around the corner, while Thomas tucked Nadine's hand into the bend of his elbow and they ambled slowly together along the winding rock pathway that led to the house.

He lifted his face to the sun, which hovered directly overhead. Although it was late October, the day was warm with a balmy breeze. Giving Nadine's hand a pat, he suggested, "Maybe we should take a walk after dinner. It won't be long now, and cold weather will keep you inside."

Nadine sighed. "Yes, I know. How I abhor the cold, damp months of winter. Yet without them, we would probably not appreciate the warmth of spring." She chuckled softly. "But then, I suppose that's the beauty of any hardship — it brings greater appreciation for the pleasant times."

Thomas agreed. He had a greater appreciation for worship and Bible-reading after his brief time of avoidance, and he felt certain his period of straying would strengthen his resolve to stay in step with God from now on. He unlocked Nadine's door and ushered her through. Before he pulled it closed behind him, however, the clatter of horse's hooves captured his attention. Who was coming down the street at such a reckless pace?

He turned to look, and to his surprise the Severt carriage stopped in front of Nadine's house. The driver hopped down and reached into the back. Thomas's breath caught when Daphne emerged from the carriage.

"What is she doing here?" Nadine sounded more puzzled than annoyed. "Did you invite her?"

His mouth too dry to allow speech, Thomas shook his head in response. They stood together and watched Daphne advance slowly up the pathway toward the house. How beautiful she looked in a matching bonnet and gown as boldly russet as an oak leaf before its tumbling fall to the ground. The closer she came, the harder it became for Thomas to breathe, as if his collar shrunk with each hesitant step of her slippered feet on the paving stones. By the time she stood before him with her hand held out in greeting, his breath came in little spurts that pumped his chest up and down.

Nadine touched his arm, and he jumped, sucking in a lungful of air. Heat rose from his neck, but the start seemed to restore him to normalcy. He took Daphne's slim, gloved hand and gave it a gentle squeeze.

"Daphne."

"Thomas." Her voice quavered, her dark eyes shimmering.

They stood dumbly, looking at one another without moving. A thousand unspoken questions paraded through Thomas's mind as he waited for her to explain her presence, but she stood mute, her gaze pinned to his. The light breeze tossed the tail of one satin bonnet ribbon over her shoulder, and Thomas automatically reached for it. But when Nadine cleared her throat, he dropped his hand and stepped back.

"Miss Severt," Nadine said, shifting slightly to stand in front of Thomas, "we hadn't planned for guests today; however, if you would care to come in, Mildred can quickly set another plate at the table."

Thomas gulped. Etiquette required the invitation, but how could he sit at the dinner table with Daphne and still keep his resolve to distance himself from her?

Nadine continued. "Your driver is welcome to join Clarence and Mildred in the kitchen, as well."

Daphne hid her hands in the folds of her gown. "I-I appreciate your kind invitation, ma'am, but I didn't intend to intrude upon a meal." She shifted self-consciously. "Truthfully, I did not realize the time. I really only wanted to see . . ." She swiveled her head to briefly glance at Thomas.

"Ah. Well." Nadine delicately cleared her throat once. "Then I shall ask Mildred to delay placing our dinner on the table and allow you a . . . moment or two." Subtle emphasis on the final words let Thomas know her patience would end shortly.

Thomas squeezed Nadine's elbow and whispered, "I'll just be a few minutes." He then stepped past her into the yard and gestured to the Common across the street. "Do you want to sit in the shade, Miss Severt?"

Daphne's brows pinched briefly, as if she experienced a stab of pain, but then she smiled and gave an eager nod. However, she didn't take his arm, as had become her habit during their time of courtship, and she sat well on one side of the carved bench with her skirts tucked close, leaving him more than enough room.

Thomas sat with his hands cupped over his knees and stared straight ahead. He disliked feeling uncomfortable in her presence, but he realized if he allowed himself to relax, he would too easily slip back into his past feelings for her. So he held himself aloof, distancing himself emotionally while a part of him longed to embrace her.

After several tense minutes of silence, she finally spoke. "I apologize for interrupting your dinner, but I could not wait one more minute to see you." Tears winked in her eyes. "When you said good-bye to me at the campaign headquarters, I couldn't imagine you truly meant *forever*."

Seeing the proof of her distress made his heart ache with regret. He would honor God, but he wished it didn't mean pain for Daphne. "I'm sorry I was terse with you that day. But . . . realities . . . became clear, and I knew there was no future for us. I thought it was best to end things quickly."

The tears that quivered on her lashes spilled, and it took all of Thomas's control not to wrap her in his arms.

"Best for you, perhaps, but not for me."

Daphne whisked her fingers over her cheeks, removing the trails of tears. "Thomas, my father's beliefs needn't come between us. He . . . he speaks harshly, but he would never cast me out." Did the tremble in her voice reflect uncertainty at her statement, or was it caused by emotion? "I am certain we could —"

"No, Daphne." Thomas held up one hand. "My decision to sever our relationship goes well beyond your father's beliefs." He angled his body into the corner of the bench to face her. Drawing in a deep breath, he prayed silently for guidance. "Do you remember the day I drove out to see you because my friend's mother passed away?"

Daphne looked remorseful. "Yes. I behaved badly. I couldn't bear the thought of you befriending another woman."

"You couldn't bear having anyone else take my attention," he corrected gently. He waited for her nod of agreement before continuing. "I should have realized the problem then, but I was too blinded by" — he gripped his knees so hard he would probably find bruises later — "your beauty. I wanted to please you, so I told you nothing else would come before you. I was wrong to tell you that. I was wrong to put you first."

Daphne shook her head slowly, the ribbons beneath her chin swaying with the movement. "But, Thomas, I put you first because I love you. D-don't you . . . love me?"

A lump of sorrow filled Thomas's throat. Yes, he loved her. As much as he'd prayed to be released, love for her still sent his heart tumbling in his chest. *Lord, help me!* He pinched his lips together, seeking an appropriate answer, and finally managed a hoarse reply. "Yes, Daphne. I do love you."

A smile broke out across her face. She put her hand over his. "Well, then —"

"But I love the Lord more."

Daphne's brow crunched, "I don't understand."

"I know you don't." He leaned his head back, looking at the sky through the leafless tree branches. "You and I . . . we grew up in two different worlds, Daphne."

"Then help me understand."

He didn't look at her, but her imploring tone roused his sympathy. "My pa raised me to serve God first, but I pushed Him aside and put you first. I knew I was wrong — my conscience tried to tell me — but I ignored it until the day I read your father's editorial about Watson. Then I couldn't ignore it anymore."

A small huff of displeasure left her lips.

"Thomas, you make too much of Father's opinion about social status. It's a common attitude. It needn't create a barrier between us."

"But it isn't just your father's opinion! It's yours, too." Turning to look at her, Thomas frowned. "You're wrong, Daphne. You're wrong in thinking one man is more important than another because of his skin color or how much money he has. In God's eyes, all men are equal, and it's through His eyes we need to view one another."

She stared at him as if seeing him for the first time. "Why did you never mention God to me before now?"

Guilt nearly buckled Thomas. Why hadn't he spoken of God to Daphne? He thought of his years in high school and college, the countless opportunities that had slipped by to share his faith, opportunities he disregarded in lieu of being accepted by his classmates. Oh, his friends all knew he attended services with Nadine, but he allowed them to assume he did it for her, not for any heartfelt desire of his own to be in church. How he must have grieved his heavenly Father by his deliberate silence. *Father, forgive me.*

His chin quivered, but he set his jaw, bringing his emotions under control. "I have no excuse. I should have spoken of God to you long ago, Daphne. I'm sorry."

Daphne rose slowly, as though her joints resisted movement. She stood beside the bench, her hands clasped, her eyes wide and brimming with tears. "But you *do* love me?"

Even though he knew it wasn't beneficial for either of them to reiterate the fact, he offered one slow nod.

"Yet you will allow God to keep us apart?"

He drew a long breath and released it, praying for the strength to do the right thing. "Yes, Daphne. I can't let my love for you take precedence over my love for God. I ignored what my father taught me, what I accepted as truth for myself when I was still a little boy, but I *will not* continue that pathway. The first commandment requires that nothing else, including an earthly relationship, come before God. I *can't* put you first . . ." His voice dropped to a hoarse whisper. "And you will never be happy in second place."

Thomas wondered if his words would cause her to dissolve into tears. But suddenly she jerked her shoulders back and raised her chin, fixing him with a look of betrayal. "I do not understand your sort of love — a love that can be relegated to second place. But you're right. All my life,

351

I've taken second place . . . to Harry or to my father's work. I thought you — I thought you were different from Father. I see I was wrong. So you're right. We . . . we're better off apart. Good-bye, T-Thomas."

A sob split his name, and Thomas jumped to his feet. But she dashed past him, crossed the street without pausing to look for traffic, and climbed into her carriage unaided. Thomas darted to the curb, but her driver slapped the reins onto the horse's back and the carriage lurched away.

26

Unwilling to return home immediately, Daphne instructed the driver to take a lengthy drive around town. He took her past the Botanical Gardens, now a dismal place with all the flowers trimmed and the trees nearly bare. When she glimpsed the swan boats, sitting in a lonely row along the pond's edge, she burst into tears. The memory of the day she and Thomas drifted gently along, his knee pressed against hers, her hand snug in the bend of his arm — the day she realized she had fallen in love — now taunted her. She'd trusted him with her heart, and he had plucked it out and thrown it back in her face, all because he was compelled to put his God first.

Finally, she leaned forward and choked out, "Take me home. At once!" Then she huddled in the corner of the carriage and covered her face with her hands while tears continued to roll. Had she truly believed seeing Thomas again would make her feel better? His ideas were so far away from the ideals with which she had been raised. Men, regardless of their station in life, equal to one another? Pure nonsense, Father would say — and she had to admit, in this case, Father was right. Why, anyone with sense knew that people were different. The colored lived one way, the poor another, and the rich yet another. Making them all equal would completely upset the balance of society. Clearly, someone had to take charge, and it only made sense that those with the most power and education should rule.

She stared out the open side of the barouche, frowning as she replayed more of her conversation with Thomas. As for placing God before anything or anyone else, Father proclaimed every man must look to himself first in order to be successful. How many times had she heard him lecture Harry, "Trust no one but yourself, son, and then you won't be disappointed." Well, today she had learned the truth of his statement. She'd trusted Thomas, and now she must bear the crushing weight of disappointment.

"Why? Why is God so important to Thomas that he would cast aside my love?" she asked aloud. The need to understand overwhelmed her. But how to find the answer? She couldn't ask Father — he would know she was asking because of Thomas. Neither Harry nor Mother would be any more knowledgeable than she was. The desire for answers made her lean forward and tap the driver on his shoulder.

"Yes, miss?" he called without turning around.

"Do you know where one would find information concerning God?"

He glanced briefly over his shoulder, his eyebrows nearly disappearing beneath the brim of his cap. "Why, yes, miss. In His holy book, the Bible."

Daphne leaned back, tapping her lips with her fingers. A Bible . . . Father had countless books lining the shelves in the library at home. He prided himself on the extensive collection. Could there be a Bible somewhere in that monstrous room?

Belinda whispered, "Sleep well, Malinda," and closed the door. She peeked into the older girls' room across the hallway from the room Malinda shared with little Lena, and gave a gentle reminder. "Girls, please stay quiet so Lena and Malinda can nap."

The girls, sitting cross-legged in the middle of their floor, looked up from their scattered paper dolls. "We'll be quiet," Abby promised, and Gussie bobbed her head in agreement.

With a smile, Belinda closed their door and crept downstairs. Summer and Peter sat side by side on the quilt-draped bench in the small front room, sharing a recent copy of the *Mennonite Review*. They looked so content together, Belinda hated to intrude, but she couldn't get to her small room without passing through the parlor. She tried to tiptoe around the corner unnoticed, but Summer set the periodical aside and called her name.

"Did Malinda eat her dinner?"

"A few bites." Belinda hovered in the doorway to the kitchen. "I left the plate for her in case she's hungry when she awakes."

Peter gestured toward Summer's embroidered chair in the corner, inviting Belinda to join them. After a moment of hesitation, she sank into the chair. A sense of contentment enveloped her, but she knew the feeling of warmth had more to do with the Ollenburgers' kind inclusion of her than the comfort of the chair's soft cushion.

"Should Malinda not be caught up on her sleep by now?" Peter asked his wife. "Since we bring her home last Friday, so much she has slept. She sleeps all through the days and nights and couldn't rise for worship services this morning. Maybe we should have the doctor to come see her."

"Oh no, don't go to that expense," Belinda protested. They'd already done so much, she couldn't allow them to pay fifty cents for a doctor's call. She assured her host, "It isn't uncommon for Malinda to sleep a lot — her weakened heart seems to require a great deal of rest. I'm sure her adventure of wandering the countryside for nearly a week wore her out." She shook her head, amazed. "I would never have imagined her walking as far as she did. The fire must have really frightened her."

"*Ja,* I expect it would frighten most anyone." Peter stroked his beard, looking at Belinda with a puzzled expression. "I have wondered what reason she gave for being in the attic."

Belinda sighed. "Malinda took to spending time up there after Mama died. I stored Mama's and Papa's clothes in the big Russian chest, so she would sit beside the chest and . . ." She shrugged. "Remember them, I suppose. Mama did the same thing after Papa died."

Summer's lips puckered. "What a dreary occupation."

Belinda forced her voice past the knot of

357

sorrow filling her throat. "I think sitting in the dark attic had a negative effect on Mama's heart. In a way, it's a relief that the clothes and trunk were ruined. Now Malinda doesn't have the opportunity to spend her time mourning over a box of clothes."

"And I am grateful she is now here, and she is safe," Peter added.

Closing her eyes briefly, Belinda offered a silent prayer of thanks that Malinda had been found unharmed. All thoughts of her sister being a burden had fled the moment of discovery. Only relief and gratitude filled her heart. She would keep Malinda close and, with the help of the Ollenburgers, lead her out of the deep mourning in which she had immersed herself.

Belinda pushed herself out of the chair. "While Malinda is resting, I believe I'll go to my room and write a letter to Thomas. I presume you'll have one ready to mail soon? Perhaps we could put them in one envelope and save the postage."

Peter nodded. "*Ja,* both Summer and me have written." He chuckled. "A very fat envelope our Thomas will get!" Suddenly a frown creased his brow. "I was glad he decided to spend time in prayer to seek God's will, but I wonder what choice he makes about the new job."

"I've been praying for him to know the right thing to do," Belinda said.

With an approving smile, Peter replied, "I thank you for your prayers. Prayers avail much." The smile faded to an expression of uncertainty. "But still I wonder . . ."

Summer took his hand. "Whatever he does, he'll choose wisely. Our son knows God's voice."

Peter's face relaxed. "*Ja, ja,* for sure he does. But" — a sheepish grin climbed his cheek — "is it all right if I hope he decides to come back here?"

Summer laughed lightly. "That's perfectly all right. A part of me wishes for that, too. But if he comes, what a full house we will have!"

Belinda's heart caught. Without another word, she turned and hurried to the little room off the kitchen. Sitting on Thomas's bed, she looked around the cramped space, suddenly realizing that if what they hoped for came true, she would be uprooted again. There wouldn't be room for her and Malinda if Thomas resided under this roof again.

She slumped forward, her heart torn in two. Although she had longed for Thomas's return to Kansas, she now realized seeing that desire fulfilled meant the loss of something that had come to mean a great deal to her. No longer would she be an honorary family member, but merely a neighbor and friend. Unless —

A hopeful thought brought her upright. If Thomas returned and — her cheeks blazed with heat — courted her, and they were to wed, she would always be an Ollenburger.

The powerful, selfish desire drove her to her knees. "Father, You have a good plan for me," she whispered against her laced fists. "If it's Your will, let the Ollenburgers . . . including Thomas . . . be a part of that plan. . . ."

A finger of sunlight reaching through a slit in his curtains awakened Thomas Monday morning. He rubbed his eyes, groaning as he fought to come fully awake. His night had been restless, the dreams confusing. Images of Daphne competed with those of people from Gaeddert, all calling out strange commands, most of which didn't make sense.

But one command — uttered by *Grossmutter* in Low German — still echoed through Thomas's head: *"Jie doone waut woare fullerene fäl bast."*

Do that which will accomplish the most good.

The most good . . . Thomas sat up, swung

his legs over the edge of the bed, and stared at the heavy curtains backlit by the morning sun. He'd prayed repeatedly for an answer to what to do next. Could the answer be within his great-grandmother's message? What would accomplish the most good — returning to Hillsboro, or remaining in Boston?

And suddenly, as if the answer was a puzzle piece dropping into place, he knew what would do the most good. Learning to be a news reporter. Expressing the truth in his articles. Articles that would reach the homes of many people.

Rising, he crossed to the window and flung the curtains wide. Sunlight flooded the room, filling him with a sense of purpose. "Ah," he whispered merrily, "the light of truth."

His spirits high, he washed, dressed, ate a quick breakfast of bread and jam, and then hailed a cab to go to the *Beacon.* He hoped Mr. Severt hadn't changed his mind about giving him the opportunity to report news stories for the paper. When the cab passed the telegraph office, Thomas called out, "Stop!"

The driver drew the horse to a halt.

"I need to send a telegram. Will you wait for me?" After the man nodded, Thomas dashed into the office. He'd promised to let Pa know what he decided. If he knew his father, Pa'd be stewing. It was best to inform him in the quickest manner. He dictated a straightforward message: "Staying to report the truth. Long letter later. Love to all. Thomas."

He smiled the remainder of the way to the newspaper office. The assurance that came from answering the call on one's heart was invigorating! His arms tingled from excitement. Or maybe, he chuckled to himself, the nip of the October breeze sent the prickle of gooseflesh over his arms. Whatever the cause, he felt alert and ready to the take the publishing world by storm.

"To the top floor," he instructed the elevator operator, then whistled as the man tugged the cables that set the car in motion. He waved to the errand boy as he strode down the hallway. Outside Severt's door, he took a moment to straighten his collar, smooth the front of his jacket, and square his shoulders. Then he raised his fist and gave two blunt thumps to the door's casing.

"Come in."

Thomas opened the door and entered, crossing quickly to stand in front of his boss's desk. The man looked at him without speaking, his face expressionless. Thomas met Severt's gaze directly and said, "I'd like to become a reporter."

A sly smile formed on Severt's face, but he smoothed his finger over his mustache, erasing the smirk. He rose. "Good choice." Rounding his desk, he passed Thomas, marched to his open door, and bellowed down the hall. "Boy! Get Pardue up here immediately!" He returned to his desk and sat, waving his hand at the chair on the opposite side of his desk. "Sit."

Thomas followed his direction, perching on the chair's edge with his hands braced on his thighs. Eagerness to get started made his leg muscles twitch.

"For now, you'll remain in your office. I will still give you the occasional editorial for review since I don't plan to fill your current position until I see how well you do as a reporter."

"That's fine, sir." Thomas had expected a period of testing.

"I'm putting you under the tutelage of Dean Pardue. He's been with the *Beacon* since the first issue of its release nearly twenty-five years ago, and he knows the ins and outs of reporting better than any man in Massachusetts. I'd wager you won't find a better teacher on a university campus."

At that moment, a clatter of footsteps

363

intruded. The errand boy rushed in, followed by a tall, reed-thin man with gray, overgrown muttonchop whiskers and a sparse tuft of gray hair shooting toward his forehead from his nearly bald scalp. The boy pointed mutely at the man and then, his mission complete, spun and hustled back out.

Severt gave a lazy nod. "Good morning, Pardue."

Thomas shot to his feet. *This* was Dean Pardue? Thomas had previously seen the man in the halls but assumed by his unkempt appearance that he performed janitorial chores. This scarecrow-like man didn't fit Thomas's expectation of a seasoned reporter. He hoped his face didn't show the surprise he felt.

The man's sharp, nearly black eyes settled on Thomas. "This the boy you told me about?"

Severt gave a brusque nod. "He's the one."

Thomas shook his tutor's hand. Although they stood eye to eye, he outweighed the older man by at least a hundred pounds. Despite his fragile appearance, however, Dean Pardue possessed the ability to make Thomas squirm with his steady, seeking gaze.

The handshake complete, Pardue stepped

back and looked Thomas up and down. The unabashed appraisal made Thomas's neck burn, but he stood with his shoulders square and his chin up, refusing to cower beneath the inspection.

At the conclusion of his perusal, a smile formed behind Pardue's bushy whiskers. He nodded in Severt's direction. "Yup. I reckon he'll do."

Severt ordered, "Dean, take Ollenburger along on your rounds today. This week, he'll observe only." Swinging his gaze to Thomas, he barked, "Ollenburger, watch and listen. At the end of the week, if Dean thinks you're ready, we'll let you use his notes to produce an article. No by-line, though. That'll come when you're on your own."

Thomas decided he'd ask Pardue what was meant by "no byline" later and simply nodded.

"All right, then. Go."

Pardue headed for the door, and Thomas trotted after him. The man's long-legged stride reminded Thomas of a stork's gait. He imagined Pardue left a lot of people behind, but Thomas had no trouble matching him pace for pace.

They stepped into the elevator, and Pardue reached inside his jacket to remove a small pad of paper and a well-gnawed pencil. He stuck the unsharpened end of the pencil in his mouth and patted his palm with the pad. "Gonna be a busy couple weeks, boy," Pardue warned, speaking around the stub of pencil.

"Oh?" Thomas's heart rate increased in anticipation. "Are we working on a big story?"

"Biggest one in four years," Pardue replied. He popped the pencil out long enough to grin. "The campaign, boy. We're covering the presidential election."

27

"Daphne, why are you hiding in here?" Mother's fretful voice interrupted Daphne's reading.

Daphne had thought the fringed chaise tucked into the window-surrounded alcove of the library a comfortable, secluded spot. Since Sunday afternoon she had spent every free moment reading the Bible she had found high on a shelf, tucked behind two other books.

Daphne repeated the statement she'd used yesterday in response to Mother's frustrated query. "I am reading."

"Still?"

At Mother's shocked tone, Daphne snapped the Bible closed over her thumb, but she didn't shift from her reclining position. "Yes, Mother, *still.*"

Mother sniffed, folding her arms and tapping her toe. "I would think you would have had your fill of that by now. Surely there is something else you could do with your time."

Daphne shrugged, riffling the page edges with her thumb. "It's not as if I have any pressing needs to which to attend." She went on in a pensive tone. "I haven't a job, or a home of my own to oversee, or even a hobby that requires my attention each day. My life, Mother, is frightfully dull . . . and without purpose."

Mother pursed her lips tightly and glared down at Daphne. Her toe continued its incessant, annoying tap — one of Mother's many nervous habits. "So you intend to liven your existence by secluding yourself in the corner of the library and reading the days away."

Flopping the Bible open, Daphne said, "Yes."

A sigh that spoke volumes came from Mother's lips, but Daphne chose to ignore it. When she returned her focus to the book in her lap, Mother spun with a swirl of skirts and left the room, sliding the pocket doors closed behind her. Daphne smiled in satisfaction, bent her knees to prop up the Bible, and picked up where she had left off.

This book, she had discovered, contained a confusing mosaic of stories, genealogies, and advice. When she'd finally located it

Sunday afternoon, she had flipped through, reading random bits here and longer passages there. Unable to grasp meaning by the slipshod method, she had decided it would be best to start at the beginning and read through to the end.

She had been reading for four days, whenever she could sneak away, and even though she hadn't yet discovered the answer to the question she sought — *Why is God so important to Thomas?* — she admitted some of the stories were intriguing. Floods and giants, wars and escaping slaves, good and evil kings, and God-bestowed blessings and curses. Some of the stories even reminded her of the fairy tales Mother had read to her when she was small.

She admitted little understanding of the rules the people followed — festivals and monument-building and sacrificing animals to experience pardon for breaking laws. A shudder shook her as she considered shedding the blood of a helpless lamb or pigeon. And to do it again and again to cover each infraction! How could the people bear to perform such an atrocious act against innocent animals?

And yet there was the other side, the tender side . . . God's protection, God's provision, God's endless mercy toward people who, quite often, seemed bent on neglecting Him. God required much of His people, but He also gave much to His people. Was that why Thomas put God first? Because he didn't want to emulate the foolish Israelites who consistently tried the patience of God and reaped His judgment? Could it be fear of judgment that motivated him?

The Bible was divided into two disproportionate halves — the Old Testament and the New Testament. A quick peek revealed she was close to halfway through the Old Testament. By the end of the week — if people left her alone and let her read — she hoped to be through the Old Testament and would be able to start fresh with the New Testament next week.

An odd rush of excitement swept over her. She pondered its source but could find no reason why accomplishing the entire read-through of this book was so exciting. Yet she couldn't deny the eagerness to proceed. At least, she concluded, reading took her mind off of her aching heart. She shifted to get more comfortable against the mound of pillows behind her back, crossed her ankles, and resumed reading.

"Practice time, Tom." Dean Pardue plopped

a stack of nearly illegible notes onto Thomas's desk. "Pick 'em apart, organize 'em, then write me four comprehensive, fact-filled paragraphs." He pointed a wiry finger at Thomas. "No opinions in there. This isn't a place to insert your viewpoint. Just *facts*." The man strode out of the office.

Thomas set to work without comment. Over the past few days, he had learned Dean Pardue was a tougher taskmaster than Mr. Severt had been. Pardue could nitpick and chide and criticize until Thomas was ready to throw the pages in the man's face and exclaim he didn't want to be a reporter after all. But one thing kept him silent and working — the desire to do that which would accomplish the most good.

If he could prove to Severt and Pardue that he had what it took to be a respected reporter, they might let him write one article about the presidential race prior to Election Day. With that opportunity, he would lay out the facts he had been collecting on his own concerning Thomas Watson of the Populist Party.

Politics often involved a game of one-upmanship, the goal being to make one's own candidate appear better than all others. For some candidates, the strategy included slinging dirt at the opponent. Thomas knew from experience an eyeful of dust hindered vision. So slinging dirt, he concluded, kept constituents from seeing the slinger's faults. He didn't much care for the practice, having been taught to be truthful in all circumstances.

"As for me," he mumbled as he drew an arrow from one scribbled note to another, indicating the placement of the information in his final draft, "if given the chance, I'll not fling dirt, but I'll certainly muddy the waters for some who think they know it all."

He considered the personal testimonies he'd gathered concerning Watson's treatment of specific groups of people. Watson had little tolerance for anyone whose religious denomination or skin color differed from his own. A person with such a limited circle of acceptance had no business pursuing leadership for a country whose population included a rainbow of skin tones and which proclaimed religious freedom. If Watson became the United States' next president, it could be detrimental to the unity of the country.

Although Thomas still approved the stance of the Populist Party concerning the Grange and its support of the farming community, he could not approve the party's chosen candidate. He could not stand quietly by and allow wrong to have its way.

He was breaking with Mennonite tradition by involving himself in political issues, and his father would frown if he knew what Thomas was doing. He might be an adult, but displeasing Pa still gave him pause. Even so, he needed to follow his own conscience this time, and his conscience clearly directed him to speak the truth about Watson before voters entered the booths on November 8. Less than two weeks away . . .

Suddenly his heart skittered to thoughts of Daphne, and the plans he had made to ask for her hand at the close of the campaign. The deep ache of missing her hadn't departed, although he had an element of peace — he knew he'd done the right thing by withdrawing from his relationship with an unbeliever.

Pa had wisely waited for Summer to recognize her need of a Savior before declaring his love for her. Thomas, as his father modeled, would follow the biblical admonition to avoid being unequally yoked. But his desire to shed the light of truth concerning God's love for Daphne, as well as God's instruction for her to love her neighbor as herself, hadn't dimmed. When the campaign ended, he wouldn't ask for her hand, but he would sit down and share his heart with her.

Lord, soften her heart in preparation to receive the truth.

But first, the campaign. He had to prove his abilities, and quickly, in order to be allowed to write his own article prior to Election Day. Writing the article he planned could very well get him fired from his reporting position before it even got started, but he would face the risk for the sake of truth.

Knowing time was of the essence, he set aside thoughts of Daphne and focused on Pardue's notes concerning the efforts to bolster the West Boston Bridge. He'd write a fact-based article that would bring words of praise from Pardue's lips, or expire trying.

As Belinda and Summer washed and dried the dinner dishes, Malinda sat with Abby and Gussie and showed them how to add and subtract by using a homemade beaded abacus. Earlier in the day she had used the same device to teach little Lena to count to ten.

Belinda's delight in observing the activity was twofold. Malinda's willingness to leave her room and interact with the Ollenburgers indicated a lifting of her deep depression. And listening to her sister's soft, patient voice as she directed the little girls let Belinda know her sister possessed kindness.

Summer stepped away from the dry sink to stack clean dishes on the shelf. On her return, she gave Malinda's shoulder a squeeze and said, "You would make a wonderful teacher, Malinda."

Malinda glanced up. "Oh, I don't know . . ." Then she tipped her head, her expression pensive. "At one time I considered getting a certificate for teaching, but my beau discouraged it. Then I got sick and . . ." She broke off and lowered her head.

Belinda's heart turned over at her sister's admission. Might Malinda's bitterness be the result of squashed hopes and dreams? The thought made Belinda all the more determined to keep bitterness from taking root. Her life was far from what she wanted right now — living under a neighbor's roof rather than caring for her own home, having to accept Thomas's decision to remain in Boston, taking care of Malinda instead of caring for a husband and children — but if she allowed regret to harden her heart, she might never gain her dreams. Who wanted to be around a bitter, unhappy person?

Summer's eyes expressed sympathy, but

when she spoke her voice sounded more matter-of-fact than sad. "You could still become a teacher. There is always a need."

Malinda shook her head. "No. I wouldn't have the patience for a roomful of rowdy children." A slight smile lifted the corners of her lips. "It's easy here because your girls are so well-behaved."

At that moment Gussie, who had leaned over for Abby to whisper in her ear, suddenly lunged and pinched her sister on the arm. Abby screeched a protest and reached to retaliate.

Summer dove between the pair. "Girls, I'm ashamed of you! Gussie, you know better than to deliberately hurt someone. Why did you pinch Abby?"

Gussie's lower lip poked out. "She said Malinda likes her better 'cause she can add higher than me!"

Belinda's cheeks twitched. How did Summer manage to remain stern in the face of such amusing naughtiness? And who would imagine children squabbling over who Malinda liked best?

"That's not an excuse, Gussie." Summer put her hands on her hips. "You must apologize to your sister."

Gussie hunched her shoulders, reminding Belinda of a turtle trying to shrink into its shell. "I'm sorry."

Belinda wouldn't have called the child's words a heartfelt apology, but Summer apparently decided it would do. She turned to Abby. "And, Abby, you need to apologize, too."

Abby gawked openmouthed at her mother. "I didn't pinch!"

"No, but you did provoke your sister with an unnecessary, untrue comment."

Abby turned to Malinda. "You *do* like me best, don't you, Malinda?"

"I . . . I . . ." Malinda looked helplessly from Summer to Belinda.

Belinda came to her rescue. "Malinda loves you all the same, Abby. It wouldn't be fair to love someone more based on what they can do, now would it? That would mean Malinda loves your mother more than you because your mama knows how to cook and sew and iron and —"

"But I'm too little for all of that!" Abby protested. Plump tears formed in the corners of her eyes.

Belinda melted. She moved behind Abby, wrapped her arms around the little girl, and rested her cheek against Abby's tousled blond curls. "Of course you are. And that's why we don't base love for each other on achievement. We love you just because you're you, the same way we love Gussie for just being Gussie and Lena for just being Lena. Right, Malinda?"

Malinda nodded slowly, her face serious.

Gussie scooted out of her chair and raced around the table to Malinda's side. Throwing her arms around Malinda's neck, she said, "And we love you just for being you, Malinda, even if you don't smile very much."

Belinda gasped and reached mutely for Summer. How would Malinda react to Gussie's innocent yet bold statement? The room seemed to hold its breath, waiting for Malinda's response. And when it came, it brought an air of relieved celebration.

Still within the circle of Gussie's thin arms, Malinda burst into laughter. She wrapped her arms around the little girl and scooped her into her lap. Rocking the child back and forth, she continued to laugh against Gussie's hair.

Belinda couldn't remember the last time she'd heard her sister laugh. For a few startled moments, she and Summer stared at each other, and then in unison they joined Malinda in hoots of amusement. Abby and Gussie added their giggles, and even Peter came from the parlor to investigate. Although no one could stop laughing long enough to explain the reason behind their outburst, he threw back his head and laughed, too.

But then, as suddenly as it had begun, Malinda's laughter transitioned to wracking sobs. Gussie pulled away, her little forehead lined in confusion. Malinda covered her face with her hands, but tears slipped between her fingers.

Gussie slipped from Malinda's lap as Summer knelt beside the chair and put her arm across Malinda's heaving shoulders. "Malinda, dear, what is it? What's wrong?"

A moan came from behind Malinda's hands. Her distress frightened the little girls, and they cowered at their father's side. He herded them into the parlor, giving Summer, Belinda, and Malinda privacy.

Belinda sat in the chair next to her sister and pried Malinda's hands down. "Malinda, please tell us what's wrong. Why are you crying?"

Malinda gaped at Belinda, her tear-filled eyes wide. "D-do you . . . love me, Belinda?"

Belinda stared back. How could Malinda question for even one moment that Belinda loved her? Hadn't she cared for her, worked to provide for her, given up her own wants and desires to make sure Malinda's needs were met?

Then she realized she had never told her sister how she felt. . . .

"Oh, Malinda . . ." Belinda reached out and drew her sister's head to her shoulder. Growing up, how often had she wished Mama or Papa would tell her she was loved by them? More times than she could accurately recall. The Bible advised to treat others as you wanted to be treated. She would no longer withhold the words from her sister. Stroking Malinda's hair, Belinda whispered, "You're my sister. I love you, Malinda. Very much."

A shudder shook Malinda's frame, but she didn't pull away. For long moments they sat, the younger cradling the older, with two hearts beating in rhythm. At long last Malinda sat up. She lifted her skirt to mop the tears from her cheeks, and then she cupped Belinda's face between her hands.

"I love you, too, Belinda." She pressed her palms to the table and struggled to her feet. Then, with short, hesitant steps, she made her way out of the kitchen and around the corner. The soft thud of her feet against the stair treads let Belinda know she headed to the bedroom. When the click of a door signaled Malinda's return to her room, Belinda looked at Summer.

The amazement in the older woman's eyes

surely mirrored Belinda's. Summer took Belinda's hand. "I believe we need to offer a prayer of thanks. We've just witnessed a wonderful breakthrough."

Belinda willingly bowed her head and poured out her gratitude for the time of sweet bonding with her sister. When she headed to her small room, she felt certain things would be different with Malinda from now on — better, sweeter.

But in the morning, when Belinda went upstairs to get Lena from her crib and wake Malinda for breakfast, Malinda's bed was empty. Her sister was gone. Again.

28

"I know where she is." Belinda slipped her arms into a knitted sweater and headed for the back door. "If I can borrow Daisy again, I'll go get her."

Peter stepped forward, his hand outstretched. "Better to go in the wagon. Wait — I will take you."

Belinda considered his offer. Malinda was her responsibility, and Peter would have to miss most of a morning's work to transport her to the little house the men of Gaeddert had built for Summer a decade ago. Yet she saw the sense of his suggestion — both she and Malinda on Daisy the last time she had retrieved her sister had made for an uncomfortable ride. Giving a nod of agreement, she said, "Thank you."

She and Peter rode without speaking. Her eyes remained on the rumps of the plodding oxen, but Peter seemed fascinated by the raucous geese making their journey across the cloudless sky. She was relieved that Peter found contentment in silence. Conversation would have been difficult.

Why, after their time of bonding last evening, had Malinda run away again? If someone needed escape, surely that person was Belinda. Her life had been one upheaval after another since Papa's death. Yet, despite being cared for and assured that she was loved, Malinda had chosen to run off. Varying emotions tumbled through Belinda — anger, frustration, bewilderment, sympathy. When she found Malinda, she would insist her sister explain herself.

Though Malinda was the older of the pair, her behavior indicated a complete lack of maturity and responsibility. Regardless of the awkwardness of taking her older sister to task, Belinda wouldn't mince words when they were face-to-face. She had enough concerns without Malinda adding unnecessary worries to the list.

Peter called to the oxen, guiding them to make the turn into the lane leading to Summer's empty house. As she had expected, Malinda was there, sitting on the steps of the wraparound porch, watching the lane as if she expected someone. When the wagon rumbled close, she pushed to her feet and stood, unsmiling, one hand raised to shield her eyes from the bright morning sun. On the ground at the base of the steps sat the little chest Belinda had seen in their attic.

Belinda touched Peter's sleeve. "Will you give me some time alone with my sister, please?"

He nodded solemnly and intoned, "Whoa," bringing the oxen to a halt.

Belinda leaped over the side of the wagon and raced to Malinda. Despite her intention to berate her sister, she found herself instead enveloping Malinda in a hug. Malinda's arms wrapped tightly around Belinda, and she pressed her cool cheek to Belinda's hair.

"I'm sorry if I worried you," Malinda said, her voice tired and raspy, "but I knew you would come. I needed you to come."

Belinda pulled back. She brushed Malinda's straggly hair away from her face. "Why?"

Taking Belinda's hand, Malinda sat on the lowest step and tugged Belinda down beside her. She reached into her pocket, withdrew a brass key, and inserted it into the tiny lock on the front of the chest. But then, instead of opening the box, she turned to Belinda, shamefaced.

"Belinda, please forgive me. Shortly before Papa died, he gave me this chest. He told me it would secure our futures, but I was . . ." Tears rolled down her thin cheeks, and her shoulders heaved with one sob. "I was selfish. I kept it hidden, because I thought if I showed it to you, you would take the contents and leave me."

Belinda's heart thumped mightily. She licked her dry lips, taking care to remain focused on her sister's face rather than letting her attention drop to the box.

"I hid it here after the fire, in the cellar. I knew no one would find it there, and I planned to keep it for myself. But when you told me last night that — that you l-love me, I knew I couldn't hide it from you anymore." Malinda's trembling chin and tear-filled eyes begged Belinda to offer understanding.

Belinda caught Malinda's hand. "I forgive you, Malinda. But . . . what is in the box?"

Slowly Malinda turned the key. A tiny *click* sounded, and Malinda lifted the lid. Neat stacks of paper money and several official-looking certificates came into view. Belinda gasped. She remembered the financial worries that plagued Mama's final days. How different things would have been if Malinda hadn't hidden this box away! Her astonishment erupted in one word: "Malinda!"

Tears rained down Malinda's cheeks and

plopped into her lap. "I-I'm so sorry!"

Sympathy replaced the shock. Belinda once more enfolded her sister in her arms. Malinda's insecurity was the root of her deceptive behavior. Losing her fiancé, her health, and her anchor — Papa — had created a fear of abandonment. Although Belinda still wished her mother's last days could have been less anguished, she did understand her sister's choice.

Against Malinda's musty hair, she whispered, "It's all right. I'm not angry."

With a shuddering gulp, Malinda pulled free. "It's yours now, Belinda. All of it. I . . . I don't want it. Not one penny."

"Oh, but —"

"In addition to Papa's cash savings, there are several surety bonds that'll mature over the next several years. Maybe now you won't have to work so many jobs." Malinda cupped Belinda's face between her palms. "Please take the box and its contents, Belinda, with my sincerest apology."

Belinda shook her head, dislodging her sister's hands. "I can't! Papa gave it to you."

"But I want to give it to you!"

"And you need money because —"

Malinda raised her hand. "I know I can't work and earn a wage. Not like others. But . . ." Suddenly she lowered her head and began toying with the folds of her skirt.

A large shadow fell across the women's feet and covered the chest. Belinda looked up into Peter's concerned face.

"Malinda, you are all right?" His deep voice held no impatience, only compassion.

Malinda kept her head down.

Belinda answered for her. "She's fine, Peter. I'm sure she's tuckered from her long walk, so if you could help her into the wagon . . ."

"Of course." Peter stepped forward.

"No." Malinda scuttled sideways on the step, distancing herself from both Belinda and Peter. "I'm not going back to your house."

Peter's brows came down, but he spoke gently. "You cannot stay here. There is no means of caring for yourself all alone out here."

Malinda shook her head fiercely, her hair flying about her pale face. "I'm not staying here, either. I just needed Belinda to come for the chest so I didn't have to carry it back to town."

Belinda looked in confusion from Peter to Malinda again. "Malinda, you must come with us."

But Malinda turned stubborn, jutting her chin defiantly. "I am not a child! I will not be forced to go somewhere against my will!"

Belinda rose, tangling her hands in her skirt to keep from reaching for her sister. "But, Malinda, you have to come back with us. Our house is gone. You can't stay here or in Gaeddert — not by yourself. There's nowhere else for you to go."

Malinda pushed to her feet. She swayed slightly, but she remained upright, her head held at an arrogant angle. "There *is* somewhere else for me to go." Taking a deep breath, she fixed Belinda with a firm look. "I am going to the Industrial School and Hygiene Home for the Friendless."

The home outside of Hillsboro for the orphaned and destitute? Malinda chose that over living with the Ollenburgers? Belinda's shoulders slumped. "Oh, Malinda . . ."

"Not because I am friendless." Malinda continued as if Belinda hadn't spoken. "I know I have friends . . . the Ollenburgers have proven that."

Peter and Belinda exchanged a quick look. Belinda said, "Then why —"

"Because I can be of service there." Malinda took two stumbling steps forward, catching Belinda's hands. "Don't you see? There are children at the home. Children who could benefit from an education. I know I can't do hard labor — not with my weak heart — but I could teach. Couldn't I, Belinda?"

For the first time, Malinda's resolve seemed to waver. Belinda squeezed her sister's hands. "Of course you could. You would be excellent." She spun to include Peter. "Don't you agree?"

"*Ja.*" Peter nodded, his face serious. "I have seen you with my girls. A very *goot* teacher you would be. But . . ." He sucked in his lips for a moment, his thick brows low. "Does the home have need for more teachers?"

Malinda worried her lower lip with her teeth. "I . . . I assumed they would."

Peter put his hand on her shoulder. "If you like, we will drive out there and ask."

"Now?"

"Now," Peter confirmed. "Come." He closed the lid on the chest and lifted it easily. Malinda took Belinda's hand and followed him to the wagon. Peter bypassed Hillsboro and drove straight to the large stone building a few miles outside of town.

When the oxen heaved to a stop in the yard, Malinda said, "Please, Belinda and Mr. Ollenburger, stay here and allow me to make the inquiries."

Although a part of Belinda wanted to argue against Malinda's idea, she swallowed her protest and nodded in agreement. She watched Malinda enter the big building and then waited, fidgeting on the seat beside Peter. It seemed hours passed before Malinda emerged, a triumphant smile on her face.

"They can use me," she exclaimed as Peter helped her into the wagon's bed. "If someone will drive me out tomorrow, I can start work immediately."

Happy tears filled Belinda's eyes at her sister's confident, enthusiastic tone. She gave Malinda a hug and offered a husky, "Congratulations, Malinda. I'm proud of you." Another thought followed as Peter turned the wagon back toward Hillsboro: What would she do now that she didn't need to take care of Malinda?

Pardue tossed Thomas's article onto the desk, hooked his elbow over the ladder back of the wooden chair that usually sat in the corner of Thomas's small office, and offered a pleased grin. "You're comin' along, Ollenburger. I marked a few word choice changes, and the third paragraph slanted toward your own opinion about the ease of using the current voting ballot, but for the most part . . . yup, you're comin' along."

Thomas decided "coming along" was a significant step up from Pardue's normally lengthy list of suggested improvements. He picked up the article and glanced over the penciled changes. Much fewer than he expected. Satisfied, he nodded. He looked forward to the day when Pardue would simply hand him back his work with no suggestions for improvement, but for today, seeing only a half dozen scrawled comments let him know he was making progress toward becoming a full-fledged reporter.

Riffling the edge of the page with his thumb, he rocked in his chair and stared thoughtfully across the desk into Pardue's whisker-dusted face. Would this be a good time to show his mentor the article that had kept him up late the past several nights? He valued Pardue's opinion, and he knew the man would be able to offer advice on making the article the strongest it could be. Besides that, if the article were going to make it into the paper in time to impact any voters, it needed to happen now. Only four more issues and Election Day would be upon them.

Pardue must have sensed Thomas's thoughts, because he leaned forward and said, "You have something weighing on your mind, boy?"

"Well . . ."

"Some writin', maybe?"

Thomas pulled his lips to the side, one eyebrow raised high.

Pardue laughed and stretched out his bony hand. "Hand it over."

For a moment, Thomas hesitated. "Can . . . can we keep it between the two of us?"

Pardue's brows raised in obvious surprise. He smoothed his hand over his balding scalp before giving a brief, serious nod. "What are you up to?"

Without answering, Thomas slid open his desk drawer and removed the pad of paper he carried back and forth from his cottage to the newspaper office. He peeled back the top layers, exposing the article titled simply, "Watson." For a moment he bit down on the inside of his cheek, wondering at the wisdom of showing the article to Pardue. Although they'd spent part of every day for the past week and a half together, and although Thomas trailed the man as he interviewed people about the campaign, he had yet to ascertain Pardue's political stance.

"Well, what is it?"

The impatient bite in Pardue's tone forced Thomas to act. He thrust his arm forward, shoving the pad across the desk. The man snatched it up, flopped the pad around, and began to read.

Thomas sat, unmoving, and watched Pardue's eyes rove from left to right all the way from the top to the bottom of the page. Pardue's forehead crinkled and his lips poked out in the now-familiar expression of deep concentration. Without breaking pace he snapped the page over the top of the pad and continued until he reached the end of the second page — the end of Thomas's editorial on why Watson would not be an appropriate choice for the United States' next president. He shot Thomas a quick, unreadable look, and then he flipped the first page back and read the entire article a second time.

Thomas battled squirming while he waited. The man's expression revealed nothing of his thoughts, no matter how hard Thomas peered into his face. But when he finished, he grimaced. Thomas's stomach turned over in trepidation.

Pardue slapped the pad onto Thomas's desk with a mighty *smack*. "You've been digging pretty deep, haven't you?"

Unable to determine by his tone whether he approved or disapproved of Thomas's editorial, Thomas shrugged in response.

"I gotta tell you, you organized that well. Good balance of facts and subsequent opinion based on the facts. There's enough passion in the lines to light a fire under the most apathetic reader." The man whistled through his teeth. "But if you're thinking Severt will let you publish that in his newspaper . . . you better think again."

Thomas shot forward, propping his elbows on the desk. "He's printed other editorials about the various presidential hopefuls. Why wouldn't he let this one go in, too?"

Pardue shook his head, his eyes sympathetic but his expression firm. "You know as well as I do, boy, that Severt wants to see Watson in office. He'll never allow one negative word about his man. Not in *his* paper."

Thomas blew out his breath in frustration. "But that's not good reporting. Withholding truth just because you don't like the truth?"

Pardue's skinny shoulders rose and fell in an unconcerned shrug. "Happens all the time. Editor of his own newspaper gets to decide what goes in and what stays out."

"But" — Thomas's voice rose with fervor — "a paper should be inclusive, not exclusive when it comes to reporting information of merit."

Pardue grinned. "You got strong feelings on this."

"Yes, I do." Thomas flopped back in his chair again, the springs protesting the force of his movement.

"Well, boy . . ." Pardue unfolded his long frame from the chair and peered down his nose at Thomas. "There's only one surefire way to get that article into print, far as I can see."

Thomas sat up attentively. "How?"

Pardue winked. "Start your own newspaper." He turned and ambled out of the room.

29

Daphne read the Bible's final words aloud:
" 'He which testifieth these things saith,
Surely I come quickly. Amen. Even so,
come, Lord Jesus. The grace of our Lord
Jesus Christ be with you all. Amen.' "

With a sigh, she closed the book, rested
both palms on the worn black cover, and let
her eyes drift shut. She whispered, " 'The
grace of our Lord Jesus Christ be with you
all . . .' " She swallowed the lump that filled
her throat, realizing after all she had learned
about Jesus Christ, she did want Him to be
with her.

Popping her eyes open, she rose from the
chaise. Reverently she placed the Bible on
the brocade seat and crossed to the window.
Peering across the grounds, now rosy from
the setting sun, she considered the reason
for her absorption in the Scriptures. She
sought an answer to one question: Why did
Thomas put God first? And in the reading,

she believed she'd found the answer: Because God had put mankind first.

God, in His infinite love, had allowed His Son to become the perfect sacrifice for sin. For *her* sin, even. The idea that someone would die to take her place created a spiral of longing that Daphne couldn't contain. Tears sprang into her eyes, and she pressed her open palms to the window, her gaze on the wisp of purple clouds in the magenta sky. "I want to believe You love me enough to give Yourself up for me."

Had anyone ever loved Daphne that much? So much that they set aside their own needs in deference to hers? No, no one. But according to the book she'd just read, God had done exactly that.

Thomas, apparently, had been taught from the Bible since boyhood. As she'd read, often she had thought, *Yes, I've seen Thomas behave in that very manner,* or *I've heard Thomas speak similar words of admonition.* The things she admired most about him — his gentleness, his honesty, his work ethic — were very much like the character of Jesus.

Her heart pounded, and she spun back to the Bible, flipping pages to locate one of her favorite parts. She read aloud, " 'Behold, I stand at the door, and knock: if any man hear my voice, and open the door, I will come in to him.' " Pressing trembling fingers to her lips, she rasped, "Oh, dear Jesus, I do want You to come in, but I don't know how to open the door —"

"Daphne?"

With a start, she spun toward the library doors.

Harry stood in the opening. "I realize the hour is growing late, but I'm going to drive in to town and see if there are any things I can do at headquarters. Would you like to ride in with me?"

If Harry transported her to town, perhaps she could hail a cab to Thomas's cottage and ask him the question that plagued her heart: *How do I invite Jesus into my life?*

Harry's face crumpled into a worried scowl. "Daph? Are you all right?"

She snatched up the Bible and flew across the glossy wood floor to her brother. "I'd like to go. But I need to change my clothes. Can you wait?"

He glanced down the length of her rumpled gown and gave a nod. "Yes, but hurry."

She scurried past him and called over her shoulder, "I shan't be more than five minutes."

She was ready in four by choosing the first

frock her hand fell upon when she reached, uncaring, into the overstuffed wardrobe. In her reticule, she carried a hairbrush that she would use on the way to town, fashioning her hair into a simple tail at the nape of her neck. It mattered not what she looked like. She nearly laughed at the thought — when had she ever been so unmindful of her appearance? Never before. Yet suddenly dressing the outward seemed insignificant when compared to satisfying the yearnings of her heart.

Eagerness sent her scooting to the edge of the barouche's backseat. She tapped Harry's shoulder and encouraged, "Quickly, Harry!"

He shot her a brief scowl, but he flipped the reins and called out, "Giddap!" The horse obediently broke into a trot.

When the carriage rolled onto the streets of Boston, Harry slowed the horse to match the speed of other traffic. Daphne fidgeted in the seat, impatience making her edgy, but she refrained from complaining.

Harry drew the carriage to a stop outside of headquarters and Daphne scrambled out, unaided. Without a word to her brother, she marched to the corner and peered up and down the street, seeking a cab.

Still beside the carriage, Harry called,

"Daphne, what are you doing?"

"Taking a cab to Thomas's."

Harry dropped his head back, released a sigh, and then strode to her side. He took her elbow and squeezed gently. "Daphne, Thomas has made himself clear. He no longer wants a relationship with you."

She peered into her brother's face, her eyes wide. "I'm not going to see him about a relationship with *him,* but a relationship with —" She snapped her mouth shut.

A tug on her arm demanded she finish the sentence.

Stubbornly, she refused to answer. She wanted to talk to Thomas — to someone who would understand her deep longing. At best, Harry would disdain it; at worst, he would contact Father to say she'd lost her mind.

"Daph?"

"I —" She pulled her arm loose. "I need to see him about a personal matter. I'll be back here well before you're ready to return home." Just then a cab rolled near, and Daphne stepped to the curb, waving her hand.

"Daphne, I don't think —"

She raced back and planted a quick kiss on her brother's cheek. "I'll be fine." She scampered to the cab and gave the driver

Thomas's address. Harry stood in place, looking worried as the cab pulled away. Daphne would explain later. But first she must talk to Thomas.

Thomas took a sip of the steaming tea and leaned his chair back on two legs to rock gently and peer at the starry sky. He angled a sideways glance at Clarence, who sat stiffly upright on the second dining room chair Thomas had carried to the front yard so they could enjoy the unseasonably warm early November evening. In the deep shadows, it was difficult to make out the dark-skinned man's expression, but Thomas sensed contentment.

"You sure you don't want a mug of tea?" Thomas asked, taking a noisy slurp of the richly spiced brew. He'd enjoyed a cup of hot, sweet tea ever since Summer had given him a cup when he was a little boy. "I have plenty of hot water."

"Oh no, Mister Thomas." Clarence shook his salt-and-pepper head, his palms flat on his thighs. "I like just sittin' here takin' in the night air." A flash of white teeth showed his smile. "Clear sky, calm breeze, and good company. A man cain't ask for much more than that."

Thomas grinned in response, then continued rocking. The men sat in companionable silence. Although Clarence was the first *en Näaja* — black man — Thomas had known, he was as comfortable with the older man as with any of his school friends in Boston or his family back home. He couldn't understand the opinion some held of colored folk. To his way of thinking, there was no justifying that sort of thinking. Clarence and Mildred were two of the finest people he'd ever known. Hardworking, loyal to a fault, never speaking an ill word of anyone. How could Watson — or anyone, for that matter — consider Clarence a lesser man?

Five more days until the presidential election — the thought destroyed the peaceful contentment of moments ago. Over dinner conversation with Nadine, he'd expressed his concern of the changes their country would see were Watson elected, but with a dismissive wave of her hand, Nadine stated firmly that Thomas failed to give the American people enough credit for their collective wisdom. "I predict Roosevelt will be reelected," she'd said, "although Parker may give him more of a run than many of my stalwart Republican friends would believe." Nadine's confident tone had eased some of Thomas's worry.

Nadine's awareness of the political figures

and events still surprised Thomas. Having grown up largely ignorant of political happenings, he thought it odd that someone who didn't have the right to vote would be so informed.

He brought his chair down sharply on all four legs. "Clarence, are you planning to vote next Tuesday?"

Clarence rubbed a finger beneath his nose and shook his head slowly. "Oh now, Mister Thomas, you know we coloreds were given the right. I joined the Loyal League way back in '67, and I been registered to vote ever since, but . . . still pretty hard, even here in the North, for most of us to put our mark on a ballot." His calm, accepting voice contradicted the unfairness of his statement.

Thomas set his mug on the ground beside his chair. "But that's not right, Clarence! If you have the right to vote, you should be able to exercise it."

A slow nod acknowledged Thomas's words. Then Clarence fixed Thomas with an interested gaze. "Is you planning to vote, Mister Thomas?"

Although it went against his upbringing, a rush of eagerness rose from Thomas's middle. "I want to, but I can't. I won't be twenty-one until January."

"Ah." For long moments they sat in silence, then Clarence's thoughtful voice carried to Thomas's ear on a whisper. "So we colored folk ain't the only ones with restrictions."

Restrictions . . . Thomas considered that word and the injustice of it. A United States citizen should have the opportunity to take part in elections. After all, the decisions made by the leadership of persons put into office affected all citizens. Things needed to change, and a desire to be a part of changing the rules that kept good men like Clarence from voting created a prompting that he couldn't ignore.

He had an idea of how to help bring about those changes, too. Dean Pardue's parting comment earlier that evening replayed inside his head, building a bold plan in his mind. He needed to pray about it, but already he believed strongly God had planted a seed that was meant to bear fruit.

Clarence yawned and pressed his hands to his knees, pushing himself to his feet. "Well, I reckon I've stayed long enough. I should probably be gettin' Missus Nadine's carriage back home 'fore she thinks I got lost somewheres."

Thomas laughed and rose. "Thank you for the ride back and for staying awhile. I don't get many visitors." His last visitor had been Harry. The memory of saying good-bye to his friend that day left behind lingering sorrow.

At that moment, a hansom cab pulled to a stop at the curb in the circle of light from the iron streetlamp. Clarence tipped his head toward the skirted passenger emerging from the back of the small vehicle. "Looks to me like maybe you got a visitor now."

Daphne? He clasped the older man's hand and whispered, "Can you stay a little longer?"

Clarence nodded, understanding in his velvety eyes.

Daphne approached as if propelled by a stout wind, her hands outstretched to Thomas. He had no choice but to take them. Her beaming smile doubled his pulse. "Thomas, I'm so glad you're here." Then her chin jerked sideways as she apparently noticed Clarence for the first time. Her smile faded. Releasing Thomas, she took an awkward backward step. "Oh. I didn't realize . . ."

Clarence backed slowly toward the cottage. "I think I'll get me that mug o' tea now. Can I fetch one for you, too, Miss Daphne?"

Daphne turned toward Clarence, her chin

angled high. "That's very kind, but no thank you."

With a nod, Clarence headed into the house. Daphne stared after him, her hands clasped at her waist. Thomas waited for her to speak again, but when she remained silent, he cleared his throat. "Would you care to sit down?"

Her gaze jerked to meet his, and her fine brows pulled together. For a moment he thought she would refuse, but then she offered a nod. He guided her to the chairs he and Clarence had vacated only moments before, and they sat. But she still didn't speak.

Thomas sneaked glances at her. Her race across the grass and her bright smile had indicated an eagerness to be with him. But now her taciturn expression and stiff posture made clear her discomfort. Females and their ever-changing emotions — how could any man understand them?

He supposed the quiet, reticent Daphne was better for his heart than the eager, warm one, but he still found himself wishing she would throw off the reserved cloak and give him another dazzling smile.

At long last, she turned to face him. "Thomas, I —"

Clarence ambled back out, a mug of tea

held between his large palms.

Daphne's back stiffened and she rose abruptly. "I must return to headquarters. Harry is surely ready to return home by now." She pressed a finger to her chin, peering apprehensively into Thomas's face. "W-will you walk me to a corner where I might summon a cab?"

"Miss Daphne," Clarence said, setting his mug on the seat of Daphne's chair, "I need to be leavin', too. So I can carry you over to the headquarters if you like. Save you the fare of a cab."

Daphne shot him a startled look. For a moment, Thomas thought she would decline his offer the way she had refused the tea. But she said, "Thank you. I would be most grateful."

Thomas said his farewells and watched Clarence escort Daphne across the grass to Nadine's carriage. When they reached the carriage, she looked back, an expression of longing in her face. Thomas's heart caught. He took one step forward, his hand rising toward her of its own volition. But then she grasped Clarence's hand and climbed into the vehicle.

30

Daphne allowed Clarence to assist her from the back of the carriage. Although she was still disappointed she hadn't been able to voice her questions to Thomas — she couldn't possibly open her heart to Thomas where this old black man might overhear — she offered the servant a thank-you for the ride.

He touched his forehead with his fingers, offering a shy nod. "You is welcome, Miss Daphne. Take care now."

She looped her reticule over her wrist as she made her way toward the double doors of Watson's campaign headquarters. The muffled sound of voices and an occasional burst of laughter carried from inside the building. It sounded as though the campaigners were having a grand time. Apparently Harry's evening had been more satisfying than hers.

Just as her fingers closed around the brass

knob, a pair of hands grabbed her from behind and spun her around. A squawk of surprise found its way from her throat before a soft, moist hand clamped over her mouth, stilling any other protest.

A second person — a man in a fashionable suit with a brimmed hat pulled low over his eyes — caught hold of her reticule and yanked. "Let it go!" The man's voice was refined yet somehow evil. "You won't be giving your donation to Watson — I'll have it instead."

Trapped by the person behind her, Daphne folded her arms across her middle and held tight, keeping the thief from taking her reticule. The strings from the small purse cut into her wrist. Pain and fear gave her strength she didn't know she possessed. With a vicious twist of her head, she managed to dislodge the hand from her mouth. She took advantage of the opportunity to yell for help at the top of her lungs.

"Stop hollering," the man yanking on her reticule growled. His breath carried the sickly sweet odor of liquor. "Stay quiet or I shall be forced to silence you with the back of my hand."

Daphne released one high-pitched, "Help me!"

Immediately, the man followed through

on his threat, striking her on the side of her head hard enough to make stars explode behind her eyes. Bile rose in her throat and her knees threatened to buckle, but she refused to be laid low by these thieves. Hunkering forward, she hugged herself and protected her purse.

Fingers bruised Daphne's shoulders. Blood seeped from a slice on the side of her wrist. The foul breath of the man who continued to tug at the velvet bag assaulted her nostrils. But still Daphne fought. While struggling, she managed a hoarse shout. "Help! Someone, help me! Help!"

And finally rapid footsteps approached. Daphne screeched, fearful that yet another thief would attack, but instead a familiar voice demanded, "What are you fellows doin'? You let Miss Daphne be!"

Daphne's head shot up. Clarence!

Mrs. Steadman's servant took hold of the would-be purse-snatcher and threw him aside. The man stumbled two steps and fell onto the bricked walkway. Clarence reached for her. "Miss Daphne, is you —"

The man behind her shoved her hard, sending her flying forward into Clarence's chest. Clarence caught her, but suddenly he was jerked away, and she lost her footing, falling hard against the foundation of the building. On scuffed hands and knees, she watched in mute horror as the man who had tried to steal her reticule caught Clarence from behind, looping his arms through the servant's elbows and holding him upright like a shield.

"Thrash him good, Melvin! Teach him not to put his filthy hands on me!"

The man called Melvin seemed to take great pleasure in pummeling the helpless Clarence. Daphne's ears rang from the blow she'd received, but the awful sound of a fist connecting with flesh still penetrated her haze. Half-walking, half-crawling, Daphne managed to clamber to the headquarters' doors. She flung one door wide and staggered into the room, shouting at the top of her lungs.

Immediately all banter ceased and several people, including Harry, raced to her side. She fell into her brother's arms.

"Daph, what —"

"Outside!" She pointed wildly. "They're killing him!"

"Who?"

"Clarence . . . Mrs. Steadman's —" Her voice broke on a sob. "Hurry, Harry!"

Crushing her to his chest, he ordered over his shoulder, "Get out there! Help the man!"

Several men raced out the door. Daphne clung to Harry's shirtfront, soaking it with her tears, while he patted her back and whispered words of consolation. After a few minutes, she gained control and rasped, "Take me outside, Harry. I must . . . I must see Clarence. I must thank him."

Harry kept his arm around her waist and escorted her to the sidewalk. Streetlamps illuminated the ugly scene — a half circle of men, staring downward at a crumpled and bloody heap. Daphne gasped and pulled free of Harry's grasp. She dropped to her knees beside Clarence. His battered face was nearly unrecognizable.

"Oh, Clarence, I'm so sorry . . ." She touched his cheek, surprised when he flinched. "He's alive!" She snapped her head up. "Quickly — his employer's carriage is over at the curb. We must get him to a hospital!"

One of the observers murmured, "I'm not going into any hospital that will take —"

"Harry, please!" Tears flooded her eyes, distorting her vision. Daphne lifted a hand to her brother, beseeching him with her eyes.

Harry crouched next to her. "Daph, I don't know what we can do."

"We can't just leave him here to die,

Harry. He . . . he rescued me from some men who accosted me and tried to rob me. He wouldn't be hurt at all were it not for me." She met the gazes of each of the men standing silently around the fallen victim. "We have to help him!"

Harry jumped to his feet. "We'll take him to Mrs. Steadman's. She can summon a doctor to care for him." He pointed at one of the men. "Jerome, you drive his carriage and I'll follow you with Daphne." Turning to two others, he ordered, "Help me lift him, but be careful. He's probably got broken ribs, the poor bloke."

Daphne trailed along beside the men, sandwiching one of Clarence's hands between hers. She heard the mumbled protests behind her, but she ignored them. Clarence was her hero. Harry and his two helpers draped Clarence across the backseat, and Daphne climbed in to kneel on the floor.

"Daphne, you come with me." Harry's stern tone demanded obedience.

Daphne shook her head, placing her arms tenderly across Clarence's still body. "No. I shall stay with him until we reach Mrs. Steadman's." She glared at Jerome, who stood stupidly outside the carriage. "What are you waiting for? Get into the driver's seat and drive! There's no time to spare!"

■ ■ ■ ■

Belinda placed the last of her sister's belongings in the bureau drawer and squeaked it shut. "Well, that's that." Though she forced brightness into her voice, underneath her heart ached. This small room in the Home for the Friendless held four cots and the single bureau. Malinda would call one drawer and one cot her own. What a change this was from the private bedroom and full wardrobe in the home they'd shared with their parents in Gaeddert.

Yet Malinda voiced no word of complaint. She sat on the creaky cot, which she had covered with a colorful quilt salvaged from their fire-damaged home. "Don't be sad."

Apparently Belinda's tone of voice hadn't fooled her sister. "Why do you think I'm sad?"

"Because I know you. Come here." Malinda patted the cot, and Belinda sank down beside her. Malinda put her arm around Belinda's shoulders and drew her close. For the first time she could remember, Belinda assumed the role of cosseted younger sister. It felt amazingly good.

Malinda spoke softly while stroking Belinda's upper arm. "This is the right thing

414

for me to do. Here, I can be useful, and you will be free to live your own life instead of worrying about me."

Belinda rested her head on her sister's shoulder. "But I don't mind worrying about you."

A soft chuckle bounced Malinda's shoulder. "I know you don't, but *I* mind." She sighed. "As much as I knew I couldn't make it on my own, I hated being dependent on you. It made me harsh and resentful. I don't want to be that way anymore."

Belinda sat up. "Will you stay here forever?"

Malinda shrugged. "I don't know. But for now, it's best for both of us." Then she asked a tremulous question. "You w-will come see me, though, w-won't you?"

Belinda threw her arms around her sister. "As often as I can borrow a wagon. I promise!"

Belinda hugged her sister long and hard. Just when she feared she would erupt into noisy sobs, a voice interrupted.

"Um, excuse me."

They pulled loose. A tall, sandy-haired man stood in the hallway, just outside the open door. Dressed in brown, striped trousers, a white shirt and collar, and a brown string tie, he presented a formal appearance despite the absence of a suit coat. The sheepish expression in his brown eyes made Belinda wonder if their emotional scene embarrassed him. He stepped just over the threshold, keeping a respectful distance, and looked directly at Belinda.

"Miss Schmidt, I'm Gerhard Wiens. I was told you would be helping with the school-age children."

Malinda rose. "I am the Miss Schmidt who will be assisting."

The man's face flooded with pink. He looked rapidly from one sister to the other. "Oh, please excuse me. The director, Mr. Goertzen, just said a young woman. I . . . I didn't —"

"It's all right. I am Malinda Schmidt, and I will be staying."

Mr. Wiens cleared his throat as his face returned to its normal color. "Miss Schmidt."

Malinda gestured for Belinda to stand. "This is my sister, Belinda. She drove me here and helped me with my belongings."

If he wondered why only one sister chose to reside under the home's roof, he kept his curiosity to himself. "It's nice to meet you, Miss Schmidt."

"Likewise, Mr. Wiens." For a moment, they stared at one another, uncertain how to proceed.

Finally Mr. Wiens turned to Malinda. "Miss Schmidt, I would be happy to escort you to the schoolroom and familiarize you with our assortment of textbooks." He shuffled his feet self-consciously. "Many of our books are well used, but all of them are still intact."

Belinda thought he had a pleasantly modulated tone — not too deep nor unnaturally high.

Malinda glanced at Belinda. "Mr. Wiens, I am rather tired and would prefer to wait until tomorrow morning to become familiar with my surroundings. Would you allow me an evening to rest?"

"Oh, of course. You can tour the schoolroom tomorrow, while the children have their Saturday break. No doubt it will be quieter. Then you can begin with teaching chores on Monday, if you feel ready."

"That would be perfect." Malinda gave Belinda a little shove that startled her forward a few inches. "Mr. Wiens, would you kindly escort my sister downstairs? She's leaving now."

Belinda stared at Malinda in surprise. Her sister's eyes twinkled mischievously. Blatant matchmaking! Who would have suspected it from her serious sister? Belinda's lips twitched with the effort of keeping her amusement to herself. She said, "Yes, I should be going. Peter's oxen have been standing outside long enough. I need to take the wagon back."

"Well, then, I'd be happy to escort you."

Mr. Wiens sounded pleased, and when Belinda stepped closer to him, she observed that his deep brown eyes and sooty lashes contrasted nicely with his light-colored hair. For a moment, Belinda was held captive by the unusual combination. Then he cleared his throat again. "Miss Schmidt, are you ready?"

Belinda snapped to attention. "Oh! Yes. Thank you." She gave Malinda one more hug and picked up her shawl from the end of the cot. "Rest, Malinda. I'll come out Sunday."

"Good. I'll see you then."

Belinda followed Mr. Wiens out of the room and waited until he secured the door. Then they walked side by side down the long hallway to the staircase. In gentlemanly fashion, he gestured for her to precede him down the stairs. Awareness of him close on her heels made her clip down a little faster than normal. Not until they stood on the wide, covered porch did the man speak again.

"I apologize for the confusion when I came up to your sister's room. I hope I didn't offend her."

"Not at all." Belinda tossed her shawl around her shoulders and tied the ends into a firm knot. "How were you to know which of us was the Miss Schmidt you were seeking?"

His penetrating gaze, which seemed to communicate he was pleased to have located her, sent a teasing tickle down her spine. She turned her gaze forward. "I-I'm grateful she's able to be of service here. It means a great deal to her."

Mr. Wiens slipped his hands into his trouser pockets, reminding her of Thomas's habit when something made him nervous. "We can always use teachers," he replied.

Mr. Wiens's height, too, was similar to Thomas's.

Stop making comparisons!

"Since we don't have the funds to pay for a regular schoolteacher, we have to rely on those who will educate the children in exchange for room and board. Believe me, your sister is a godsend."

Belinda's heart turned over at the sincere statement. "I'm so glad."

Tugging one hand free of his pocket, he held it toward the wagon in a silent query.

419

She nodded, and he walked beside her. She noticed that their strides matched perfectly. When he offered his hand to assist her, fire filled her face, but she placed her hand in his.

Once on the seat, she smoothed her skirts over her knees and picked up the reins. "Well . . ."

He stood looking up at her, squinting against the afternoon sun. "Well . . ."

Belinda hunched her shoulders as a chilly breeze whisked around the school and ruffled the edges of her shawl. With regret, she said, "Well, I'd better be going."

"Yes." He took a step backward, lifting his hand in a wave. "Drive safely, and we'll see you Sunday."

"Yes. Sunday."

All the way back to Hillsboro, Belinda thought, *Did I just flirt with that man?* She felt certain he assumed she was returning on Sunday to see him as much as her sister. Then she wondered if he was right.

She left the wagon and oxen at the livery and walked to the Ollenburgers', eager to be out of the wind, have some hot coffee, and enjoy a few calm moments before dinner. But when she stepped through the door, those hopes were dashed. The sound of weeping carried from the kitchen. Abby and Gussie sat together on the sofa, their little faces sad.

Belinda dropped to her knees in front of the little girls. "What's happened?"

Abby's eyes brimmed with tears. "Papa came home with a telegram. He made us come in here. Then Mama started crying."

Gussie's lower lip quivered. "I'm a-scared, Belinda."

Belinda took time to hug and comfort both girls, her own heart pounding in trepidation, before she cautiously peeked through the kitchen doorway. Summer and Peter sat at the table. Peter held Summer to his chest, and sobs shook her slender body. A floorboard squeaked, announcing Belinda's presence, and Peter looked up.

"Oh, Belinda. You got Malinda delivered to the orphans' home all right?"

Of course he would ask about Malinda. Belinda stepped closer. "Yes, she's fine. But . . . Abby and Gussie said you received some bad news." *Did something happen to Thomas?* Her fleeting attraction toward Gerhard Wiens now made her feel traitorous.

Peter patted Summer's back and she sat up, wiping her eyes with an apron. She sent Belinda an apologetic look. "I'm sorry to fall apart like this. But . . . but he means a great deal to me." Pressing her fist to her lips, she jumped up from the table and rushed around the corner, closing herself in her bedroom.

Belinda looked at Peter, fear holding her silent.

Peter lowered his head. He fingered a folded square of paper. "We get a telegram from Thomas. A good friend of his — Clarence — was hurt. Summer takes it very hard. Clarence and Mildred helped care for her when she lived with her mother-in-law. She has known Clarence and Mildred for many years."

"Was he in an accident?" Belinda sat at the table, and Peter pushed the telegram across the surface to her.

"See for yourself. Not an accident. He was beaten." Peter shook his head, clicking his tongue. "A man older than me. Too old to be fighting, for sure."

"Beaten?" Belinda couldn't imagine something so horrendous. The Mennonites were firm believers in nonviolence. She read the brief telegram, noting the statement about Clarence and the plea for prayer. Then she read the final lines, and her heart leaped. Her chin shot upward and she gaped at Peter. "But . . . but Thomas is . . . ?"

Peter's mustache twitched, and his eyes

suddenly brightened. "*Ja,* you see the other part he tells us."

"*When Clarence is well, I am returning to Kansas. Tell Belinda I need to speak with her.*"

Peter nodded. "*Goot* news, *ja?*"

31

Thomas added another log to the fireplace in the corner of Nadine's best guestroom. He crouched in front of the flickering flame, staring at the reflection in the molded brass cheek. Although the image was distorted, he could still make out Daphne's slender form leaning forward to place a cool rag over Clarence's swollen forehead.

His hands trembled at the sight of self-important Daphne Severt ministering to a humble, black servant. Pressing his palms to his knees, he pushed to his feet and turned just as Daphne turned from the bed. Their gazes collided. Although her face was pale, her lips unsmiling, and her eyes sad, her beauty still made his breath catch.

He crossed slowly to the bed and stood beside her. "You could use a rest," he whispered. His fingers itched to smooth the purple smudges beneath her eyes. "You don't have to stay here."

"Yes, I do, Thomas. I can't leave until he wakes up. I must . . . I must thank him for what he did."

Thomas nodded. He looked at Clarence, and the anger he had been trying to hold back cut through him once again. When Nadine had summoned him because Clarence had been injured, Thomas assumed there had been a carriage accident or perhaps a fall in the house. But to discover that two men beat Clarence because he dared to defend Daphne . . . How could men be so cruel to another human being?

"Thomas?"

Daphne's soft, wavering voice captured Thomas's attention. "Yes?"

"I have something I need to discuss with you."

Thomas gestured to the small settee that faced the fireplace. They sat side by side on opposite ends of the settee, and Daphne fixed him with a serious look.

"I came to your cottage yesterday evening to talk to you. But with Clarence there . . ." She paused, glancing toward the bed. "I was so foolish to refuse to talk in front of a servant. In front of a colored man. I feel so ashamed, Thomas." Tears swam in her eyes.

Thomas resisted taking her hand. "It doesn't matter what you did then," he as-

sured her. "What matters is what you're doing now."

She looked at him and nodded. She licked
her lips, swallowed, and spoke again. "In
the Bible —"

Thomas's heart nearly stopped with those
words.

"— a man asks Jesus what he must do to
inherit eternal life, and Jesus tells him to
give up all he possesses and follow Him.
But I know there is more to it than giving
up material wealth. I know the heart is
somehow involved." Her words tripped out
quickly, almost uncontrolled, like a brook
splashing down a mountainside. "The Bible
also talks about God sending His Son to
save the world." Drawing back, she clasped
her hands beneath her chin and implored
him with her dark eyes. "I want to be saved,
Thomas. I want to know God like you do.
Please, please tell me what I must do so I
can do it quickly."

Shifting so his knees touched hers,
Thomas leaned forward. "All you have to
do is believe that Jesus is the Son of God
who died to be your Savior and ask Him
into your heart."

Her eyes widened. "That's all?"

He grinned. "That's all."

"Then I must do it. Right now. Should I kneel?"

Although Thomas knew Daphne's prayer would reach God's ears regardless of her position, he understood the importance of humbling oneself before God. He nodded and watched her slip unhesitatingly to the floor. He marveled that Daphne — the Daphne who had so recently proclaimed her superiority — would be willing to kneel where Nadine, Mildred, or the doctor could walk in and see her. Her action convinced him of her genuine desire to become a child of God.

He joined her on the carpet and bowed his head. Tears stung his closed eyelids as he listened to her say the words that would impact her soul for all eternity. When finished, she raised her tear-stained face to Thomas. The light shining in her eyes brought a rush of delight so overwhelming Thomas laughed out loud.

She laughed, too, the sound light and joy-filled. Pressing both hands to her chest, she said with awe, "He's in there. I *feel* Him, Thomas. He's with me."

"And He'll never leave you or forsake you," Thomas promised. Taking her hands, he helped her to her feet. She didn't even brush the wrinkles from her skirt.

"Thank you. Thank you for helping me."

Thomas couldn't reply. His heart ached with regret for not sharing God with Daphne sooner. Yet at the same time, he celebrated the decision she had made. God had worked His wonder despite Thomas's failings. *Thank You, Father, for your endless mercy.*

Behind them, someone cleared her throat, making both Thomas and Daphne whirl around. Nadine and Mildred stood in the open doorway. Nadine held her arm protectively around Mildred's sloped shoulders. "How is Clarence? Any change?"

Daphne shook her head. "Still sleeping." She took a few stumbling steps toward Mildred. "I'm so sorry."

Mildred puckered her face. "You didn't do nothin' wrong, so you don't need to say sorry to me."

Daphne closed the gap between herself and the older black woman. She enfolded Mildred in her arms. Her cheek pressed to Mildred's, she whispered, "Thank you for your kindness." She pulled back. "May I . . . may I stay? Thomas, will you teach me how to pray for Clarence?"

Nadine gave a start, her eyes widening. Thomas understood her reaction. He would never have expected such unselfishness from

Daphne.

Nadine quickly regained her composure. Taking Daphne's hand, she said, "We never refuse prayers. Do we, Mildred?" Shifting her gaze to include Thomas, she lifted her chin. "Let's all combine our hearts in appeal to the heavenly Father for Clarence's full recovery."

"You will not spend another day at the bedside of that servant!"

At Father's explosive order, Daphne bit down on the end of her tongue. For the past four days, Harry had transported her to Nadine Steadman's, where she helped care for Clarence as he recovered from the vicious attack. Not until this evening at dinner had Father casually questioned her whereabouts over the weekend. Her truthfulness had brought about an abrupt change in his demeanor.

Now a war raged in her soul as she pondered her alternatives. During the hours Clarence slept, she and Mrs. Steadman studied and discussed the Bible. She knew she was expected to honor her parents. She also knew she was to love her neighbor as herself. Which admonition should she follow in this situation?

Apparently Father read her silence as

consent, because he released a satisfied grunt, picked up his knife and fork, and cut another bite of roast. As he lifted the bite of beef to his mouth, Daphne found her compromise.

"May I just go for this week, Father?" By the end of the week Clarence probably would have recovered enough to have no more need of around-the-clock care. Despite the doctor's grim prognosis, the prayers of Thomas, Nadine, Mildred, and Daphne were being answered. Clarence showed daily improvement.

Father threw the fork onto his plate. The piece of meat bounced from the prongs and landed on the linen tablecloth.

Mother sucked air through her teeth. "Stanton, please pick that up before the gravy stains the cloth."

The servant stepped from the serving table to Father's side while Father grated through clenched teeth, "No daughter of mine will lower herself to care for a mere household servant!"

Stanton's face remained emotionless, but Daphne noticed hurt in his eyes as he plucked up the fallen piece of meat with a folded napkin. Daphne gave the man an apologetic look and waited until he left the dining room before softly addressing her father. "Surely you won't deny me the honor of caring for the man who risked his life to assist me."

Father's lips pinched together, his jaw muscles twitching. His initial outrage upon learning of Daphne's rough treatment at campaign headquarters had changed to excuse-making when she described her attackers. "Ah," he had said, "college lads, no doubt, with too much ale in their systems. An unfortunate incident, certainly, but no real harm done."

Daphne felt indignation rise once again as she remembered not only her fear that night but the very real harm done to poor Clarence. She took a slow breath, prayed for guidance, and continued in a low, passionate voice. "There is a verse in Matthew in which Jesus instructs His disciples to love your neighbor as yourself. Clarence cared for me by coming to my rescue. I only wish to repay him by —"

Father roared to life. "You have amply repaid him by transporting him to his home where his mistress could see to his needs!" He pointed at her, his brows forming a stern line. "And I forbid you to speak again of the Bible. We wouldn't be dealing with that religious nonsense had I curtailed your friendship with Ollenburger from the beginning." He settled back in his chair, tossing his napkin from his lap to his plate. "Ollenburger . . ." He sent a frustrated look across the table to Mother. "At least we needn't be concerned about him anymore."

Father's gaze swung to Harry, who continued to eat in silence as if oblivious to the battle being waged around the table. "Your chum submitted his resignation this morning, and after all I've done for him! He offered to remain for a few weeks until a replacement could be found, and I told him to pack his belongings and get out. I can tell you, I was angry at the time, but now I'm glad to see the boy go. The sooner, the better! Maybe once he's back in Kansas, things will return to normal."

Harry's nervous glance flitted from Daphne to Father and back to his plate. Without a word, he put another bite of potatoes in his mouth, but Daphne's appetite fled. Thomas was leaving Boston? Why hadn't he told her? She had seen him each day when he'd come to visit Clarence, yet he'd never said a word. She swallowed hard to maintain control of her emotions. She would mourn the loss of Thomas, but first she must deal with something else — Father's mistaken idea that with Thomas's departure, her "religion" would disappear.

"Father, as I told you the other evening, I have accepted Jesus Christ into my heart. Thomas did influence me, but the decision was entirely my own. Jesus is now a part of me, and He's not going away."

"Bah!" Father pushed away from the table. His red face glowed with barely controlled fury. "And as *I* told *you* the other evening, you're a foolish, impetuous girl going through a religious phase. It will pass."

"Please, Father, I —"

He rose, leaning toward her. "Remember your place, Daphne. If you cannot do that, you will not be welcome at my table. Harry!"

Harry sat upright.

"I'm going to headquarters. Come along."

Without a word, Harry followed Father from the room. The slam of the back door signaled their departure.

Daphne looked toward her mother, but Mother turned away from her. "I will not defend your actions, Daphne. Your father is right — you've always been impetuous and selfish."

Daphne jumped up from the table and made her way to the library. She crossed the darkening room to the settee — the place where she had first encountered Jesus through the words written in God's book.

Dropping to her knees, she bowed her head and closed her eyes. "Lord, why does doing the right thing hurt so much?"

"So you're leaving us, hmm?" Pardue leaned his shoulder against the doorjamb, his arms crossed, and watched Thomas pack the contents of his desk.

"You still here?" Thomas had chosen the late hour to clean out his office because he thought all of the employees had gone home.

"I'm still here. I'll be visiting the different campaign headquarters over the evening, interviewing people, getting their thoughts about the election. Always interesting how every group thinks their own candidate will win."

The man pushed off from the door and ambled to Thomas's desk. "So . . . Severt said you're not only leaving the paper, you're leaving Boston. That true?" He picked up a glass paperweight and bounced it in his hand.

A rush of eagerness washed over Thomas. He was going home. Kansas . . . Pa and Summer . . . his sisters. He knew he would miss many aspects of Boston, yet returning to Kansas felt right. He had remained in Boston long enough to learn what he needed, and now he would follow the pathway God had outlined for him.

"Yes, sir, it's true. And it's partly because of you."

Pardue stopped tossing the paperweight, his eyebrows shooting high. "Me?"

"Yes. You told me the way to make sure I could write what I wanted to was to start my own paper. So that's what I'm going to do. I plan to start a paper in Kansas, aimed toward the Mennonite population."

"Kind of a limited readership, isn't it?" Pardue asked.

Thomas answered with a light chuckle. "Not where I grew up. And who knows? Maybe it'll spread to other Mennonite communities, as well. Until it does, I'll also be working with my father, helping him establish a chicken farm at our old homestead. You see . . ." He paused, chewing the inside of his cheek thoughtfully. "I've figured out we Mennonites need to make some changes — increase our awareness of what's going on in the world. We live in the United States, and that means we're affected by the decisions made by the leaders of the country, yet we don't involve ourselves in the process of choosing leaders." He considered the battle he might face when church leaders realized his intent. Change didn't always

435

come easily, but sometimes it was needed. "I think we need to be informed. So that's what I plan to do — publish a newspaper that will provide necessary information while honoring our Mennonite heritage."

Pardue whistled through his teeth. "Sounds like a mighty big undertaking."

Thomas shrugged and returned to packing. "I suppose."

"Well, boy" — Pardue thumped the paperweight into Thomas's box and stuck out his bony hand — "I wish you well. It's been an honor getting to know you. You've got the talent and drive to make this paper of yours a success. Send me a copy now and then, but make sure you blow the chicken feathers off beforehand. Feathers make me sneeze." He chuckled, pumping Thomas's hand up and down.

Thomas wondered briefly if Pardue would share the paper with Mr. Severt, but he didn't ask. "Thanks, Mr. Pardue. I appreciate everything you've taught me. I'll put it to good use."

"Oh, I know you will, boy." Pardue backed up two steps. "Good luck to you." With a wave, the man headed out the door.

Thomas reflected for a moment on all he'd learned from the lanky reporter. Mr. Severt had told him he'd learn more from

Pardue than from most college professors, and the man's statement had proved true. Thanks to Pardue's tutelage, Thomas felt ready to take on the responsibility of his own small-town newspaper.

There was already one newspaper in operation in Hillsboro, but he planned a different kind of paper — one that focused solely on politics and events that could affect the simple lifestyle of his people. He'd start small by necessity, maybe one page, but as his readership increased, the coverage could increase. He had contacted the editor of the Hillsboro paper and asked permission to use his printing press until he had enough money to purchase his own. It would be inconvenient — for both of them, he was sure — yet it was his best option for the moment.

As he emptied the last drawer, he wondered if Belinda Schmidt would accept his offer of working for him. Based on her letters, he knew she possessed the ability to communicate well in written form. And from Summer's letters, he knew Belinda wanted a job. He wouldn't be able to pay much at first, but maybe eventually . . .

Suddenly, he felt very eager to get home, to get started, to make a success of this plan.

32

Belinda awoke with a start. She blinked in confusion, trying to make sense of the hour. The room was dark — not even a sliver of light beneath her closed door from the kitchen's lantern, which told her it was too early to rise. She lay on Thomas's rope bed, peering into the murky darkness. What had brought her from sleep to full wakefulness? Likely it was the same question that had plagued her daytime hours ever since Thomas's telegram about Clarence's injury arrived: *What did Thomas want to speak with her about?*

In a recent letter, he had shared his realization that he must sever his relationship with Daphne due to her unbelief. He had asked her to join him in prayer for the strength to wait and the discernment to recognize his God-chosen mate. Could he have decided to turn his attention to her? Considering the possibility now sent her heart into wild fluttering.

She flopped her arms outside of the covers, pinning the rough blanket across her chest in an attempt to calm her racing pulse. It didn't help. Why did Thomas's comment bring worry instead of elation? When, she wondered, had her infatuation with Thomas waned?

She couldn't identify a time, but she knew it had changed. Her reaction to his message coupled with her response to Gerhard Wiens's attention offered the evidence. If she were truly in love with Thomas, no man would intrigue her for even a moment of time. Yet, regardless of the fleeting minutes they'd shared, Gerhard had captured her heart and mind. Had she received Thomas's telegram prior to meeting Gerhard, would it have conjured excitement rather than apprehension?

"I would still be apprehensive," she whispered, allowing herself to acknowledge the truth. Receiving the message had forced her to examine her feelings for Thomas, and she had reached an uncomfortable conclusion.

Although she cared for Thomas as a friend and brother in Christ, she didn't want him as much as she wanted the family he possessed. Peter and Summer Ollenburger were everything her own parents were not —

open, loving, accepting. Living with them had given her a taste of being a member of their family, and it had filled the long-held need for unconditional love and acceptance. Having received their care, she no longer had the need to be with Thomas. She already had his family.

"Lord, if Thomas proposes marriage, I must say no," she rasped to the shadowed rafters, "yet how can I hurt him when I care so deeply for him as a friend?"

A soft clank, followed by the pale band of lantern light beneath the door, told her Summer was starting the day. Immediately Belinda slipped from the bed, pawed the dresser top to find the box of matches, and quickly lit one. The flare allowed her to locate her own lantern, and in moments the room was illuminated enough for her to dress and open the door to join Summer in the kitchen.

To her surprise, rather than finding Summer starting breakfast, she saw Peter Ollenburger stoking the woodstove. He finished placing kindling on top of the tightly woven corn husks that fed the stove, dropped a match in the middle of the tiny bits, then turned. He gave a start when he spotted Belinda.

"Belinda, you are awake."

Only then did she realize he still wore his sleeping clothes. He crossed the flaps of his plaid flannel robe across his belly and tied the belt with a sharp yank. His hair stood up in wild waves on his head, and his eyes were heavy-lidded. Belinda had never seen the man in such a state of dishevelment, and embarrassment made her entire body feel hot. She surmised by his red face, he was as uncomfortable as she.

"I-I'm so sorry. I thought Summer —" Belinda backed toward her room. "I'll leave you alone."

"No, no." Peter waved his hand. "I could not sleep, so I thought to make some coffee. I am sorry to have wakened you."

Belinda's backside collided with the closed door, bringing her to an abrupt halt. "It's all right. I was having trouble sleeping, too."

Concern etched his brow. "If you are not sleeping, there is a reason. Would you like to tell me about it?"

Appreciation for this man's fatherly attention to her needs once more bathed Belinda in gratitude. But something else occurred to her. "You must be worried about something, or you would be able to sleep."

At that moment, Summer rounded the corner, rubbing her eyes. "I heard voices. Is something wrong?"

Peter opened his arms, and Summer stepped into his embrace. He smoothed his large hand over Summer's tumbling hair and kissed the top of her head. "I could not sleep, so I thought to make some coffee. I woke Belinda with my banging around."

Summer chuckled softly, then pulled loose. "Yes, my great big mouse, you woke me, too." She balled her fists and stretched, yawning. "As long as we're all up, we might as well all have coffee." Giving Peter a gentle push toward the table, she said, "Sit down. I'll get the coffee started. Belinda, why don't you put some of yesterday's *zwieback* in the oven to warm?"

Soon the scents of fresh coffee and toasted bread filled the room. Peter broke a *zwieback* into two halves and dunked one half in his coffee. "Belinda, what worry keeps you awake?"

Belinda bit down on her lower lip, unwilling to risk hurting this tender man by confessing she had been trying to find a way to refuse his son's proposal. She couldn't find appropriate words, so she formed a question of her own. "I'd rather know why you're awake at this hour." She gestured to the kitchen window, where the moon seemed to rest within the branches of the backyard tree. "It's far too early to be up."

Summer put her hand over Peter's. "Were you thinking again of the chickens?"

Peter chewed a bite of bread, his beard bobbing with the movement. "Always I seem to be thinking of chickens." His expression turned dreamy. "So many things go right for me to start the chicken farm. We have land to build a chicken house, and land to plant grains to feed the chickens. My mill could grind those grains, so we would not need to spend money for feed. Then the eggs and grown chickens we could sell and have a good income." He raised one brow and shook a piece of toasted bread at his wife. "The Plymouth Rocks, they are popular roasting hens."

Summer grinned. "I know. You've shown me the brochure. Several times." She winked at Belinda.

Belinda smiled in response, but then a selfish thought hit her — if the Ollenburgers moved back to their homestead outside of Gaeddert, she would be alone. She'd already lost a set of parents, and she wasn't prepared to give up the surrogate ones who had come to mean so much to her. She sputtered out the realization. "You're really leaving Hillsboro?"

"Yes, I believe we are," Summer replied. Then, seeming to sense Belinda's melancholy, she added softly, "But we wouldn't make any changes until the spring."

Belinda lowered her head, fingering the handle on the coffee cup. "Spring . . ."

"*Ja.*" Peter nodded. "Time it will take to make a house for the chickens and ready the land for seeds. I must have feed first, then chickens. So while the grains grow, I will build *en Heenastaul* — my chicken barn. And when the barn is ready, then the chicks can come on the train." He sighed, his lips curved upward in satisfaction. "*Goot* it will be to be on my own land again, to put my mill to good use."

He had everything worked out. Belinda wondered how she could have been so oblivious to their plans to return to the Gaeddert homestead.

Summer gathered their empty cups and carried them to the sink. "Well, there will be time for us to discuss all of this. After all, spring is a few months away!" She dropped the cups in the dishpan and turned to face the table. "But, Belinda, if we return to Gaeddert, that will leave this house open for someone's use. If you are interested in renting it, we should mention that to the owner."

"Yes . . ." Belinda would need a place to stay. Summer's suggestion was worthy of exploration. "But for now . . ." She yawned widely. "I think I might try to get a little more sleep before the sun rises. Excuse me."

Back in her little room, Belinda curled on the bed. More changes. . . . Hadn't her life been one change after another for the past year? She longed for life to settle into a routine that would provide security and stability.

Once more her thoughts drifted to the telegram and Thomas's message to her. Thomas, she knew, was a stable man. Life with him would offer the security she sought. If he did propose marriage, would it be wrong to accept him to avoid losing her newly adopted family? That question kept Belinda from drifting off to sleep.

Daphne set the Bible aside. The peace she'd sought in the pages of the book had been delivered in an unusual way. Reading in Matthew, she had come upon Jesus' bold statement that He did not enter the world to bring peace, but a sword. *"For I am come to set a man at variance against his father, and the daughter against her mother . . ."*

Odd words to deliver a sense of peace, yet the recognition that her very belief in Jesus would create a division as clearly defined as a sword's swath helped her accept her parents' continued refusal to allow her to speak of her new relationship with Christ. They weren't rejecting her; they were rejecting her Savior. The condemnation still hurt, yet she could separate herself from it knowing it was a price she paid for the privilege of being God's child.

God's child . . . She smiled, absorbing the words. As much as she loved Father, her relationship with him had never been the close, loving one she desired. But with her Father God, she felt loved, accepted, valued. Even if Father and Mother cast her out, she would always have a home waiting in heaven, and she found complete contentment in the thought.

Dear God, keep knocking at the door to my parents' and brother's hearts until they allow your entrance. Although Harry hadn't openly scorned her, he kept his distance. Actually, he had little choice. Daphne had been ordered by Father to stay in her room until she came to her senses, and Harry was hustled to the office each day, so their paths didn't cross.

Since the election had ended with Thomas Watson bringing in less than one percent of the popular vote, Father kept Harry busy editing his scathing editorials containing his view of the winning candidate, Theodore

Roosevelt. Daphne sensed Harry's views on racial issues had been altered somewhat by Clarence's heroic efforts on her behalf, yet he wouldn't go against Father's wishes. She understood and didn't hold any ill will toward her brother. He was being groomed to take over the newspaper.

Being alone had one advantage: undisturbed time. She used it to read her Bible and study and pray. And think. In some ways, asking Jesus into her heart had been the easy part. Now she wanted to discern how His presence should affect her daily life.

She slipped from the pillowy nest she'd created and crossed to her large window. The grounds were brown and dismal now in November, and the sky dull as an old nickel, yet a sliver of silver outlined the edges of the heavy, dark clouds, letting her know the brightness of the sun still existed. Just as her joy existed despite the censure of her family.

Still at the window, she allowed her thoughts to drift past her parents and Harry to the other person who held a portion of her heart. How she longed to see Thomas one more time, to thank him again for opening the door to God's love to her. Who would have thought that by sending her away, he would have sent her straight into the arms of God? But that is what had happened, and although Thomas's dismissal of their relationship had brought incredible pain, the end result brought joy.

"God's ways are not man's ways." She spoke the words aloud. Mrs. Steadman had made the comment when Daphne had shared how her view of colored people was altered by Clarence coming to her rescue. Nadine had suggested perhaps God allowed the situation as a means of changing Daphne's heart. Daphne disliked the means of the change — Clarence had paid a mighty price for her heart-change — but again, she celebrated the end result.

She sighed. How she wished she could tell Thomas she no longer believed in one man's superiority based on race or wealth. Rather, it was the heart of a man that mattered most.

She started to turn from the window, but a movement on the road leading to the estate caught her attention. A carriage, she realized, pulled by a sorrel mare that reminded her of Nadine Steadman's horse. She craned her neck, squinting for a better look, and to her shock she recognized the carriage's driver.

With a little cry of excitement, she raced

out of her room, down the stairs, and out the front door to meet the carriage as it pulled up next to the house. She held both hands out to the man, exclaiming, "Clarence! How wonderful to see you looking so well!"

Swelling along the right side of his jaw gave his face a misshapen appearance, but his crooked smile was bright. He climbed down slowly from the driver's perch but kept his hands clasped to his middle rather than taking hers. "Thank you, Miss Daphne. It's good to see you, too. Wanted to come out, say thanks to you myself for getting me safe back to my home. And for taking care of me."

"Oh, Clarence, what I did was very little in comparison to what you suffered for me." Daphne linked her hands behind her back and smiled. "I'm just so very grateful you're well enough to be out of bed!"

"Prayers do work wonders, Miss Daphne, and I've had a-plenty of them, I know."

"Yes, you have." Daphne suddenly realized she felt a kinship with this elderly black man as a result of the prayers she had uttered on his behalf. How different their appearances were — him with his dark, leathered skin and humble shirt and trousers, her with skin as creamy as milk and attired in a day dress of russet satin — yet they were bound by petitions offered to a shared God.

A longing to embrace him, to publicly acknowledge him as her friend, welled up, but she squelched the desire. His reluctance to even take her hand in greeting communicated their need to remain within social dictates. She wouldn't make him uncomfortable by stepping outside of those bounds to satisfy her own need.

Forcing a cheerful tone, she said, "Thank you for taking the time to drive out and see me. It means a great deal to me." Since Father's outburst at dinner, she hadn't had a conversation of any consequence with anyone. Talking, and being spoken to, refreshed her spirits.

"Well . . ." Clarence scratched his head, assuming a sheepish expression. "I confess, Miss Daphne, I did want to thank you, but there's another reason I come out today."

Daphne tipped her head, waiting for him to explain. Instead of speaking, Clarence turned and walked to the enclosed carriage. He took hold of the doorknob and gave it a tug. Daphne, curious, peeked inside the coach. Her heart somersaulted in her chest, stealing her breath. Thomas!

33

The springs squeaked as Thomas stepped clear of the carriage.

"I brought Mister Thomas to see you, Miss Daphne," Clarence declared with a chuckle.

"Oh . . ."

Daphne's breathy reaction sent a tingle of awareness across Thomas's scalp. Her deep brown eyes flooded with tears, and she danced forward two steps, stopping short of flinging herself into his arms.

"Thomas!"

How she managed to convey everything he was feeling in one simple word, Thomas couldn't explain. He only knew he heard in that quivering utterance the same mix of joy, despair, and desire that filled his own heart with one look into Daphne's beautiful face. Her name tumbled from his lips on a husky whisper: "Daphne . . ."

They stood, looking at each other, while

Clarence shuffled from foot to foot, examined his thumbnails, and finally cleared his throat. At the sudden sound, Daphne jumped.

"I's gonna go sit under the tree there, Mister Thomas." He pointed to a bench beneath a towering, leafless maple in the center of the front yard. "You and Miss Daphne, you talk long as you want to." He chuckled again. "Your train don't leave 'til tomorrow noon anyways."

Thomas bit back his own laugh as Clarence ambled away. "Are you sure I'm not interrupting anything important? Maybe I should have called first . . ."

Daphne shook her head, her thick, dark hair bouncing across her shoulders. "There is nothing more important than time with you, Thomas. Except maybe time with God in prayer. And I feel like praying is all I've been doing for the past three days! I don't think God will mind me talking to you now."

Thomas couldn't stop a grin from growing at her bold words. Although very new in her faith, it seemed Daphne had grasped Christianity with both hands. He nodded, then pointed to the little wicker settee nearby. She led the way, and they perched side by side.

"As Clarence said, my train leaves tomorrow. I'm going back to Kansas."

"Yes." Her voice sounded tight, although her smile remained serene. "Father said you had turned in your resignation. What do you intend to do for a living?"

Thomas took a few moments to share his plans with her. She listened intently, never interrupting, her hands clasped in her lap, her gaze pinned to his. When he finished, she reached out and placed her hand over his.

"I'm so proud of you, Thomas, for being brave enough to follow your heart."

He turned his hand to grasp her fingers. Being linked with Daphne sent his heart careening. *My heart led me to you, Daphne.* The words formed on his tongue but remained unspoken. He loved her — he knew that — but he couldn't take her away from Boston and everything that was familiar. He'd hurt her once by walking away, and he loved her too much to hurt her again.

Knowing their time was short, he pushed his own desires aside to focus on doing what was best for Daphne. "Before I go, let me encourage you to find a good, Bible-teaching church. Nadine said she would be glad to have you accompany her to services, if you would like."

"How incongruous." A coy smile curved

Daphne's lips. "Could you have imagined her inviting me to spend time with her?" She laughed softly, shaking her head, but Thomas recognized no malice in the humor. "Tell her I'd be grateful. If Father allows me to leave the house on Sunday, I shall most certainly attend service with Mrs. Steadman."

Thomas frowned. "If your father allows you . . . ?"

Her cheeks reddened, and she turned her head away.

Gently, Thomas caught her chin between his thumb and finger and brought her face around. "Daphne, has your father been abusive?"

Tears appeared in her eyes. "He's angry with me. He thinks me foolish for reading the Bible and praying, and he has banished me to my room until I stop."

"Oh, Daphne . . ." Thomas pulled her to his chest, resting his chin on her hair. He should have known, based on the harsh statements thrown at him by his former boss, that the man would react severely to Daphne's decision to become a Christian. "I'm sorry."

"I'm not." She pulled out of his embrace. "Some of the people in the Bible faced far worse. I pray continually for Father, for

Mother, and for Harry to come to know Jesus as I have."

"I'll join you in prayer," Thomas vowed. "Every day."

Suddenly the tears that welled on her lower lashes spilled down her pale cheeks. "Oh, Thomas . . . I shall miss you dreadfully."

Only a few months ago, on the day of his graduation party, she had made the same proclamation. That day, he'd viewed her statement as a manipulative tactic. Today, however, he read a sincerity and anguish that matched his own. "And I . . . I will miss you." His voice broke as the truth of his statement struck hard. He didn't want to leave her.

He drew her close again, breathing in her citrusy scent, memorizing the feel of her slender form in his arms. His eyes slipped closed to hold back his own threatening tears. His heart pounded so hard his breath came in spurts, stirring the fine wisps of hair along her temples.

"I don't want you to go," she whispered against his neck.

"And he ain't wantin' to leave you."

Thomas jerked back, swinging his gaze over his shoulder. Clarence stood only a few feet away with a crooked grin creasing his face.

"I's right, Mister Thomas, ain't I? You love this girl and don't want to leave her behind."

Thomas nearly groaned. He loved Daphne, but Clarence didn't understand the sacrifices she would have to make for him.

Daphne pressed her hand to Thomas's beating heart. He looked into her hopeful face. "Do you still love me, Thomas?"

"Yes, I do, but —"

"But what?" Clarence interrupted again, taking another step closer. The grin faded, his expression becoming serious. "Love's not something to be taken lightly. If you love her, don't leave her."

Thomas rose, sending Clarence a silencing look. "It's not that simple, Clarence. I'm going to build my life in Kansas, and Daphne's family is here."

"Please do not speak of me as if I were absent."

The tart tone reminded Thomas of the old Daphne. He looked at her. She stood and hooked him sternly with her gaze.

"You're right that my family is here, Thomas, but you're forgetting something important. I now follow the guidance of my heavenly Father. I wish to seek and discover

His will." She moved forward, catching his hand and holding it between both of hers. With her shoulders squared and chin high, she spoke in a confident tone. "I would not presume to force you into a relationship you don't desire, but it occurs to me that, given my upbringing, I am familiar with the newspaper business. Although my father has openly disdained me due to my gender, I am educated and capable of assisting in such a business."

Suddenly her haughty air crumpled and her shoulders wilted. Her fingers quivered even as she continued to hold to his hand. "That is, if . . . if you believe you have need of . . . assistance . . . and if you believe God ordained us to do this work . . . together."

Thomas stood in stunned silence. Could she possibly love him enough to leave her opulent home? To be days' distance from her family? To live in a simple community in a clapboard house and spend her days serving as his assistant? *Lord, could I ask it of her? She'd be giving up so much.*

Clarence's whisper carried from behind Thomas. "Mister Thomas? The thing to do now is to go see this girl's daddy."

His suggestion, uttered with an amused undertone, was just what Thomas needed to spur him to action. Giving Daphne's hand a gentle tug, he said, "Is your mother inside?" At her nod, he continued. "Then go get her. We'll all ride in to the newspaper office, and I will ask your father for his blessing on our marriage."

How could one heart contain so many differing emotions and still keep from bursting? Daphne held tight to Thomas's broad, strong hand. The joy of being hand-in-hand with the man she loved juxtaposed the heartache of facing the stern, unyielding glares of her parents. Even Harry stood silent and seemingly disapproving while everyone waited for Father to form an answer to Thomas's humble yet impassioned request for Daphne's hand in marriage.

Thomas's fingers twitched on hers, and she knew the wait was as excruciating for him as it was for her. She longed to look into his face, give him a smile of assurance, but she knew no assurance would exist until Father made his decision. *Oh, please let Father say yes, dear Lord.* Her thoughts formed a prayer, and a bit of the heartache melted away with the knowledge that her loving heavenly Father would never withhold His care from her.

Father cleared his throat, and everyone in

the room jumped. Daphne's hand rose to her throat, and she felt her pounding pulse beneath her fingertips.

"I must first say, Ollenburger, that I find your request unfathomable considering the way you betrayed me."

Thomas didn't flinch in the slightest. "I'm sorry you see my decision to return to Kansas as a betrayal, sir. I believe my time under your tutelage prepared me for the pathway God designed for my life. I appreciate all you've taught me here, but I can't allow my appreciation to you to keep me from following God's will."

Thomas's surety in the face of Father's wrath filled Daphne with pride, but Father released a loud harrumph that made Harry cringe.

"God's will?" Father crossed his arms, his glare fierce. "And you think taking my daughter away from her family is God's will for her?"

Thomas opened his mouth to answer, but Daphne squeezed his hand in a silent message to allow her to respond. He looked tenderly into her face, his gentle smile encouraging her.

"Father, no matter where I live, I will always be your daughter. I will always love you and Mother. But I believe I am meant to go with Thomas and help him. Who better than I can understand the newspaperman's life? I do believe with all my heart we are meant to be together, and if that means —" Sorrow struck hard as she realized the distance that would separate her from her family if she went to Kansas with Thomas, but she swallowed the bubble of sadness and bravely continued. "If that means going to the plains of Kansas with Thomas, then I will go willingly and gladly."

Releasing Thomas's hand, she took a hesitant step closer to Father's desk. He sat in his chair like a king on a throne, his arms crossed, his face stern and forbidding. Resting her fingertips on the desktop, she whispered, "But I would very much like to go with your blessing."

"Daphne, what do you have in common with this man? On what will you build your future?" He barked the questions, an attempt to intimidate and dissuade her, she was sure, but she knew the answer and it tumbled from her lips effortlessly.

"We share a common faith and a strong love for each other. That faith and our love will be the foundation of our lives together."

Father's derisive snort filled the room. "Faith and love . . . As if that will put food on the table. . . ."

Mother nibbled her lip, her eyes sad. Harry stared off to the side, the muscles in his jaw tense. Her family's obvious distress pierced Daphne's heart. She didn't want to hurt them, but neither did she want them hurting her — destroying her with their censure. She glanced at Thomas, and the love shining in his eyes gave her the courage to face her father once more.

"God has promised to meet our needs, and Thomas will work hard to provide — I know he will. I will never be wanting if I go with this man." She leaned forward, her chest aching with the desire to finally receive her father's approval.

"Father, please . . . I love Thomas and wish to marry him. But I don't wish to go against you. Won't you give us your blessing?"

For a moment, she saw her father's expression soften, but when he spoke, his voice remained harsh. "If you go with him, you'll go without dowry. You'll be his financial responsibility."

Thomas stepped forward and slipped his arm around Daphne's waist. "Sir, we don't want your money. We want your blessing."

Father looked at Mother, and Daphne glimpsed a brief, nearly indiscernible movement of her mother's chin — a nod —

coupled with a plea in her eyes. Turning to Thomas, Father snapped, "When will you be married?"

Thomas suddenly looked uncertain, causing Daphne's heart to pound. But when he answered, her anxiety washed away on a wave of love and appreciation.

"As much as I know my parents would like to witness our union, they can't afford the train trip to Boston. And I know you're a busy man — coming to Kansas would be inconvenient for you. I'm sure Daphne wants her parents at her wedding, so we'll be married here before we leave for Kansas."

Daphne turned excitedly, grasping her mother's hands. "Mother, might we be married in the library, tomorrow at midmorning, when the sun pours through the big bay window on the east side of the room? A quiet, private wedding, with just a minister and you, Father, and Harry present? It would be so special to me."

Mother held tight to Daphne's hands as she sought her husband's approval. "Harrison?"

Father didn't relax his frown, but he gave a brusque nod. "I suppose I could take an hour tomorrow morning."

Daphne danced around the desk to embrace her father. He remained in his chair, but he raised one arm to give her a brief pat on the back. "Make the arrangements."

Mother and Harry left the office. Thomas took Daphne's hand and led her to the doors. Just before stepping into the hallway, she paused and glanced back. Father sat at his desk, his shoulders slumped, an expression of dejection on his face. But when he lifted his head and caught her looking, he immediately sat upright and assumed a formidable air.

"Go, Daphne. I've work to do."

Daphne closed the door behind her. Despite her father's austere command, her heart sang. She glimpsed his reluctance to let her go. It was the closest she'd come to hearing words of affirmation or love from her father. For today, it was enough.

34

Belinda stirred the thick stew with a long wooden spoon, inhaling the pleasant aroma rising from the pot. The scent of meat and vegetables combined with the heady fragrance of fresh bread sent her stomach into spasms of desire. She could hardly wait for Peter, Summer, and the girls to get back so they could sit down and eat.

The unexpectedly warm mid-November afternoon had enticed the family out for a walk around the neighborhood. Now that plans were set for them to return to their farm outside of Gaeddert, they knew their time in Hillsboro was short. For the past week, Summer had been making visits to neighbors, gifting each with jars of jam or loaves of cinnamon-laden raisin bread in appreciation for their friendship.

Belinda retrieved bowls from the shelf above the dry sink and began setting the table. Her life would soon undergo another great change. A sigh found its way from her throat, but the sigh was one of satisfaction more than discontent. She would miss the Ollenburgers very much — how dearly she loved her surrogate family — but she knew she could let them go. She may not have parents or a home of her own, but God had met her needs at every turn. She trusted Him to continue to do so, so she need not fear the future.

With thoughts of the future came thoughts of Thomas's return to Kansas. Her hands paused in their task as a tiny twinge of discomfort wiggled through her middle. She had practiced various ways to let Thomas know, despite her faithful letter-writing, that she only loved him as a brother in Christ. She hoped he wouldn't be crushed when he returned and discovered he had no sweetheart waiting, yet she knew she would be dishonest if she pretended to care more deeply for him than as a friend.

She had written him a letter, telling him on paper that he mustn't make his proposal, but in the end she had torn it up and thrown it away. Sending her message through the mail was the coward's way — she would tell him face-to-face as soon as he returned.

The lid on the stewpot jiggled, and she

hurried to the stove to move the pot before their dinner burned. Just as she shifted it to the warming part of the stove top, someone knocked on the door. Had the Ollenburgers accidentally locked themselves out? She hurried through the parlor and swung the door wide.

Instead of the Ollenburger family, she found Gerhard Wiens on the stoop. He beamed at her, and she noticed he held his hat in one hand and a cluster of bedraggled mums in the other.

"Good afternoon, Miss Schmidt. These are for you." He thrust his hat forward. She sent the straw boater a startled look, and the man's clean-shaven cheeks flooded with color. Yanking the hat back, he jammed the flowers forward. "I mean . . . these . . ."

Belinda bit the insides of her cheeks to keep from laughing. Reaching out, she took the cluster of red and yellow blossoms and managed a quick nod of thanks. She hugged the flowers to her apron bib as Gerhard erupted with words.

"I'm sorry to burst in on you unannounced, but I don't get to town very often, so it's hard to stand on formality. Your sister, Malinda, told me where I could find you, and she seemed to think it would be all right for me to stop by. I hope you aren't offended, and I hoped you might enjoy a walk. It's a pleasant evening for November."

Regretful, Belinda gestured toward the back of the house. "I have a stew on the stove, and the Ollenburgers aren't here right now. So I can't leave."

"Oh." His face fell. He put his hat on his head. "I understand." He took a step backward.

"But maybe —" Belinda stepped through the doorway. Before she could complete her suggestion, a joyous shout came from somewhere nearby.

"Belinda! Belinda!" All three girls charged across the yard, their faces shining. Gerhard moved aside to avoid being plowed over.

"Belinda! Papa got another telegram from Thomas!" Abby reached Belinda first and grabbed her hand, tugging her off-balance in her excitement. "He got married!"

Belinda's knees nearly gave way. "W-what?"

"Thomas got married!" Gussie clapped her hands.

Little Lena echoed, "Thomaf got married!"

Summer and Peter came up the walk, and Belinda looked at them in confusion. "Thomas . . . is married?"

Summer's curious glace skipped over Gerhard as she said, "Yes — to Daphne Severt, at the Severt home yesterday morning."

Peter shook his head. "I wish we could see our son be married, too, but Boston is far away. And he could not bring her to Kansas without being bound as husband and wife, so . . ." He held his big hands outward, raising his shoulders in a shrug. "He says in the telegram they would like to make a reception here. You will come to the reception?"

Both he and Summer seemed to hold their breath while the little girls continued to dance in circles and giggle with excitement. Belinda understood Peter and Summer's reticence — she could imagine them each thinking, *How will Belinda take this news?*

She remembered all the worrying she'd done, the letter she'd written, and her careful plans to let Thomas down gently. She swallowed a giggle. How ridiculous she'd been! Thomas didn't want to propose to her; he was in love with Daphne Severt!

"Of course I'll come. May I bring a guest?" She held her hand toward Gerhard, inviting him to move into the circle. When he stood near, she said, "Summer and Peter Ollenburger, please meet Gerhard Wiens. He works for the Industrial School and Hygiene Home for the Friendless."

Summer and Peter exchanged handshakes

468

with Gerhard, and Belinda stifled another giggle when Peter gave the man a deliberate up and down examination. Gerhard stood tall without cringing beneath the perusal, which pleased Belinda. Apparently Gerhard met with Peter's approval, because a grin split the big man's face.

"*Wellkom* to our home." He sniffed the air. "I smell something good cooking. Would you like to join us?"

Gerhard looked at Belinda, as though seeking permission. She nodded, and Gerhard graciously accepted Peter's invitation. "I would like that very much."

"*Goot!* Then come." Peter gave Gerhard's shoulder a smack that sent Gerhard through the doorway. "We do more celebrating when Thomas and Daphne come home, but for now — let us eat!"

Thomas looked down into his wife's face. Relaxed in sleep, she looked fully content. He shifted his arm, drawing her a bit closer, as peace washed over him.

The train rumbled onward, carrying them ever closer to Hillsboro and home. *Home . . .* Had only half a year passed since he'd graduated from college, wondering where he would make his home? He could scarcely believe all that had transpired in such a short amount of time, yet he recognized God's hand in every twist and turn.

With a jolt, he realized he'd been granted a legacy. Pa had wanted so much to leave his son the mill. How he had mourned its loss. Yet what he had given to Thomas was of much greater importance than a means of income. Pa had lived daily a faith as big as the man himself. Thomas, in witnessing it, had adopted it as his own. If he were fortunate enough to have a son someday, he would teach his child the same lesson of dependence on God that he had learned. Then his son, too, would have the strength to face whatever battles he found in the world and would always carry the promise of eternity with God.

Closing his eyes for a moment, he offered a silent prayer of thanks for the time of testing. He might have strayed, but all he faced had forced him to examine the root of his faith. He now knew without a doubt that God was deeply imbedded in his soul.

Daphne sat up sleepily and rubbed her eyes. Their gazes locked, and a sweet smile lit her face. She tipped her chin upward, a silent invitation for him to bestow a kiss. Thomas willingly obliged, his heart thrumming as their lips met. Although their high-backed berth afforded some privacy, anyone could walk by and see them, so they kept the kiss agonizingly short.

By late this evening, they would pull into Hillsboro. Thomas would take Daphne to the little house Pa had helped build ten years ago for Summer, and then they would have all the privacy they needed. Fire filled his face at the bold thought.

Daphne angled her head in puzzlement. "What are you thinking?"

He laughed self-consciously. "I'll tell you later, when we're alone."

She burrowed against his chest. "Oh, Thomas, I can hardly believe that we're married and we're on our way to Kansas."

"We're *in* Kansas," Thomas corrected, pointing to the passing landscape outside the window.

Daphne sat up eagerly and looked out the window. After a few moments, she caught Thomas's hand. "Will they like me?"

"My family?"

She nodded, her lower lip caught between her teeth.

Thomas shook his head. "No."

Her eyes flew wide.

He smoothed a strand of hair from her cheek. "They will *love* you." He risked another quick kiss. "How can they not? You're beautiful, you're kind, you're intelligent, and —"

"And I'm nervous." Daphne's brows pinched together. "I've never kept a house. I don't know how to cook or wash clothes or . . . or anything! Thomas, I want so much to be a good wife to you, but I'm afraid —"

"Don't be afraid." Thomas gathered her in his arms, holding her to his beating heart. "You're everything I want, everything God wanted me to have. Housecleaning you can learn — Summer will teach you. But all I need in a wife you already possess."

"Oh, Thomas . . ." She sank into the circle of his arms. "I love you."

"I love you."

They sat, arms entwined, for several more minutes before Daphne pulled back, her nose wrinkled. "Phew. You're musty."

He laughed. "So are you!"

Her grin let him know he hadn't insulted her. "So . . ." She sat straight up and folded her hands in her lap. "Tell me about the place we'll live."

Thomas laughed, shaking his head. "We've discussed this already."

Her smile turned impish. "I know. But I like hearing it."

Thomas settled into the corner of the seat, tugging Daphne into the curve of his arm. "We'll live in a little house in the country, built as a labor of love by my pa and the men of Gaeddert for my stepmother, Summer. It's a perfect house for us, with a wraparound porch where we can sit in the summertime and watch the sun set. The Cottonwood River flows behind the trees, and birds sing with the river's music. Wildflowers grow everywhere, and I'll pick you a bouquet every day."

She closed her eyes as if picturing it. "Oh, it will be so lovely!" Then she fixed him with an attentive look. "Where will your newspaper office be located?"

"In Hillsboro, since Gaeddert is nearly empty." Sadness tried to wiggle its way in, but he pushed the feeling aside. This was not a time for sadness — it was a time for rejoicing.

"And what is the town like?"

He pictured Boston and its vast, bustling expanse. Daphne was in for a surprise. "Small, very quiet. But it has everything we need — a butcher, a dry goods, a telegraph office for me to send and receive information. With that check your father gave us as a wedding gift, I'll be able to rent a space and purchase a small printing press to get our newspaper started."

Thomas still marveled at Mr. Severt's change in attitude concerning Daphne's dowry. The unexpected check, added to his savings, would insure an easier start to their lives together.

"So Hillsboro will have two newspapers," Daphne mused.

"Well, Hillsboro has two hotels." He winked, then changed the subject. "Do you think you'll mind me smelling like *heena* — like chickens?"

She wrinkled her nose. "Is it worse than your current odor?"

He laughed. "Probably." Sobering, he added, "It means a lot to my pa to have my help getting his farm started. And I know it will take a while for my newspaper readership to build, so working together with the chicken farm makes sense for both of us."

"I'm sure it will be fine," Daphne replied, smoothing her skirts over her knees, "and I shall do whatever I can to help, even if it means smelling like chickens." A grin twitched her cheek. "My mother would be mortified by what I just said!"

"Are you missing your family?"

Her face clouded. "Yes." She grasped his hands, holding tight. "But you're my family now. Besides, Harry and Mother both promised to write every week, and Harry even said he wanted to start going to church

474

with Mrs. Steadman to learn about the Bible."

Gratitude welled up in Thomas. Harry's attitude had changed following Clarence's heroic rescue of Daphne. Thomas and Daphne had committed to praying that, with Clarence and Nadine's influence, Harry would come to a knowledge of Jesus as Savior. They also prayed daily for Daphne's parents. Thomas sensed Mr. Severt would be the hardest to reach, but he would be more likely to listen to Harry than anyone else. They wouldn't give up hope.

Outside the window, daylight faded, bathing the plains in a rosy hue. The sky bore streaks of pink and yellow with purple clouds hovering on the horizon. Daphne sat up and gazed out the window, seeming to absorb the scene. "It's so beautiful, Thomas."

"Yes, it is," he agreed, looking at her enthralled expression.

"How much longer until we're there?"

He glanced at his pocket watch. "About two more hours, and we'll be home."

The train swayed along the track, the steady *clack-clack* measuring the miles that brought them closer and closer to Hillsboro. Closer and closer to their future. Daphne relaxed in his arms, her eyes closed, her cheek against his shoulder. He kissed the top of her head and then rested his chin on her silky hair. From within her nesting spot, she whispered, "I'm so happy, Thomas."

He nodded in agreement, Happy . . . and blessed. He had everything his heart had long desired: faith, family, and a place to belong. Pressing another kiss on his wife's hair, he whispered, "Welcome home."

ACKNOWLEDGMENTS

Don, Mom and Daddy, my precious girls: Thank you for sharing this journey with me. I love you all muchly!

Ramona, Eileen, Margie, Darlene, and Donna: You're terrific critters — thank you! And Ramona, you went over and above on this one . . . bless your heart!

Connie, Kathy, Cynthia, Carla, Rose, Phil, First Southern Choir: Your prayers and endless support are an incredible blessing to me. May God repay you in kind.

My soul sister *Kathy:* The refreshment of our laughter provided the impetus I needed to bring Thomas's story to a close. Your timing was perfect, as always. Love you!

Irv Schroeder and Mrs. Warkentine: Special thanks for the *Plautdietsch* translations. *Ekj räakjne jie* — I appreciate you!

Charlene and the wonderful people at Bethany House: Thank you for the opportunity to live out my childhood dream. And thanks especially for this story — revisiting Gaeddert and these characters was like going home.

Most importantly, thank You, *God.* You have blessed me beyond the scope of imagination. Every day with You is a joyous adventure — thank You for your immeasurable love. May any praise or glory be reflected directly back to You.

ABOUT THE AUTHOR

Kim Vogel Sawyer is fond of C words like children, cats, and chocolate. She is the author of eleven novels, including the best-sellers *Waiting for Summer's Return* and *My Heart Remembers.* She is active in her church, where she teaches adult Sunday School and participates in both voice and bell choirs. In her spare time, she enjoys drama, quilting, and calligraphy. Kim and her husband, Don, reside in central Kansas and have three daughters and six grand-children.

The employees of Thorndike Press hope you have enjoyed this Large Print book. All our Thorndike and Wheeler Large Print titles are designed for easy reading, and all our books are made to last. Other Thorndike Press Large Print books are available at your library, through selected bookstores, or directly from us.

For information about titles, please call:
(800) 223-1244

or visit our Web site at:
http://gale.cengage.com/thorndike

To share your comments, please write:
Publisher
Thorndike Press
295 Kennedy Memorial Drive
Waterville, ME 04901